SUMATRA

A Story From The Kenya
That Barrack Obama's Father Knew

NORMAN NABUTOLA

Dedication

This book is dedicated to Hadji

Purchase of additional copies of this book

To purchase additional copies of this book go to
www.CreateSpace.com/1000252177

Charitable Donations

Profits from the sale of Sumatra will be donated to Born Free Foundation in
the UK, (bornfree.org.uk). The Foundation supports the Mt Elgon Elephant
Monitoring program, run by the Kenya Wildlife Service, which is designed to
improve our understanding of the elephants and prevent poaching on the
mountain through regular monitoring and involvement of communities
bordering on the Mt Elgon forest.

If you wish to make a donation for this purpose please make the cheque pay-
able to 'Born Free Foundation', and note on the back "For Mt Elgon Elephants", then send it to Born Free Foundation, 3 Grove House, Foundry Lane,
Horsham, West Sussex, RH13 5PL, UK.

In the United States, please make your tax-deductible donation out to
Born Free USA and note on the check that the donation is "For Mt Elgon
Elephants," then send it to Born Free USA, PO Box 32160,
Washington, DC 20007.

Another book by the same Author

Tip and Spot, The adventures of two young cats travelling from Mt Elgon to
Kitale. To purchase this book go to Xlibris.com, then click on Bookstore and
enter Tip and Spot in box headed Xlibris Book Search.

Apology

As this book is being first published in America, the spelling is American rather than English to accommodate the sensibilities of American readers. Sincere apologies are made to Kenyans and the English whose desire for correct spelling will be met in any publication in those countries.

Sightseeing

Many of the places in this story really exist. If you are interested in visiting Mt Elgon to see them please contact: Normannabutola@aol.com

Disclaimer

This book is a work of fiction. Names, characters, behaviors, places and incidents are either the product of the author's imagination or are used fictiously and not as a record or representation of actual events or any person now living or dead.

ISBN: 1-4392-5796-5
ISBN-13: 9781439257968

Kiswahili Glossary

Akili	skill.
Askari	policeman.
Backsheesh	pocket change, bribe.
Banduki	gun, rifle.
Boma	enclosure, usually of brush for cattle and goats.
Bwana	sir or master, honorific.
Chai	tea.
Chumvi	salt.
Dawa	medicine.
Duka	small shop.
Dume	male, or bull.
Farasi	horse.
Habari yako?	How are you doing?
Mpishi	cook.
Jambo	hello.
Kali	sharp, fierce.
Karai	big saucer shaped metal bowl.
Karibu	close, "Come in," after a knock on the door.
Kidogo	small.
Kisharani	hot headed person.
Kitambaa	small piece of cloth, napkin.
Kuja	come, arrive.
Kwa heri	goodbye.
Lakini	but.
Mali	wealth.
Mamlambo	South African term for a root acquired by a witch that becomes a snake
Manyatta	Masai huts in a *boma*.
Maziwa	milk.
Mbuzi	goat.
Mchanga	earth.
Mdomo	mouth.

Memsahib	'madam' in an honorific sense.
Mganga	witch doctor.
Mpagazi	farm laborer, porter.
Msituni	forest.
Mtoto	child.
Mtu, plural Watu	person.
Mwekundu	red color.
Mwanamke	woman.
Mwrani	young man, warrior.
Mzee	old man, a respectful term.
Mzungu,	
plural Wazungu	white man.
Nzuri	good.
Panga	machete.
Posho	ground maize meal.
Sana	very, very much.
Sawasawa	good, OK.
Sema	say, speak.
Shifta	bandits.
Shimu	a hole, or cave.
Siafu	fierce red ants, safari ant.
Sirkali	government official.
Sufuria	saucepan or cooking pot.
Sukari	sugar.
Sululu	double headed pick.
Tatu	the number three.
Tamu	tasty, sweet.
Tokolotsi	South African term for a shape shifting animal, usually a dog or baboon, created by magic.
Tumbo	stomach.
Ugali	cooked maize meal, grits.

TABLE OF CONTENTS

Chapter

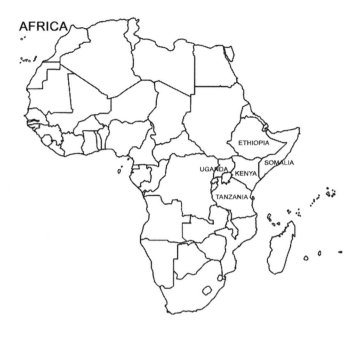

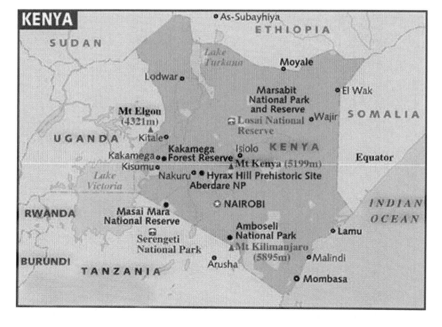

1. Introduction.

In the beginning was the force that always was, is now, and ever shall be. A force that is as restless as a stormy sea, ever changing, ever moving. This force is found throughout creation. It holds the earth in orbit around the sun, the moon in orbit around the earth and the electron in orbit in the atom. It is the force of the universe. It has infinite power and infinite wisdom. It reaches across space and warms the earth, it drives the storms, it makes the lightning flash and thunder roll. Its manifestations are more than the eye can see or the human mind can understand. It can make continents move and mountains rise, and it can make a tiny blade of grass push up through asphalt. It is the power of creation that takes many forms, as when a cloud gives birth to rain drops, or hail stones, or snow flakes. Each of these is part of, and responds to, the force that created it, as does mankind. The force that creates the rain drop pulls it down to earth, granting it a separate individual life for a crystal flash of time; then it rejoins the unity from which it came. And so it is with us, and all life that embodies a small part of the force. We have our own separate manifestation of electro-chemical energy for a little while and then fall back to the arms of the force whence we came.

We could think of that force as the power of God or God itself. But this is not useful since it gives no guidance to man. Man who alone, amongst all the manifestations of the force, needs to look outside himself to know why he is, why he exists and how he is different from other creations of nature. The force of the universe has no morality, gives no meaning, no purpose, to the life of man, no goal to strive for, no hope of eternal life. The force just is. All that man can do is respect the many manifestations of the force that are reflected in nature and know that he is but one of those manifestations. From the earth he came, and to it he will return. The energy that is gathered in him for a while, will rejoin the totality of all energy and man will be separate no more from whence he came. He will arrive at Nirvana, where the flame ceases to flicker, passions end, suffering is no more and transcendental calmness gives him peace.

You will understand this if you sit on the edge of the Great Rift Valley in Kenya and look over its vast wild splendor. You cannot help but feel insignificant, a mere speck in the universe, in awe of the majesty of time and continents rolling on for ever. Your own personal situation may have great drama for you. But if you clear your mind and are honest, you know that your troubles and triumphs are no more than an unnoticed blade of grass to be forgotten as it bleaches in the sun as though you had never been. If you are lucky, sitting on the edge of that vast trough in the surface of the earth, you will have to hand a rifle and water bottle, products of man's industrial ingenuity, to keep you safe and comfortable. If not you will appreciate how man struggled to live and survive through all the millennia save the last blink of geological time.

The story I have to tell you began 10 million years ago, long before man first appeared in East Africa. At that time the Great Rift Valley was already there running all the way from the Red Sea south to what is now Tanzania. At that time it was raw and fresh, like a wound still open, hardened, but not healed. Volcanoes were active along its edges where the earth's skin cracked open to let out its smoking blood. One of the biggest was Mt Elgon on what is now the Kenya Uganda border. It grew from a weak spot in the earth's mantle forty miles west of the Rift Valley. Elgon rose like a giant flat boil spitting ash, rock and gas in a twenty mile diameter circle around the crater. The first eruption built an enormous, relatively flat, cone spreading wide and low across the plateau which was already six thousand feet above sea level. All the animals on the plain died, if not from the blasts of hot gas then from starvation as hot ash covered the grass and trees, first ten, then hundreds of feet deep. The trunks and branches of the trees are still there in the stone today for any one to see. Later eruptions built a huge volcanic cone fourteen thousand feet high surrounding a crater nine miles across. It is said to be one of the largest volcanic masses still existing.

Modern science says that mitochondrial Eve, the Mother of us all, originated in East Africa, possibly on Mt Elgon. If this were the case, it is very likely that Eve first came to be in one of the caves on Mt Elgon. So this story is of the place where man began. When Eve began she was wild like any other animal of the forest and the plain. As the waves of time rolled by, her descendants evolved as one must if one is not to be overwhelmed by changes in the world from millennia to millennia. Developing a capacity to wonder why things happen was the biggest part of that evolution. The answer for ancient man was forces that can be seen only in the mind. Since the earliest days of man he has known there are spirits. These he has personified and envisaged as reflections of his own strengths and weaknesses. That is why god and the devil are often both made in the image of man. For the African there are many spirits. He has always understood the elemental importance of earth and air, fire and water, each connected to the other in a circle of life. Each of these has a mother spirit who brings forth as many children as there are locusts in the sky. These spirit children are to be found in the rivers and rocks, in the trees and on the plains, in the animals and the bush fires they flee. You can hear their feet pattering on the thatch of your hut roof at night. You respect and fear them as you fear the unknown. These forces are very much a part of this story.

Eve's African descendants of mountain and plain also evolved by coming to understand that what separates man from animals is the knowledge that man can, and must, control the selfish impulses inherited from the wild, although those impulses are always in him. This is the bedrock on which human civilization is founded, essential to live successfully in a group, a society. But it is always a struggle for man because in his genes are the animal instincts of greed, male sexual promiscuity and aggression. In animals these instincts are not moderated by a sense of fairness and empathy towards others, or by rules of the herd or flock. How many animals share their food? Controlling impulses harmful to the groups in which man lives requires conscious effort and self discipline. So also do good impulses, such as empathy, kindness, hard work, and, not least, a sense of honesty and fairness. If these things have not been taught to a child by the age of ten it is extremely difficult for him to acquire these virtues later in life. This is because the programming of the organic computer that is the child's brain becomes hard wired at an early age. What he has learned in childhood becomes part of his 'operating system', his world view, his general approach to problems and life. What he learns after that time is information and application software; programs that are turned on for specific tasks then turned off; unlike the operating program which is always on. A feral child brought into human society after the age of ten will never fit comfortably because his operating system is animal.

This story is of a foundling child who started life on Mt Elgon with a stranger for a father and a goat as a surrogate mother. This made the child at least half animal. Man can accept anomalies, but nature does not. So forces that are understood by the African, if not by the European, moved to eliminate the anomaly of a child who was human in form but not wholly human in mind. The tale I tell is of how it all came to pass, and what happened.

Mt Elgon-Kenya

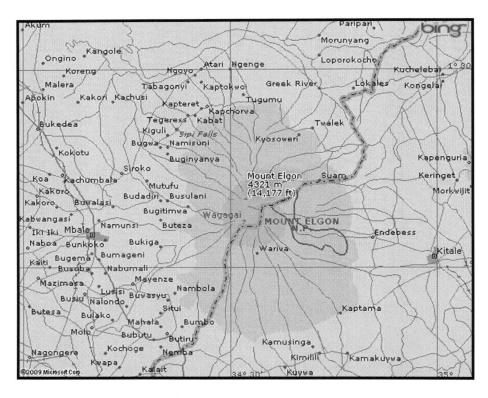

Chepnall cave is ½ an inch left of Endebess

2. Sumatra the Elder

Sumatra the Elder was a short, stocky, powerful man. His story begins when he was in his prime. It is part of the history of Africa. It is a story of a man's man because he was the kind of man who would have been respected on any frontier. But his story is a sad one, as he was ground between an irresistible force and an immoveable object; his tribal code and values on the one hand, and the British colonial administration's rules of justice on the other. As a result he lost the better part of his life. But his legacy was a young man who was one of the best that Kenya has ever seen.

A long time ago in the early part of the last century Africa was still wild. Elephants, buffalo and antelope roamed the bush on the plains, in the forests and on the mountains. Man lived in tribes and clans, usually miles apart. In those days man was a small part of the panorama, dotted in groups and clans, here and there, with vast expanses in between. Cattle grazed among the antelope and young warriors (*mwrani*) guarded them against hyenas, lions and raiding parties of other tribes. One such clan was home to Sumatra the Elder.

The night this all began he did not sleep well in his thatch roof hut 6000 feet up on the foothills of Mount Elgon. By the way, if you want to find Mount Elgon in your atlas, look half an inch from the top right hand corner of Lake Victoria, almost on the equator in East Africa. Sumatra the Elder could remember only bits and pieces of his dream. It was a restless, troubled dream, haunting his sleep, keeping him tossing and turning half way between sleep and wakefulness. He was anxious and not happy. He woke as the cocks crew just before dawn, as is their want. He lay there awhile turning the dream over in his mind seeking its meaning. He realized that his spirit, free from his conscious mind while he slept, had roamed the forest in the night. He remembered going to and fro like a branch swinging in the wind. As so often happens the details were forgotten in a general awareness of restlessness and trees.

Then gradually there crept into the consciousness of his memory the sharp acid smell that wild bees give off when disturbed near the hive. The smell drives the others into a furious frenzy of attack on the threat. Whether by instinct or design they attack the head and eyes.

As the smell came to him, Sumatra the Elder knew that something, a honey badger perhaps, or some one, had disturbed one of his beehives. He would have to find out what and why. In Africa you take a hollow log, block the ends with slices off a smaller log, and leave a mouse hole as a front door. This log you hang in a tree in the forest. Soon enough a swarm of bees will take up residence and honey combs will hang inside along with others full of bee grubs and places for the workers to rest. Each man knows his own hives and where he put them. In those days, beehives had a value and ritual significance undreamt of by today's western supermarket shoppers. Perhaps this is because for centuries the only sweetener known in Kenya was honey. Sugar cane and sugar were to come later.

When he understood his dream Sumatra the Elder rose and crossed the ten feet to the door of his hut. There he untied the rawhide leather strap that held it shut. His woman, Watumba, still slept. He did not wake her. What he had to do was man's work. He had chosen and taken her about six months before. Many cows it had cost him, for she was a desirable young woman. He looked out and saw that it was one of those beautiful clear mornings with a few small fluffy white clouds floating in a blue sky. They were all that was left off the heavy rain in the night. He turned back in and gathered the few simple things he would take with him; his spear, a *panga,* and his blanket knotted over one shoulder where it would hang down around him like a toga. In addition he had a bag of *posho* which is maize meal and a small metal cooking pot or *sufuria* in which he would make his *ugali,* similar to grits in America. The *sufuria* was a real prize so much lighter and more convenient than a clay pot to cook in. Not often did one find its way so far in land. They came from the Arab traders on the coast. This was five hundred miles away. The Arabs were better known for trading slaves than pots and pans. But by then the British had put an end to Arab slaving in East Africa. Two fire sticks from the *Dombier* bush were the only other things he carried in a little quiver hung over one shoulder. Matches were unknown. But with the fire sticks he could always have fire unless it was raining in which case a hollow podo tree or a cave would be his only shelter.

Sumatra the Elder had lived so long in, and on the edge, of the forest he was a natural part of it. No man in the area knew it, and all the creatures in it, better than he did. Though he did not know it then, his son, yet to be born, would know it even better, but would not learn it from his father. Indeed he would not meet his Father until he was a grown man and he would never know his Mother. But the future is not ours to know. So with the grass wet and cold on his feet, Sumatra the Elder started up the path towards the forest. He had no idea that this day would set in motion a chain of events that would make him a longtime guest of his Majesty King George VI and then his daughter her Majesty Queen Elizabeth the Second who succeeded him. This day would also make him a lifelong friend of the only white man, (*mzungu*), in the area whom he knew as Bwana Paws. It was also a chain of events that would deny him the knowledge that he even had a son until he became truly an elder, a *Mzee*.

He set out at dawn when it was light enough to see under the trees, but before the sun came up over the Cherangani hills thirty miles to the East. His beehives were about two hours march away across the Kassowai River, high up the mountain near the bamboo line. This was where flowers of the mountain made the honey sweeter. In fact, it took him about three hours to get there because of a herd of elephants on the path. He was a long time finding his way around them because the undergrowth was very thick and there is nothing more dangerous than coming around one of those creeper laden trees and bumping into a cow with calf. The maternal instinct means an instant charge. With a fifty yard head start and open ground a fit young man can keep ahead of a charging elephant. But with a ten or twenty yard start in thick undergrowth a man has no hope. The undergrowth traps a man but is no more than grass around the ankles to an elephant. Even the most athletic young man has little chance. The trunk swats him like a lead pipe, the tusk goes through him and his body squishes like a grape as the foot crushes him. So Sumatra the Elder was sensible, careful, testing the wind, listening for five minutes at a time to locate stragglers and young bulls on the edge of the herd, invisible in the thick forest. When he was sure of the edges of the herd he cautiously made his way around it with no sound except an occasional zing of his *panga* as he cut a "wait a bit" thorn in his way.

As he went up the slope to the big trees on the edge of the glade where his hives hung Sumatra the Elder moved forward very cautiously. He was like an antelope testing the wind, his eyes moving all around at every step. He was nervous. His dreams had been very troubled. As he came closer, however, he had that intuitive sense we get when a place is empty. He knew that whoever, or whatever, had been there, had gone. And so it proved. As soon as he reached his first hive and saw it lying on the ground split open down its length by ax blows, his anger arose. Only man could have cut the hive down. Even if the rope had broken, no animal could have made the ax marks and wood chips he saw. It was theft of his honey, pure and simple. The unwritten code of the forest had been violated. A man's honey barrel is unprotected, unguarded as it hangs in the branches of the forest. It is there on trust in the trees which no man owns. Because any man can take it, no man may touch it. A young warrior may raid another tribe and fight them openly for their cattle and young women. That is to be applauded and is natural for a young man. But to creep through the forest and steal what is unprotected is the act of a coward, a sneaking hyena. If the thief is of your tribe you will not kill him. The elders will decide his punishment. If the thief is not of your tribe you may blood your spear and wear three small scars on your right cheek by your right ear so that others may know that you have faced and overcome one of life's defining moments, kill or be killed. Those scars you wear with honor. They make you a man among your own people. Young women will admire them too. With an instinctive knowledge, developed over thousands of years of evolution, a young woman knows that a man who can fight has a better chance of protecting her and her children. That is what men are for. It is important when fear of attack by man or beast is constantly with you, like background music is in the West. On occasions, such fear is at the front of consciousness, but mostly it lies buried in the mind just behind the eyes, and so not seen, but always there.

Sumatra the Elder did not think of these things. They were already programmed into his mind. His anger was part of an unthinking, automatic response system, rather like the perception of sexual or racial slight today in the West, which triggers the same spontaneous aggression, although flavored in the West with financial greed. With a sinking feeling in the hollow of his stomach Sumatra the Elder studied the ground around the hive. He knew at once there was more than one thief. The grass and leaves around the hive were trampled too much to be one man. He could see easily where they had left. He had no difficulty following the trail. To his dismay it headed towards his second hive. Whether by accident or fore knowledge he could not tell. Two hundred yards away the question became irrelevant. His second hive also lay on the ground like a giant broken calabash. And so it was also with the third. There he found the bundle of sticks tied with creeper all burnt black at one end. This had been used in the traditional way to smoke the bees, blunting their attack making them choke and splutter and back away; the effect of smoke on the bees being like tear gas thrown into a crowd of protesters.

The smoke sticks were cold and had been rained on, so he knew that the deed had been done the previous afternoon before the rain in the night. Now he knew there were three, one wearing a sandal made from an old car tire which must have been carried up from Nairobi, one with a large bare foot and one with a small narrower foot. Tracking them was not difficult in the wet leaves and mud after the rain, except where the trail led over a glade in the forest covered by a rocky outcrop. There he had to use all his skill from years of tracking in the forest. The faintest mark, from a turned stone, to a blade of grass with the dew knocked off, was enough for him. The trail led up the mountain.

After a mile or so Sumatra the Elder decided that this was the thieve's true direction not just a detour to reach another elephant trail down the mountain. It was then that he knew the men were not of his tribe. These men were going up over the crater of the mountain towards Uganda. This meant that they were Wagishu not Elgon Masai. It was then that the anger in him turned to resolve. He had no choice. When a warrior finds his property violated and stolen by men of another tribe, honor leaves him no alternative. Sumatra the Elder knew that from that moment that if he caught up with them before they reached the safety of their territory and clan, either they or he would be dead. He did not have time to go home and gather a raiding party of a dozen or more young men. That would take all day. By then the thieves would have too much of a head start. Besides, Sumatra the Elder was by nature a man who did not need, or seek, group support before taking action. He had no desire to cajole or persuade others to his point of view. He would not massage their egos with unfelt goodwill, act like a political creature, not out of conviction but to curry favor and gain influence. When he reached a decision on a course of action he would do it himself thank you. This was part of his character that was genetic. It was nature not nurture, and a trait that his son would inherit unbeknown to him.

Sumatra the Elder did not think about making a will, even though odds of three to one are not very good. Anyway no one in his clan could read or write, nor could he. Due to this fact, his language had no word for such a concept. If his spirit were to leave his body, tradition and rules handed down verbally from generation to generation would govern who came to have what he owned.

Quite soon the trail led to a small cliff about 20 feet high, part of a rocky outcrop in the forest. There a huge slab of stone lying at an angle made a small triangular cave where it was dry. It was here that the three men had taken shelter from the rain in the night before. All that was left were small pieces of charred sticks between three stones where they might have placed a small pot. Sumatra the Elder wriggled his bare toes in the ashes just as he would in elephant dung to see if it were warm. The ashes were cold but the stones still just warm. From this he knew that they must have left about the first hour of the day, an hour after dawn. What the white man, the *mzungu*, with his complete absence of simple logic, would call seven o'clock rather than one o'clock. Now that it was the fourth hour and the sun well up in the sky the thieves had at least a three-hour head start. Sumatra the Elder hurried. Whenever the trail was clear enough he jogged along with that long easy stride that eats up the miles like a bush fire on the plains, steady and inevitable. He could cover enormous distances with that tireless lope of the wild hunting dog. Running long distances was a tradition of his people. Years later Kenyans would regularly win international honors as a long distance runners in numbers quite out of proportion to the country's size.

So he pushed on as fast as he could. Once he disturbed some buffalo. They thundered away through the undergrowth with a huge crashing and breaking of branches. Other animals saw him come and pass. The bush buck, the duiker, the water buck and the colobus monkey, they all slipped silently aside and hid, watching as he went by. Only the baboon barked a warning to his band. Hour after hour he pushed on, stopping only to drink from one of the cold mountain streams.

About five hours later when the sun was well past its peak Sumatra the Elder knew he was getting very close. The moisture squeezed out of the wet ground by the weight of a footprint was still glistening and not yet dry. This meant they were only minutes ahead, perhaps three hundred yards, but invisible through the thick forest. Now the reality of what he was about became immediate and urgent in his mind. He knew that it would be too dangerous to simply come up behind them. One might turn around and see him. If they were armed with a bow and arrow, as the Wagishu often were, he could be shot down long before he came within spear or *panga* range. If the hindmost man did not turn around Sumatra the Elder could spear him from behind, but in all probability he would cry out and the other two would run or fight. So he decided to wait until they made camp and catch them by surprise sitting on the ground no weapons in hand. It was now later in the afternoon, only a couple of hours before dark. He knew that they would stop at least an hour before the sun went down to give themselves time to gather wood for the camp fire. It is quite impractical to gather fire wood in the dark even if there is a moon, which there was not. So now he followed carefully not crossing an open space until he was sure they were well beyond it.

The path they took was part of the well established trail over the mountain to Uganda. Soon it climbed out of the forest and bamboo onto the more open moorland. This starts at about ten thousand feet. There in a park like setting one finds tussock grass, flowering lobelias looking like ten foot high hollyhocks, and giant groundsel as big as small trees similar to the Joshua cactus found in southern California. For some reason that just is, the moorlands cover the crests and sides of the hills while the forest pushes up the valleys. Here Sumatra the Elder had his first good view of the three. As he had assumed they were men. A woman has no business traveling so far from home. His fear about a bow and arrows was also correct. The lead man had a bow hanging from his shoulder down to his knee. The other two carried spears and though he could not see them he assumed each had a *panga* in a sheath. They also carried two large rawhide bags which were stuffed with the stolen honey combs.

About half a mile into the moorland the Wagishu left the path and headed diagonally down the hillside towards the forest and stream in the valley bottom. Sumatra the Elder lay on the ground so that if they looked back his black head would look like a rock on the ground. He peered between two tussocks of grass and watched the men about three or four hundred yards away until they disappeared into the bushes that fringed the taller trees in the valley bottom. This was misty country, high and cold and often in cloud. The trees were not large, only about thirty feet high and covered with moss and lichens so that a branch as thick as your arm looked as thick as a man's leg above the knee.

When they disappeared Sumatra the Elder did not dare to cross the open ground where he would be in plain view. He went back about a hundred yards down the steep rise he had just come up. When well out of view he too, turned down the hill to the trees in the valley bottom. About fifty yards off the path he stopped by a giant groundsel which stood alone about twice the height of a man. He chose it due to its unusual shape. Instead of branching at random as was normal, this one was shaped like a candelabra. Three branches, each the thickness of milk gourd, went straight up like three fingers on a man's hand. This he could recognize easily if he walked this path again. In the thick shrubbery at the foot of the groundsel he put down his blackened metal pot, his bag of maize meal and his fire stick quiver, everything except his spear and *panga* and of course the brown blanket he wore. He tightened the cord of this around his waist until it hung like a belted tunic not a Roman toga. Carrying only what he needed for the fight he went on down the hill towards the trees in the valley.

Had he been a modern man he might have stopped to consider the drama of what he was about. He had left home without telling his wife. It was at least an even chance that he would never come back. If he did not come back she would assume he was dead in the forest killed by an animal. The forest was the only place he would go routinely without telling friends. His body would almost certainly not be found. The hyenas would eat it. Any way how would one go about looking for it with hundreds of square miles of forest to search in. After one rain, tracking him would be impossible even if you knew where to start. Like many a woman before her, all she would know was that her man went out and never came home. It was a story that has been told many times. The missionaries did not understand this when they preached romantic love between one man and one woman blessed by their God. When you know there is a very real chance that fate may take you from one beach and toss you up on another, you do not become too attached to any one island. If you are inherited by your husband's brother, that is in the nature of things. To be owned by a man is better than being alone. You expect your new man to build you a separate hut, and you hope his first wife is not too unkind to you. If your sons are old enough they will care for you with a stronger sense of duty than would be the case in the Missionary's tribe.

Being a man of his time and place, Sumatra the Elder thought of none of these things. He simply knew what the code of his tribe required him to do. He would do it because that is the way things had to be. He could lie and say he could not find the thieves. But he was a powerful young man in his prime, built like a short Hercules. His tribe would expect him to fight. His honor and his self respect were at stake. But he was alone. His stomach felt hollow. His hand quivered, or did it tremble. Fear and excitement gripped him in equal measure. Had he been a cat, or a lion, his tail would have twitched wildly with excitement and strain. As it was his short muscular body slipped silently between the bushes with careful, hesitant, but smooth movements. He passed like a shadow under the trees, each footstep chosen the instant he made it, to avoid breaking a twig or rustling a leaf. Slowly he moved up the valley invisible in the thick undergrowth. Then he heard their voices. He did not speak their tongue and could not understand what they said. What was important to him was that they were not of his people and they did not know he was there.

They had stopped where a small lava flow jutted out from the side of the valley and made an overhang not deeper than a man's arm. Small thought it was, they knew from experience that if the camp fire were five or six feet away the heat would reflect off the rocks and they would be much warmer than they would be in the open. Above the tree line it freezes every night even on the equator. So a good camp fire is a must, especially when you travel with no more than the clothes you wear. But a good camp fire means gathering enough fire wood. That is why they had stopped and hour before the sun would go behind the crater's crest in the West, when this side of the mountain would be in darkness. In front of the overhang there was a small open area about fifteen feet wide where the stony ground would not support any bushes, just very short grass and African violets with their flowers like blue stars on the ground. One of the men started a fire in the middle of this open space, while the other two pushed through the bushes towards the bigger trees looking for larger pieces of dead wood that would keep the fire going while they slept.

The two hunting for firewood went slightly up the valley at first. This mislead Sumatra the Elder. He thought they were sixty yards away when in fact the camp site was about thirty feet in front of him. Fortunately, the man making the fire had his back to Sumatra and did not notice the change of light and shadow in the bushes behind him. When he glimpsed the man, Sumatra the Elder stopped in mid step and very carefully put his foot back where it came from, turned and crept back ten paces where he knelt down and inserted himself under a thick tangle of morning glory type creepers growing over two bushes. He had no plan of attack. He just knew that when you hunt you must take the hunted by surprise if you hope to be successful. While he was thinking about creeping up and spearing the fire maker from behind he heard the other two come back dragging wood. So he stayed where he was listening to their movements, waiting for some development that would give him an opportunity. It came much sooner than he expected.

Having dumped his load of dead branches by the fire, one of the men started down the slope with his eye on a small dead tree about fifty yards from the camp fire. His mind was on the task at hand. He was not cautious. By now any big animal near the camp site would have crashed away through the underbrush. He was relaxed, his eyes on the dead tree. He almost trod on Sumatra the

Elder as he pushed around the bushes with the morning glory. Sumatra the Elder crouched in the gloom under the creepers, his *panga* in one hand and his spear in the other. He could smell the sour smell of sweaty unwashed body as the man brushed by. Letting go of his spear Sumatra the Elder stood up with a rustle of leaves and took two steps forward. The Wagishu heard the rustle and instead of running forward, turned to see what creature he had disturbed. Out of the corner of his eye he was aware of something behind him. It was not a duiker or bush buck, but something big, as tall as he was. Instant fear swept over his body. He opened his mouth to cry out, but no sound came except the thud of the *panga* into his skull as the hemispheres of his brain were separated. He collapsed like a bull when the Matador's sword cuts its spinal cord.

The thud was heard by the two Wagishu at the fire. One called out and hearing no answer called again. He looked down the rays of the setting sun. The bushes were tipped with orange and cast long shadows as the light went on down the valley, over the trees in the forest and across the plains to the Cherangani hills, now purple in the distance. He did not know that he loved that view. It was just part of life, his reality. He did not know he was going to die. He was just wondering what had happened to his companion. If an animal had been alarmed he would have heard it crashing through the bushes. If his friend had tripped and fallen, why did he not answer? With anxiety born of uncertainty, and the fear of the unknown rising within him he unsheathed his panga and followed in his friends footsteps. Meanwhile Sumatra the Elder wrested his panga out of the dead mans skull with a powerful twist of his wrist. Then he crept quickly back to the same bush and crouched behind it this time, rather than under the creepers. In his right hand he grasped his spear lying flat on the ground, and in his left his *panga*. He could see sideways, but not in front of him because the bushes covered with morning glory creepers blocked his view. The dead man's body lay about ten feet behind him. When the second Wagishu was about twenty feet from the body he stopped in his tracks as he saw the brown length lying like a log in six inches of grass. He knew instantly that this was no tree trunk, but rather his friend. He could not yet see the split open skull. So he looked around for a buffalo or perhaps an elephant that might have swatted his friend with its trunk. But no, there was nothing. As he stepped very carefully forward he still did not suspect another man. Then he came up to the side of the bush where Sumatra the Elder hid. He had enough time to let out a yell as Sumatra the Elder rose up out of the ground his spear point moving like the nose of a striking python. The black blade, with edges of sharpened silver, began its trajectory towards the Wagishu's chest. The spear left his hand as Sumatra the Elder pushed up hard with his knees and his legs straightened. The Wagishu reacted instantly, without thought. His *panga* made a sweeping arc as he swung it across his body. The *panga* caught the spear with a ring of steel on steel. The spear blade missed his chest and sliced across the top of his left arm near the shoulder. That cut was not fatal or even serious. But the momentum of his swing took his *panga* over to the left side of his body. It was only beginning to come back when Sumatra the Elder's *panga* came down into the right angle where his neck rose from his chest. He fell with a gurgling cry as blood ran like water from a hose. He was unconscious in seconds and dead in less than a minute.

When the third Wagishu heard the cry of alarm he knew they were under attack. Who and why did not matter. Obviously it was some one of another tribe. He snatched up his spear and *panga* backing up against the overhanging rock. He felt safer with his back protected. In front of him it was open for fifteen feet. He could see anything coming. No sneak attack was possible. He made a mistake in not taking up the bow and arrow of his dead colleague. With it he could have shot down Sumatra the Elder as soon as he appeared. At miss at those very close ranges, fifteen or twenty feet, would not have been likely. As it was, he and Sumatra the Elder were each equally armed with spear and *panga*, and neither now had the advantage of surprise. But Sumatra the Elder had the psychological advantage. He was prepared. He knew he now faced only one man. The third Wagishu was full of surprise, fear and uncertainty. Sumatra the Elder was on a roll. Two men down, one to go. His blood was up. He felt half fury, half exultation. His enemy was justifiably afraid. Two companions probably dead and who knows how many attackers. When Sumatra the Elder appeared out of the bushes in front of him, the Wagishu's fear led to his mistake. He hurled his spear at Sumatra the Elder with a force born of desperation. Had his aim been true, it would not have been a mistake. As it came about Sumatra the Elder side stepped about six inches to his right to avoid a rock on the ground as he rushed in to the attack. The Wagishu's spear went under his upraised left arm and through his blanket slicing across his ribs. The white of his bone showed at the bottom of a six inch long gash and his blood ran freely down his side and leg. None of this slowed his charge. Sumatra the Elder's spear took the Wagishu in the pit of his stomach and passed through his body as he swung wildly at his attacker with his *panga*. But, Sumatra the Elder's body was out of range of the *panga*. His hand and arm were not, so he let go of the spear and pulled his arm back as the *panga* whistled down and chunked into the shaft of the spear. From there it fell on the ground as the Wagishu collapsed backwards. In a half sitting position, he pushed on the ground with his hands trying to stand up. He barely raised his backside from the earth when dizziness and darkness made him sink back. His life force, the electrochemical energy that moved his spirit, flowed into the earth where it would travel to familiar places to be with his ancestors. No longer separately encapsulated in a human body, it had rejoined the force of the universe, just as a rain drop joins the waters of the ocean after a brief flight as a separate thing traveling through clouds and winds, the light and darkness of its life.

Sumatra the Elder stood still for several long minutes, trembling until the excitement and fury of the fight subsided. The sun was passing down below the rim of the mountain crater. Where he stood was already in shadow. In half an hour it would be dark.

He knew he had to hurry. First he went back to the giant ground-sel to get his things which he brought back to the Wagishu camp site. Then taking his water gourd he went down to the river to get water for his evening meal. He stepped over the two dead bodies on his way down and made a mental note to take their spears, and *pangas* and anything of value in the morning. He had some trouble getting through the tangle of the forest in the gathering darkness, but made it in the end with only a few scratches from the wait-a-bit thorn. Breathing heavily in the thin air he came back to find the camp fire burning well. He dragged the body of the third man off to the side of the little clearing. Then he sat on a stone by the fire and put the water on to boil in his little pot so that he could make his *ugali* of boiled maize meal. As he waited he began to notice the throbbing of his ribs. The blood had dried and had been flaking off his side and leg as he moved. Now it just hurt. In the white man's hospital they would have put ten stitches in the wound. Alone on the mountain it just hung open, dried, and hardened.

As he ate his *ugali*, he contemplated the flickering orange yel-low flames of his fire, the occasional spark floating effortlessly up until it shrank and then was gone like the life of man, leaving only the grey smoke twisting and curling into a blue black sky. The warmth of the fire felt good on his face and front. But, the cold of the night began to bite into his back and his rib throbbed pain-fully. Now that the hunt and the fight were over, he felt a little at a loss. If he had been hunting an animal he would be cutting it up, cooking some over the fire and making a bush back pack to carry home as much as he could, to feed his family. The victory over the Wagishu did not serve such a practical need. Recovering the stolen honey was a minor part of the drama. At the heart of the matter was his honor, his sense of self, as a man, as a warrior. This he felt had been well proven and he looked forward to the admiration of his tribe. He had demonstrated his courage and strength. He was pleased with himself. Now he just wanted to get back to a warm hut and his woman.

In the morning six feet from his camp fire a ring of frost whitened the grass and African violets. Sumatra the Elder shivered and poked in the grey ashes of the fire until he found a few embers still glowing under the end of a blackened branch. These he gently fed with tiny twigs and knelt blowing them into flame. When he had the fire going he warmed the remains of his *ugali* from the night before and ate. Then he gathered together the spears, and *pangas,* and the bow and arrows, of the dead men and tied them in a bundle. Finally he cut off each dead man's ears and put them in one of the raw hide bags with the honey. Gathering it all together he set off on the long march home. He felt proud of himself and looked forward to the admiration of his clan. He decided to go first to the big podo tree where all important matters were discussed. From there he would send a boy off to spread the news and tell his wife to bring him something to eat.

And so it was that about the tenth hour of the day, what the *Wazungu* would call four o'clock, he walked past the huts of his clan up the hill from the podo tree and gathered a small entourage of young people curious about his load, where he had been and what he had done. Soon the word was all over the hillside, "Sumatra has killed three Wagishu on the mountain. He is wounded you can see the white of the bone on his ribs." A small crowd gathered. The story of the hunt and the fight was told and retold around the fire under the podo tree. As evening fell, Sumatra the Elder was buoyed by the admiration of the men, young and old. Feeling good and expansive, that this was his moment, he ordered one of his goats to have its throat cut so that all men could eat meat as warriors should, in celebration. The women brought some *ugali* and green vegetables already cooked and the men roasted bits of goat over the fire, their women standing behind them. For two hours after the sun went down the murmur of voices rose out of the darkness around the circle of light that flickered on the branches of the big podo tree. When the smoke began to go down the hill with the cold air of the night, Sumatra the elder went back to his hut. There he slept in the warmth and familiar smells of cow dung, smoke and home. Though his rib throbbed, he was exhausted, so he slept soundly untroubled by dreams, secure in the admiration of his people and what he had achieved.

For the next week or so the triumph of Sumatra the Elder was the main topic of conversation in his village and along the whole side of the mountain. The story spread with the speed of what the white man called the "bush telegraph". Pretty soon the story reached the ears of corporal Kigei at the Endebess police station. To sergeant Kiprono, the man in charge, corporal Kigei was a tiresome and ambitious young man with a big disadvantage from the Sergeant's point of view. Some missionaries had taught the corporal to read and write. This was something the sergeant could not do. Because the corporal could read and write he believed that he should have a senior position and not have to carry a rifle and actually go out and keep the peace arresting drunks or thieves. Much to his annoyance, the District Commissioner had said that he must start at the bottom and work his way up the ranks. Now he had moved up a notch to corporal.

When corporal Kigei heard the story of Sumatra the Elder and the Wagishu, he wrote a short report saying that the talk was that a man called Sumatra had killed three Wagishu on the mountain up by the crater. He wrote this report not out of any sense of duty to police work, but to embarrass the sergeant who could not read it. Sergeant Kiprono sighed when he saw the report written in pencil on a sheet of school boy note paper. His first instinct was to use it to make roll up cigarettes and then stub the buts out on corporal Kigei. When the first wave of irritation passed he reflected that one source of the white man's power seemed to be all the writing he did. It was like a universal magic giving people power and authority. He suspected that corporal Kigei would try to use the report to gain favor with the District Commissioner and show up the Sergeant. So he made a practical and sensible decision to make the report his own and steal Corporal Kigei's thunder. A week later he took the report to the District Commissioner's office in Kitale about fifteen miles away. There he turned over two prisoners accused of stealing maize and reported on the shooting of a rabid dog. Then he addressed the question of the report on Sumatra saying; "Bwana Commissioner, I heard that a man called Sumatra killed three Wagishu up on the mountain. So I had corporal Kigei investigate a bit further and write a report for you. It seems that the story is probably true. What would you like me to do"? The Commissioner replied "Send corporal Kigei and another man out to this man's village and if the story is true arrest the man for murder."

So it came to pass that corporal Kigei and a private went to Sumatra's village arriving in the mid afternoon. The people of the village knew that these policemen, the "*sirkali*" as they were called, did the bidding of the white man. Bad things could happen if they were disobeyed. So corporal Kigei and his companion were directed to the big podo tree and a lad sent to summon Sumatra the Elder. He wondered why he was being honored with a visit from emissaries of the white man, but could think of no reason. Perhaps the DC wanted to use him as a tracker to go hunting buffalo on the mountain like the white man Bwana Paws. Perhaps he could make a little *baksheesh*. So he came willingly enough to the tree where a knot of people were gathering to see what was going to happen. The lad who had been sent to fetch Sumatra said to corporal Kigei, "This is Sumatra." "Is that true?" asked corporal Kigei. "Aii," said Sumatra the Elder. At this the private moved to stand behind Sumatra the Elder in case he might run away. He hitched his rifle sling over his shoulder so that both hands were free. Corporal Kigei lent forward looking very serious with both his hands around the muzzle of his rifle which was standing with the but on the ground in front of him. "They say that you killed three Wagishu," said the corporal. "Is this true?" "Yes indeed, said Sumatra, "They stole my honey barrels and nearly killed me." As he said this he lifted his blanket to show the not yet healed scar on his ribs. "It is against the orders of the DC to kill people. We will take you to the DC who will decide what to do to you. Private tie this man." With that corporal Kigei leveled his rifle at Sumatra the

Elder who knew that a rifle spat the death of fire. He had seen it when hunting with Bwana Paws. So he stood quite still while the private took a rawhide cord out of his pocket and tied Sumatra the Elder with his hands in front of him. Then they put a longer heavy cord between his tied wrists so that they could lead him away rather as one might a dog on a leash. Sumatra the Elder protested that he had only done what was right, but corporal Kigei said only, "Shut up and tell it to the DC." Corporal Kigei thought of himself as a superior person. He liked the feeling of power that carrying a rifle gave him, especially as it was backed up by the authority of the white man. Telling this tribesman man to shut up, felt good. Even the villagers knew that if they intervened, the KAR, the Kings African Rifles, would be sent out and any who opposed them would be shot. So they muttered darkly at their hero being arrested and lead away, but did not overwhelm the two *askaris* as they could have done. The consequences would have been too severe.

Corporal Kigei knew that they could not walk back to Endebess that day. So he headed for the Kassowai camp where there was a hut that police and forest department workers could use when they needed a place to stay overnight. They arrived there about five o'clock and set about gathering wood and getting a fire started in the hut. There they cooked their *ugali* and boiled some tea made thick with sugar, another privilege of police rations when on patrol. They did not offer any to Sumatra the Elder. He was a prisoner. They had no intention of sharing their rations with him. If he was hungry that was too bad. He should not have done anything to annoy the white man, the *wazungu*, and get himself arrested. In fact he must be bad and deserved to suffer. He was lucky they did not cuff him and hit him. So they left him hungry and tied in the back of the hut. After two or three hours corporal Kigei felt tired and told the private to sleep lying in front of the only door to the hut. The corporal himself went to sleep on the floor with his feet by the fire to keep them warm.

All this time Sumatra the Elder watched them darkly in the uncertain light of the fire in the middle of the hut. He squatted as motionless as cat over a mouse hole, waiting. He was so quiet the two policemen ignored him. When they were both asleep, Sumatra the Elder lifted his hands to his face. In fifteen minutes he had chewed through the rawhide cord and was free. The door of the hut opened inwards and the private was lying in front of it. Sumatra the Elder could have picked up one of their rifles, but he had never handled a gun. He would not have known how to take off the safety catch. Any way it was not a good idea to kill a policeman appointed by the white man. So he came up with a less dramatic but effective plan. He took up one of the sandals that the private had left lying near his feet and used it as shovel to pick a pile of hot embers from the fire. These he poured on the sleeping private and instantly kicked the other embers and smoldering remnants of wood over the legs and stomach of corporal Kigei. The effect was immediate. Both policemen leaped to their feet cursing and hopping around the hut slapping at the burning patches on their shorts and jerseys. Sumatra the Elder quietly opened the door and slipped into the darkness.

He ran, heading back down the path they had come by. He was about a hundred yards away when corporal Kigei burst out of the hut brandishing his rifle. He fired a quite useless shot in the dark. Sumatra the Elder hurried on. A new moon was just beginning to come up, so he could see the outline of the trees, black against the sky. He knew the mountain and all its trails so well he had no difficulty finding his way. But he did stub his toes every now and again against unseen rocks on the path. Once he impaled his thigh with one of those huge two inch long thorns from a waist high young white thorn tree. He pulled it out, painfully, and jogged on. Once he heard a snort and drumming of hooves and knew that he had disturbed a group of waterbuck which are bit bigger and heavier than a donkey. Apart from this his flight through the night was uneventful.

The moon was overhead when he arrived back at is hut. He knocked on the door saying in an urgent and low voice, "Watumba it is I Sumatra". He had to knock again before he heard an answer from his woman, in a small frightened voice, "I am coming". Then he heard her working on the cord that held the door. In a moment it swung open and he felt and smelt, rather than saw, her in the glow left by the embers of the evening cooking fire. Watumba put new sticks on the fire and soon there was enough light to gather up and warm the remains of the *ugali* she had cooked earlier. She waited for him to tell her the story of what had happened since the policemen had taken him away. It was not that she was not intensely curious. That she was. It simply is not a woman's place to ask about things that are a man's business. When he was warm and fed Sumatra the Elder told her the story. She laughed heartily at the description of the policemen dancing and cursing as they brushed hot coals off themselves and slapped the burning patches on their clothes. She fell silent however when he said, "I know they will come again for me." She had a sinking feeling as she thought of this. A woman who loses her man is like a buffalo calf that loses its mother. She faces a very uncertain future.

Sumatra the Elder slept soundly. He was tired. He knew the policemen would not come at night through unfamiliar territory. If they came in the morning it would be midday before they arrived. He was right. It was about eleven thirty when the dogs down the hill began barking and a ten year old boy came panting up to the hut to warn his hero, "The sirkali are coming," he said. "I was expecting them," said Sumatra the Elder somewhat to the boy's surprise. "Where are they going?" "To the big tree," said the boy. "There they will ask the mzee where I live and then they will come for me," mused Sumatra the Elder. And that is exactly what happened. By the time the policemen arrived Sumatra the Elder was well hidden in the nearby forest. Though too far away to hear anything, he saw the two policemen walk up to his hut. Soon Watumba came out and was obviously in conversation with the policemen. After a minute or so she threw up her hands as if to say, "I don't know." Corporal Kigei pushed her aside, leveled his rifle at the door and went inside. Finding the hut empty he came out and smacked Watumba across the face demanding, "Where is he?" "He ran away into the forest when he heard you were coming," said Watumba quite truthfully.

Corporal Kigei gritted his teeth in anger and frustration. It was quite obvious that the woman was telling the truth. That meant he would have to go back to Endebess without his prisoner. Sergeant Kiprono would mock him, "Two men with rifles and you can't even hold one man," he could hear him say. For a moment he wondered if he should try to swear the private to silence. He gave this thought up when he considered that he would have to explain the burn holes in their clothes at the next inspection. He knew he would have to face Kiprono's scorn. So he left thinking dark thoughts about Sumatra the Elder who was embarrassing him so.

Just as he had expected, sergeant Kiprono ridiculed him and due course reported to the DC that corporal Kigei had arrested the man and then allowed him to escape. The DC listened to the story attentively and reminded himself that Sergeant Kiprono was a good trooper. He was a man without the gift, or was it a curse, of education. A man of little imagination, but one who would do exactly as he was told. So the DC said, "Sergeant Kiprono, go yourself with three men and the iron handcuffs. This man has no other place to sleep. So go in two weeks and arrive at his hut at the third or fourth hour of the night and then arrest him." I will not burden you with the details of this second arrest other than to say that it went as the DC had instructed. The malice of corporal Kigei ran true to form. As soon as the hand cuffs were on Sumatra the Elder he began to beat him with his rifle but to vent his anger. Sergeant Kiprono promptly ordered him to stop, not out of sympathy or for reasons of principle, but for the common sense reason that if the prisoner could not walk they would have to carry him. So Sumatra the Elder walked to Endebess. The last two miles were along the old Karamoja trail which Arab slavers had used a generation before until the British put an end to slave trading by the Sultan of Zanzibar. This they did at the end of the nineteenth century. Sumatra the Elder was too young to have seen slave caravans although he had heard of them. So he was unimpressed by the history of the red dusty road that he walked in handcuffs as others had walked before him. Three days later he found himself in a stone walled cell in the Kitale prison waiting on the decision of the District Commissioner.

The District Commissioner, a Charles Fotheringham, had read classics at Oxford before joining the British Colonial Service. He had started his career enthusiastically with a genuine desire to bring the benefits of English civilization to His Majesty's colonies, wherever they might be. Between the two world wars England had not yet lost its belief in self. Of course there was a Fabian Society and a Socialist party. But they had not yet degenerated into apologists for their culture. The left had not generally begun to denigrate what was then perceived as, "civilization". Particularly for the Socialists it was then a drive for power that concerned them. They alone knew how to govern society and create a working class utopia. But at that time the English ruling classes still ruled. They believed in Empire and the superiority of their civilization and ideas. The decadence and self destructiveness of moral and cultural relativism was to grip the intelligentsia and the media only as civil rights became fashionable in America in the sixties and later. Fotheringham was a man of his time. He truly believed in the benefits of British rule and *pax* Brittanica. Stopping savages slaughtering each other was part of the white man's burden as he saw it.

As District Commissioner he reported to the Provincial Commissioner, who reported to the Governor, who in turn reported to the Colonial Secretary and the British Cabinet which ran his Majesty's government. He was in fact a representative of the British Crown and saw himself as such. Benevolent though the Crown might think it was, within his territory Fotheringham's word was law. To back it up he could call first on the police force. It was a paramilitary force armed with rifles. If that were not enough, the white officered Kings African Rifles (the feared KAR) were there to be called on.

In those days to be, "booked," at a police station meant what it said. The prisoner's name, tribe, date of arrest and charge against him were recorded in the big book. This was done in ink by a clerk using a goose quill, or pen with a metal nib. Both were dipped in an ink well on the desk. When a man was, "booked," no lawyers came rushing to the door waving writs. There were no lawyers in Kitale. So no one paid any particular attention when the name of Sumatra the Elder was entered in the book with the charge that he had disturbed his Majesty's peace by killing three Wagishu. Good riddance thought the captain in charge who did not like Wagishu. But he said nothing. The penalty for murder was automatic and British, "To be hung by the neck until he be dead". The captain understood well that Sumatra the Elder was proud of what he had done in the circumstances, and was sympathetic. But the captain worked for the white man and the white man's orders must be obeyed however irrational they might seem. The white man was called in Swahili, "*Mzungu*," meaning the mad or unpredictable one. To most Africans of that time they might as well have been all powerful Martians so strange were their ideas to men who lived tribal lives in the bush. But one thing Sumatra the Elder did understand, the white man was all powerful. So he fully expected to die, not in years but in a few weeks.

There was only one place in Kitale where the white man then ate and drank. It was the Kitale club, a big rambling colonial building with wide verandahs, green lawns, and a golf course. There was a men only bar, another room where women and men were allowed to have a drink, and a big dining room. One wing had guest rooms, the other, the kitchen and utility rooms. All *wazungu* who went out to lunch, went there. So it came to pass that District Commissioner Charles Fotheringham found himself sitting at the same table as the man known to Sumatra the Elder as Bwana Paws. In the course of conversation Fotheringham said, "You know Buster old chap, I have a man in jail who says he knows you." "Who is that?" replied Bwana Paws. "His name is Sumatra. He said he is your tracker and guide when you go hunting on the mountain." "You mean

Sumatra the Elder the Elgon Masai, not very tall but very broad and strong?" "Sounds like the same man." "So what's he in jail for?" "Murder!" "What do you mean murder? He seems to me to be a good man, reliable, always on time and a great tracker." "Well he admits to killing three Wagishu." "Was he cattle raiding?" "No, he said they stole his honey barrels that he had hanging in the forest." "So what are you going to do?" "Hang him of course. I can't have a chap going around in my district killing people over honey barrels." "Well," said Bwana Paws, "I don't know the story, but I want to look into it and talk to you." "If you want to get involved you can," replied Fotheringham, "But I cannot talk to you about a case outside the court room." "When is the hearing?" "A week from next Thursday at ten in the morning in the police station court room." Fotheringham's tone of voice clearly said no more conversation about Sumatra the Elder. So they talked of maize crops, cattle dipping and the problems of native cattle spreading disease because they were not dipped, the wet weather and similar topics of interest in a farming community.

Bwana Paws went over to the police station after lunch and asked to see the prisoner Sumatra. The desk officer was very surprised at a white man wanting to see a prisoner. He went in to the back and said to the Captain, "There is a *mzungu* here who wants to see Sumatra." "Why?" said the Captain. "He says that Sumatra is his hunting tracker," said the policeman. That satisfied the Captain as to why a person as important as a *mzungu* would have any interest in a no account forest man like Sumatra, so he said "Let him talk to him through the bars." A few minutes later Bwana Paws saw that it was in deed Sumatra the Elder, the man he knew. His heart sank. He liked him. If there is such a thing as a noble savage, a man of and in nature, Sumatra the Elder was it. Bwana Paws could not help visualizing the grayish tone the black skin on his face would have at the end of a rope. He had seen a number men hung from trees after lynchings in the Northern Frontier. He knew immediately that he would do his best for Sumatra the Elder, but he had little hope. The killings were not denied.

Bwana Paws spoke the Kings English with no accent, in other words as the King would speak it. He had grown up in a very small English village in Suffolk. His home there was known as the Old Rectory. He lived there because his Father was, for forty five years, a "gaming parson" for the parish church. That meant that during the week he was a game keeper for the local big landowner and on the weekends and holy days he administered to the spiritual needs of his small flock. Bwana Paws father had no money and could not send the young man to university to read law as he so earnestly wanted. So the young Bwana Paws had to sublimate his interest in the law. Instead he became an army officer. In the early nineteen twenties believing there would never be another major war he abandoned the army and at the suggestion of Lord Howard de Walden, whom he had known as a boyhood friend, went out to pioneer the British Empire in Kenya with the backing of his patron. When he first went there, the railway had not yet reached Kitale, so he drove his ox wagons forty miles from Eldoret to the foothills of Mt Elgon and began the long fight to establish a cattle ranch and grow wheat and maize on a farm known as Chorlim. Hyenas, locusts, cattle raiders, rinderpest and elephants in the maize fields were routine. But Bwana Paws' childhood yearning to advocate for the accused remained unrequited. Growing up in a small English country village he would never have guessed that the yearning would be met in a room with a concrete floor and galvanized iron roof on the very frontier in Africa.

Bwana Paws listened to the story told by Sumatra the Elder and realized at once that the fact of his having killed the three men was not in issue. Sumatra the Elder readily admitted it and was proud of the three fresh scars on his cheekbone. He ended his story saying, "Bwana Paws you are a *mzungu*. Why does the DC want to strangle me? I have not done him or any *mzungu* any harm." To him his logic was impeccable. He said to himself, "I have not hurt you or yours, so why do you want to hurt me? If you wanted to kill me in order to take my woman or my cattle or even my honey barrels, I could understand. But you want nothing from me except to end my life which is then of no use to you." Bwana Paws did his unsuccessful best to answer. He struggled to explain in Kiswahili their only common language. Kiswahili had no words for concepts of British law for the good reason that such concepts did not exist in tribal Africa. All that Sumatra the Elder could understand was, "The DC has a rule, you may not kill anyone, even of another tribe. If you do then the DC kills you." This much Sumatra the Elder understood even though he did not understand why the *wazungu* had such a rule punishing the traditional killing of another tribe. So he prepared himself to die and hoped, as did Bwana Paws too, that he would not lose his courage and would die like a man when the moment came. He appreciated Bwana Paws wanting to help, but did not expect anything. The DC was a more important man than Bwana Paws and wanted him dead. His emotion was not sorrow for Watumba or pity for himself. It was simply fear. Fear of dying, the despair of not being able to run or fight.

Bwana Paws parked outside the police station at 9.45am the next Thursday. In the old model T Ford with running boards and headlights he had three elders from the village of Sumatra the Elder. The police station court room was a large depressing sort of room with the flavor of a warehouse. It had a plain concrete floor with white washed walls going up to bare rafters and a galvanized iron roof with no ceiling. The windows had no glass in them, just iron bars where the sparrows hopped in and out. At one end was a big desk for the DC. On his right was the dock and on his left a table and chairs for the translator and native assessors. The three men Bwana Paws had brought sat at the table. About fifteen feet in front of the DC's desk were several backless wooden benches for witnesses and any public spectators. There were no desks or chairs in front of the bar for lawyers, although there was one for the clerk who kept a short record of the proceedings and judgment in each case. The clerk also kept the "book" and called all cases.

Bwana Paws had the clerk bring him a chair which was placed at one end of the DC's desk. Several off duty constables came in to see what was happening. It was the first time that a *mzungu* had appeared to help, instead of prosecute, a black man. That created quite a stir and rampant speculation as to why a *mzungu* would waste his time to do such a thing. Sumatra the Elder was not a chief, not a man of importance. The constables felt no compassion for the death of a person of another tribe. That a white man might have compassion for a black man about to be put to death by another white man was not even within the realm of speculation. Does the warrior feel sorrow for the lion he spears, or the lion for the antelope he kills? The powerful kill the weak. That is in the nature of things. So the constables decided, correctly, that Sumatra the Elder must be a very good hunting guide for Bwana Paws. For his part Bwana Paws was moved only a little by that consideration. If the truth were said, he was moved by compassion, but he would not admit that even to himself. He knew that compassion could be a weakness stopping a man from doing what must be done, unpleasant though it might be. So he rationalized his involvement as being on legal grounds.

Promptly at 10.00am Fotheringham came into the court room. All stood including Bwana Paws. The police sergeant on duty saluted. Fotheringham bid Bwana Paws a friendly, "Good morning Buster," and then directed the sergeant to, "Bring in the prisoner." Sumatra the Elder was brought in with his hands cuffed in front of him, still wearing the same brown blanket. He was relieved to see Bwana Paws there. It gave him hope. Faint though it was, it kept him from the abyss of total despair. "Read the charge," Fotheringham told the clerk. "Sumatra son of Sirengo you are charged with the killing of three Wagishu on Mt Elgon when the time of the rain was there." "Translate it" said Fotheringham to the court translator. This and all conversation was translated. Fotheringham took an active part in the case, not seeing himself as the referee of a contest between lawyers as is the practice in America. He saw himself as a representative of the Imperial Crown bound to apply the law and do justice as best he could see it. There being no lawyers in the room and no formal prosecutor he somewhat informally asked Sumatra the Elder, "Did you kill the Wagishu?" "Ahee yes

I did," replied Sumatra the Elder, "And they very nearly killed me."
"Why did you kill them?" asked Fotheringham. "Because the stole
my honey barrels," was the reply. Fotheringham then turned to
the table where the three old men sat and said, "Is this true?" "Yes
Bwana DC," the eldest replied. For Fotheringham it was an open
and shut case as he had expected. "Then I find you Sumatra son of
Sirengo, guilty of murder of three Wagishu as charged," said Fotheringham. "The penalty for murder is death by hanging. Before I
pronounce sentence do you have anything to say?"

After this was translated there was a long silence, then all eyes
turned to Bwana Paws as he spoke very formally. "Your Honor I
wish to refresh your recollection, should that be necessary, con-
cerning the white paper on the East African Colonies that was published by His Majesty's Government in 1923. In relevant part it
reads as follows:

> *Primarily, Kenya is an African territory, and HM Government
> think it necessary definitely to record their considered opinion that
> the interests of the African natives must be paramount, and that
> if and when those interests and the interests of the immigrant races
> should conflict the former should prevail....*

> *In the administration of Kenya HM Government regard
> themselves as exercising a trust on behalf of the African popula-
> tion......*

> *In administering this trust native law and custom shall pre-
> vail except when contrary to natural justice.*

I wish to speak to the last sentence in particular. We do not
prosecute the native for bigamy when he has more than one wife,
though we certainly would a European. We do not presume to
tell them what form marriage must take or how their land will be
inherited. What the prisoner did was entirely in accordance with
native law and custom. As the prisoner and his tribe see it, the

prisoner has done no wrong. I have the elders of the prisoner's village here to testify to the law and custom of the forest and the honey barrel. Very respectfully your honor I submit to you that native law and custom should prevail in this case". "Thank you for your observations," said Fotheringham. "As you know tribal warfare was the custom before British rule. Slavery by the Arabs was too. Both have been stopped by the British. That is part of Kenya's recorded history. The prisoner would not have killed a man of his own tribe for stealing his honey barrels. He used the theft as a pretext for a tribal killing."

"As you say," replied Bwana Paws, "He would not have killed one of his own tribe. That is part of native law and custom. The theft was not a "pretext", it was a justifiable reason for the killings as he saw it. He never denied the killing. Nor has he ever admitted any wrong doing. He is illiterate. He speaks no English. He was ignorant of the white man's law. Ignorance of the law may be no excuse to us, but for him that rule is unfair".

"I have to administer the trust imposed on me by His Majesty's Government," replied Fotheringham. "I cannot quash a murder conviction just because the man killed was of another tribe. What if he had killed a white man? I have no doubt he felt he was justified, but in law and in principle I cannot condone it, cannot allow it. As Lord Mansfield once observed, 'Hard cases make good law.' The prisoner's conviction must stand".

"Then you honor may I address you on the question of sentence?" "The sentence is clear," replied Fotheringham, "To be hung by the neck until he be dead". "I accept that is the penalty for murder provided by the penal code," responded Bwana Paws, "However, section 293 of the Code provides in part that:

"Notwithstanding any other provision of this code, the judge or magistrate may vary any penalty provided for, taking into account all the facts and circumstances of the case."

I urge you to exercise your discretion and mitigate the penalty in this case. Even the English criminal justice system does not hang a lunatic, who does not realize what he did was wrong. In this case the prisoner thought he was doing right. I have brought the elders of his village here to give you evidence of this".

"Very well I will ask them," responded Fotheringham. He then engaged in a dialogue with the elders through the interpreter. After ten minutes or so he stopped questioning them and was silent. In the court room there was not as sound. Outside, as though on a distant planet, the usual murmur of voices and chirping of birds could be heard. Inside all waited as life and death hung in the balance. A corporal coughed and the chair on which Bwana Paws sat squeaked with the sharpness of a knife cut across the silence as he shifted his weight. All eyes were on Fotheringham as he struggled with his thoughts. Then he turned to Bwana Paws and said, "All right I won't hang him. I will decide later on the jail time."

Bwana Paws breathed out audibly, then he stood and said, "Thank you your honor." He then walked over to Sumatra the Elder and said simply, "They will not kill you. They will put you in Hoteli ya Kingi Georgi for many years." Sumatra the Elder lifted his cuffed hands and took Bwana Paws hand. The two men said nothing as they looked in each others faces for a long, long moment. Each knew what the other felt. Between the two men emotions were not expressed. That would have shown weakness. It was the frontier. Man's country. Bwana Paws did not see Sumatra the Elder again for twenty years.

Bending Twig

3. Birth and Death

About nine months after District Commissioner Fotheringham had sentenced Sumatra the Elder to twenty years in prison for spearing three Wagishu who stole his honey barrels, he chanced to have lunch with Bwana Paws in the Kitale Club. "Buster, you remember that tracker of yours, Sumatra, who killed the three Wagishu, I want to tell you that he will be sent to the Northern Frontier as part of a road gang. There is a prison camp at Marsabit where he will be based." "Thank you for letting me know Charles, but why are you telling me this?" "Well he won't be back for a long time, so if he has any family that want to see him, next week is the last opportunity." "The case has bothered you, hasn't it?" "Yes." "Well I'll let his wife know and bring her into to town if she wants to come." The conversation then drifted on to club finances and the number of Afrikaaners who were applying for membership in that predominantly English institution. Prejudices still lingered from the Boer War at the turn of the century thirty years before.

When Bwana Paws came home he gave instructions that Sumatra's wife Watumba be informed that Sumatra was to be sent to the Northern Frontier and if she wanted to see him he would take her to Kitale next week. This option was rephrased by the messenger as a command from the white man that she must visit Sumatra. This rephrasing gave the messenger the status of an order giver not simply an informant; made him feel important. Although the messenger was pleased Watumba was not. She had given birth to her first son about two months before and would have to take him along. Also, she had never before been more than a mile or two from home, had never been in a car and knew that in that distant place called Kitale there were all kinds of bad people who would trick you and steal from you. The messenger enjoyed bullying her, however, and insisted that she be at Bwana Paws house on the hill not more than two hours after sunrise next Monday. Reluctantly she said she would be there. On the appointed day she was running a fever and felt very sick. But she did not know what might happen if she disobeyed. The fact that the *wazungu* had taken her man from her very recently, reminded her that they had powers beyond her understanding. Better to please them, than oppose them. So she started off at the first sign of dawn and was sitting by Bwana Paw's garage at 8.00am when he was ready to go to Kitale.

Watumba had no idea how to open a car door; she had never used a door handle in her life. Her hut door was tied with a rawhide strap at night. She was at a complete loss when told to get in. She stood there uncertainly wondering if she could squeeze in through the partly open window. Seeing her confusion, the driver Mahindi opened the door and put her in the back of the van. They left and after half an hour of driving over dusty, bumpy dirt roads arrived at Bwana Paws' office in Kitale. The office was a building designed by Bwana Paws himself. With its clock tower, two stories and red tile roof it would have fit well on the high street of an English country town. In remote Africa it looked quite out of place surrounded by the flat or galvanized iron roofs of Indian *dukas*. To Watumba it was as strange as a Martian city would have been to Bwana Paws. She was happy to hide in the back of the van and not have to face the strangeness she saw.

After dropping off Bwana Paws at the office Mahindi drove Watumba to the prison. There, with some empathy for her nervousness, Mahindi walked her into the front office. When Watumba did not see Sumatra, she was at a complete loss. She had been told to come to the prison to see him. She was at the prison and he was not there. So she stood silent looking around in fear as though seeking an escape route. Mahindi explained to the prison desk officer that she had come to see a prisoner called Sumatra and she was his wife. The desk officer grunted and told her to wait outside. She was too frightened to ask for water though her fever flamed within her. So she sat on the ground under a tree, nursed her baby and waited, feeling sicker than the stray dogs that looked on. After an hour or so she was summoned to go inside to a room with one door and no furniture at all. There Sumatra the Elder waited for her. The door clanged shut and she was told she had half an hour. They did not kiss Western style partly because it was not their custom and partly because Watumba had taken the baby from the cloth carrying scarf on her back and held it in her arms. This was the first time Sumatra the Elder had seen or heard of the baby. Surprised and wondering if it was his, he asked "How old is it?" She had not been visibly pregnant when he was arrested. "About two months," she said. He was silent for a moment as he calculated that she must have been carrying the child when he left. He smiled and reached out to hold it saying, "Is it a boy or a girl?" "A boy," she answered. On balance he was pleased. A man who has only girls leaves nothing behind him. Richer with cows he may be, but his seed is lost to another man. "Name him after me, and go live in my brother's *boma*. I am to be sent far away beyond the mountain that is shaped like the end of a spear." He was referring to Riwa whose peak rose in a diamond point, blue in the distance to the North. "Yes, the Bwana has told me. I am very ill I must sit."

So saying she sank to the floor and with great effort took back the baby that had started crying, finding itself in strange hands. He squatted in front of her and they talked of things on the ridge where his hut was. He could see it in his mind's eye and it gave him comfort. What he did not know was when he would ever see that hut again. He did not know Watumba would never get there. She fell silent with her head lolling against the wall as though she were asleep. Sumatra realized she was indeed very ill. There was nothing he could do and he knew better than to ask for sympathy from the prison staff. They delighted in making life in prison harsher and more painful than life on the outside. If the white man in his madness would house and feed wrongdoers, instead of fining or beating them, then the prison staff would steal half the prisoners rations, give them no water all day and make them understand the meaning of 'Hard Labor'. Soon the door opened with a metallic scrape and Watumba struggled to her feet to leave. She sat under the same tree until Mahindi came at noon and took her back to sit under another tree outside Bwana Paws' office. Mahindi gave her water from the office cup. She thanked him and looking at the baby said, "His name is Sumatra." The remark was perhaps a premonition of what was to come. It was so out of context Mahindi remembered it when it became relevant some time later.

Watumba waited until four thirty when Bwana Paws' office day was done. Except when the baby nursed, she slept. Then Mahindi loaded her sluggish body into the back of the van and drove Bwana Paws home. The red dust that billowed up under the van penetrated everything especially in the back where Watumba was. She had a fine red covering all over her by the time they arrived back at the house on Mt Elgon. This was two hours march away from her hut up the mountain to the North. It was now five o'clock. The clouds had come up from over Lake Victoria and the thunderheads rose ten thousand feet high. The malaria had been coming over Watumba's body in waves every few hours as generations of filarium multiplied repeatedly in her blood stream. Her head pounded, her temples were on fire and every step was an effort. But she knew no one on Bwana Paws' farm. She had never been there before. The people were strange to her. In the morning she had met only one who spoke her language, that of the Elgon Masai. In the evening he was not there. The Nandi, the Luo, Kitosh and Kikuyu she could not understand, and she did not speak any Kiswahili. In the midst of people, she was alone, frightened, and feeling awful. Under those towering black cumulus clouds, she started out for her own little spot of safety and security, her hut on the hillside far away. She never made it. She had struggled along the path through the forest for about an hour when the storm broke. The rain came down in enormous cold, cold drops as the lightning crashed. In less than a minute she was soaked and trembling even more violently with the fever burning in her. She took shelter in the hollow of an old podo tree so big five men could not put their arms around it. Fire from honey hunters of another year had burnt out the old dead wood at the centre leaving a cone about five feet high and three feet deep. Watumba crawled into this hollow and put young Sumatra on her lap. She barely felt him as he pulled at her breast. She leant back shivering, trembling, but no longer pounded by the rain. Her eyes closed in relief and her headache faded as she slipped into unconsciousness. She never woke up. The evening turned to night and some time before dawn her body went cold. Young Sumatra began to howl as though he knew.

Watumba's spirit still lives in that enormous tree. She was a woman of the earth, the bush and the forest, so her spirit was comfortable there. If you sit under that tree and clear your mind of daily things until it is quiet, you can hear her sighing softly. If you are still for some time, you will be at peace, as she is, and you will become aware of the creatures that live there. The sensitive timid duiker, a tiny deer with delicate hooves. The waterbuck taller than a cow with its great curving horns and white rump. The colobus monkey, the aristocrat of all monkeys, black with large white whiskers and flowing sides of white, always a courteous gentleman. The sly, small blue monkeys, and baboons, always thieving and not be trusted. From the plains may come ever helpful painted dog and, not so welcome, hyena who thrives on the misfortune of others. Overhead you will see the iridescent green and blue parakeets eating the acorns of the podo tree and hornbills with huge yellow beaks. All these live there and are part of the natural order of things.

Snitch, one of the blue monkeys, was sleeping in the podo tree when Sumatra started crying. He woke up and wondered why a man child should be crying under his tree. Such a thing had never happened before. But it was dark and Snitch was scared to explore in the dark even though his curiosity was burning him up. In the end the man child stopped crying and Snitch wondered if he had died. As soon as it was light he went down the tree to a low branch where he could see the hollow where Watumba lay. He thought they were both dead, but lacking in courage he did not go close to them. Instead he ran to break the news to his band and soon they were all chattering about it. "Let's tell hyena," said the unsympathetic Snitch always wanting to ingratiate himself. "He will clean up the bodies." "You do it if you want, Hyena is not for me," said the biggest of them. "All right I will," said Snitch setting off down the hill to where Hyena had his lair in a tunnel made by an ant-bear. As he left Sumatra started crying again, though weaker now. The blue monkeys all gathered around to see, chattering and waiting for Hyena to come and finish the affair. They made such a noise that a troupe of colobus monkeys heard them and came to investigate. The blue monkeys fell silent as the much larger, regal, colobus stalked haughtily through them. Without hesitation a small group came carefully down from the branches and walked over to the hollow at the bottom of the tree. They saw at once that the big human was dead, but the child lived. One of the colobus, known as Bending Twig, because of her flexible nature, had recently lost her half grown child to a leopard. So her heart went out to the man child. She went to their leader, the old Wise One. She was their guide by common consent in such matters. "Can I take him? I am sure I can keep him alive," she said. The Wise One thought for a minute then looking kindly into Bending Twig's eyes said, "It would not be good." "But why not?" asked Bending Twig. "I think you could keep the man child alive," she answered, "But he will never be able to leap and run with us through the tree tops. He will have to stay on the ground where you cannot help him. He will be eaten and you probably would be too. Even if you live, you will almost certainly lose again." "When he grows I can turn him over to the man tribe," said Bending Twig. "You could, if he lived that long," said the Wise One, "but they grow very slowly. Even if you could keep him safe for that long, once he is half grown he will think and act like one of us, as best he can. Then the problem will be that at that age he will not be able to change to be really man. He can never be a monkey like us nor would he ever be completely man. He would be a misfit, an out cast forever. Let man raise man. If you wish we can tell the old man of the forest who lives in Chepnall cave. Perhaps he will save him and raise him as man." Bending Twig gritted her teeth and sighed as she accepted the decision. Then in a burst of passion said, "Let me tell him." "Go, fly like a bird," said the Wise One with a smile. So Bending Twig dashed off through the tree tops. She did not know that Snitch had gone to tell Hyena and time was short. As it was, Hyena arrived at the tree quite a bit before the old man of the forest who was known as the Mzee ya Shimu, meaning old man of the cave, or Simu for short.

Snitch and Hyena got along because they shared a common characteristic, cowardice, or as they would prefer, 'sensible caution'. Hyena had more reason than Snitch to fear man. He and his clan were in constant conflict with man, eating their sheep and goats if they could and biting off the tails of sleeping cows. The other end of the cow had horns so Hyena would not dream of attacking there. When he came to the podo tree he could see and smell man. All the alarm bells in him went off. He circled the tree keeping well away expecting some kind of trap. Perhaps the man person was just pretending to be dead. He sat and watched and waited to see if there were any movement. Only Sumatra moved and cried. Hyena knew that he would be a couple of gulps only.

He made some short rushes at the tree to see if he could provoke a defensive response like a cow swinging its horns at him. Nothing happened. So each time he came closer and more confident, until he was able to reach out with those most powerful jaws and grab Watumba's foot. He began to drag her out from the hollow of the tree and Sumatra cried louder as he rolled off her lap.

So intent had Hyena been on his task, he did not notice the arrival of Simu. The first he knew was a burning pain as Simu's spear, almost missing its target, cut off his hind paws. With a howl he reared up, turned, and fled with a horrible shuffling gait, as Simu charged him with his *panga* glinting in the early morning light. Some say Hyena's cry of "Ooowump," dates from that day. Certainly, since then he has always shuffled and looked deformed with his hind legs shorter than the front. No one felt any sympathy for him, not even Snitch, whose loyalty was only to himself.

One glance told Simu that Watumba was lifeless. Having heard Sumatra cry he knew the baby still lived as Bending Twig had said. But his cry was weak, and the child exhausted and cold. Bending Twig hovered in the branches above him, elated at the narrow escape from Hyena, but full of anxiety about Sumatra's condition. She knew how quickly a young one can die when it is wet bedraggled and cold. She watched with hope and an intense desire to shout, "Hurry," as Simu studied the scene. First he took Watumba's carrying scarf from her and wrapped the baby up. That done, he noticed and admired her leather skirt decorated with small red white and blue beads, and some *cowrie* shells. He saw too the copper bangles on her wrist. Without embarrassment he took all these off and rolled them up in her dirty brown shawl. These things had value and he was a poor man. For him it was 'finders keepers'. He hesitated as he thought about what to do with Sumatra. He remembered his pain when his own children and wife had died of the disease of many spots a long time ago. The emotion rose up his throat as though it would choke him. He stood quite still, holding Sumatra as he fought for control, thankful that no one could see the shame of a man's tears. Gradually he mastered it, as Bending

Twig wondered what on earth was wrong. Simu was not sure if he wanted to see another child die, even one that was a stranger to him. He knew that such a death would make him relive the grief that had caused him to leave and live alone in Chepnall cave, an, 'out of sight out of mind', escape. He owed this child nothing, did not know his name or where he came from. He could just leave right now. He knew that if he did not, if he intervened, tried to save this child, then by sundown he might be carrying a reminder of what he had worked hard to forget. Also, if he saved a life he would become responsible for it. Sumatra's future hung in the balance until Bending Twig said, "Take him and let him be man. You said you would!" Simu looked up at Bending Twig, and said to himself, "What a handsome one." In that moment he remembered that he had indeed told her he would try to help. He wanted to please her, but knew he did not have to live to that casual commitment. Then he realized that though he loved the rocky Bluff, the forest and the animals in it, he missed the companionship of his fellow man. He remembered the pleasure of giving learning and guidance to a young child and being rewarded by his growth and co-operation. At an almost sub-conscious level he knew he had to do this, to love again if his life was to have meaning, even if, with loving came the risk of losing. So he swallowed hard, got a grip on himself, and moved decisively. Bending Twig heaved a deep sigh of relief and followed him.

Knowing he had no milk in Chepnall cave, Simu headed for his old *manyatta* above the tree line, three thousand feet up from where he was now. He knew he did not have much time. So, with Bending Twig racing through the tree tops behind him he hurried up the side of the Bluff before Chepnall cave and through the open park land on the flat spur that runs for three kilometers behind the Bluff. That land is studded with enormous trees. It is a place of grand beauty and solitude too. About half way to where the mountain rises sharply again, the bamboo starts. It is, of course, like giant yellow grass, long, straight and bendy with no real branches. It could not take the weight of a colobus monkey without bending right over, making it impossible for a monkey to run and jump. So Bending Twig stopped at the bamboo line and sadly watched Simu disappear. In less than fifty yards he was out of sight.

The bamboo, and the trees scattered through it, end at about ten thousand feet where the alpine moorland starts. Reaching this point, breathing heavily, Simu saw his old *manyatta* across a valley about half a mile away. As he came closer he smelt it too. It was the smell of wood smoke, mud and cow dung. It stirred in him a warm glow of good feeling and happy childhood memories. He had grown up in one of three huts there, and had personally helped build the other two. One of these substituted as a shed for the cattle. Unlike the traditional African hut which is round with a conical thatched roof, these huts were rectangular with slightly domed roofs. There being no thatching grass above the tree line, the roofs, like the walls too, were made of woven branches daubed with a mix of elephant dung and the same red mud that made the walls. For building, elephant dung is better than the usual cow dung because it has a larger amount of fiber in it, two or three inches long. This holds the mud together as straw gave strength to the mud bricks the Israelites made for the Egyptians. Simu remembered many a happy elephant dung collecting trip into the forest as he was growing up. Converging on the huts were foot paths and tracks cut like wavy ribbons into the red earth where the cattle and goats came home at dusk and left again in the morning.

As the low roofs came into sight over the crest of the rise in front of him, Simu hurried on. Sumatra lay still. He had not even whimpered for some time now. Simu headed for the hut where Maziwa lived, calling out as he came so all would know he came in peace. Maziwa was his brother's daughter, now nursing her third child. She was a thick set, strong, well built woman with a cheerful smile and big breasts which was fortunate. In the West she would definitely have won a wet T shirt contest. "Greetings Uncle, what is your news?" she said as custom required. Equally formally he responded, "Greetings Maziwa, my news is good, but I have a problem. I need milk for this baby who is near death." "What are you, the forest hermit, of all people, doing with a baby?" she replied, adding "all the cows are out grazing until sundown." "I will tell you, but first will you feed him?" As he spoke his eyes left her face and traveled to her bosom. Maziwa looked him right in the eye for a long moment, then slowly and thoughtfully said, "For the baby's sake I will do it now, but Kisharani will not let me share my milk with another man's child. Is this your child? Why is it not with its Mother?" "His Mother is dead. First feed him then I will tell you all." So Maziwa took young Sumatra to her breast. She noted that he was too weak to hold and knead her breast with his fingers, but he did drink, and she judged correctly that he would live. As she fed the baby Simu told her the story

That evening the lowing herd came up the hill from watering at the river, and headed for the night safety of the cattle shed. The main concern was leopard and hyena, although there was then the occasional lion. Maziwa's husband, Kisharani, came behind them. He had spear in hand, shiny *simi* (double sided short sword) on a leather thong around his naked waist, and his ochre colored blanket knotted over one shoulder hanging down to his knees. His relationship with Simi had never been warm, correct at best. Kisharani was a muscular, brash, opinionated, not very bright and rather lazy young man. He had paid the bride price to Maziwa's Father, who was Simu's brother, but had not built her a hut, as tradition required. Instead he had taken over the huts left by Simu. A stand up man would have taken the woman into his family and built his own hut, not moved into her Uncle's hut. Kisharani had a justified, if underlying, feeling of inadequacy. He attempted to drown out his nagging doubts about himself by adopting a defiant and defensive attitude to others. Maziwa would have preferred to have belonged to a more principled man, but that had not been her choice to make. At least, she reflected, she had fetched the highest bride price in recent years.

Kisharani put the cattle at one end of the shed used for that purpose, and the sheep and goats behind a dividing wall at the other end. Then he came to Maziwa's hut. He was taken aback to see Simu. "*Jambo*, what are you doing here?" he said breaking etiquette by not asking "*Habari yako?*" or, "What is your news." "*Jambo*, my news is good," responded Simu ignoring the breach of etiquette in failing to ask how he was. "He has brought a baby to our house," interjected Maziwa pointing to Sumatra sleeping in a corner. "Quiet woman! I was not speaking to you," said Kisharani hesitating as he absorbed the fact that there was another baby in the hut. "I found a baby in the forest and brought him to Maziwa so he would not die," said Simu. "Why should my woman feed another man's baby?" replied Kisharani. It was a statement not a question. "When a cow dies you ask another to take its calf and sometimes it will," said Simu. "I have asked my niece and she is willing to do this for me." "It is for me not her to decide," replied Kisharani. "Of course that is true," said Maziwa tactfully, "Perhaps my Uncle should discuss it with the Elders." She was not afraid of Kisharani and quicker than he. She knew he would be embarrassed to have the whole clan know that he had refused his Uncle by marriage in whose hut he was living. Kisharani glared at Maziwa not wanting to admit his discomfort at the idea. "I do not want another man's child ruining my children," he said nastily. "He will not be here long enough to do that," said Simu confirming in his own mind a decision that he had only half acknowledged earlier. "When he is recovered I will take him," he said. "Make sure you do," said the ever charming Kisharani.

Without thinking it in so many words, Simu had intervened to save a life, and thereby taken on a duty to care for it. He accepted this without debate. At a time and place where each family would periodically struggle to survive famine and disease, there were no social services to which one could shift such a responsibility. If one assumed an obligation, made a mistake or suffered a misfortune, one could not pass the burden on to one's fellow man by transferring it to a government agency. As a consequence, without thinking about it, African people were not irresponsible; they were strong and self reliant. The current Western concept of blaming your problems on others, of having other people pay to solve either the personal mistakes you make, or the obligations you assume, and then don't care to carry out, would have struck Simu as being quite wrong. But, then that is why the white man is called "*Mzungu*" or crazy one. He did not know it, but Simu had in effect adopted a helpless child. In the West he would have found, to his surprise, that his fitness to raise the child would have been investigated and, in his case almost certainly denied as he lived alone. As a responsible man of good will, he would have been even more surprised to find that the people who denied him his wish to love and care for a child would vehemently advocate the unlimited right of unmarried women to have as many children as they wished whether or not they could care for them well. When it concerned such things Simu was fortunate to live in a less, 'progressive', society.

But Simu did not know of these things and so did not think about them. He spent the rest of the evening in conversation mostly with Maziwa, with Kisharani listening, telling about how he came to find Sumatra and had driven off hyena. How there was nothing on the dead woman but the dress she wore and some bangles which he had. He had no idea who she was. All agreed that is was very strange that a woman should be going through the forest alone. She had no strap to put around her forehead to hold firewood on her back and carried no *panga*. So she was not a local looking for firewood. She must have been traveling, but where from, and where had she been going? No one could guess. Kisharani soon demanded to know how soon Simu would take the child away. He pushed, of course, for next morning. Maziwa made the valid point that the baby could not yet eat solid food and Simu had no milk. Kisharani adamantly refused to have another man's baby in his house a day longer than absolutely necessary. In the end, some time after they had finished their evening meal, it was agreed that when the baby was recovered Simu would take a nanny goat of his choice on loan and young Sumatra would be raised on goat's milk. In return for the loan of the goat, every time the moon was round,

Simu was to bring a bag of wild honey to Kisharani. When this arrangement had been made Simu left to sleep in the hut used as a barn for the cattle and sheep. Years before Simu had built a sleeping platform there with sticks. He did this because a leopard had been trying to claw through the walls to eat the sheep. The platform was nobly and uncomfortable, and the smell was pungent. It was also totally dark as there was no fire there. But Simu carried no blanket and the hut had the great advantage of being very warm from the body heat of the animals, while outside it froze most nights, as is normal in equatorial montane environments.

Simu lay on the sleeping platform oblivious to the heavy breathing of the cattle and occasional bleat from calf or kid. It was something his mind registered but took no notice of, like cocks crowing in the morning, or, for a *muzungu*, traffic noise on a road in a European city. But his mind was not at rest. His thoughts were troubled. He was not particularly adventurous or risk taking by temperament. He liked routine, the certainty that tomorrow would be pretty much like today. He would rather his life be predictable than exciting. The loss of his family to sickness some years before Bending Twig's call for help had been a blow that made him withdraw into seclusion rather than go out and seek new opportunities after a period of mourning. Now the events of this day had come to change the even tenor of his daily life in Chepnall cave. He was aware that a child would entail a major change in his routine, although he did not yet appreciate just how major. He was not quite sure why he had saved the child. As he lay in the dark and reviewed the happenings of the day, he began to have misgivings. Why didn't I just walk away, he thought. No one would have known, and I owe the dead woman nothing. If I had not brought the child here only Bending Twig could reproach me. Now I will have to watch over this child all day, every day. At least there will be no one to see and laugh at me for doing woman's work, but do I want to do it? I really do not know how to do it. I felt strange enough carrying the child here. Will I ever be comfortable holding it as Maziwa is? Will the goat let the child nurse? Will the

child die any way? Thank goodness the child is with Maziwa tonight. I wish I could leave it with her. On the positive side Simu was
glad the baby was a boy. The thought of raising a girl would have
been even stranger. There was, of course, no answer to Simu's anxieties. So in due course exhaustion of the day caught up with him
and he slept. The only part of his dreams that he could remember
in the morning was one in which he was threatened by a giant in
the forest.

Simu woke when Kisharani came to let the cattle and goats
out in the morning. He walked stiffly over to Maziwa's hut and
was first pleased to find that the baby had survived the night and
then burdened again by his anxieties about caring for it. He did
not have much opportunity to talk with Maziwa about his concerns
because just after sunrise Kisharani brought his mother over from
her nearby *manyatta*. She had once been a big woman but now
age had left her tall and thin, almost gaunt with bangles hanging
loosely on skinny arms and an animal skin skirt that rattled around
her bony legs as she walked. She had mixed feelings about Maziwa.
The woman was strong and healthy which was good, but not ad-
equately subservient to Kisharani which was not good. Kisharani's
mother immediately supported his refusal to allow Maziwa to care
for the baby a moment longer than necessary. "We don't want this
foreign child spoiling our children," she said. "It's quite likely he
is not even a Masai. Why should my son care for a child from another tribe? Simu should have left it to hyena as nature intended.
Any way a man can't care for a child, especially not a man living
alone in a cave. It won't be long before something gets it." She
said this matter-of-factly, almost hopefully. The fact that she was
probably right did nothing to make Simu feel any better. Secretly,
Maziwa shared her mother in law's concerns about Simu caring
for a child, but she liked her uncle and knew him as a very steady
man. She knew she would always back him against Kisharani's
mother. She simply said to her, "You may be right, but we cannot
know what the spirits will bring. They must have brought Simu to
the child for some reason. Obviously they do not intend for the

child to die just yet. Who knows, he may live to be as old as you."
"Not in this house," replied Kisharani's mother, a little miffed at
Maziwa. And so the talk went on, with no one foreseeing the dark
role that Kisharani and his mother would play in young Sumatra's
future.

Bossy

4. Chepnall Cave.

Two days later, Simu set off with the young Sumatra and a nanny goat on a tether. When Simu left Maziwa said simply, "Uncle you are doing right. The only answer to your loss by sickness is new life. May the rains bless you and the baby." In her heart she knew she would always be there for that baby no matter what Kisharani said. If the rains failed people starved, so Simu appreciated Maziwa's blessing and the simple sincerity with which she offered it. "Truly a good woman," he thought a little wistfully, remembering only the good times with the woman he had once had.

Before he left, and feeling somewhat self conscious, Simu put the baby in a sling on his back as a woman would. Maziwa helped and showed him how to do it. It made good sense as it left his hands free. In one he held his *panga* which he would use to slash off scratchy fronds of wait-a-bit thorn overhanging the path in the forest. In the other he carried his short spear, mostly out of habit rather than the thought that it would be useful. He could not expect to stop a dangerous animal like a buffalo or an elephant with it. The other animals, the bush buck, giant forest hog, serval cat and the like, would move silently away when they heard or smelt him coming. He was more worried about the unfamiliar baby on his back than about any animals he might meet in the forest.

It was one of those beautiful mornings that you can get at 11,000 feet on Mt Elgon. The air was cool and clear, the morning sun warming the dew on the grass and giving a touch of fire to the wisps of cloud over the Cherangani hills. Simu appreciated the clean fresh smell of the start of the day. The sheep and goats and cattle were just moving out for the days grazing. The lams 'baaed' for their mothers and the cattle moved slowly and sedately down well worn trails, the leader's neck bells making ding dong sounds. It was all familiar and very comfortable to Simu. So he started his journey in good spirits. At first they went over the open moorlands where the cattle grazed. The goat came along willingly enough reaching out to take a mouthful of grass here and there. Downhill the going was easy. The baby slept comfortably on Simu's back, lulled by the steady rhythm of his pace. As he traveled, Simu thought about names for both the baby and the goat. The goat was easy. He called her Busi which was short for *mbuzi* meaning goat. I will call her Bossy in English because bossy she was, and much more determined than any sheep would be. The child was more difficult. Eventually, when no inspiration came to him he called the baby 'Dogo', an abbreviation of *kidogo* meaning small or little. It was a term of affection which Simu used even after it was known that the child's true name was "Sumatra".

After traveling comfortably downhill for about an hour they came to the tree line where the moorland ended and the forest began. The trees and thickets of bamboo made the path dark and gloomy. Bossy was on a raw hide lead about eight feet long with a loop around her neck. She was used to being handled by man and happy enough going over the moorlands, but all her instincts were against going into the forest and bamboo. There were dangers in the darkness and gloom of the forest. Everything she had learned as young goat said one should never go alone into brush or forest, where you were one, and all the eyes of the forest were on you. She hesitated and dug in her front feet when Simu pulled on the lead. After a couple of minutes Simu realized he could not drag her all the way to Chepnall cave. He could have beaten her with a stick until she co-operated, as Kisharani certainly would have done, but he did not do so because he was a gentle man, and one who had lived in the forest long enough to have learned to work in harmony with nature not against it, whenever possible. He did this instinctively and not out of any philosophical consideration that he should not beat or bully one he was going to live with, and one who was to be so important to the child he carried. He understood Bossy's fear of the forest. Having lived in it for so long he shared her instinctive sense of caution. He too believed in its dangers, and he was as sensitive to them as any of the wild animals there. But he also believed that he could avoid them if he was alert and careful. So he sat down next to Bossy and was silent as he stroked her neck until she was less rigid and nuzzled his hand. Then in a low voice he talked to her, telling her that although they had to travel through forest and bamboo, he was with her and would protect her. Also there were many big open glades on the path they had to take. There the grass was short because it was rocky underneath and she could see any danger a long way away. He told her that the animals he was afraid of, such as the buffalo and elephant were no threat to her. All she needed to worry about were the cat tribe; the leopard and the serval cat and that nasty slope-backed hyena. They all feared man. Were any of them foolish enough to come close they would not survive his spear and *panga* which were bigger and more dangerous than any tooth they might have. He told her this speaking very quietly in cadences. As he spoke, a fly buzzed around them annoying Simu as it tried to settle on his eye seeking moisture. The movement of branches above them dappled the sunlight on the ground while birds chirped and sang in the trees. But for Bossy's anxiety, it was as peaceful a scene as one could have wished. Bossy may not have understood every word Simu said, but she did understand that this man had no fears and was with her and for her. She could not visualize the needs, wants and plans of man, but like all domesticated animals she knew that when darkness came, or the dangers of the bush threatened, man would try and protect her. In his gentle quiet way Simu reaffirmed this basic understanding. So her fear lifted slowly like darkness leaving at dawn, until she was able to follow where Simu might lead her. When he did rise in the end, and started down the path again, Bossy followed without resistance, but with her nose twitching and her ears cocked for any sign of danger.

While Bossy relied mainly on her nose, Simu relied on his eyes more than anything. He was constantly interpreting marks and footprints he saw on the ground. As he walked he would turn his head and scan the forest on each side every few yards. An animal hidden behind a bush at first might be in view ten yards further on. In the forest neither Simu nor Bossy felt entirely safe, so both were on full alert. In fact it was Bossy who first gave the alarm. The sun was well up in the sky when they were traveling through one of the patches of forest between the glades that run for three or four miles on top of the Bluff on Mt Elgon. Because it was a warm day the breeze was blowing up the mountain as they were coming down. So Bossy was able to smell many things drifting on that breeze from some place in front of them as they walked. These scents were to her as a ballad set to pleasant music would be to man. They told a story and drew a picture in her mind. Although Simu's sense of smell was superb by human standards, by animal standards it was as weak as his eyesight was strong. So when Bossy snorted and stopped so that the lead tightened as she sniffed the air, Simu knew instantly that there must be good reason for her alarm. He rightly knew that her fear would be of a meat eater not a grass eater. That would mean leopard, hyena or serval cat, in all probability. He could see nothing. Some what to her dismay, Simu tied Bossy's lead to a bamboo and then stood for a long minute, spear in one hand, *panga* in the other, listening, waiting. He did not expect any frontal attack, or really expect an attack at all. But he had to know what Bossy smelt that alarmed her. They were in bamboo where there were no large trees. There was no possibility of a leopard on a big branch over the path. Also, visibility through the bamboo was twenty or thirty yards and nothing showed. This simply meant that what Bossy smelt was further away, out of sight and directly in front of them as that was where the wind came from. So Simu went forward very quietly and carefully leaving a very anxious Bossy tied where she fretted with a strong urge to run back down the path they had just traveled. This, of course, was exactly why he had tied her. Forty yards down the path Simu found the source of Bossy's alarm. A fresh footprint, very faint on the ground, one with soft edges not made by a hoof, told Simu that one of the cats or a hyena was close by. In a moment he found the flattened grass and weeds where the animal had been lying, and realized that their coming had disturbed it and caused it to move quietly away. From the shape and size of the flattened area he thought it was probably hyena that they had come upon. Whatever it was, Simu knew instinctively that it had retreated and was no threat. So he went back to Bossy, untied her and told her that whatever it was had left. Quietly he coaxed her into following him again, although she was very hesitant until they came to the next open glade.

An half hour later, without any further incident, they crossed the small stream that falls over Chepnall cave and reached the track down over the rocks on the North side of the Bluff. This was a bit beyond Chepnall cave, but the easiest way to get down to the path to the cave. The top of the track is a rocky open glade, but it soon descends into the dark shade of podo trees growing tall and slim, straining up to the sun above the top of the cliff side. Simu went very carefully over the rocks at the top feeling slightly unsteady with the unaccustomed weight of Dogo on his back. Once in among the podo trees his only concern was slipping and sitting down heavily on the very steep muddy path. This happened only once. Bossy had no problem. She was as surefooted as the proverbial mountain goat. By noon, when the sun was well up and they were glad to be in the shade of the trees, this odd new family had reached the cave. It was at the end of a little valley where a small stream had cut into the cliff on the side of the Bluff. Tall cedar, podo and other trees carpeted the bottom and sides of the valley. Standing out from the rest was a giant euphorbia about one hundred feet high, its leafless thick branches a stark contrast to the other trees. The cave itself was really two caves. There was an upper chamber and a lower each about twenty feet high and as wide as a house. Both reached back deep into to total darkness in the mountain. Simu headed for the upper chamber which opened about fifty feet below the top of the cliff where a waterfall came over it. At the cave mouth was a jumble of enormous rocks often covered with vegetation and interspersed with shrubs and flowering hibiscus. The entry was under an overhang of rock on one side. Here there was a dry and dusty pathway about fifteen feet wide between the cliff wall and huge fallen boulders. More boulders narrowed the path to a point where one had to duck around a boulder reaching to within eighteen inches of the cliff. A man and a goat could scramble this boulder, but that was quite impossible for bigger dangerous animals like buffalo and elephant. They would go into other caves to dig out the salty rock, but not this one. Chepnall cave made a good home not only for this reason, but also because it was not too large, about twenty feet high at the very front, rapidly coming down to head height and going back a long way into darkness. Looking in on the right hand side, the roof came down even lower, to about four feet from the floor and then ran nearly horizontally back to a cul-de-sac against the cliff wall. It was here that Simu had built a little fortress. Very laboriously he had piled up rocks and built rough dry stone walls from the cave floor to the low roof. This made an enclosure about ten feet by eight feet. At night Simu would crawl in with Bossy and Dogo and fill the small door way by pulling in the top of a young thorn tree. Neither Hyena, nor any of the cat tribe either, could penetrate those two inch long white thorns. If they tried, Simu had his spear to bloody an inquisitive nose. After Bossy arrived Simu built a little wall of sticks to separate Bossy's sleeping area from his. It was the custom of his people to often keep the cattle in the same long low building where the humans slept, but separated by such a wall. When there were many animals their warmth kept the whole area comfortable as he had experienced on the sleeping platform in Kisharani's cattle shed.

Simu made his cave fire at the very front of the cave where the smoke could rise with the hot air going up the cliff above during the day. At night it would fall down the valley when the cold air came down the mountain. Sitting on a stone by the fire he could look down the small valley towards the Elephant Platform where one can sit on top of an old lava flow that makes a cliff across the valley lower down. From there one can watch the elephants in the valley below when they are on that part of the mountain. On the left, over a shoulder of Mt Elgon, the distant triangle of Mt Riwa rose blue in the distance out of the hot dry plains of the Northern Frontier. Although Simu did not know it, this was where Sumatra the Elder now toiled making roads. These roads were to allow the Kings African Rifles, the KAR, to patrol the borders with Ethiopia and Somalia. Then, as now, *shifta* (bandits) were in a constant state of evil doing, in those semi desert wastelands. In the middle Simu could look across the foothills of Elgon to Kapenguria where the escarpment falls two thousand feet to the hot, flat, thorn scrub plains below. On the right the Cherangani hills rose misty blue in the distance across the plains.

That first day when they arrived at the cave, Bossy was as sure footed as any mountain goat. She had no problem following Simu up to the cave mouth. "This is your new home," he told her. "You will sleep in my little *boma*, my enclosure, where you will be safe, but first you must feed the little one." So saying he tied Bossy's hind legs together gently with a strip of bark from the *Dombier* plant. This was to stop her natural reflex of kicking when a buffalo fly bit her stomach. Then he put Dogo down to one of the two nipples on Bossy's udder which was so long it hung down near the ground.

Dogo drank reflexively and without hesitation. Bossy stood still and soon understood she could not kick at the biting flies because it might hurt Dogo. Instead she would swing her head around and try to knock the fly off. Without any fuss a pattern was established that would continue until Dogo was weaned.

As soon as Simu arrived, he gave Dogo to Bossy to feed, while he gathered wood and then started the cave fire. The blue grey smoke curled up into the sky and was seen by Bending Twig a half mile away. She knew at once that Simu had returned; but had he brought the child, had it lived? She ran, and jumped, and raced through the tree tops, her heart in her mouth all the way. When she arrived on top of a large rock at the cave mouth her stomach felt like a bottomless pit as all she could see was Simu sitting by his fire. She looked at Simu, trying to hide her anxiety, as the darkness of the cave seemed to reach out ready to engulf her, she felt so worried. "Hello beautiful one," said Simu. "Good afternoon," said Bending twig very formally from the top of her rock. "Do you have the child, did you bring him, is he still alive?" "Yes to all your questions," said Simu with a smile. "Then where is he?" Simu turned and called out to the *boma*, "Bossy we have a visitor please come out." "What is that?" asked Bending Twig, in a disapproving tone of voice, as a black and white goat appeared, looking pregnant with its stomach swelling out wider than its shoulders on each side. "That is Dogo's wet nurse," said Simu. "She will feed him, but I would like you to help care for him." "Thank you, but where is the child, can I see him?" requested Bending Twig. "No," said Bossy firmly. "He is sleeping." Bending Twig was a bit taken aback by the abrupt answer from some one she was not even speaking to. But she was a good hearted creature who instinctively lived up to the gentlemanly reputation of the Colobus. "Well, good afternoon to you too," she said to Bossy. Simu interrupted, "Bossy this is Bending Twig. She brought me to the child when hyena was going to eat it." "Oh," said Bossy, looking at Bending Twig with interest, but not acceptance. Bending Twig looked directly at Bossy and in a very even tone said,

"If he is sleeping, you are quite right he should not be disturbed." She then turned to Simu and asked, "May I wait until he wakes up?" "Of course," was the answer. As Bending Twig accepted her authority Bossy began to feel warmer to her. By the time Dogo woke up Bossy had decided that she would not have too much trouble with Bending Twig. As Dogo learned to crawl, then walk, Bossy came to be positively glad that Bending Twig was there to help her. The challenge to her authority came not from the ever courteous Bending Twig, but from the strong willed, impulsive, inquisitive Dogo himself. But much was to happen before Dogo reached the age of childish defiance.

First was Simu's dawning realization that his worries that night on the sleeping platform at Kisharani's *manyatta* were valid. He had taken on a very large task; one that he had never before had to think about in any detail. In this he was no different than any other man. He had never been the sole care giver to a child, or even much of a helper. By tradition that was not a man's function. Also he was hampered by the fact that Dogo had no siblings who could help. In a normal family, as soon as a child could walk and leave its mother for a while, it would be taken out by an older brother or a neighbor's child to play or help herd the sheep and goats. Only bigger children could herd cattle. Herding sheep and goats was simple. Mostly it involved sitting and watching them graze. If several in the herd had neck bells that made *ding dong* sounds like an xylophone there was little need to round up stragglers. One who lost sight of the others in the brush would simply head for the ding dong noise and rejoin the group. Herding was not a physically strenuous task. If there were a routine problem it was amusing oneself as one sat in the shade. Simu had deep nostalgic memories of this as a child, when he idled the time away marveling at the stupendous views over the plains to the hazy blue mountains and hills beyond, wondering what is was like there. Simu ruefully realized that in Chepnall cave there were no siblings or older neighbor children. There were no animals to herd either. Every moment that Dogo was awake Simu had to be there and alert. He found it to be an enormous change in his daily routine, both tiresome and exhausting. So much so that he left it more and more to Bossy.

It was not long before Bossy truly became Dogo's surrogate mother. Obviously she could not meet all his needs, particularly before he could crawl. But she did feed him regularly, and at night she kept him warm against her stomach behind her fence in the rock *boma* where they all slept. He became used to the smell of her body and the touch of her tongue. They became part of his subconscious. When they were there, he felt good, felt safe. He experienced what every baby needs in the first two years of life, unconditional love, leading to a subliminal belief that the world is more good than bad and that your care givers can be trusted. As he grew older he would of course resist and argue more and more with his caregivers Simu, Bossy and Bending Twig, and their love would grow more conditional. But such defiance as he had would never be pushed to the point of destroying relationships, running away, or even violence towards those who cared about him. Unusual though his start in life was, Dogo was not to suffer the attachment disorders of so many children neglected in the ghettos of the West. Indeed Simu, Bossy, Bending Twig and the animals of the forest never failed him in any way that he understood as failure. As a consequence Dogo grew to be a most optimistic, creative and productive young man. But he had trials along the way. The first, nearly fatal, trial of his life came to pass when he had just started to be able to roll over. It was this new ability that was the cause. Simu was not paying attention because he was digging for rock salt.

It came about this way. Simu had to dig salt rock in the cave and sell it to cattle owners in Endebess in order to earn enough money to buy his *posho* (ground up maize meal), *sukari*(sugar) *chai*, (tea) an occasional *sufuria* (metal saucepan) and a *sululu* (a heavy double headed pick) with which to dig the salt rock. Endebess was then just a cross-road six miles away with a police station, a *duka* (small shop) and some trees in whose shade people would come to trade and barter. Simu would barter his salt rock for *posho*, or some dried ears of corn and for coins if he needed to buy something from the *duka*. In those days most people wore blankets, or wrap-arounds, not shorts with pockets, so the coins all had a hole in the middle. This allowed Simu to put them on a cord and hang them around his neck like a necklace. This was very convenient and one of the many sensible ideas of the *wazungu* who had introduced the concept of coin money in order to pay the Indians they imported in the late 19th century to build the railway from Mombasa to Lake Victoria. This had been done as part of their effort to put down the Arab slave trade and as part of the expansion of empire, to control the head waters of the Nile. Simu was ignorant of this. He was aware only of the fact that the *duka* was run by an Indian and never closed during daylight hours.

About two months after he had returned with Dogo and Bossy to Chepnall cave Simu made his first trip to Endebess with Dogo. He carried the salty rock in a large basket whose strap went around his head, like a woman carries firewood. Dogo he put in the space above the salt rock. He was always teased by the regulars under the trees at Endebess, usually in a good natured way. Carrying a basket with a strap around your head was woman's work. This time, hearing Dogo cry, they called out, "Hey *mtu chumvi* (salt man) what have you on your back today? Now you have a baby. Did you become a complete *mwanamke* (woman)?" They spoke in Kiswahili as they were of a different tribe, but what they said was pretty insulting. Simu was not a big man and there were several of them, so he was silent. When Simu said nothing they carried on, "Where's the mother. Are you a Wagishu, did you eat her?" They all laughed heartily at this as the Wagishu had a reputation for cannibalism. Simu answered them shortly, "I found the baby in the *msituni* (the forest), on its dead mother." "Did you kill her?" they asked, interested now. It was not an unreasonable or provocative question as killing a person of another tribe was common, and often applauded, among the Pokot and Turkana tribes not far to the North of Endebess. In fact Dogo's father had killed the three men who stole his honey barrels. "No," replied Simu. "I heard hyena about to eat the woman and went to investigate. She had died of some sickness and lay under a podo tree. The child was still alive, so I saved it." "Too bad you did not kill her, better buy another woman and get her in that cave of yours," was the answer as he made his way to the barred window through which the *duka* transacted business over a counter polished brown by many dirty hands. They assumed, correctly, that he did not have a woman in the cave. If he did it would have been she who carried the salt rock and the baby, this being woman's work. Donkeys were not used much in those days to carry things. Simu ignored them and began his business with the Indian *duka* owner.

His business done in Endebess, Simu returned to Chepnall cave arriving late in the day. The next morning he was back at work digging salt rock slowly and laboriously. He had laid Dogo not far from the fire at the cave mouth as the morning was cold. Bossy had gone out to graze and Bending Twig had not arrived yet. In any event she was not really comfortable in the cave and definitely afraid of the fire. Not thinking that Dogo could move, Simu went to the back of the cave to dig. About half an hour later he was startled to hear screams, not cries, from Dogo. By now Simu could recognize the difference between an attention getting cry and one provoked by pain. This cry was pain. He rushed to the front of the cave and found that Dogo had rolled over once, perhaps twice and now had his naked buttocks too close to the fire, not in it, but close enough to burn. He grabbed him away from the fire and put Dogo on his stomach, feeling distraught and helpless as Dogo howled for the next hour. He brought some cold water from the stream in his *sufuria* but it did not seem to help. Ultimately Dogo cried himself into exhaustion and slept. Meanwhile the black skin on one buttock turned a deep red and later in the day came up in a huge blister. By morning the blister had burst. Then dirt from the cave floor went in and an infection started. By the end of the next day yellow puss was oozing out. Simu made a poultice out of the ashes of the burnt leaves of a guriot tree. It did not help. By the morning of the second day Dogo was feverish and not eating. Simu had traveled that road before. He knew the signs and what they foretold. His heart felt as heavy and hard as the obsidian stone he used to make arrow heads. With a desperation born of despair, he spent the day invoking every spirit he knew and practicing as much magic as he was capable of. It was all to no avail. By nightfall Dogo had not improved, if anything he was worse. In the end Simu too fell into an exhausted sleep, but it did not bring oblivion. His mind fretted and worried with visions of fire and yellow buttocks. He was half awake, restless with anxiety, knowing he had an insoluble problem.

Then Simu's dreams became focused on one image so bright and clear it was in color. He dreamed that he was in a green glade. It was unlike those on top of the Bluff as it was perfectly level and smooth with no rocks. Around it were strange beds of flowers of a kind he did not know. An elephant made of smoke stood in this glade. He knew it was smoke because he could see through it and beyond it there was a *mzungu*, a woman with flowing flowered dress and wide straw hat. She came towards him walking right through the elephant as though it were not there. In her hand she held things that he did not recognize. One was a small white stick made of glass with a shiny silver end. Another was a tube with a long thorn on the end like that of the white thorn tree. As he watched her coming towards him, a puff of wind bent the flowers on one side of the glade, both the *mzungu* and the elephant were blown away like down on the wind. As they disappeared Simu found himself standing there holding in his hands a huge dried leaf that knew had been Dogo. Then his dream changed and he looked up and saw the podo trees in front of Chepnall cave. The he woke up. The image had been powerful and frightening in its strangeness. The implied death of Dogo he understood. But why the *mzungu* in a green glade with flowers. Why a ghost elephant. He struggled to know what it meant. The vision was so beyond his experience he knew it had to have meaning. Awake now, frightened, and in the dark, Simu pushed back the thorn branch that blocked the entrance to his rock *boma*. He crawled out, *panga* in hand, to stoke the cave fire and drive back into the darkness the spirits that had come into the cave and entered his consciousness. Sitting in the flickering fire light he wondered why he had dreamed of a *mzungu*. He knew that dreams were what your own spirit saw as it wandered outside the body when one slept. Then he remembered that a few days before, when at Endebess, a young man relatively well dressed in shirt and shorts, rather than a blanket, had approached him in a friendly way not laughing at him like the others. After the usual greetings, the young man asked where Simu lived. He had seemed disappointed when Simu said, "Several hours walk away on Mt Elgon. Why?" "I would like to teach you about the great spirit of the *wazungu*, their God," he said. "He can be your God too, your Great Spirit, because he loves all people not just the Masai or the Luo or the Nandi. If you believe in him all things are possible. He is the king of kings, master of all spirits. He is as big and powerful as the elephant. From him the *wazungu* get their power." The idea of having the powers of a *mzungu* interested Simu. "Do you believe in this Great Spirit? Do you have this power?" asked Simu. "I believe," replied the young man, "but I do not have the powers of a *mzungu* because I am an African and young. Only recently have I learned to read. I still have much to learn. But I will learn. As they say "*Akili ni mali*," (a clever mind is wealth). Simu was disappointed by the young man's admission that he did not have the powers of a *mzungu*. So he said "I do not know the Great Spirit of which you speak and I cannot afford to buy any book to read even if I could, so *kwa heri* (goodbye) and let me alone." "Wait, take this, until we meet again," said the young man earnestly as he held out a little wooden Christian cross no longer than Simu's finger, "it will bring you the magic of the *wazungu*." Simu had put the cross in his basket with Dogo and forgotten about it.

When Simu realized that the only mention of a *mzungu* had been by the young man in Endebess, he knew where his dream had come from. Then he remembered the cross and recognized it for what it was; a symbol of *wazungu* belief, *wazungu* magic. Hesitantly and fearfully, he now went to look for it in his salt-rock basket. He fumbled in the dark with a shaking hand until he found that small cross. Holding it gingerly, as one might a little snake; he took it back to the fire. Then he put on more branches to get more light. He examined the cross carefully, and felt goose bumps start at the back of his neck and run down his back, then his arms, then his legs, as he came to realize that whatever spirit the young man had spoken off was small enough to fit in that strangely shaped cross, and big enough to give the *wazungu* power to rule the land. This spirit had brought him his dream of the *mzungu* woman. There he sat, on a rock, in a cave, with a Christian cross his hands, alone except for a goat and a very sick baby who was likely to die soon. He felt very small, lonely, afraid, and extremely unhappy, sitting in a small patch of flickering light, surrounded by a ring of darkness and the sounds of the African night. He felt the cold on his back. He sensed all around him unknown powers, unseen forces that he could not control. He looked around at the blackness surrounding him, half hoping that he might glimpse the spirit if it were there, as it must have been. He started when he heard a scuttling sound, and then relaxed as he realized it was one of the hyraxes that lived in the rocks at the mouth of the cave. As he fingered that cross he repeated to himself over and over the words of the young man, "It will bring you the magic of the *wazungu*." Simu recognized that his magic was powerless to deal with Dogo's hurt and illness. He knew that the spirit of the cross had brought him the dream to tell him only the magic of the *wazungu* could help him. He had to go to the *mzungu* woman, whoever and wherever she might be. He had heard of only one who helped Africans with her white magic. She was the one who lived in a big white house with a red roof amongst thorn trees on a hill about an hour's walk down from the Bluff. The woman was in fact the wife of Bwana Paws, who was just a name to Simu. Simu had no idea that Dogo's mother had left for home from behind that white house the night she died. But the spirit knew. So as Simu's fire burnt down, all he understood was that in the morning he would have to go there. He would have to overcome his anxiety at going into a strange place to ask for help from a *mzungu* he had never met. In fact he had never spoken to a *mzungu*. They were as strange to him as Martians would be to a European. He had no idea if this white witch doctor woman was the right *mzungu,* or what she would want for helping him, even if she would pay any attention to a man of no consequence such as himself. He had no cattle to give, only a goat that he had to have for Dogo. He had no chickens either. In the end he decided to take the only gift he could afford, honey, from one of his honey barrels in the forest. Having made his decisions, he then gradually dozed off by the fire.

As soon as light began to brighten the Cherangani hills and streak the cold sky with red, as the morning chorus of bird song began, Simu was up and out into the cold air of dawn, traveling to his nearest honey barrel with his *sufuria,* that aluminum two quart pot blackened by his cave fire. He left Dogo in Bossy's care. He had no other choice. Dogo was comatose, but still living. When Simu reached the tree with his honey barrel, he started a small fire with his two dried fire sticks, made from the *dombier* plant. One stick had a slightly rounded end. This end he put on a flat patch cut in the other stick. Then he twirled the upright stick between his hands until it bored a small circular hole in the second stick. The sawdust, if one could call it that, coming from this drilling process leaked out of a notch cut in the side of the circular hole. It built up like a small heap of cigarette ash. As smoke began to rise from the drilling, a tiny red ember appeared in the sawdust now glowing like the lit end of a cigarette. This ember he covered with the finest of dry grass on which he breathed ever so gently until the ember grew, and spread, and ultimately burst into flame. This done, he soon had a small fire going. As the fire grew he tied together a bundle of dry sticks and put one end in the fire until it was alight. When the bundle was burning well at one end he removed it from the fire and blew out the flames leaving a smoking stump about six inches across. With this he smoked out the bees who buzzed furiously around his head and arms. Surprisingly, only half a dozen actually stung him, mostly on his face and some on his hands. He ignored it, almost as though he did not feel it.

Perhaps he didn't because his face did not swell up like a *mzungu's* would. Pretty soon Simu had all the honey combs there were, about half a *sufuria* full. The combs full of unborn bee grubs he left, except for one that he munched on appreciatively, spitting out the waxy comb residue. Then he hurried back to the cave where he had left Bossy to watch over the very groggy Dogo in the rock *boma* where they slept.

Between the first and second hour of the morning he was on his way to Bwana Paws' farm and the big white house on the hill. He went carefully around a small herd of elephants under the Bluff and then down over the Chiparelwe stream onto a track alongside a field of maize. At the end of the maize was a small plantation of pine trees planted by Bwana Paws. There Simu could hear cattle lowing and calves calling as morning milking progressed in the milking shed in the trees. These familiar sounds made Simu feel less anxious. He told a man there, Kibore, that he was carrying a sick baby in his basket and wanted to see the *Memsahib*. "Go up the road to behind the house and ask some one there," said the man. Simu did, and there met Wanga one of the houseboys. Wanga was a Luo, which is why the four front teeth on his bottom jaw had been removed with a knife when he was about ten, in accordance with tribal custom. By tradition this was to make it possible to feed a person with soup if he got lockjaw, known to western doctors as tetanus. Wanga described the extraction of his lower teeth as the most painful experience of his life, causing him to defecate 'in mounds' as he put it. Wanga was a tall gangly young man with big knobby knees, thin legs and huge protruding front teeth on his upper jaw as though to make up for the four missing below. Although he looked odd, Wanga was good natured, and this was to Simu's advantage.

When Simu arrived, Wanga was putting the *Memsahib's* bed sheets in an old blackened four gallon paraffin can sitting over a small fire in the yard behind the kitchen which was in three separate rooms at the back of the house. He looked up in surprise to see a stranger dressed in a blanket with a big basket on his back.

At first glance he thought the man had come to sell something. Rather than simply say, "No," and tell the man to go away, he was polite and went through the normal greetings of, *"Jambo, habari yako,"* meaning "hello, what is your news?" and the ritual answer "good and how are you." Simu did not feel well at all, and now the formality was out of the way quickly said, "I have a very sick child and would like to see the *Memsahib* for some *dawa* (medicine)." So saying he took Dogo out of the basket and showed Wanga the large reddish raw patch with a yellow rim on Dogo's buttock. It looked pretty bad, so Wanga said "Wait here I will tell her." The *Memsahib* was in fact giving the morning instructions to the gardener. She said to Wanga, "Tell the man to wait; I will be with him shortly." She was quite used to dealing, as best she could in the wilds of Africa, with the ailments of wives and children of farm labor who came to see her when their own traditional remedies had failed. Usually this meant the condition had progressed to a serious stage. Simu's case was no exception. Wanga waited until the *Memsahib* finished her instructions to the gardener and then went to fetch Simu. They came around the side of the kitchen then down a verandah to where Simu could see a green mown lawn and an herbaceous border of bright flowers running all along one side, with thorn trees standing on the lawn. The thorn trees had not been in his dream, but he knew at once that this was the place.

The *Memsahib* walked across the lawn and then had Simu put the naked Dogo on a plain pine table on the verandah overlooking the lawn. My God what a mess she thought, looking at Dogo. She took his temperature with a glass mercury bulb thermometer which Simu recognized from his dream. It read one hundred and four. She did not bother to tell Simu this because she knew it would be meaningless to him. Kiswahili had words for 'hot' and 'cold' but not for degrees and temperature because instruments to measure degrees of temperature did not exist. The *Memsahib* simply said, "The child is hot, he is very, very sick, how did this happen?" "He rolled too near the fire," said Simu most unhappily. The *Memsahib* did not try and explain what an infection was, or how her

72

medicine might help. She simply said "I will give him *dawa,* but he will die if you do not keep the wound clean, and quite likely will even if you do." She went into the house and came back in a few minutes with the small glass stick with a thorn on the end that Simu recognized, and a white jar which had not been in Simu's dream. He was less surprised than a European would have been, because he believed in spirits and magic. That he recognized things from his dream simply confirmed to Simu the helpful nature of the spirit who inhabited the small cross he had been given. He began to feel more confident of the superior power of the *wazungu's* magic. He watched in fascination as the *Memsahib* gave Dogo an injection in the other buttock and put an antiseptic ointment on the burn as Dogo howled. "You must keep it clean," said the *Memsahib.* "How?" asked Simu simply, thinking of the dusty floor of his cave and Dogo sleeping against Bossy's stomach. The *Memsahib* did not answer. She sent Wanga to the kitchen to get a clean dishcloth, a *kitambaa,* as Wanga would say. When he returned with one she put a gauze pad over the burn and wrapped the *kitambaa* around Dogo, as you would tie a scarf around one's head. Then she said, "I do not have enough *dawa,* the Bwana will get more in Kitale tomorrow. If the child lives bring him back tomorrow when the sun is here," and she pointed to the western sky at an angle indicating four o'clock. She knew Simu had no means of telling time and everything would be an approximation. Simu agreed to come back. As they went back around the house to behind the kitchen where visitors waited, he brought his *sufuria* of honey out of his basket, saying, "*Memsahib,* I am a poor man of the forest, all I can give you is this honey." The *Memsahib* glanced at the sticky mess with some leaves and bee grubs mixed in, and thought, I don't want that stuff. But she said, "Thank you," to Simu and turning to Wanga said, "Have the *mpishi,* (the cook) put it in one of my *sufurias* then wash his and bring it back." The *Memsahib* was a thinking and educated woman. She understood the dignity and self worth of a man who did not ask for something for nothing, a man and a culture that had not yet been taught that welfare and free medicine are your right. She accepted the honey, not because she wanted it, but to leave Simu with his dignity. In fact she gave the honey to the household staff.

That afternoon when Bwana Paws came back from Kitale the *Memsahib* said, "Buster, I want you to get some penicillin in Kitale tomorrow, tablets and injectable. I suppose you will have to get a prescription from Dr King." Bwana Paws was not surprised. His wife had been raised to believe that if you are more blessed than others in wealth or education, you had a social obligation to give to the needy. She did not think of her life being feudal, but in reality it was in some respects. She and her husband were more blessed than many in England, their home country, and certainly much more so than any one on that farm in remote Africa. They were, in effect, the Lord and Lady of the manor house, while every one else lived in huts. As such they instinctively felt some responsibility to the one hundred and twenty men who lived and worked on the farm. Together with wives and children they made up a community of six hundred souls; though that community was fragmented into several different tribes. Each man was given a daily *posho* (maize meal) allowance, allowed to build himself a hut, or two, or three, if he had more than one wife, and cultivate two acres of land. Bwana Paws also paid the teacher for the farm elementary school and the *Memsahib* tended to ailments that did not respond to African traditional remedies. They were always concerned not to allow intertribal clashes and ran a moot court under a tree to settle disputes that led to bloodshed. The rule was "No blood no case." They usually enforced the recommendation of the elders running the court. This might be, for example, that a man should be dismissed because he was always practicing witchcraft and being troublesome, or he should pay a fine to the aggrieved party. Given this background, when the *Memsahib* asked for more penicillin, Bwana Paws simply said, "Of course Dear, what happened?" "A man who said he lived in the forest brought in a child with a badly burned buttock. The infection has progressed for several days. I think it will die, but I want to do what I can." "Oh not one of our men?" asked her husband. "No. He's some man from the forest. It's horrible how they let their babies roll into the fire. Is there anything we can do to stop it?" asked the *Memsahib*. "This has happened before". "Tell them to bring more stones up from the river and build a ring around the fire," was the Bwana's practical answer. "I suppose so. I'll suggest it to the man when he comes to-morrow, if he does." "He will," said the Bwana, "if he let the child get this sick, he is worried and knows our *dawa,* our magic, is more powerful than his." "I suppose that is the way he thinks of it," said the *Memsahib*. "We haven't yet started teaching them science in our school have we?" "One step at a time," replied the Bwana, "first they must learn to read and write."

When Bwana Paws returned from Kitale the next day to have his five o'clock tea at home, Simu was waiting with Dogo. To Simu's great relief Dogo was no worse. The penicillin shot seemed to have arrested the downward trend. This time Bwana Paws' driver, Mahindi, accompanied Wanga when they and Simu took the baby to see the *Memsahib* on the same table. After another injection and redressing of the burn, the *Memsahib* gave Simu a small bottle of what looked to Simu like white round seeds or beans. He thought they were magic seeds from some strange plant. She told Simu to give the baby one in the morning and one in the evening until all were gone. As the baby was not eating hard food he should grind the seeds up with a stone in his *sufuria* and put the powder in milk. She went on to add that a small cup made from a bamboo stem would probably be better than the one he used for his *chai*. When these instructions were finished and understood, Simu went to the backyard behind the kitchen. Mahindi joined him to try and satisfy his curiosity. Who was this stranger, where did he come from and why was there no mother. To break the ice, so to speak, he offered Simu a cup of tea from the kitchen. He did not invite Simu into the kitchen block, that was reserved for the inner circle of people who worked directly for the *wazungu*. The kitchen, an adjacent room used as a staff sitting room, an ironing room, and a pantry were in a bolck separate from the main house. As it looked like rain, Mahindi and Simu moved under the galvanized iron roof of the open sided shed that the Bwana used as a garage, behind and to one side of the kitchen block.

Simu gratefully took the *chai* appreciating the friendly gesture even from a man of a different tribe, which Mahindi obviously was once they exchanged names. "Do you have far to go?" asked Mahindi. "About an hour's walk," was the answer. "Where?" "To the cave that is over there," replied Simu pointing to the right hand side of the Bluff. "Where is the mother, is the child yours?" asked Mahindi. "The child is not mine, but I care for him," answered Simu, who then went to explain that not so long ago when it was still the days of the rains he had found the child with its dead mother in the forest, and had decided to care for it. He confirmed that the woman had been alone, she had died of natural causes and there were no tracks of any one else present. There was not much more to say, so the conversation ended and Simu went on his way, and Mahindi went back into the kitchen to talk about it with Wanga and the cook. It was very odd story. Why would a woman be traveling alone in the forest. No woman living on the farm had gone missing, so the woman was obviously a stranger. The only stranger Mahindi had seen any time recently was the woman he had taken to the prison to see her husband, the one who had sat outside the office in Kitale, looking sick holding a child. He wondered if it was the same woman, and same child. He remembered the out of context statement she had made to him that the child's name was son of Sumatra. He thought no more about it mostly because there was no way he could think of to identify the woman who died in the forest, and it was not important to him anyway. In those days if you died in a place where people did not recognize you, then you were just a body; and to your family somewhere else, you were simply some-one who never came home. Usually it was men traveling alone who sometimes just disappeared.

Simu was half a mile from Chepnall cave in front of the Bluff when he was met by a very worried Bossy and Bending Twig. Bossy was grazing in the long grass by the path and Bending Twig was eating leaves in a large tree fifty yards away. As the wind was still coming up the mountain they smelt him coming long before they saw him. Bossy ran up to him and nuzzled his hand until he brought the basket down of his back and lifted Dogo out. Bossy disliked the smell of the antiseptic ointment on him. It had an unnatural quality to it that she could not define and had never met before. But the medicines of man were beyond her understanding. If it had been something to eat, she would have understood it. As it was she had a surge of delight as Dogo seemed recovered enough to want to feed. So she and Simu sat under a tree as Dogo drank and Bending Twig heaved a sigh of relief and then chattered away happily. "He is getting a little better," Simu said simply. "The white man's *dawa* works, but the *Memsahib* says it will be a week before he may be cured." When Dogo had finished with Bossy, Simu got up and started out again for Chepnall cave with Bossy following behind and Bending Twig overhead. He had not gone more than five minutes walk when he stopped in amazement looking at the footprints of the elephant herd he had avoided the day before. In one of those foot prints there was the rough outline, but still clear shape, of a cross pointing in the way the elephant was traveling. Simu shivered as he remembered the ghost elephant of his dream. This was beyond his understanding, so he hurried on back to the cave and built the fire a little larger than usual. That night he did not put the flat stone on top of his *ugali sufuria* and brought out the cross saying to it, "If you are hungry in the night please eat." In the morning the *sufuria* empty. Every night since he had gone to the white house with the red roof, Simu had held that small wooden cross and had invoked the powers of the spirit that he believed lived in the cross, and in the pills, although he was not be sure how the spirit could be in both. Perhaps the pills were the eggs of the spirit in the cross. How the ghost elephant was involved was beyond Simu. That was *wazungu* magic not to be understood by him. All that mattered was the magic was working! And so it was that a week later when all the pills Simu had been given were finished Dogo was out of danger. Now he had a hard, large scab covering his wound and no puss coming from it. Before the scab came off Simu stopped invoking the spirit of the cross not wanting to bother it too much. He put the cross with Watumba's things in the little stone locker he had made at the back of his rock *boma,* and resumed the task of raising a child. Many years later, in boy's locker rooms at school, Sumatra would have the nick name *kovu nyuma* or "Scarbut". But that is another story.

Tumbo

5. Growing up

As soon as the burn on his buttock was healed, Dogo began to grow apace. In what seemed like no time to Simu, Dogo was crawling all over the floor of the cave. Simu was even more worried now about Dogo getting burnt again. He let Bossy know of his worry. She was completely on side with Simu because she felt very strongly about fire. She feared it, like all animals, because she could not use it or control it like man. Man sitting next his fire did not need to fear animals, they stayed away. Indeed control of fire is what separated man from animals. Bossy tried to get Dogo to understand that if she said to stay away from something he had better listen or he would get hurt. When he did not understand or would not listen to her, she allowed him to get hurt, a little bit, just to teach him. This happened for the first time after she told him repeatedly not to go near the fire. Dogo was fascinated by the movement of the fire light. He kept crawling towards it not remembering his burnt buttock, which happened when he was too young to have memories. Whenever he went near the fire Bossy, tried to stop him stamping her hoof and nudging him with her muzzle. When he persisted in seeming not to understand, or perhaps did not want to listen, she let him push by her. In a minute he had burnt the tip of his finger. He howled then, which brought Simu running from the back of the cave. "It's all right," said Bossy, "he is learning and it's just the tip of his finger." "His cry frightened me, let me see," replied Simu looking at the finger of the still howling Dogo. It was not serious so Simu put Dogo down and let Bossy tell him again to listen to her. Dogo caught on, pain being a great teacher. After that he stayed away from the fire until he was older and learned to sit by it without touching; appreciating its warmth in the cold of the evening and early morning.

Simu and Bossy took turns stopping him falling off the rocks outside the cave. Bossy would kneel down in his path and block his way. Simu would simply pick him up and carry him back. This was a big strain on Simu who could not dig his rock salt in the back of the cave while he was on baby watch duty; which seemed to him to be most of the time. The scared buttock was a reminder of what happened if he was careless. In was not long before Simu became totally exasperated constantly stopping Dogo from falling off the rocks outside the cave. He began to regret he lived in a cave where falling was a real danger for a child. He began to understand, as he never had before, why a woman with a young child has to be there all the time, why she is dependent on man not only during pregnancy but also for two or more years after the child is born. He wished he did have a woman in the cave to the share the burden of both child care and providing the necessities of life. He even thought of going back up the mountain to live with his clan again. But he was uneasy about Kisharani's cold, or even mildly hostile, attitude toward him. Besides he was used to his life in the cave.

As Simu pondered on these things he hit on the idea of taking both Dogo and Bossy down below the rocks about a hundred yards in front of the cave to where there were no rocks to fall off, and some buffalo grass left by the waterbuck for Bossy. Full grown buffalo grass was tall enough to hide a man. It was like miniature bamboo with hard dry stems as thick a pencil. But there were always patches where it had been grazed down making way for new growth. There Bossy could graze on green shoots no more than her head height. She liked this idea and Simu thought he had solved his problem. In reality he had merely substituted one problem for several others. He thought of the obvious, the possible danger from large animals. To satisfy himself that this was not a problem, he walked around the area in a large circle as best he could, following buffalo and other animal trails through the bush, grass, hibiscus, brambles, and small thorn trees, and then moving more easily in the open areas under the podo trees on the edge. He also asked Bending Twig to keep watch from the vantage point of the podo trees. She was only too happy to oblige, though secretly dismayed at how helpless a human child was compared to a young colobus monkey. She began to truly appreciate the words of the Wise One, "let man raise man." When Simu was comfortable that there were no large animals in the area, he put Dogo down next Bossy saying, "Stay close to him." Bossy gave a Baa of acknowledgement and began happily nibbling on a rather luscious large blade of very green grass coming up by her ear.

Dogo felt beneath him something quite different than the soft very dry dust of the cave floor that he had grown accustomed to. Here the ground was rough, scratchy and much harder. Also he was used to dark and light; dark when facing into the cave or one of its walls and light when facing the entrance. Here all was light, no dark in any direction. It was much warmer too as the sun was out. Instinctively he blinked. The smell was quite different also. Although he did not yet have words to describe them, Dogo's developing mind registered several smells in the cave. Dust and goat were dominant, but the smell of the cave fire came a close second. In the back of the cave the sharp acid smell of bat droppings was dominant. Out in the glade below the cave the smells were grass, leaves and damp earth. For some this might have been frightening, but by temperament Dogo was more fight than flight, inquisitive rather than cautious, risk taking rather than fearful. These were the inherited default settings of the operating program that ran the organic computer that was his brain. They could be over ridden by the many application programs that his mind would learn in due course. But he had not yet learned fear, except for heights, so he immediately set about exploring this new environment. On all fours, like some clumsy animal, he crawled forward until a clump of grass brought him up short. He reached out and tried to pull himself up only to find that the grass bent and broke. That seemed like a fun game which he indulged in for a while. Some of the grass he put in his mouth and spat out when it was not satisfying. Only Bossy's nipple felt good. So he gave a cry that Bossy immediately understood and came over to meet his need, giving him a raspy lick on his face. Satisfied and with the bits of dry grass out of his mouth, Dogo started off in a different direction. This time the clump of grass that stopped him had a young thorn tree growing in it. Dogo cried at the first prick and looked without understanding at the dot of blood on his thumb. A weaver bird with a bright yellow breast came and sat on a branch in the thorn tree. Dogo immediately forgot his thumb and stared in fascination at the color and movement of the bird. When the bird flew away, he again tried to pull himself up, and pricked himself again. His mind was just developed enough to register the idea, don't do that again! So he turned and started off in a new direction that was to lead to a much more painful problem.

Bossy was grazing and browsing no more than fifteen feet away from Dogo when he began to howl. She immediately trotted over to see what the matter was. At first she did not notice anything and was at a loss to know why he was howling. Then she noticed him picking at his face and looking more closely saw that he was covered in ants. These were not the little black ants you may find in your sugar bowl: these were fiery red *siafu,* or safari ants. *Siafu* are notorious as the most predatory and aggressive of ants. They go hunting in long columns about an inch wide. Everything edible they attack and eat, no matter how large. They have no fear. In an attack, thousands will sacrifice themselves. They have workers and soldiers. The workers are normal size, but in relation to the soldiers they are as small as a sheep is to a cow. The soldiers are as long as the last joint on your finger with huge square heads and massive jaws that can bite into your skin. That is why Dogo was howling. He had crawled onto one of their trails and they were now swarming all over him. The first thing to do if you happen to stop on one of their trails is move away so more cannot get onto you. Bossy tried to get Dogo to move away, but could not get him to understand, or move. So she let out strident cry for help to Bending Twig who was dozing in a podo tree about fifty yards away. She came awake with a start and heard Dogo howling. Throwing caution to the winds she raced down the tree onto the ground and dashed through the brush and buffalo grass towards the sound. One glance and she knew what to do. With great effort, because he was too heavy to carry, she put Dogo under one arm and dragged him away. Her instinct was to carry him up a tree like she would with her own child who would hang onto her fur. With Dogo this was impossible. So she stopped a few yards away from the *siafu* trail and asked Bossy to stand guard while she attended to Dogo. She was absolutely the right person for the job; picking ants off Dogo with dexterity born of long practice. She killed each one she pulled off with a quick bite that left a sour taste in her mouth but gave her with the satisfaction of knowing that what hurt Dogo was now dead. Her fingers were nimble and sensitive. She had no trouble pulling a soldier ant off Dogo's eyelid, much to his relief. Bossy knew how nervous Bending Twig was when she was on the ground, so she made a big showing of her guard duty as she circled around Bending Twig and Dogo. Bending Twig was genuinely appreciative and let Bossy know, as she held and stroked Dogo to calm him down. On her side Bossy now realized that Bending Twig could do things for Dogo that she could not do, however much she might want to. From then on Bossy and Bending Twig had a relationship of genuine mutual respect and affection as they shared a common purpose. Bossy no longer felt that Bending Twig was an intruder and Bending Twig responded by no longer feeling shut out and jealous of Bossy's much closer contact with Dogo. Each knew they had a role to play and accepted their own limitations.

"We have to teach him to move better, to walk like man, get away from *siafu*," said Bending Twig. "I wish he had four legs," said Bossy, "then perhaps he could be like my children and walk the same day he was born and run the next." "He looks more like me, more like a monkey, than you do," said Bending Twig, but he certainly doesn't act like one. If he were mine he would have been up in a tree long ago." "He is too upset to listen now," said Bossy, "tomorrow let's try and teach him to walk, even if he can't run. At least he'll be able to move out of a *siafu* trail." Bending Twig nodded and said "I'm going to get Simu, you watch him." So Bending Twig went back up to the cave and told Simu to stop digging and come to help Dogo who was hurting. When Simu arrived he thought the little red marks on Dogo were thorn pricks until Bending Twig explained and showed him the *siafu* trail. I should have thought of that, he said to himself. I can't leave him down here with Bossy right now. I will have to wait until he is old enough to walk and understands. I hope that will be soon, I really need to be able to get on with my digging for rock-salt. I can't do it at night when Dogo is sleeping because it's dark and I have no light. I'll have to ask Bossy to spend more time in the cave during the day. Bending Twig won't come far into the cave, she is afraid. With these thoughts Simu carried Dogo back through the afternoon sun and into the lengthening shadows coming over the cave. The motion lulled Dogo to sleep. So Simu put him down close by and went back to digging.

The very next day Bossy started teaching Dogo how to walk. She bent her head down until her six inch long horns were parallel to the ground and an inch or two above it. Dogo loved being near Bossy, so he grasped both horns and Bossy slowly lifted her head until Dogo was standing holding on. Then she moved back one step, then another. When Dogo stumbled, he did not let go of her horns. He was determined by nature and did not give up easily. He hung on tight, a habit that was invaluable when Bending Twig was teaching him tree climbing. But holding up his weight gave Bossy a stiff neck after a while. So she put her head down and let Dogo sit in the dust. He pawed the air trying to reach her horns and play the game some more. Bossy left him with Simu and went out of the cave to graze. The game was repeated every day, usually twice a day. Dogo never seemed to hurt himself even when he tripped over a stone and Bossy's horns pulled out of his hands. He loved playing this game. It made a big impression on him; he had so much fun pulling Bossy's head down. It is not surprising that one of his earliest visual memories was of Bossy's black nose, the white patch running up between her eyes to her horns, and the black ears with white tips that twitched. In a week Dogo was walking unsteadily about the cave, propping himself up on the wall, and falling over stones, but walking.

As soon as Dogo learned to walk, Simu taught him to respect little heights and fear larger ones. This he did by letting him clamber up and fall off ever bigger rocks in the cave. Dogo was a quick learner. It did not take too many bruises and scrapes for him to be afraid of falling from any significant height. Perhaps experience merely enhanced instinct. In any event soon there was no longer any worry about him falling over the rocks at the cave mouth. He understood that he would hurt if he fell off. This was a great relief to Simu and Bossy and above all to Bending Twig who had worried about how clumsy, and seemingly unaware of heights, this human child was. Bending Twig could race along a branch and leap ten feet to another, her long black and white hair flashing in the sun. But then she was more at home in the trees than on the ground.

Pretty soon life fell into a routine which started with the rising of the sun. The end of the first hour after sunrise is known in Africa as one o'clock, the first hour of the twelve hours in a day. Noon is known as six o'clock. This way of counting time was common not only in Africa, but also in many ancient and medieval cultures where the division between night and day was what truly mattered. The twelve hours in a day represented the twelve finger bones on one hand; a convenient way of counting when one could not read or write, which was true of Simu. Being on the equator, as Kenya is, night is as long as day, so it too always had 12 hours. Who knows why some mad *mzungu* decided that the 24 hour day/ night cycle should start at midnight. Some things make no sense. Having no calendar or clock Simu did not think in terms of weeks or months, or for that matter days of the week. The passing of time was noticed only by changes in the phases of the moon. When it was a new moon Simu knew it was time to take his salt rock to Endebess for sale. When it was a full moon he had to take honey to Kisharani in payment for Bossy. The new and the full moon were Simu's primary points of reference. He thought in terms of seasons not years. Being right on the equator, there was no summer or winter; only a dry season and a wet season. The beginning of the rains was a time for celebration, when cattle frisked and kicked up their heels at the promise of fresh grass and their owners were thankful they and their cattle had survived the dry weather. The beginning of the dry season was a time for anxiety, as grass turned hard and dry and one could see a dozen dust devils whipped up on the plains on a hot day. If the dry season lasted too long water holes could dry up. Even if they did not dry up completely, all grazing within walking distance might be eaten down to the ground, so that animals could not both eat and drink in the same day. Starved and weakened they would then not have the strength to struggle out of the mud around a water hole and would die there to become standing skeletons.

For Simu, Dogo and Bossy the day began when the dim rays of dawn crept over the Cherangani hills and spread across the plains lying dark in the shadow of those hills. It ended when the blue of the distant hills turned to red, then purple, and then faded from view leaving the cave in darkness, but for the little pool of firelight where Simu sat. Some things were repeated every day because that is in the nature of things. They would have breakfast at about one o'clock, (African time), then lunch when hungry near six o'clock, and eat once more at dusk. After breakfast, Simu would call Bossy in from her grazing so that she could watch Dogo while he went out. Nearly every day Simu spent half an hour collecting or cutting firewood, though in wet weather he used a supply stored in the cave. Except in the dry weather, he went out into the forest to gather pigweed to boil as a vegetable. When these chores were done he let Bossy go out to graze again. After Dogo had learned to walk, and heed warnings, Simu let him go with Bossy while he laboriously dug salt rock for several hours. The experience with the *siafu* being fresh in his mind, he was quite apprehensive at first, but he had to dig and could not watch Dogo as he did it, so he took the risk. He enlisted the help of Bending Twig to help Bossy by watching for bigger, dangerous animals. She was very well suited to this having the advantages of excellent eyesight and a bird's eye view from the tree tops.

Every morning Bending Twig would jump down from the trees above the cave on to the rocks in front, with a big chortle that only a colobus can make. Bending Twig was against going into the cave. She was a creature of the tree tops and open skies. Caves to her were nasty dark gloomy places where leopard would hide. So Simu would walk out and give her a 'good morning' piece of his *ugali*. She always gave him a polite, "Thank you," but in truth she preferred green leaves and podo berries from the big podo trees nearby. She gave the *ugali* to the hyraxes that lived in the rocks at the cave mouth because they enjoyed it so much more than she did. Her arrival was the signal to Bossy that she could go out to graze with Dogo in tow and Bending Twig keeping watch from above. Twice in the first six months Bending Twig had to pick *siafu* of Dogo because he was careless and stood on a *siafu* trail. But soon he learned to look down at his feet before stopping any where, to make sure that there were no ants there. He also learned quickly to recognize stinging nettles. In fact there was some right alongside the path out of the cave, so he was stung every time he went out until he learned not to touch them. That did not take long. The stings hurt for a little while, but, fortunately, did not bring up violent itching blisters like poison oak or ivy would in the Northern hemisphere.

Usually Dogo and Bossy went down to the open area below the cave where he had his first experience with the *siafu*. He liked being with Bossy and playing in the stream as she grazed near by. On warm sunny days he delighted in squishing mud between his toes and fingers and was thrilled when a butterfly would come and sit on his muddy foot to get the moisture. Later he learned from Simu to build a little dam and make the water deeper. He had a surprise the first time he put his face in the water. He did not know what was happening, but he did know that it was not nice and it happened when he put his face in. So he instinctively withdrew, coughing, and did not drown as a small baby might have. This was a time of unconscious learning for Dogo. Bossy taught him to recognize goat talk and ideas. A stamping hoof, a snort, a nuzzle, many inflections of bleat, they all had their meaning. Though he did not know it, some human languages, such as mandarin, were similar, giving the same syllable up to five different meanings, depending on how it was pronounced. By the time he was two years old Dogo could mimic a goat so well that goats other than Bossy would respond to him when he went with Simu on his monthly visits to pay his honey dues to Kisharani. Bossy also taught Dogo to use his nose and his ears, as well as his eyes, to know what might be in the bush or forest around him. Like a muscle that grows when it is much used, the neural circuitry in Dogo's brain grew to register sounds and smells that would not have been heard or smelt by the ordinary person. He learned too what a sound or smell meant. As he grew older, he could distinguish the bark of a baboon from the bark of a bush buck, and know whether a smell was a buffalo or a domestic cow. Often in Elgon's thick forests, he could smell an animal long before he could see it. In this he was like many other creatures of the forest. He became as attuned to the forest as any wild animal because he lived in it. Bending Twig taught him to use his eyes like a hawk and climb trees better than most men. But in tree climbing he was a total disappointment to Bending Twig. As a tortoise is to running against a hare, so Dogo was slow and clumsy in trying to match a monkey climbing. Bending Twig soon came to see the truth of the Wise One's statement that no human could ever begin to climb, balance and jump like a colobus.

In the dry weather when the stream over the cave did not flow any more and its stones baked hard and hot in the sun, Dogo would sit by the water hole that Simu dug in the deep shade just above the old elephant path that went around the flanks of the Bluff. It started out as a bucket size hole just big enough for Simu to dip in his cup and fill the large hollow gourd, with raw hide carrying strap, that he used to carry water. Almost immediately, the animals of the forest came too. Their hooves broke down the sides pushing earth down into the water and filling it up with mud until Simu dug it out again. This was repeated many times until keeping the water hole deep and clear became almost an obsession with Simu. It slowly grew until it was a shallow pond about six feet across and ten feet long lying in deep shade beneath an overarching green canopy, kept well above head height by the elephants that sometimes came to drink there. They often drained the pond temporarily dry, but helped to enlarge the pool with the enormous holes left in the soft mud by their huge feet. Every animal coming to drink left his signature in that mud with his feet. The hoofed animals left sharp prints and were easy to recognize. The smallest were the duiker, a tiny deer standing no taller than Simu's knee. Next in size came the bushbuck who was deer sized. Above him, and two or three times his weight were the water buck who were as big as an elk and had harped shaped horns as long as a man's arm. One of the heaviest though not the tallest was the giant Elgon forest hog. The largest were the big black buffalo that would go crashing through the forest like a run away train when disturbed. Far softer footed were the creatures with padded feet. Many of them were hunters, like hyena, the leopard, the jackal and various fox and cat like animals including the large serval cat that looked like a small leopard. The mongoose and the gennet were long and slinky. The honey badger was short, squat, and very thick skinned.

A non hunter, all on his own, and left alone by all, for good reason, was porcupine. Then there were climbing animals like baboon, the grey monkey and colobus. Of these the colobus were by far the most handsome and aristocratic. Their bodies were covered in black hair, but their faces were white and they had capes of flowing white hair running from the shoulder all the way down the flank.

The first animals Dogo became more aware of, and made friends with, were the hyraxes at the mouth of the cave. There are rock hyraxes and tree hyraxes. These were rock hyraxes. A hyrax is a gentle leaf and berry eating creature that looks like a cross between a rabbit and a prairie dog. If you like, you can visualize him as a rabbit sized guinea pig. Of course, rock hyraxes make their homes in the cracks between large rocks. They are a pale brown in color like a rabbit and have black button noses, and beady brown eyes. Like Bending Twig, they loved podo berries, holding them up in their delicate paws and nibbling a hole in the hard outer shell like a squirrel eating a nut. Bending Twig re-assured the hyraxes that there was nothing to fear from the clumsy man child who could not yet climb on the rocks, much less run over them as they did. The hyraxes slowly came to believe her. They would come out from the cracks in the rocks in a little band and carefully watch Dogo as they ate their podo berries sitting in the same place every day; throwing the shells onto a heap that grew bigger and bigger. One of the young boy hyraxes was more adventurous than the rest, and perhaps braver. He would come right down off the rocks and cross the dusty floor of the cave to where Dogo was sitting watching them. At first he just sniffed Dogo's foot to find out what he was. When nothing happened he became more confident and soon was running over Dogo's legs and jumping on his shoulder to Dogo's great delight. Dogo tried constantly to catch him but did not come close. His hands were too small and much too slow. In the end he satisfied himself with stroking the little creature on the head. Simu was not as enamored of the little hyrax as Dogo. Simu called him *chokosa* (or Chok, for short) meaning one who annoys or provokes, because this little devil became brazen. If Simu did not put a flat rock on top of his *sufuria* of *ugali* Chok would get into it as soon as it cooled down and then gorge himself. Simu could easily have whacked Chok with a stick which would probably have killed him. But he didn't, thinking, Chok was harmless and he did amuse Dogo. Also the hyraxes were good watch dogs. Whenever any thing came near the cave they gave out short sharp cries of warning, even if it were only Bending Twig or Bossy coming in. As was his nature Simu was happy to put up with some annoyances and live and let live.

In the third dry season since he had come to the cave Dogo was traveling with Simu through the huge trees that make the forest on top of the Bluff. They were on their way back from delivering honey to Kisharani; a task that had become increasingly unpleasant. Simu was absorbed in his thoughts about Kisharani, paying less attention than usual, when he was jerked out of his reverie by Dogo saying, "Look Baba," as he pointed at a tan patch about thirty feet to one side of the path. It was out of place in the dark green of the underbrush, and not very large. It did not move when Dogo spoke so Simu was not alarmed. He knew at once that it was a patch of fur, of some kind of animal. He wondered why it did not run or move when so close to humans. Curious, he went around some underbrush to get a better view. It was a very small animal, about the size of a house cat, lying on its side, motionless, as though dead. As he came closer Simu noticed the mouth slightly open as though in a gasp, with some dry pink tongue showing between small white teeth. The cord of the snare had pulled very tight around its neck, leaving a raw red band with dark patches where the blood had dried. Flies sucked eagerly at the blood. The animal lay exhausted or dead after its long struggle to escape. Simu had often seen duiker and bush buck caught in snares set by hunters. This was different. He wondered if it were a jackal or hyena cub. The thought that the mother might be near made him grip his *panga* a bit tighter. As he came closer he realized that this was neither. The long legs, black face, rounded ears, patches of tan and reddish brown and black, over its body and the white tail told him that this was a very young wild hunting dog. Such dogs were often called Painted Dogs, because of their coloring. Dogo ran up wanting to pet the small animal as he did the hyrax Chok. Simu held him back saying, "Be careful, be careful, it may bite you." He poked it with the end of his *panga*. The only reaction was the slight movement of one eye and the buzzing of flies. The moving eye told Simu that the pup was alive but only just.

After a moment, Dogo said, "Is dead Baba?" "Almost," replied Simu. Dogo knelt down and reached out a tentative hand to stroke the flank of the motionless pup. Surprising in a child so young and in a place where pain and suffering were commonplace, Dogo felt empathy surge up from his heart to his moistening eyes, "Take home Baba," he said looking up earnestly at Simu. Simu's first thought was, "No, what do I need with this half dead piece of fur that will just be more work." Then he caught the pleading look in Dogo's eyes, sighed, and said, "I will take him but I do not think he will live." Then he too knelt down beside Dogo and used his *panga* to slice the snare cord. He slipped the flat of the blade under the pups head so that he could lift it up without getting bitten and slid the noose over its head. The pup made no sound as Simu had to break the cord away from where dried blood stuck it to the raw ring around its neck. As he lifted to pup from the ground, Simu stopped as if frozen in place. The pup had been lying on an elephant footprint which was now clearly revealed in the damp earth. "The spirit elephant," he said half audibly to himself. "What is it Baba?" asked Dogo. "Look, see this mark on his foot, this elephant is protected by the spirit of the *wazungu.*" He pointed to a mark on the ground a bit longer than his hand in the rough shape of a cross. "This is the spirit that saved you when you would have died from the fire. Now it has brought us here to save this young one." He did not feel the same empathy that Dogo did, but now believed that the finding of the pup was no accident. As was always the case in the presence of unseen forces Simu was afraid. A chill ran through him and he looked around anxiously to be sure the elephant was not near, as though some dark spirit might be hovering in the gloom under a big tree. Seeing nothing, he quickly put the pup in his carrying basket and set off at a brisk pace not thinking any more about his troubles with Kisharani, but rather about getting the pup to water, to save it as he now knew he should. He correctly assumed that the pup had been in the snare several days and was dying of thirst. He also thought, "The pup's family must have left in order to save themselves. I wonder whey they were up here on the Bluff; normally they are plains animals that hunt down there not in the forest?" No rational answer came to mind, so he carried on to the bed of the stream that fell over Chepnall cave in the wet weather. It was dry now, but Simi simply followed the stream bed into the forest on top of the Bluff until he found a small pool under the trees. The buffalo had drunk from it leaving big hoof holes in the mud and buffalo pats with a strong smell on the ground. A few gnats and small forest flies rose from the mud as he knelt down and brought the limp pup out of his basket. He put its bottom jaw in half an inch of water and watched to moisture change the whitish pink color of the pup's tongue to a brighter healthier looking pink. As the water soaked up into its parched mouth the membranes softened and a few minutes later he saw a small swallowing motion in the pup's throat. Dog cried out excitedly, "See Baba, see." Ever so slowly, as though rising from a deep sleep, the pup came back to life, until its eyes blinked and its tongue began to move. In five minutes it was lapping at the water, very weakly, but drinking. It drank a long time, not stopping even when Dogo stepped into the mud and reached out to stroke its head. He bent down to lick it on the head as sign of affection as Bossy had shown him so many times, but Simu put his hand in the way saying "Not yet;" for this was still a wild animal even if very weak. When the pup stopped drinking he put its still limp body back in his basket and the little party made its way back to Chepnall cave.

The new arrival was not greeted warmly by Bending Twig and Bossy. Bending Twig sat on the rock at the front of the cave and tried to make out what this new creature was. After Dogo, with Simu's help, had given it some goat milk to drink and a small piece of dried meat, it was able to stand for a few seconds when Simu lifted it up. Bending Twig saw at once that it was, as she thought, a young jackal of some kind. She was horrified that Simu would bring such predator into the cave. Young monkeys were always at risk from jackals when on the ground. Only a leopard or serval cat cub would have been worse; particularly the leopard because he could climb trees and lie in ambush for an unwary monkey. "What do you think you are doing bringing that creature to live with you?" she demanded. "Don't you know it will grow into a hunter? When it's grown up it will eat Bossy." "Not likely," said Bossy, shaking her horns. "This one will grow up knowing who is in charge around here. I have had quite a bit of experience keeping young dogs in line. He won't mess with me, and I'll make sure he doesn't bother you either," she said turning to Bending Twig. With great foresight, Bending Twig said, " When he grows up he will go roaming, he is a boy isn't he? Then he will bring his family here. What then? You can't fight a pack of wild painted dogs." Bossy was quite used to the dogs of Kisharani's *manyatta* and knew they would not think of attacking man's sheep and goats. She had never met wild dogs. It was too cold for them above the tree line on the mountain. She recognized that they might be a problem, but she was a strong willed creature, not as concerned as Bending Twig. So she said, "You'll be alright up in the trees, and if there is a problem I will take care of it when the time comes." She had pricked enough rambunctious young dogs with her horns to be quite confident she could meet the challenge if it came. "Perhaps," said Bending Twig who quite respected Bossy's determination, "but I still don't like it."

Dogo was enthralled with his first pet. He constantly tried to feed it, and when darkness came he took it into the *boma* where it slept against his side so that it would be safe and warm. No mother could have been gentler or more attentive. Caring for the animal seemed to come naturally to him, young as he was. In three days the pup was up and about as though nothing had happened except for the slowly healing scar around his neck. That ring was to be his trademark all his life. When he was still very young, the pup saw Dogo as his care-giver. As he grew up over the next year he came to see Dogo as his friend, and when he was a full grown hunting dog he saw Dogo as some one to be protected by him as well. Dogo was quite used to black and white markings on an animal. Bossy and Bending Twig had nothing else. He found the reddish markings of a painted dog quite strange. Simu said they were, "Like earth that is red," or *mchanga mwekundu* in Kiswahili. That was too much of mouthful for Dogo so he called the pup *mchanga* which became shortened to Changa. It rolled off the tongue and it was easy to call "Changa, Changa, Changa." So that became his name, although when Bossy or Bending Twig were angry at him they would refer to him as, "That Painted Dog," which of course he was.

The call of the wild was deep in Changa. His first wild instinct showed itself early as he began to stalk Bossy when still a playful pup. He jumped at her in a mock attack. Though he meant no harm, Bossy swung her head hard so that he slammed into her horns and forehead. Changa fell back to the ground with a yelp and Bossy put her foot on him pressing down hard until he wriggled free and retreated to where Dogo and Simu sat by the cave fire. There he turned and stared hard at Bossy who snorted a "watch yourself," message. Simu put his hand on Changa's head and said, "No, not Bossy." After a couple more similar set backs with Bossy, Changa gave her a respectful birth. His next target was Chok, the little hyrax. Fortunately Simu saw him flattened to the cave floor behind a stone, ready to rush Chok. Again Changa yelped when the pebble Simu threw at him struck his ribs. "No" said Simu and Changa understood the tone of voice, the disapproval, if not the word itself. By the time Changa was half grown he knew he could not play hunting of Chok or Bossy or Bending Twig. By the time he was fully grown he understood that if a creature had the smell of man about it, like the sheep and cattle, they were to be left alone as part of the extended family of man.

Changa's second wild instinct began to show when he was about half grown. This was the roaming instinct of a plains hunter. Chepnall cave was to him the lair where he came when he was rescued. It had the familiarity and security of home, but nomads do not have homes, do not live in lairs tied to pieces of geography. They wander all over the place, and Changa was built for wandering. Although he was already quite a big and powerful dog when half grown, it was in a tall, lean, long limbed way. He was built for running immense distances, like a racing car not a truck, a thoroughbred not a cart horse. Nature had designed his kind to run tirelessly for miles, exhausting the antelopes they hunted. So he was light rather than heavy, but hard and tough as raw hide. He had huge, black, pricked up, Mickey Mouse ears, rounded rather than pointed at the top making his head look half as wide again as it really was, and instantly recognizable as Painted Dog. Those ears enabled him to hear a mouse fifty feet away in the grass and the sound of hooves a mile away on the horizon. His head was unusual for another reason too, the power of his jaws. They were a hunter's jaws, designed not just to catch but to kill. He had a dappled coat of black tan and reddish brown that let him blend in with the red earth and dry grass of the plains, and the dark shadow under a bush. It was perfect camouflage clothing for hunting.

The moon had waxed and waned five or six times since Simu had rescued Changa. Now he was big enough to begin to indulge his other basic instinct, which was to range far and wide, to roam as his ancestors had across the African plains, from generation to generation before him. He was already used to roaming up to half a mile from Chepnall cave. He had begun to lift his leg and leave his mark on the rocks and tree stumps along the animal trails and by the water hole that Simu had dug out below the cave. So it came to pass that when his family made another circuit of their territory and revisited the mountain, they smelt Changa's presence in the area immediately. There were eight of them when they found Changa at the water hole. Six were adults, the other two were Changa's brother and sister who had survived, and were now a bit over half grown as he was. They came silently like mist drifting between the trees, coming upwind to the water hole. Their first instinct was to attack this intruder in their territory that they could smell long before they saw him. But they were very cautious because there was also the smell of man at that water hole. Like all animals they distrusted man. But the smell of Painted Dog was stronger and fresher than that of man, so they came on ready to expel the stranger. They would not kill him because dog does not eat dog, but they would drive him away. Like ghosts flitting between the podo trees and around clumps of buffalo grass they moved upwind until all of a sudden they stood in a group on one side of the water hole looking at Changa drinking ten feet away. Changa had not heard them coming. When he lifted his head from the water he froze, seeing that he was the center of their attention. He realized they could catch him instantly, so flight was not realistic. A wave of fear ran over him making his hackles rise unconsciously along his back. They looked at each other silently for what seemed like a long time, but was really a moment. Then the familiarity of Changa's smell suddenly fell into place in the memory of Changa's mother. Recognition came to her just as a hidden antelope suddenly takes shape in your eyes, for what it is, when it moves even an ear. In an instant her territorial hostility changed to the instinctive affection of mother for child. She was second in hierarchy in the pack, so they followed her lead as a school of fish or flock of birds will all turn together as if guided by some soundless, invisible, telepathic command. The aggressive tension of the pack that menaced Changa a moment before evaporated like a drop of sweat off a hot rock. Not a sound passed between them, but Changa too became immediately aware of the change in atmosphere. His hackles sank as his mother stepped forward.

Changa waited as she came slowly round the pool. Now he was more curious than afraid. She sniffed his nose in greeting, and then nuzzled him on the neck wrinkling her nose in disgust at the smell of Dogo on him. At that moment Changa felt more comfortable, more at peace, than he had at any time since he recovered in Chepnall cave. The memory of his mother, buried for so many months in his subconscious, took over. Without thinking he lowered his head and front paws towards the ground in a friendly submissive gesture, and then reared up on his hind legs as though he would wrestle playfully with his mother. She responded in kind and used her front paws to push him down with an affectionate growl. At this the whole pack came around Changa until he was overwhelmed with sniffs and nuzzles. It was his brother and sister who said, "You stink of man," as they began to romp with him. When the pack had drunk at the pool and began to move on, he went with them as though it were the most natural thing in the world; which it was for him. He was young and impetuous. As is often the case with the young he was careless about the feelings of others, in this case Dogo. By evening that day Dogo sorely missed Changa. He was used to Changa going roaming for an hour or so, but not for a whole afternoon. When the shadows lengthened and the tops of the trees took on a golden glow from the setting sun, Dogo was frantically looking for Changa. The small valley in front of Chepnall cave rang with his shrill calls of "Changa, Changa, Changa." But by now Changa and his pack were several miles away. Soon Dogo's calls were joined by the deeper sound of Simu calling his name. But it was useless. Their voiced echoed off the cliff above the cave and the floated down the wind into the trees. There was no answering bark and no Changa racing up the path as he had so often before. Simu did not say it, but wondered if Changa had been caught in another snare. He was distressed by Dogo's plea, "We must find him Baba, we must find him." They searched near the cave along the paths they used, but saw no sign of Changa. It was getting too dark to see footprints on the ground when they went along the path by the watering hole on the way back to cave. So Dogo sat and cried by the fire that night not knowing what had happened. He said, "Leopard has eaten him, I know it. He would come when I call if he could." Simu replied, "I do not think so. I have not seen any traces of leopard near here, even at the water hole, but I will look some more in the morning."

Dogo was not at all convinced. That night he curled up in the *boma* next to Bossy, his stomach feeling hollow and silent tears on his cheeks. He woke Simu as soon as the dawn calls of the great yellow beaked hornbill echoed into the cave. Simu shivered in the cold and went down to the water hole to replenish his water gourd which had not been filled the night before. It was just light enough to see the ground when he came to the water hole. Dogo came anxiously with him. One glance at the footprints in the mud told Simu the whole story. Pointing out the many marks he said, "Look Changa's family came. There were two young and as many big ones as you can count on one hand." "But where is Changa?" asked Dogo. Simu pointed to the side of the pool where three sets of smaller footprints led out to the path around the Bluff. "He went with his family," he said. "No Baba, he can't, will he come back?" asked Dogo. "Perhaps he will when he has learned to hunt like Painted Dog. When he is grown up and cannot be top dog he may wander away from his family, or be driven out if he is bad mannered. Then he will look for a girl to start a new family. In his wanderings he may come to visit us." Dogo did not really understand all this and Simu did not really believe what he said. He just wanted to give Dogo some comfort in hope. Dogo sat in the mud by the pool and cried. "At least we know leopard did not eat him," said Simu.

Simu's speculation turned out to be prescient. Changa went with his family without a thought of looking back. He fitted into the pack like a finger in a well worn glove, warm and comfortable. Now he had his own kind to wrestle and play with. His hunting instincts, far from being thwarted and criticized, were encouraged, guided, directed. He learned to work with the pack. He became part of the current that flows among creatures that think of themselves primarily as part of a group, and secondarily, if at all, as individuals. There is an energy that flows through them all without conscious thought or will, moving them all to the same action. This was especially true of hunting. One dog would start running the antelope, staying a bit behind and to one side so that the antelope would naturally veer away to the other side. After a mile the antelope would have kept veering away and run in huge half circle, when another fresh dog would pick up the chase. As the antelope became exhausted and began to slow down the whole pack would converge for the kill. Not so friendly nips and growls quickly taught Changa to wait until his elders and betters had eaten before he tied to get close. He, with his brother and sister, were always the last to eat, even behind their mother. When survival was always a struggle, maternal protection of the young ended early, forcing the pups to face the harsh realities of life. Only the strong survived drought, starvation, hyenas, injuries and sickness. Fortunately for him, Changa was strong. He quickly established his dominance over his brother and sister. He did not challenge the adults until he was fully grown which was about six months after he rejoined his family. When the wet season had come and gone he was a strapping powerful young male. The females did not care to challenge him. The two grown males in the pack were a different story. Whether Changa could have beaten either one alone we will never know. He never had the opportunity, because they worked together. Changa could not challenge one without the other joining in. He came to learn the true meaning of 'back biting', as he faced one and the other came up behind him. The leader and his friend maintained their dominance. Changa was obliged to accept the reality that he could not command the pack, but he never accepted that he could be commanded against his will. So an uneasy truce developed. Changa did not contest the leader's authority over the others, but claimed the right to do his own thing. For the pack as a whole, their cohesion as a group, their willingness to work together and be guided by a leader, was an important part of their survival strategy. Changa never worked against them, but he often stood aside, except in the hunt. Frequently he was aloof and went his own way. When he lost his struggle to dominate the pack, he came back to visit his other family, rather as Simu had foreseen. But now he was a fully grown dog, experienced with many hunts, fights and hungry nights.

While Changa was growing up with his family and learning to become a fully fledged Painted Dog, Dogo was growing up also, but much more slowly. He was moody and downhearted for several days after Changa left moping around the cave ignoring Chok and not going out to play with Bending Twig. But young children tend to look forward not backwards, so in a few days he was out and about looking for amusement. In came in a rather surprising way. He had gone down the mountain with Bossy more than half a mile from the cave to where there was a little plateau of bush, buffalo grass and acacia trees some alone, some in little stands. It was a place where the elephants loved to browse on the trees and pull up clumps of buffalo grass. On the lower side of the plateau, where the underlying rock came close to the surface, there were no trees or even bushes, just short grass with bumps of grey green lichen covered rocks, and here and there tiny bright blue African violet flowers tight to the ground. Bossy rather like grazing here on the much finer short grass. She and Dogo had been here often before. So often in fact, the elephants had become used to the smell of Dogo. The elephant's trunk is so sensitive to smell it can distinguish one human scent from another if the smell is not mixed up with too many other human scents. If there are too many then it is like mixing several distinct colors, you just get a uniform brown, or in this case, just a smell that says, "man". Dogo and Simu never bothered the elephants, who came to recognize their distinct smells and accept them as part of the natural, non threatening, order of things. One very small elephant, not more than a few months old, was called Tumbo (meaning literally stomach) because of his barrel shaped belly. He had not yet learned fear of humans, so he ambled over and sniffed Dogo with his trunk just out of curiosity. Dogo tried to hold the end of it, which delighted Tumbo who easily wriggled it free and then held it out to play the game again. In no time Dogo was holding onto Tumbo's ears and then climbing on his back. This bothered Tumbo at first, so he learned to run into the bushes which did not slow him down at all, but did brush Dogo off his back. Soon this too became a game. Dogo was bored with Chok, and without Changa had no companion of his own maturity, so he came to look forward to playing with Tumbo as often as he could. That was not every day as the elephants frequently browsed in other places, but they did come back often to drink at the Chepnall cave stream that ran past one end of the plateau in the wet weather, which it was when Dogo first met Tumbo.

At first, Tumbo's Mother disliked the relationship between Tumbo and the man child, because instinctively, and correctly, she did not trust man. She could have squashed Dogo as one might tread on a grape, but for some reason did not do so. Mostly, this was because Tumbo was amused by Dogo. But in part it was because the mama *mzee* of the elephant herd, the old leader, told her that one day this man child who liked elephants would be the elephant's best friend, would try to protect her clan from man. So she did not put an end to the game of, 'leg running' that this man child began with Tumbo. The leg running game drove Bossy absolutely frantic. It was quite a simple game really. It involved Dogo and Tumbo running under the stomachs of the big elephants, and around their legs, without getting kicked or trodden on. When the elephants were in the open glade without any underbrush it was just dangerous enough to be great fun. If they became tiresome Tumbo's Mother would just tell him to stop and give him a swat on his rear end with her trunk if he didn't. Though tempted sometimes, she never did that to Dogo, it would have been like hitting him with small tree trunk. Instead she would put her trunk up to his shoulders and send him flying by sneezing, though to us it would sound more like a foghorn.

It was elephant sneezing that caused Dogo to have the greatest of admiration for the striped field mice that were no bigger than his hand. He was sitting in the short grass with the elephants near by one day, when he saw a little group of field mice running in single file towards an elephant that was pulling up tussocks of grass and eating them. When they were about ten feet away they all stopped, then slowly and hesitantly one went forward right up to the elephants trunk. When he next put it down, the mouse made a running jump into the trunk. With scrabbling feet he disappeared up one nostril. The trunk continued to curl around the clump of grass and pull it up. Then when the grass was half way to its mouth the elephant dropped the grass, straightened out its trunk like a tapered tree trunk, and sneezed an almighty sneeze like a trumpet blast. The mouse shot out of the trunk like a lead ball from a muzzle loading musket. He described an arc fifty feet long in the air and landed with a bump in patch of grass where he made a little trail about a foot long as he slid to a stop. Then, slowly, he struggled to his feet and began to move a bit groggily towards his friends. They rushed over and congratulated him by sniffing and licking him. Dogo was fascinated. He had never seen such a thing before. The elephant went back to eating grass. When he came back the cave that afternoon Dogo said to Bending Twig, "Why do mice run up elephant's trunks?" "Only boy mice do that," said Bending Twig. "But why?" reiterated Dogo. "Oh that's how a boy mouse proves that he has become an *dume* a real man mouse. It's quite dangerous. If he's unlucky he can be blasted into a rock on the ground or even worse impaled on one of those two inch long thorns of a white thorn tree. I've found quite a few there shriveling and smelly in the sun. They have to do this as a rite of passage, to be accepted into the elite few of the bravest, and have the right to father the next generation. It's called the 'trial of the trunk." "I think it must hurt," said Dogo with feeling.

It was about a month after this, when the dry season had just begun, that Changa came back for a long visit; a visit that lasted until the rains came again. Simu and Dogo were sitting in the mouth of Chepnall cave one evening brewing *chai* over the cave fire when the hyraxes cried a warning and Bossy pricked up her ears. What had disturbed them were strange sounds, part heaving breathing, part rustling leaves and an occasional breaking twig. Most animals went smoothly, almost silently, through the forest and made almost no noise coming up the path to the cave. Here was something making no real attempt to hide its coming. That was sufficiently unusual to be almost a challenge, a statement that said, "I'm coming and I don't care if you know it." Only man was that arrogant. But Simu never had visitors. If a man were coming, was he alone? Did he come in peace? What tribe was he, friend or foe? Simu got up quickly and reached for his spear. He held his *panga* in the other hand and then went to where he could see the path leading to the cave mouth. Bossy stood stock still listening and Dogo crawled up by Chok on the big rock in front of the cave. All eyes were on the path. Then suddenly two big Mickey Mouse ears and a black face appeared around a turn in the path. In his mouth Changa was dragging the remains of a duiker that he had half eaten. Dogo recognized him instantly, jumped down off the rock and raced down the path to throw his arms around Changa's neck. Simu called uselessly, "Wait! Slowly!" He saw a full grown Painted Dog carrying its kill, probably ready to fight any one who might try and take it away from him. He thought it was Changa, but in that moment was not sure. Even if it was Changa, had he become totally wild in the many moons since he had left? A wild dog could tear off half of Dogo's face without difficulty. Simu held his breath as Dogo's arms went around that big dappled neck. He breathed out a sigh of relief as Changa put down the half duiker and licked Dogo's face before rearing up on his hind legs high above Dogo to playfully wrestle and push him down as he had so often before. Boy and dog were all tangled up rolling around in great mutual affection for several minutes before they stood up and came up the path with a dance in their footsteps. Changa carried his kill and left it at Simu's feet before going off the romp with Dogo again. Simu was astounded. Never before had he seen a wild animal share its food, except only a mother with the very young. "He must have eaten all he can eat," thought Simu. He wasted no time cutting up the remains of the duiker. The bones he put in his *sufuria* to stew, the rest he put on green sticks that he used as skewers that he stuck in the ground at an angle leaning over the fire. Meat was always a feast for Simu and Dogo. That night they ate well. Their stomachs hung almost as low as Changa's. For the next few months it was as though Changa had never left. But it was different. Just by the way he behaved and carried himself, Changa gave a clear message that nobody was going to tell him what to do. It was different also in the fact that Dogo was no longer simply Changa's friend and playmate; he was now also a younger one who did not always know what to do, one who needed guidance and protecting. The change in Changa became very evident the next time Simu went to pay his monthly honey dues to Kisharani and Changa came along.

Changa

6. Trouble with Kisharani

Not long after Changa came back, Dogo seeing an almost full moon said, "Baba when will we go up the mountain?" By this he meant go Kisharani's *manyatta*. He was anxious to go because he liked playing with Maziwa's children and she was woman who treated him with great affection, as women may do even with children that are not their own. A young boy being raised by a man alone may live a life that is incomplete because there is no woman. Simu answered, "Yes, you are right; tomorrow I will get the honey." So the next day he left Dogo with Bossy, Bending Twig, and now Changa too, and raided one of his honey barrels to get Kisharani his due. He did it reluctantly because his visits were becoming less and less pleasant. He always took Dogo with him, but had to walk slowly so that Dogo could keep up. This meant he could not make a round trip in one day. He had to spend the night. Although he too looked forward to being with his niece Maziwa, Kisharani and his mother were another story. On this occasion he took Changa as well as Dogo, or more accurately to say, Changa just came along. He would not have stayed at the cave even if Simu had told him to. He would co-operate with the elders of his pack and with man in a common endeavor, usually hunting, but listened to no one, and made up his own mind about everything else. He remembered not to hunt Bending Twig or man's domestic animals like Bossy, but now he was proud of his ability to hunt and kill, to be independent of man, unlike the yapping curs of the *manyatta*. They made a big mistake when Simu arrived with Dogo and Changa at Kisharani's place.

As usual, half a dozen of the *manyatta* dogs started barking when they saw or smelt Simu approaching. When Changa came into view the territorial imperative in the *manyatta* pack went into high gear. They rushed out growling to drive off this stranger, or make him submit to their many bites. Though he did not think of it in those terms, Changa's pack had taught him the value of a strategic retreat to a better defensive position when one was outnumbered. So, with a wolf like lope of his long legs, he went ahead of the barking pack to where two giant lobelias, as big as small trees, grew about two feet apart with a thick tangle of old dead leaves and branches at the bottom. He backed his rear end into that gap so that his sides and rear were inaccessible. Only his head and shoulders stood out. This made good sense, but was unnecessary as things turned out. The leader of the *manyatta* pack was a young brown colored male of medium size, with a long tail that curled up almost over his back as is common with mongrels. He expected Changa to run further. The leader was totally confident, twenty yards ahead of the others, and going to show them how to see off an intruder. He did not notice that Changa was somewhat bigger than he was and not afraid at all. Changa waited with a certain tension in him, but calm and calculating. When the dog was ten feet away he made a fake move as though he would go to the left. The move was withdrawn in an instant, but the charging dog turned a quarter turn to go after Changa and could not turn back in time. His shoulder hit Changa's chest as Changa's jaws closed around his neck. A canine tooth pierced the lead dog's jugular. He was already dying as Changa dropped him, choking blood, at his feet. The second dog managed to get a mouthful of the loose skin with the ring scar around Changa's neck. It hurt but did no real damage. Changa twisted his head and tore off the dog's ear. He ran yelping back. The five or six other dogs were demoralized by the yelping and the sight of their leader now motionless on the ground. Changa came out from between the lobelias and started toward them, deliberately, purposefully and fast. They broke and ran. He gave a hunting howl which terrified them even more as he set out in pursuit. They fled past the *manyatta* as Maziwa came out to see what all the noise was about. It was then that Simu called Changa. He looked back as though to say, "I hear you," but kept on going until the *manyatta* dogs disappeared around the curve of the hill. Then panting a bit heavily he came back and fell in line behind Simu and Dogo.

"Uncle, what is that fierce dog? I have never seen one so big and with so many colors," asked Maziwa. "He is a Painted Dog, a dog of the plains, and his name is Changa," replied Simu. "Hello and what is your news?" Maziwa ignored the formality of greeting and said with some concern, "Looks like a wild dog to me." "He is," said Simu. "Dogo and I saved him from a snare many moons ago when it was a puppy. He was Dogo's best friend until he was half grown, then he left with his pack. Now he comes and goes. Today he came along. Your dogs better leave him alone." "Kisharani's going to be very angry about the dead one," said Maziwa. "Where is he?" asked Simu. "Out herding the cattle. He will be back at dusk." "Then we have some time," said Simu. So they talked comfortably and Dogo played happily with Maziwa's children until Kisharani came home behind the cows. As the afternoon wore on the *manyatta* dogs came back in ones and twos, silently, subserviently, avoiding Changa or overtly letting him know they would not challenge him. This held true even when Changa spend a couple of hours enjoying one of the females in season. Instinctively she submitted to the top dog until he could do no more. Changa had a good afternoon. After that, whenever Simu went up the mountain to Kisharani's, Changa came along too.

When the evening shadow of the mountain began to reach across the plains, the sound of bleating sheep and lowing cattle brought Maziwa and Simu out of the hut they were in. They sat on two rocks and watched the herd go by to the night *boma* and cattle shed. All too soon, Kisharani appeared behind them. He had seen the dead dog fifty yards off the trail and had gone to investigate. Ignoring Simu, he addressed himself to Maziwa. "Why is my best dog dead with blood on its throat?" He demanded. "He and the others attacked Simu's dog. He was too pleased with himself, and not good enough," replied Maziwa calmly, drawing a mental parallel with her husband. "Since when did Simu have a dog? Where is this animal?" "Over there under the bush," said Maziwa pointing. "Kisharani saw Changa and began to walk in his direction, spear not trailing at the length of his arm, but held shoulder height ready to throw or lunge. With a wild animal's sensitivity to the basic feelings of others, including man, Changa was immediately aware of Kisharani's aggressive intentions. One of the *manyatta* dogs would have put its tail down and slunk away hurriedly, but not Changa. Kisharani was quite taken aback when a big long legged dog, dappled in many colors, stood up and growled with its hackles rising. He pulled back his arm as though to hurl his spear at it, not realizing that Simu had followed behind him. Simu now grabbed the end of Kisharani's spear behind his shoulder and said, "No." quite firmly. Kisharani turned with a burst of anger, thinking, first the dog, now this cave man will challenge me. Simu did not let go of the long metal spike at the back end of the spear even as Kisharani jerked it violently with a scowl on his face. Kisharani was a bigger, rougher and much younger man than Simu. In a fight without weapons it would have been no contest. So he snarled, "Let go, that dog is dead." "That dog is protected by the great spirit of the *wazungu* that travels in the ghost elephant and can be called by the sign of the cross. If you attack it, the elephant will walk on your *manyatta*." He said this very solemnly, without fear, look-ing directly into Kisharani's eyes. Kisharani thought of himself as strong and brave. Like many young men he thought, or possibly just hoped, this was all he needed to be. He realized however, that he was not very knowledgeable, especially about spirits and magic. Deep down he knew that they could do bad things to you, and that he had no idea how to protect himself. Also he had heard of some white people called the *wazungu* who were very powerful, but he had never met one. So now he hesitated, and to cover his uncertainty said, "I know nothing of the spirit of the *wazungu* or the ghost elephant, so let go of my spear." He had stopped tug-ging on it so Simu knew the battle was half won. He replied, "You should learn of these things. Know that the power in that dog is the power not only of his teeth, but his spirit and those that pro-tect him." Kisharani looked again at the large growling wild dog and saw him as bigger now and imbued with evil powers coming from his malevolent yellow eyes. A shadow of fear flitted across his consciousness as he asked, "Are you now a witchdoctor that you threaten me with spirits?" "Not a witch doctor, but I have met the spirit of the *wazungu* and know its power. It saved the child who is with me." Kisharani now remembered Masziwa talking about Dogo's near death experience when he burned his buttock. So he stayed silent as Simu rather generously said, "When you see this footprint, know that the spirit is near." Then he drew the outline of an elephant's footprint on the ground and in it a small cross. Pointing to the cross he said, "That is the *wuzungu* sign for their great spirit. Its magic is more than our magic. It would not be wise to anger it." Leaving Kisharani feeling uncertain and discomfited, he walked over to Changa and told him without a spoken word that the confrontation was now over. Changa's hackles went down, but his instinctive dislike of Kisharani remained.

Simu kept behind Kisharani as he walked back to the hut where Maziwa stood waiting. She had kept Dogo next to her as Kisharani went after Changa. Dogo had cried out in alarm, "He is going to hurt Changa!" "Baba will stop him," replied Maziwa with far more confidence in her tone than she actually felt. She had then watched the altercation between Simu and the man who had bought her as his wife. He had bought and paid for her, so he thought of her as belonging to him, his property. He had seen her as a big breasted sex object who was also well built, strong, and capable of hard work, not the least of which was carrying water up the hill on her back from the stream five hundred feet below. She had seen him as an athletic well built young man with no first wife to lord it over her. So she was not unhappy about the union. She had enjoyed him sexually as much as he wanted her, though perhaps a little less frequently. Now, two children later, the mutual physical attraction had faded, like thirst disappears when there is plenty of water. "He used to drink like a bull at the water hole in dry weather," she thought to herself, "now I don't care, and he doesn't much either. He used to want to please me, now he just pleases himself." As Maziwa's attention gradually turned from Kisharani to her children she began to see her man as stupid, short tempered and arrogant, good for herding cattle, but not much more. His mother became more and more of an issue, as he complained constantly to her about his woman. Maziwa called his mother, 'mdomo kali' meaning sharp mouth. 'Kali' means sharp in the context of a knife, and fierce when used in relation to an animal. In Maziwa's mind both meanings were appropriate for this poison tongued woman whose words burned like a scorpion's sting on a hot rock. Maziwa wished she would hurry up and die, but Mdomo Kali would not cooperate. Vinegar is a good preservative and she had plenty of it. These thoughts flashed across Maziwa's mind as Kisharani walked back with Simu following. "Where is the honey," he demanded as he walked up. Maziwa showed him the *sufuria*. "Why so little?" he asked accusingly, turning to Simu. "The rains were small and the flowers few this year," replied Simu. "Then take from two barrels not one," said Kisharani angrily. "They must have time to repair the damage, and have some thing to eat themselves in the dry weather," said Simu. "If I take too much or too soon the hive will die." "That's your problem not mine," said Kisharani nastily, adding, "you're probably eating half of it yourself. Make sure the *sufuria* is full next time." Simu did not deign to answer, but gave Kisharani a steady look that said, "To me you are as donkey pee is to honey." He walked away and sat under a small tree, while Maziwa went in to cook the evening meal. While she did this, Kisharani walked over to his mother's house around the curve of the hill. He always went to her to dump his feelings when he was upset. She enjoyed joining in his bad feelings, in fact she reveled in bad mouthing others. She saw him coming and went out a little way to greet him. "*Jambo*" she said, "what is your news?" "Good, but..." and Kisharani went on to complain about Simu. Mdomo Kali responded, "That man is no good. I knew it when he went to live in a cave. What does he think he is, a bat? He's ruining the child you know. Probably does not care as it's not his. Look at the way it behaves, like an animal. I don't want it around your children spoiling them, teaching them to lick each other like dogs." As she paused for breath, Kisharani interjected, "Have you heard of the spirit of the *wazungu*?" "No, why do you ask?" "Because that cave man says his dog is protected by the ghost elephant." "You talk like an idiot of *wazungu* and ghost elephants," replied Mdomo Kali unkindly, continuing, "since when did the cave man have a dog?" "He has a giant wild dog that came with him for the first time today," said Kisharani. "It killed our best dog. When I went to kill the wild dog the cave man claimed that it was protected by the ghost elephant that has the mark of the *wazungu* spirit on its foot, like this," he said drawing a little cross on the ground. "So? Did you kill the dog?" she asked. "No," he replied. "Good," she said, "then you have not angered any spirit and we can find out what magic this cave man is practicing. What does this mark you made mean?" "Do I know why the cock crows? All I know is he told Maziwa the spirit in this mark healed the boy when he burned his buttock. A *mzungu* woman gave him *dawa* which carried the spirit into his body and drove out his sickness." "So what is this talk of an elephant?" asked Mdomo Kali. "It is not any elephant. It is the one that carries the spirit of the *wazungu* when it travels in the forest, that is why it has on its foot the mark I showed you, the mark of the spirit. He says this is the spirit that gives the *wazungu* their power." "Has the cave man learned the magic of the *wazungu* has he learned to use the power of this spirit?" "I do not know," replied Kisharani. "I doubt it," said Mdomo Kali. "That cave man is simple. What would a powerful spirit want with a man like him," she said nastily. "But we should be careful until we know," she continued. "You are right my mother," replied Kisharani, " I will not provoke him or his dog for now, but please find out about this magic he speaks of. I am not good at such things." "You let it be, say nothing, I will find out. Now go back to your house," replied Mdomo Kali. As Kisharani left for home, Mdomo Kali retired to her hut to plot and plan. Simu had never threatened Kisharani or his family. The concern of Mdomo Kali about Simu's knowledge of magic was not because she felt threatened, but rather because she was concerned about retaliation if she were nasty to Simu, as she intended to be. She felt quite justified in this intention, telling herself it was her duty to support her son who was always complaining about Simu. In reality she took pleasure in other people's misfortunes and felt only envy at their successes.

When Kisharani came back to his *manyatta* he found Simu and Dogo chatting happily with Maziwa around the fire. At Maziwa's suggestion they were waiting for Kisharani to return before eating. She saw no point in needlessly provoking him and making the meal more uncomfortable than it already promised to be. Her good intentions were frustrated by Kisharani. It took a minute for his eyes to adjust to the gloom in the windowless hut. When they did he exclaimed angrily, "What's that dog doing in here," pointing at Changa. Dogo got up and went over to put his arms protectively around Changa. That stopped him from standing and giving Kisharani a warning growl. As it was he just raised his head and bared his teeth in an unmistakable message. "Get that dog out of here," said Kisharani raising his voice. "No," cried Dogo in a small child's voice. Simu stood up and took two steps to stand by Dogo and Changa. He did not want to be embarrassed by Dogo or

Changa refusing to leave, or arguing with Dogo about it. "We are guests, he said by way of preface to his next words, "come, we will all go out." Also he wanted to take the pressure off Maziwa who said, "I will bring it to you." Then he, Dogo and Changa went out of the door without another word. In due course Maziwa brought out what was left of the meal and they ate under the stars with the cold of the night beginning to shrink their ribs. As they sat there they heard Kisharani's voice raised again in complaint, but no answer from Maziwa who simply went on about her business. Today she withdrew rather than used her tongue as a weapon because she felt embarrassed to fight with Kisharani when her uncle Simu was present. When Simu and Dogo finished eating they went to the cattle shed where they climbed onto the sleeping platform. The total familiarity of the smells, the heavy breathing, muffled bleats and sound of many animals acted like a potent soporific on Simu. Dogo lay awake a little longer, missing the feel of Bossy next to him. Changa slept in the cold starlit bowl of night as he had so often before, but at first light he went and found again the bitch in season, something that was noticed by Kisharani.

In the morning Simu let the cattle, sheep and goats out, helped Maziwa milk a cow into a gourd, had breakfast, thanked Maziwa very genuinely and set off back to Chepnall cave. On the way back Dogo asked, "Baba why was Kisharani angry?" Simu really did not know as he had been careful not to give offence personally. "Perhaps it was as he said, because Changa killed the dog, but I do not think so. He has not worried about a dog dying before." "Then why Baba?" repeated Dogo. "In every man there is good and bad. The good is like a leopard, the bad like a hyena. They are constantly fighting each other," said Simu. "The hyena has more powerful jaws, but the leopard has claws as well as teeth." "Well, which one wins?" asked Dogo. "The one that you feed the most," replied Simu. He did not know that Kisharani had decided to feed the hyena.

Later that week Kisharani went to find his brother Kiretu and asked him to watch his cattle, sheep and goats as his children were too small and he had matters that he needed to attend to. His brother said, "Of course," and thought nothing more of it. Kisharani went off to his mother's *manyatta*. Her husband had died some years before. She now lived in one of the smaller huts in the *boma*, an enclosure which had a wall of branches and brush around it. Several of her other grown children lived in the larger huts. They, or their wives, took care of her needs such as collecting firewood and bringing water up from the stream. The wives had long since learned to be attentive to those needs and obedient to her wishes. She had a cutting mouth and a relentless drive in pursuit of her goals. Maziwa was one daughter in law who had been fortunate enough to escape her tyranny by living some distance away and ignoring her criticisms of child raising and personal behavior. Maziwa being nice to her uncle Simu was one behavior that did not please Mdomo Kali. So she listened sympathetically as Kisharani complained about Maziwa. He had done this often before, but this time he had a deeper concern. "Mother," he said, "I am worried about Simu and his magic that I have told you about. Do you think that Maziwa might be possessed by evil spirits sent by Simu which cause her to do what she otherwise would have no reason to do? As I have told you many times she ignores me, she has no sexual desire for me, she defies my orders, and even when she says nothing she makes it clear by her expressions and slow movements that she does not care what I say." "My son, ever since you told me about the ghost elephant and this cave man's *mzungu* magic, I have been looking into it. No one here knows what the *mzungu* magic is, or how to make it work for them. The white woman that cave man went to may have given him the healing of *mzungu* magic. That magic could have healed the child, but the cave man did not create it. So he does not have the power to use it against you." "Well if the cave man cannot create *mzungu* magic is there any other way he could he put evil spirits into Maziwa?" asked Kisharani. "He may have learned our magic; how to make and use *tokolotsi* and *malambo*. Or it could be Maziwa who makes the magic, or they may both do it when they are together and you are watching the cattle.

She may be deceiving you. She is a well built healthy woman. If she has no sexual interest in you, it is a problem of the spirit or the mind, not the body. She has desires. Some one, or something, is satisfying them." "How could that be Mother? My brothers would not steal her from me, not even for an hour, and if she went to another man's hut every one would see her and we would know." "You forget Simu," his mother replied. "Go and ask the children if they have seen anything while you are not there. Do not let Maziwa know you suspect *tokolotsi*. Go now," she said shooing him out. She expected that the idea she had planted would grow in his mind and take over his emotions. She knew that if this happened he would see in many little things abundant evidence of a conspiracy between Simu and Maziwa. May be then her son would gather the strength of will to put this upstart woman in her real place, and drive out of his life the bad influence of Simu, a recluse of no significance with a wild child. The first steps of her expectations were well satisfied.

Even as Kisharani walked back to his *manyatta* the idea of a conspiracy between Maziwa and Simu began to grow in his mind. They do like each other, he said to himself. Whenever I see them together they are laughing and talking. When I come close they fall silent. It must be because they know I should not hear what they say. With these thoughts he hurried home. On arriving he said to the two elder children, "Come with me, we will go see what Kiretu is doing with the cattle." A mile or so around the mountain, when they could see the herd across a valley, he sat down saying, "Let's watch and wait for them to come back." So the children sat down with him on a small outcropping of rock, watched a red wattled lizard scurry away and then did their best to answer his questions. They did not understand what it was about because one child was seven years old, the other five. "When Simu comes does he talk to you?" he asked first. "No, not more than to say *Jambo*." "Does he talk to your mother?" "Oh yes he is nice to her and to us." "Does he touch her?" "No, he does not need to, she is not old, she can stand without help." "Where do they sit?" "Mostly outside in the shade except when she is cooking." "Does she make anything other than food?" "No, only the honey she takes out of Simu's *sufuria* which she washes so he can take it back." "How is that new big dog of his?" "He's very fierce with the other dogs, they are scared of him now. You know he won the fight." "Are you scared of him?" "No, he's friendly unless we knock Dogo over, then he growls unless Dogo tells him not to." "Is anything different when Simu and Dogo are here?" "No not really, just that they are here and it's fun." Not getting anything he wanted, Kisharani gave up and said, "Soon Kiretu will bring the cows. We will wait here. See if you can find a rabbit." So the children went off pretending they were hunters, while Kisharani pondered his frustration. Then it came to him; perhaps Simu was putting some black magic, some *dawa,* in the honey, but if he is, what would that do? He decided to ask Kiretu. Half an hour later, when Kiretu came up the hill behind the cows, he fell in step and asked, "Could some one use *dawa* in honey to make themselves, or some one else, into *tokolotsi?*" "What do you mean by *tokolotsi?*" responded Kiretu. "You know, when a *mganga*, some one practicing witchcraft, turns himself into an animal such as a baboon which he uses to guard his house, or entice his neighbor's sheep into his hut so he can kill it and eat it secretly." Kisharani did not mention the most common use of a *tokolotsi* which was as a secret lover. They were very well suited for this because they could be invisible when they wanted, but even when invisible they could give and receive all normal human sense of touch. Men who made themselves into *tokolotsi* often seduced other men's wives and unmarried young women in their sleep. Women who changed themselves into *tokolotsi* could travel unseen into men's huts and play with them in their sleep, so they would wake up with an erection or even a wet dream. Kiretu was not taken in. He said, "Yes, but *tokolotsi* are mostly lovers. Surely you do not want to turn yourself into a baboon to be a lover?" "Of course not" replied Kisharani indignantly. "I do not hide in an animal if I want a woman. But I am not so sure about that strange cave man who brings me honey once a month. He has no woman, yet he does not seem thirsty. Do you think it possible he could turn himself into a dog? He came with a big wild dog, that seems to be part of his family even though it is wild. This morning I saw that dog mounting one of mine for over an hour. Could he have been in the dog?" "It's possible," said Kiretu, "but *tokolotsi* usually have intercourse with humans not animals." A new thought then flashed into Kisharani's mind, "But what if a woman became *tokolotsi* to have intercourse with another?" Kiretu was no fool, "You think that Maziwa makes herself into a *tokolotsi* in the form of a dog?" "I do not know, perhaps she and the cave man both do," replied Kisharani, fast making up his mind. "Could *dawa* in honey be used to make some one *tokolotsi*?" "Probably," replied Kiretu, "but don't you eat most, if not all, the honey he brings? You don't look like a dog to me and you're not invisible." "Don't get smart," replied Kisharani a little angrily. "Alright," said Kiretu, "but Maziwa's not that kind of woman. She is a good person. Where was she this morning when you saw the dogs together?" "She had gone to get water from the river, at least that's where she said she was going," replied Kisharani thoughtfully. Kiretu had no answer to this inference, so he remained silent as they listened to the cattle lowing as they moved contentedly towards home, which was more than could be said of Kisharani whose mind was churning.

When he came back to his *manyatta* Kisharani immediately went to look at the water container. It was emptier than usual. He demanded of Maziwa, "Why is the water jar so empty, why did you not go to the river this morning as you should?" "I did," she replied succinctly. "Then why is it almost empty?" "Because I used more water than usual to wash out the *sufuria* that Simu uses to bring you honey," replied Maziwa. Kisharani changed paths and asked, "What *dawa* does Simu put in the honey?" "What are you talking about? He does not put any *dawa* in it. It comes straight from his honey barrel to you." "How would you know that if you have not talked to him about it? You are admitting that you and he have spoken of putting *dawa* in the honey." "I am doing nothing of the kind. I just don't believe he puts any *dawa* in it. Why would he want to?" Kisharani could not contain his himself, "So that he can make you into *tokolotsi* and mount you like an animal." Maziwa looked at him in utter disbelief. "I do not think you are drunk, so why do you say such stupid things? Have you gone mad?" "You have no more desire for me and are now satisfying yourself secretly as a *tokolotsi,*" said Kisharanai. Maziwa was now getting angry with his outrageous accusation and childish jealousy as she saw it. "You may be right that an animal would be better than you," she said cuttingly. "You can't see that what I want is not sex, but an end to your complaints. No! All you can do is think in terms of sex, because that is the only way you can express your manhood, and then not much, you *safari moja* man (one time man). We have no enemies to fight here so you can't even be brave in battle to show you are a man. All you can think of sex. So you think I must too. Well, I don't, and if I did, I would not have to make myself into a magic animal like a *tokolotsi* to get it." The *safari moja* barb had enough truth in it to badly hurt Kisharani's ego. For a moment a surge of anger swept through him causing him to raise his fist as if to strike her, then it subsided and he continued. "If you do not become *tokolotsi* then it is that cave man. The children said they saw a baboon walking around on its hind legs like a man. It had an enormous penis that it carried over its shoulder." It was true that the children had said they had seen a baboon. The walking on its hind legs, and penis size, were exaggerations consistent with folklore. As he repeated them in the days to come they became truth in Kisharani's mind. Maziwa responded, "Yes the children have seen a baboon, there is nothing unusual in that." "Then why was it that when I reached out to touch you in the night a month ago you were ice cold and hairy like an animal. When I spoke to you, your answer came from outside the hut. You were there with that cave man." "This story I have not heard before," replied Maziwa. "You were drunk or dreaming, and probably touching that piece of dried cow hide we have." Then with a woman's intuitive perception Maziwa said, "You are getting all this nonsense from your mother." Without denying it Kisharani said, "She was right when she said you had been with a *tokolotsi* when your child was born dead three years ago." Maziwa responded bitterly, "She is evil. If my child died because of a *toko-lotsi* then she was the one who kept it and sent it when I was asleep. Many say she practices black magic. You leave this nonsense before I denounce her, you fool!" Kisharani was aware of his mother's reputation as some one who practised witchcraft. He knew that Maziwa was popular with the women of the clan. The possibility that Maziwa might denounce his mother had a very chilling effect on him because his mother would be very angry that he had not followed her instructions. She had told him not to mention *toko-lotsi* to Maziwa and now he might have provoked his usually good natured wife into denouncing his mother for keeping one. So he said, "It is that cave man who talks of *mzungu* magic and ghost elephants, not my mother, and you support him. It is the two of you who practice magic." With that he left the hut. Not knowing what else to do, he went to report to his mother.

Kisharani did not repeat to his mother all the details of his conversation with Maziwa, but did report that the children had seen the baboon, adding his own his own exaggerations that it had been walking on its hind legs with its penis slung over its shoulder. He also told the story of reaching out to touch Maziwa and finding something cold and hairy that flew up in the dark and out of the door of the hut, and Maziwa's voice coming from outside when he cried out in alarm. He said all this as fact, and affirmed his belief that Simu and Maziwa were practicing black magic on him. He blamed the *dawa* supposedly put by Simu in the honey for the fact that when angry, and trying to dominate Maziwa by penetrating her, he was unable to do so. He did not mention that he often fermented the honey, either intentionally or accidentally, and was usually in a drunken rage on these occasions. His mother encouraged him, saying, "I knew it. She had that miscarriage because of the baboon. That child he picked up in the forest is part of this you know. It's really an animal in human form. It licks your children in greeting like a dog and bleats like a goat. When your cattle stampeded and three were pushed over a cliff and died wasn't that child with your eldest boy who came with you?" "Why yes mother he was. Why do you ask." "Don't you see? It is a clear sunny afternoon and all of a sudden the cattle stampede for no apparent reason. That child turned himself into a leopard or hyena and deliberately spooked the cattle." "Now that you mention it," said Kisharani, "it is strange that my dogs will sometimes growl and act scared when I can see nothing to be afraid of. It only happens when that cave man is visiting. Do you think the child could be *tokolotsi* and make itself invisible in the form of a hyena?" "Hyena, leopard, baboon, something," said his mother. "I'm sure of it. You're lucky more of your cattle haven't been killed. That wild dog the cave man came with this last trip may be the child's brother, he acts like it. Didn't you find a sheep's bones a few months ago?" They carried on in this vein and warming to the theme came to realize that black magic was behind all the unexplained problems they had over the last few years. Man's malevolence expressed through witchcraft was behind cattle deaths, miscarriages, sores that would not heal, fevers that attacked them and unusual stomach pains. "How could we have been so blind to this man Simu, how are we going to protect ourselves in the future, what are we going to do?" asked Kisharani. "Leave it to me," answered his mother with tight lips.

A few days later Mdomo Kali sent word through one of the other women that she wanted to see Ol Kinyei about a serious matter. Ol Kinyei was a much respected elder of the clan who lived about a mile away. He knew every one in the clan by sight and in the normal course of contact and conversation had a reasonably good idea of the reputations and personalities of them all. Simu was no exception to this, but contact with him had been negligible for all the years that Simu had lived in Chepnall cave and abandoned cattle herding as a way of making a living. Ol Kinyei knew Mdomo Kali as a woman with an abrasive tongue who seemed to relish rather than avoid confrontation with neighbors. He was flattered by the deference to his wisdom and authority implied by Mdomo Kali's request, but this small pleasure was more than offset by his expectation that she wanted to discuss some relatively insoluble problem. If it were a manageable problem he knew she would have handled it herself. Ol Kinyei sent word back that he would see Mdomo Kali the next day when the sun was overhead. He took the precaution of moving to a nearby large overhanging rock out of earshot of any one in his compound. He did not want pressure from others about any decision he might have to make. He sat in the shade of the rock and admired the stupendous view down the foothills of Mt Elgon and over the plains to the Cherangani hills hazy and blue in the distance. He had never been there and wondered if those hills were like the mountain he lived on.

These thoughts were interrupted by the sight of an old woman coming slowly up the path to where he waited. He recognized her when she drew close. It would have been normal for a woman her age to have had one of her sons with her in a supportive role. Ol Kinyei wondered what problem could be so personal, or so embarrassing that she did not need or perhaps want family help. He had no idea, but became more curious as she approached. "Greetings *mzee*," she said respectfully, "I hope your news is good." "Greetings," he replied, "sit over there," and he pointed to place a few feet away, "tell me what matter troubles you that you wish to see me." Mdomo Kali sat on the stone indicated and curled her toes nervously in the dry dust under the rock where no rain came. "It is a matter of witchcraft," she said. "Is this witchcraft against you?" asked Ol Kinyei. "No it is against my son Kisharani," she replied. "Then why did he not come to see me?" "The witchcraft has taken away his manhood, he cannot bring himself to speak of it to any one but me." "What do you mean, taken away his manhood? Whenever I see him he looks healthy and whole to me. Was he attacked?" "No the injury is not to his body which is normal, but to his ability to act on a man's desires." "You mean that the bull can no longer mount the cow, yet his body is unhurt?" "That is his trouble," replied Mdomo Kali. Ol Kinyei tried to draw a mental image of an impotent Kisharani, but saw only a handsome strapping young man who did not look in the least impotent. So he countered, "Kisharani has several children and has been known to look at other women too." "The children are not babies any more. They were born before that cave man Simu found the child in the forest and started bringing honey that he gives to Maziwa, who, as you know is Kisharani's wife." "Are you saying that Kisharani's problem is because he puts honey on his organ?" asked Ol Kinyei incredulously, but laughing silently. "The problem is not that he puts honey on his organ," relied Mdomo Kali without smiling. "It is the *dawa* that the cave man and Maziwa put in the honey, so that he loses his powers as a man." Ol Kinyei looked at Mdomo Kali thoughtfully as he said, "What good would come to Simu or Maziwa from taking away Kisharani's powers as a man? Simu is much older and Maziwa's uncle." Mdomo Kali was quick to answer, "Maziwa is most disrespectful to Kisharani and refuses him many times. She has no desire for him because she and Simu become *tokolotsi* in the form of a baboon or dog and satisfy each other. They have learned how to change their shape and form and even become invisible. This is the magic they practice. The child that Simu keeps is half animal too. You should see how it behaves." Ol Kinyei now understood that there were difficulties between Kisharani and Maziwa and they were blamed on a witchcraft conspiracy between Simu and Maziwa. But he was a wise old man who had seen more dry seasons come and go than one could count. In his experience poor sexual relations were usually a consequence, not a cause, of other problems, so he asked, "What other bad things come from this magic?" Mdomo Kali was only too happy to launch into a harangue covering a long list of matters. She carried in her left hand a bundle of twigs which she put down one by one as she made the points she wanted to make. Her malevolence was organized. Ol Kinyei listened in amazement as she spoke of Dogo's burnt buttock being healed by *mzungu dawa*, of the ghost elephant carrying the symbol of the great *mzungu* spirit in the form the mark of the cross on its foot, of Maziwa's miscarriage, her explanation for the cattle stampeding, the sheep that was eaten in the bush, the sores that would not heal, the baboon, the dogs, the cold hairy touch in the night and other things that must be the workings of *dawa, maganga* and *tokolotsi*. When she seemed to be finished, Ol Kinyei asked gravely, "If this is all as you say, what do you want me to do?" Mdomo Kali answered without hesitation, "That cave man Simu should be told he may never come here again on pain of death, and Maziwa should be tied to a tree and beaten until she begs for mercy and forgiveness from Kisharani, besides agreeing she may be beaten again if she is ever insolent to him." "You know very well I could make no such order without the approval of the clan," replied Ol Kinyei. "I will look into the matter and let you know what I will do." He said this in a tone of voice that said the conversation was ended. So Mdomo Kali said *kwa heri* and left Ol Kinyei to his thoughts.

Ol Kinyei was, at first, a little overwhelmed by the litany of sins alleged for Simu and Maziwa. He set about his inquiries quietly and discreetly. It was not long before he learned of Kiretu's conversation with Kisharani, which Kiretu had happily shared with his wife to her great amusement. The story had spread quickly from there as was inevitable with any gossip of a titillating nature told to a woman. Kiretu said he did not believe Kisharani's claims, but could not be sure. As he said, in matters such as this involving allegations of magic, truth is as elusive as a rat in the grass, as difficult to prove as it is to hold onto smoke. Like every one else that Ol Kinyei spoke to, Kiretu spoke well of Maziwa saying she was a woman without guile who did what a woman should. Thus encouraged, Ol Kinyei sent for Maziwa. She was worried by the summons, but not surprised as word had begun to circulate that Mdomo Kali had made witchcraft accusations against her. She took her best friend with her for moral support. Her manner of speech was frank and open, without secrecy or guile and lacking in nasty comments about Mdomo Kali, although they would have been fully justified. Ol Kinyei was impressed. She openly agreed that the children had seen a baboon, as had other people. It was a perfectly ordinary baboon on the edge of a troop. If it stood on its hind legs at any time that was undoubtedly to reach something above its head. There was nothing unusual in that. Baboons are great climbers and it may have been going to climb up a rock or tree. The cattle had indeed stampeded about two years before, but that too was not unheard of if they smelt a leopard or hyena. The idea that a child then aged three could have done it was ludicrous. She frankly admitted, however, that Dogo was an unusual child in his closeness to animals. She attributed this to the fact that a nanny goat was his surrogate mother, no woman was in the home at the cave and he lived in the forest like an Ndorobo. Here she was referring to people of the tribe that were forest dwellers. It was well known that their bush craft and knowledge of animals was unsurpassed. She could not explain how *mzungu* magic and *dawa* had cured Dogo, and neither could Simu. She retold the story of the young man at Endebess, the sign of the cross and Simu's dream. These were beyond her understanding, but Simu could not control them, he was merely the beneficiary of white magic, good magic, for which she was happy. Yes she did have a miscarriage and most painful it was. She would hardly use a *tokolotsi* to bring herself such pain. If it were not in the ordinary nature of things then some one hostile such as Mdomo Kali might be the initiator. Coming to Kisharani's alleged loss of manhood Maziwa first pointed out that she knew and accepted a wife's duty to accommodate her husband's sexual desires. She regularly kept silent, biting her tongue, as she submitted to him. Yes it was true that on occasions he was unable to perform the act, and it was true that the honey was responsible, but not because of any *dawa* in it. Rather Kisharani's problem lay in the fact that she put water in the honey as he wanted so that it fermented. Then he would drink too much and be drunk. She hated this because when drunk he was always abusive to her and making sexual advances he could not then fulfill. This explanation struck a chord with Ol Kenyei. He saw it as totally believable and, from his own experience, a very compelling explanation of incapacity. From that moment on he knew he would not denounce Maziwa or Simu for practicing black magic. In fact he respected Simu for living religiously to his commitment to bring Kisharani honey. Everything he had heard was a normal occurrence without black magic.

The child might be a bit strange, but that was not surprising given his situation. The only thing that intrigued, but did not bother, Ol Kenyei was the story of the ghost elephant with the mark of the cross on its foot. His mind made up, he sent for Mdomo Kali and truthfully told her no one supported her charges of black magic against Simu and even less against Maziwa who was well liked and a good woman. He then made a comment to the effect that, "People in glass houses should not throw stones." He left her with the idea that if she created any more trouble he might denounce her for witchcraft. Mdomo Kali did not dare to argue with so respected a man. So she winced and gritted her teeth saying she would talk to Kisharani. This she did reporting the bad news to Kisharani who exploded angrily, saying, "How can they not see we are right. I will denounce that cave man myself." "You will be a voice crying alone in the forest with no one to listen to you. Worse than that remember that the sheep you send out in the morning comes back at night, even if from a different direction. If you make witchcraft accusations they may be thrown back at me and you. Ol Kinyei said as much." "What! That's ridiculous," fumed Kisharani who had repeated his suspicions often enough that he had come to believe them to be absolute truth. Mdomo Kali sighed as she looked at her simplistic son, saying, "Promise me you will not say anything foolish. Do not speak of these witchcraft accusations and let me deal with the cave man a different way. "How can you do that?" asked Kisharani. "I know of some one in the Ndorobo tribe who knows this mountain and all the spirits in and on it. He may be able to help. Now do not ask me more." She did not want Kisharani to know what she had in mind because he would inevitably talk about it, if not when sober, then when drunk. So it was that Maziwa was unaware of the visit Mdomo Kali paid the Ndorobo *mganga*. She did not know about the one heifer fee that he charged for what he promised to do, nor his promise to Mdomo Kali that he would have Simu and Dogo removed from the mountain. The *mganga* misrepresented his powers. In truth he could not direct the spirits of the mountain; he could only bring their attention to things that existed. What they might then do with the information was their decision. It usually helped if the person targeted knew what the *mganga* had asked the spirits to do, because the target might believe that the spirits could be directed. If the target had such belief, then he might, consciously or unconsciously, act in a way that would bring about the desired result. The reputation for success of many a *mganga* rested on this self implementation principle. Of all this, and of the Ndorobo *mganga*, both Maziwa and Simu were blissfully unaware.

White house with Red Roof

7. Attacks on Dogo.

When Simu next came with honey, Maziwa naturally told him about the attempt by Mdomo Kali to have him, and her, denounced for witchcraft, and how it failed. Simu was greatly astonished to hear of this, and he was aggravated. "Why do we have to be plagued by that idiot and his poison tongued mother?" "Uncle," said Maziwa, "that is the shape into which the tree of life has grown, who knows why. Remember that the stars come out at night, without darkness there can be no light. If they are the darkness, let us be the light." "She's darkness all right," said Simu, "she should stay in the dark so that I never have to see her." "You are not the one who has to," replied Maziwa with feeling. "You are right," answered Simu a little sheepishly, adding "do you think I should go to see Ol Kinyei?" "You should see him," said Maziwa, "let him know that you are an honest man and thank him. It will help him to see with his own eyes that he is right." So the next day he went to see Ol Kenyei to thank him and express his regret that Mdomo Kali had bothered him with such nonsense. Ol Kinyei was impressed by Simu's above board sincerity and with the courtesy and respect that Simu showed. He thanked Simu for coming to see him and in parting said, "If it is possible, without surrender of your honor, try to be on good terms with Kisharani and do nothing to give offence." "I hear you," replied Simu, "you know me, that is the way I am." His commitment to this was sorely tested on his first visit after the attempted denunciation. Kisharani said to him loudly and angrily, "I know that you put *dawa* in the honey that you bring, and with this *dawa* you take away my strength and with your magic you become an animal when you wish, just as that child is an animal in human form. Give me back my goat, bring no more honey, and never darken my door again."

Maziwa and Simu had anticipated and discussed the probability of this outburst. They had talked before Kisharani came home with the cattle. Discussing Kisharani's expected demand for the return of Bossy, Maziwa said, "I do what I can for Dogo when he is here, but the goat is like his mother. You cannot take Bossy away from him and give her back to Kisharani. The boy is too young to be separated. You have to refuse. What can Kisharani do?" "But it is his goat," said Simu. "Bossy is Dogo's mother, you cannot take her away from the child," replied Maziwa firmly. "You are a woman and mother yourself," said Simu, "so I accept that you know better than I and will do as you say. But I am worried that Dogo is too much of an animal as Kisharani says; too much goat and monkey, and more recently wild dog. I wish I could teach him more of the ways of people." "That is difficult because you live alone," replied Maziwa kindly. They left the matter there. When the time came Simu spoke his truth quietly and clearly to Kisharani, "You distress yourself with things in your imagination. As our people have told you neither I nor Maziwa use any *dawa* against you. My honey is pure from the bee. The matters of which you complain all are in the nature of things that come about because accidents happen and life is never certain. You made an arrangement with me that

I have honored in spirit and in deed. I intend to continue to honor it. You forget that these houses were mine. You live in them only because I gave my consent. This I did because Maziwa is my niece and I had no use for the houses when I went to Chepnall cave. You cannot ban me from the house in which I was born and came to me from my father." "It is my house now because I live here not you," responded Kisharani. "It is true that you live here, and for that reason I would not enter alone, but come I will, and if invited in, I will enter." "I should beat that Maziwa for inviting you in, and you too," retorted Kisharani. "That would not be wise," Simu responded in a tone of voice that left a chill in Kisharani, believing as he did in Simu's powers of magic. The resolution of the matter was that Simu kept bringing honey every month, Kisharani did not eat it, and Maziwa fed Simu and Dogo outside when they visited. The *ugali* was sweetened with the honey to Dogo's great delight.

Life continued for Simu and Dogo in its usual pattern for the next several months. Simu was quite unaware of Mdomo Kali's rather difficult visit to the Ndorobo *mganga*. It was difficult because Ndorobo and Elgon Masai do not mix comfortably. Also when the *mganga* demanded a heifer in payment for such a difficult and major assignment, Mdomo Kali realized she would have to tell Kisharani about the *mganga* so that he could bring the heifer. She very solemnly swore him to secrecy. For once he lived to his commitment. When Kisharani left to bring the heifer demanded by the *mganga*, Kisharani told his *manyatta* that he was taking it to Endebess to sell it. So only he and Mdomo Kali knew of the visits to the *mganga* and that the *mganga* had promised to remove Simu and Dogo from the mountain. True to his word, once he had the heifer the *mganga* began to contact the spirits of the mountain.

Dogo's problems started when the rains had come. The morning it began, it had rained in the night. All the animal footprints on the trails near Chepnall cave were filled with water. That morning had a wonderful fresh smell of wet earth and green shoots reaching for the sun. The air was so clear there was no haze even over the Cherengani hills forty miles away. Little cotton wool balls of infant cumulus clouds dotted a bright blue sky. It was likely that they would grow ten thousand feet tall with dark bases full of thunder and lightning, but that would come in the afternoon. The cave was its usual cool shadow with a splash of warming sunlight on the rocks outside. But Dogo was not cool. He said, "Baba my head hurts with a great pain, and I feel hot." Simu put his hand on his own forehead first so that it would know his temperature, then he put his hand on Dogo's forehead. As Dogo said, he felt hot. Simu went out of the cave and picked some of the nettles that grew by the path. These he boiled in his *sufuria* and poured the greenish water into his cup, straining out the leaves with a makeshift hand-carved wooden spoon. When it cooled, he gave the potion to Dogo. He drank it reluctantly and only because Simu said it would make him feet better. It didn't. A couple of hours later he felt even hotter. He went to the back of the cave where it was cooler and lay down on the dusty floor his hands on his temples as if to squeeze the pain out of his head. Nothing helped. After about an hour in the back of the cave, he felt less hot. In two hours he was shivering and came back to the fire at the front of the cave to keep warm. "More wood Baba," he said, "more wood." Simu obliged until the fire was too hot for him to sit on the rock he usually used as a stool. Dogo kept so close to the fire Simu was afraid he might be burned, but still he complained of the cold. He shivered and his teeth chattered. About four hours later the cycle was repeated, cold shivering giving way to hot dry burning temples. He was in the third cycle when darkness came to cave. Simu saw in the flickering firelight, hollow cheeks and a skin now dull gray not healthy black as usual. As each cycle came and went Dogo seemed weaker. But that might have been because he did not eat anything. Simu knew that this was the 'hot and cold' illness that killed many children and some grown ups too. His people had no cure for it. The illness had to just run its course. If you did not die you would be too weak to run for many weeks. If you were a child you were more likely to die.

That night Simu remembered Dogo's burnt buttock when he was just a baby, and the spirit of the cross that had saved him. He knew his *dawa* was powerless against this illness. So he went to the back of the cave where he kept the clothing and bangles he had taken from Dogo's dead mother, and where he also kept the small cross given to him by the young man in Endebess. He brought that cross out, dusted it off and laid it on his hand as he sat by the fire. He shut his eyes so as not to be distracted by visual images and then concentrated on clearing his mind as he might when speaking through his mind to animals. But now he focused all the energy of his mind on the cross until it filled his mental vision. He hoped that he might be able to see and speak to the spirit of the cross that had helped him before. But nothing came. Exhausted he laid the cross on Dogo's brow as if to ease his pain, but it soon fell off as Dogo moved and spoke strange words in a strange voice. He spoke of black things in the sky which Simu did not understand. He wondered if they were the evil spirits bringing the illness to Dogo. Then he put the cross on Dogo's chest and watched him sleep and wake and sleep again. Very early he made up his mind that he would have to go again to see the white woman, the *Memsahib*, whose *dawa* had healed Dogo's burnt buttock when he was a baby. He decided to hurry as children could die from this illness on the third day. Dogo was now too big to carry and too weak to walk. So Simu knew that he would have to leave Dogo with Bossy and Bending Twig. All that Bossy could do for Dogo was lick the salty sweat off his face when he was hot. For her sickness was something that came and, hopefully, went like the cold of the morning went when the sun came out. You suffered and waited for a better time. In truth it was not much different for Simu and Dogo. Knowledge of germs and medicine was relatively new even in Europe, although, there, quinine, the 'Jesuit bark,' had been used for centuries to cure fevers and the ague without any understanding of malaria as a disease.

The next morning as soon as it was light enough to see under the trees Simu set off for the white house with the red roof in the thorn trees on the hill below the Bluff. The *Memsahib* had seemed so unconcerned about payment five years before, and he was so anxious to go and return to Dogo as soon as possible, Simu did not waste time collecting any honey to take. He jogged along the paths easily as it was mostly down hill. He stopped only once to examine fresh elephant tracks on the path. They had been made in the night after the rain. Simu lifted his head and looked around in alarm and astonishment when he saw in one of the footprints the unmistakable image of the cross. He knows! He is here, he whispered to himself. Up until that moment Simu's heart had been very heavy. He had been expecting the worst. When he looked forward he had seen only the darkness of the death, because his hope was very small. Now, with this omen, hope once again surged up his throat in a wave and brought tears of joy to his eyes. He no longer jogged, he ran to save a life he loved so dearly. Sweating and panting he arrived at the *Memsahib's* house at about eight in the morning.

Simu was much more comfortable this time. He knew where to go. Behind the kitchen he met Wanga as he had before and asked to see the *Memsahib* about a sick child. He was told that the *Memsahib* was having breakfast. When she was finished she would be informed of his request. Disappointed and fidgeting with impatience, Simu waited. About half an hour later the *Memsahib* appeared, not on the front lawn this time but on the verandah between the main house and the kitchen quarters where the staff stayed. They went through the usual formalities in Kiswahili of "*Jambo*", "*Jambo,*" "*Habari yako?*" "*Nzuri*" "*Na habari yako?*" "*Nzuri, lakini..*"The last meaning "Good but..." Kiswahili has a 'count your blessings' approach. When asked, "*Habari yako?*" or "What is your news?" one would never say, "Awful." Convention required that one first say, "Good," and then qualify it with whatever was troubling you. So Simu said, "Good, but my child, the one who had a burnt buttock, is very sick." "I am pleased to hear that he lived," said the *Memsahib*. "I did not think he would. Why do you think he is sick now?" "First he is very hot, then he is very cold and he shivers, and now he is very weak," replied Simu. This was enough for the *Memsahib* to make an instant and correct diagnosis. "He has malaria," she said. Then looking around asked, "Where is he?" "He is in the cave where I live. I could not carry him because he is too big now, and he is too sick to walk so far to come here." "I will give you *dawa* that looks like seeds," said the *Memsahib*. "Give the child two when the sun is overhead, two at night and two when wakes in the morning. How long has the child been sick?" "This is the second day," replied Simu. "You did good to come quickly," said the *Memsahib*. Then turning to Wanga she said, "Please give him a cup of *chai* while I get the *dawa*. As before Wanga took Simu behind the kitchen and told him to wait there. There was no way he would invite this forest man into the kitchen quarters which were occupied by important people who worked for the *Wazungu*. As she went to get the *dawa*, the *Memsahib* met her husband on his way back from the 'long drop" toilet at the other end of the lawn with the flowers. She said, "Buster, that forest man who is not one of ours, the one who had a child with a burnt buttock a few years ago, is here again. The child has malaria." "Do you want me to take him to the native hospital in Kitale?" asked Buster. "No," she replied, "the child is not here, he is in a cave in the forest. The man says he is too big to carry and too sick to walk. I hope he will be all right with quinine. Thank goodness he did not wait until the last minute like they usually do. I know you have to go to work now. Please get some more quinine." "Right," said Buster and went out the back where Mahindi was waiting to drive him to Kitale. Mahindi recognized Simu standing behind the kitchen and was curious, as he had been the first time. After the usual exchanges of 'hello, what is you news,' he asked, "Did you ever find out who the woman was who died when you found the child?" "No," answered Simu a bit surprised as he had not thought about it in several years. "Well" said Mahindi, "about the time you found the child, the *Bwana* took a woman with a child to Kitale and back. She said her child's name was Sumatra. She also said she had to walk up the mountain to get home. Why don't you ask your people if there was any woman who had a child with such a name?" "Thank you for your information," said Simu, "I will ask." He said this as a polite formality and not because he had any interest in finding some unknown family to claim the child.

With the bottle of quinine pills clutched in his hand, Simu hurried back to Chepnall cave. He found Bossy grazing below the cave and Bending Twig eating podo berries on the big rock at the mouth of the cave. Dogo was lying where he had left him on the cave floor looking glassy eyed and hollow cheeked, his skin a rough dull gray. Simu sat beside him, put an arm under his shoulders and lifted him into a sitting position. Then he gave Dogo two pills to swallow with water from his bamboo cup. With some difficulty Dogo swallowed them, making the mistake of chewing on the first pill. "It tastes awful," he said in a small voice. "That is what will drive the illness out of you," replied Simu. Then he made some *chai* which he tried to share with Dogo, but without success. In fact Dogo did not eat anything until the afternoon of the next day. Meanwhile he slept and tossed, muttering in his restless sleep. Late in the next day be began to slowly recover to Simu's indescribable relief. At the end of a week he could walk out of the cave to relieve himself, an activity happily watched by Bending Twig. It was three weeks before Dogo was back to his normal self, and six weeks until Dogo faced his next life threatening crisis. As they say, troubles seldom come singly.

As you know a large family of rock hyraxes lived in the rocks in front of Chepnall cave. Dogo's friend and favorite was the one called Chok. Chok spent a lot of time with Dogo as he was recovering from the malaria. When Dogo became stronger and started leaving the cave they were together less, but always exchanged greetings as he came and went. One day Chok said, "Have you seen Scratchy Foot? He has been missing since yesterday." "No," said Dogo. The next day it was Black Ear who was missing, then three days later the twins were gone. The hyrax family was distinctly smaller. Chok and Dogo did not realize that the cause was an eight foot long python. They had never seen one before and did not recognize it for what it was. The python would lie on top of a big rock basking comfortably in the sun looking like a grey and black, lichen covered, fallen branch. He really enjoyed lying in the sun without moving for hours. You could not see him breathing and even his eyes did not blink. He was like a dead branch blown down by the wind. He would wait on a rock very comfortable in the sun, until dinner walked by under the rock, or a young and foolish hyrax played on the rock not seeing death in a dead branch. Lizards and mice he just swallowed. Rock hyraxes and bigger things he had to squeeze a bit until he broke them into limp rag dolls that would slide comfortably down his throat. He could eat things much wider than his body by unhooking his bottom jaw and opening his jaws so wide you could see how all his teeth were curved back down his throat. Once you were in those teeth, there was only one way to go, down.

Bossy had heard that something was eating the hyraxes, but she did not know what it was, because she had never seen a python and did not know what the word meant. She just told Dogo to stay away from the hyraxes. But Dogo liked them and was at an age, and of a temperament, that led him to ignore instructions when he thought he could get away with it. And so it was that one day Bossy and Dogo left the cave and turned right through the narrow gap between the cliff and a rock on the ledge at the cave mouth. This put them in the dark shade of the tall trees that stood like arrows going up the side of the mountain. The slope was as steep as the roof of a house. So Bossy and Dogo slithered and scrambled as they went down to the flatter open area where they came out into the sun below the rocks in front of the cave. Bossy browsed happily there while Dogo played in the stream, tried to catch butterflies, and then wandered up to the big rocks to call on his hyrax friends. Bending Twig was about a hundred yards away eating leaves. Changa was off hunting. Later Bossy was to console herself by saying that even if she had been next to Dogo, she could not have seen on top of the rocks which were taller than she was. She could not have smelled the python either, partly because they give off much less scent than warm blooded creatures, and partly because she was below him and hot air rises on a warm morning. The first thing Dogo knew was the thump of the python falling on him knocking him flat on the ground. Bossy heard the note of surprise and terror in his cry. From this she knew instantly it was a crisis. Unaware of the burst of adrenalin that made her impervious to pain; she drove through the underbrush like a miniature buffalo. In ten seconds she was there. Ten seconds may seem like nothing if you are having fun, but it is a long time if you are being hurt. In two seconds the python had locked his tail around Dogo's left ankle. Then as Dogo tried to get up he whipped three coils around him and began to tighten his muscles. You could see them rippling up from his tail around Dogo' body. First his stomach was squeezed up into his chest, then his ribs began to bend and he gasped for breath. Bossy burst onto this scene with no thought for herself, only a furious urge to do everything she could.

There was not much she could do. She had no hands and even a strong man could not unwind a python of that size when it began squeezing. She had teeth, but they were designed for grass and leaves. Fortunately she had those six inch horns she used to help teach Dogo to walk. She was as quick and accurate with those horns as you would be with your hands. With the loudest Baaaa a goat can make and a powerful swing of her head alongside Dogo's fallen body she drove one horn into the first of the three coils of the python around Dogo's middle. The python was most surprised. He had never been attacked before. With a hissss of pain and anger he swung his head around and locked his teeth in Bossy's shoulder. She cried out in pain, but strained to lift her head and drive the horn in further. No wilting violet she. As they struggled the python forgot to keep squeezing Dogo. His attention was all on the horn in his side which hurt terribly. Dogo's and Bossy's first cries were heard by Simu sitting in the cave. Like any parent he too knew these were no ordinary cries. If you have ever seen a kangaroo leaping over rocks then you know what Simu looked liked coming down with *panga* glinting in the sun. He leaped the last four feet down off the rock where the python had been lying and landed next to Bossy who was still standing, though with plenty of blood running down her shoulder. With his left hand he grabbed the serpent around its neck and with a long smooth stroke sliced off its head with his *panga*, putting a small cut on Bossy's side as he did so. In the heat of battle she did not feel it. As you know a snake never dies until sunset, but without its head, its body has no direction. It just twitches and writhes aimlessly. Simu was worried that its convulsions could hurt Dogo, so he left the head with its curved teeth still locked in Bossy's shoulder as he used all his strength to unwind the body from Dogo. A minute later, somewhat to his surprise, he saw that Dogo was breathing. He was as limp as a wet rag, but he was alive. Greatly relieved Simu turned his attention to Bossy as Bending Twig sat on a branch above them frantically biting the tip of her tail. Putting one hand on each jaw of the snake he pulled them open until the teeth came out of Bossy's shoulder. Then he threw the head on the ground. Bossy was in red hot, fighting mode. She stomped and kicked that head until she stood panting over a muddy red mess. Then she became aware of the pain in her shoulder and side. She was grateful as Simu led her back to the cave, carrying the limp Dogo in his arms. Back at the cave Simu was somewhat surprised to find that Dogo did not have any broken ribs or pelvis, at least he did not cry out if Simu gently squeezed him. So he turned his attention to Bossy and put on the wound a poultice of wet ashes from the fire. When calm returned to the group and every one rested, he began to wonder who had sent the snake. Simu was not particularly introspective or philosophical. He was a practical forest man. He knew that if unusual things happen there has to be a reason. That afternoon he was still pondering what this might be, when his thoughts were interrupted by Chok, the bravest of the hyraxes, coming in to the cave and leaving some podo berries as a gift on a rock by the fire. Simu knew they were not good for humans to eat, but he appreciated the gesture.

That evening Simu was even more convinced that the events of the day had not been a mere accident. As darkness settled over the forest outside the cave, Simu's thoughts became darker too. Never before had he seen a python so high up the mountain. It was too cold at night for them. No, he thought, this python was acting unnaturally. It had been sent. His attack on Dogo had not been just for food. He had plenty of that in the hyraxes. There was a deeper, more malignant reason. This snake had been an emissary of some dark force. The more he thought about it the more he became convinced it was a *mamlambo*. He knew that *mganga,* or witches, were said to acquire the *mamlambo* in the form of a small root no longer than your arm. This root had very strange qualities. It would seem to be alive, because it was. If you attempted to cut it, it would jump from your hand. After some time the root would grow into a snake which was hard and slimy with huge fangs and eyes like shiny stars. When grown it could be hidden in a hollow tree or amongst rocks. It liked to live near water. The *mamlambo* could be changed by the *mgana* in to human form. It could also fly like an owl. Witches sometimes used the *mamlambo* for personal sexual satisfaction like they did *tokolotsi*. But more than this, men and women practicing black arts, used it, in particular, to steal wealth from others and cause harm to them. Unlike *tokolotsi* which were used mostly for sexual purposes, the *mamlambo* was also commonly used to attack other people, prevent women from having children, and even kill others in ways that looked like an accident, such as snake bite and lightning strikes. The *mamlambo* was greedy possessive and dangerous. Many witches found that they became unable to control the *mamlambo* which might come to dominate and enslave them. The *mamlambo* often demanded sacrifices of chickens or goats in exchange for the wealth it brought the witch, or in payment for the evil done to others at the witch's request.

Simu began to think of who might bear him a grudge and send a *mamlambo* to hurt him or Dogo. Kisharani came naturally and immediately to mind. Simu decided to put him aside while he considered if there were any other less obvious candidates.

He thought of the people he traded with at Endebess, where he sold or bartered the salt rock he dug from Chepnall cave, and the wild honey he collected. There the local louts insulted and teased him, but this was just for their amusement, not because any one had a grudge against him. They thought it odd that he lived alone in the forest with a child, but it made no difference to them. At first when Dogo was still a baby Simu had taken the child with him. As Dogo grew bigger, he began to leave Dogo with Bossy and Bending Twig when he went on these trading trips. Dogo certainly had not made any enemies at Endebess. In fact for a couple of years no one there had even seen Dogo. They had probably forgotten about him. Besides Simu himself had no quarrels with anyone there. So Kisharani was the only person he could think of who might take the trouble to do something so serious and dangerous as to send a *mamlambo* to attack Dogo. "But," thought Simu, "Kisharani is too simple, he does not know anything about magic, he could not control a *mamlambo*. Only a witch doctor, a *mganga*, could do such a thing without great risk to himself." Then he thought of Kisharani's mother and it came to him. Only she with the tongue of poison was capable of such malevolent action. She was the one who had wanted to charge him and Maziwa with witchcraft, imputing to others what she herself would do. As this thought settled in his mind he became a little less anxious, although he had no idea what he would do about it. It had been a long day, he was tired and the fire was dying to a dull red glow, so he patted Changa on the head, and then went back to his rock *boma* where Dogo and Bossy were already sleeping. He pulled the thorn tree branch into the doorway and joined them.

In the morning Bossy's shoulder was very stiff and quite swollen from the snake bite. She moved slowly and painfully but was in good spirits. Dogo was his usual cheerful self and seemed none the worse for his near dearth experience. His was not of an hysterical temperament. He treated it an isolated incident. Something scary had happened, but it was done and gone and he was not hurting, so where is breakfast? Like Bossy, Bending Twig and Changa,

Dogo did not worry about the future. His mind was too young to visualize spirits, *mamlambo* and dangers waiting for him another day. Worrying about tomorrow was for an adult human mind like Simu's, and worry he did as he made his morning *chai*. In the cold light of dawn he was not as confident as he had been the night before that Kisharani's mother was the source of his problem. Was that old woman, screech though she was, capable of owning, controlling and sending a *mamlambo*. He had killed the snake, but could its owner collect it and revive it to come again. With this thought he went down below the rocks in front of Chepnall cave to see if the body were still there. His heart sank when he could not find it. Something had come and taken it in the night. Simu saw in his mind a large shape, a black cloud many times taller than a man, moving through the trees like smoke in the dark, a spirit come to gather and carry away one its own. He could deal with a human being like Kisharani's mother, but what if the sender of the snake were not her, were not human, how could he fight the forces that lived in darkness. The very idea made fear grip his stomach. He had to know what he was dealing with. Without much hope he decided to seek an answer by calling on the most powerful of the benevolent spirits that he knew, the spirit of the earth. This was the spirit that made the forest grow. He had been told it could make the mountain tremble, but this he had never seen. To bring his plea for information to the spirit's attention he went to the drum rock. This was a boulder about two feet across that lay on top of a rocky outcrop on the elephant platform, the lava flow that made a cliff across a valley near Chepnall cave where one could sit and look down on elephants below. The boulder was curved on the bottom. You could rock it and the rocking made a deep booming sound like a huge bass drum. That afternoon, when the bright sunlight gave him confidence, Simu went to the rock. He took Dogo afraid to leave him alone. Changa naturally came along.

The booming of the drum rock was enough to wake any spirit. He rocked the boulder for several minutes to get the attention of the earth spirit and then called our repeatedly, at intervals, "Spirit of the earth who sent the python, who sent the python, who sent the python?" But no one answered. So he rested and then repeated the process. He did not expect to hear a voice, but he did hope that the spirit would give an answer to his mind. He tried for a long time until the shadows lengthened. In the end he gave up tired and discouraged and started back to Chepnall cave. As he travelled, the sky became dark with a thunderstorm. He hurried on with Dogo even as lightning began to crack and rumble and a downpour made him and Dogo shiver. He started violently, and almost gave way to terror, when a thunder bolt hit a tree about a hundred yards away on the path ahead. There was a tremendous flash and overwhelming crash of noise that almost threw him to the ground as the tree trunk exploded. Dogo clutched Simu's leg in fear. Simu took it as an omen. He believed that he had angered the earth spirit by drumming on the rock and calling out to it, disturbing it when it did not want to be bothered. He was sorry he had done it. I should have known better than to venture into the world of the spirits, he said to himself. That evening as he huddled closer to his fire feeling the chill on his back, and looking into the flickering flames he tried to find an answer to the question, "Who sent the *mamlambo?*" Nothing came to his mind. All he heard were the usual night noises. In the end he concluded that this was a problem too big for him alone, too serious to be ignored. He would have to get help. He decided to ask Maziwa for her thoughts. She was always insightful and sensible. He looked forward to visiting with her again and felt good that Dogo would be delighted too. As Dogo was already asleep he decided to tell him in the morning.

As he made his *chai* the next day, Simu said to Dogo, "Today we are going to visit Maziwa. Dogo smiled happily at the news. He always enjoyed playing with her children. "Can Changa come?" he asked. "If you tell him to stay away from Kisharani," replied Simu. "Is that because Kisharani tries to do bad things to him?" asked Dogo. "Yes" was the answer. "Why is he bad to Changa?" asked Dogo. "Because he wants to control everything in his *manyatta* and Changa won't listen to him." "I don't like Kisharani either," said

Dogo. "You will be a guest in his *manyatta* and must be polite to him," replied Simu. "If I have to I will, Baba," said Dogo. "You have to," was the answer. So they set off on another clear fresh morning, the sun warming their backs as they crossed open glades in the forest. Dogo was full of delight and anticipation of fun. Simu was depressed and anxious. He kept an especially sharp eye out for snakes, and was prepared to be extra cautious in looking out for dangerous animals who might charge them, really only buffalo and elephant. He told Dogo "We must be extra careful today." "Why Baba?" asked Dogo. "Because I am worried that something in the forest or on the mountain wants to attack you. The snake may have been sent by some one to squeeze you." "But I am not hurt and I am not afraid," said Dogo bravely. "That is good, but it is more than I can say. I am afraid because I understand more than you." "Changa is with us," said Dogo, "he knows if there is anything bad nearby. He will growl and his hair stand up. Let me send him down the path first." "Good idea," replied Simu. So Dogo motioned Changa ahead saying, "Go see what is there." Changa was only too happy to do so, hoping he might catch a duiker or bushbuck unawares. But that was not be. They arrived at Kisharani's *manyatta* without incident except that the dogs slank away without barking when they saw Changa leading the little party. Changa made no attempt to associate with them. He did nuzzle Maziwa's hand when she came out to greet them, and in return was given a pat on the head. She said to Simu, "You know I think Changa is now almost better company to Dogo than Bossy. "You're right," said Simu, "man is a hunter like Changa, not a grass eater like Bossy. But, I have come to talk to you about more serious things." Is that why you came early and brought no honey?" asked Maziwa. "Yes. I am sorry I forgot about the honey, I was too worried." "Come tell me about it," replied Maziwa looking at him curiously, "it can't be that bad. You are both alive and well." "Only just," replied Simu with some exaggeration. Dogo had already left them to find and play with Maziwa's children.

Maziwa did, of course, already know of Dogo's bout of malaria. Simu had told her about it in all its details on a prior visit. She listened without interrupting as Simu now told her of the attack on Dogo by the python just in front of Chepnall cave. He ended by saying, "I think the python was a *mamlanbo* sent by Kisharani's mother. I can't think of any one else who bears me or Dogo a grudge, and it was he and his mother who accused both you and I of witchcraft." "You are right that many accuse others of things they themselves do, but why do you think this was not just a python who was hungry in the nature of things?" said Maziwa. "First Dogo gets malaria and nearly dies. Then as soon as he recovers he is attacked by a python, and this all happens after Kisharani and his mother are shamed by false witchcraft accusations against us," replied Simu. Maziwa looked at him thoughtfully and said, "People often die in the night which follows day, but because one follows the other that does not mean that the darkness killed them. Malaria and a python would not seem to be connected." "Only if both were sent by the same witch," said Simu. "Kisharani would have no idea how to keep and control a *mamlambo*," said Maziwa, "and I don't think his mother could either. She is too old and does not have the knowledge. Besides, I'm not sure the python was a *mamlambo*." "Pythons like warmth," said Simu. "They belong on the plains and especially in hot dry country. I have never before seen one in the forests of the mountain. Would you go where it was cold if you did not have to? No! This snake came for a reason. It was sent by some one, or something, but who or what?" "Have you done anything to offend the spirits of your ancestors?" asked Maziwa. "I have given it great thought and cannot see anything that I might have done to invite misfortunes," replied Simu. "Well," said Maziwa, carefully, "either it was just a matter of chance or you are right. If you are right we have to find out why the python came." "How do we do that?" asked Simu. "Let me think," she replied walking back into the hut while Simu stayed outside to avoid confrontation with Kisharani when he came home.

When Simu heard the cattle lowing as the light on the plains turned gold and the Koitobos peak on Elgon cast long shadows, he moved away to his usual tree and called Changa and Dogo so as to avoid their meeting Kisharani coming back behind the herd. There he lit a fire to ward off the chill of the darkness that would soon close in. He felt warmed by the fire and calmed for some nostalgic reason by the flickering flames. He knew Maziwa would know how to solve a puzzle that was beyond him. That would have annoyed an egotistical man like Kisharani, but not Simu who was an unassuming, practical man. He was happy to get help wherever it was available. He instinctively knew that women understand intangible things better than men. Woman's strength was in software, things of the mind, whereas the strength of men was in hardware, spears, bows and arrows and beehives. He was not disappointed. After she had fed Kisharani, Maziwa came out to bring dinner to Simu and Dogo. It was less tasty for Dogo than usual because there was no honey, but he had been trained by Simu to thank Maziwa, and so he did. She was delighted and gave him some more. "Don't spoil the child," said Simu smiling. "Oh I'm not," said Maziwa. "Didn't he and Changa bring you most of a duiker the other day?" "Well they were together, but I think Changa was really the one who caught it," said Simu. "The boy is getting bigger and stronger," said Maziwa, "you should make him a bow and arrow so that he can hunt. If he wounds the animal Changa can catch it. He doesn't catch duiker now unless he is very lucky." "Please do Baba," interjected Dogo. "Good idea," said Simu, "I will see if I can buy two or three arrow heads in Endebess." "Tomorrow when Kisharani goes out with the cattle I want to talk to you about Endebess," said Maziwa mysteriously. "Why? What is it about Endebess?" "Wait until we are alone in the morning," replied Maziwa. "If I must," said Simu. "Thank you and good night." He watched her go back to the hut and wondered how much abuse she took from Kisharani. He felt for her, but knew he could not intervene. She belonged to Kisharani. As he went off to the cattle shed with Dogo to sleep, he thought, at least she is a strong woman, and rightly or wrongly, he believes she has powers of magic, so he will be careful.

In the morning, when Kisharani had gone off with the cattle and Dogo went to play with Maziwa's children, Maziwa joined Simu by his rekindled fire. "I have been thinking about the python attacking Dogo," she said. "I really do not know if it was a *mamlambo* or not. I have never seen one, although I have heard of them of course. That the body disappeared so quickly is suspicious. If hyena had eaten it, one would expect to find a bit of skin or bone left behind, but you could not find anything. So I just don't know." "In my heart I know it was a *mamlambo,* said Simu, "but I do not know who sent it. Do you think Kisharani could have done it?" "He would have to find some one else to do it," said Maziwa, "and he would not ask any-one without his mother's approval. She herself does not have the necessary skills and knowledge. She would have had to find a *mganga*." "But who?" asked Simu. "Well Ol Kinyei would not have co-operated with her, he was embarrassed by her accusations against us. Any way he is not a practitioner of black arts. Lolmara Lenkoko is the only clan member who might have sufficient knowledge, but he is a healer, a medicine man, a practitioner of white rather than black magic. He would not do such a thing. Besides every one knows he does not get along well with Kisharani's mother." "Could Kisharani and his mother have gone outside the clan and found a *mganga?*" said Simu. "If they are involved, and I am not sure they are, then they would have had to go outside the clan," replied Maziwa.

"There is one thing that makes me wonder though," continued Maziwa. "What is that?" "Well a few months ago Kisharani took one of the cattle, a young heifer not yet with calf, to Endebess saying he was going to sell it to get money. He left very early in the morning and came back much earlier than I would have expected for so long a trip." "Did you ever see the money," said Simu. "No, and that surprises me too, there is no place in the hut he could put it where I would not find it just cleaning up. Perhaps he gave it to his mother. But then why would she need it, what is there to buy up here on the mountain that she would need so much money? We have no *dukas* here. Also Kisaharani did not come back with any-thing, no new clothes, or spear or blankets. I think that perhaps he did not go to Endebess and did not sell the animal," said Maziwa. "Are you saying that he might have given it to a *mganga* we do not know of?" asked Simu. "That is what I am saying," replied Maziwa. "How could I come to know if what you say is true?" asked Simu. "You could go to Endebess and ask if a man from the mountain came there to sell a heifer," replied Maziwa. "If they say no, that a man from the mountain did not come to sell a heifer then you would know that he had lied to me and done something he could not speak of openly; that he probably gave the animal to a *mganga* to put a curse on you and Dogo." "I suppose so," replied Simu. "If you reach that conclusion," continued Maziwa, "then you must realize that you will have to pay a *mganga* to protect you. You have to fight fire with fire. You cannot fight magic with a spear." "I real-ize that you are right," replied Simu gloomily, "but I do not know of a *mganga* I could go to." "Well Lolmara Lenkoko would not be the right man," said Maziwa. "He does not practice black magic and even if he tried to help you with white magic, Kisharani or his mother would know you were seeing him and take steps to counter his spells." "So what can I then do?" asked Simu. "My suggestion is that you go to a different *mganga* and ask him if he can find out if you have been cursed, or if he does not know, whether he can protect you any way." "Whom could I ask?" replied Simu. "Well, my suggestion is that you go and see Kakere Kaito," replied Maziwa. "He is a very powerful *mganga* who lives down the mountain on the Kassowai river at a place called *miti tatu* or three trees." "I have heard of it, but never been there," said Simu. "How much would he want to be paid?" "I have no idea," said Maziwa, "you would have to ask him and trust him to tell you if he has already been visited by Kisharani or his mother. But you realize he is a black magic *mganga*. You can never know if they speak truth." "I will do it because I have no choice. I believe that I and Dogo have been cursed. I only hope that I can protect Dogo until I can counter the magic sent against us." "If you go back to Chepnall cave today you could go to Endebess tomorrow," said Maziwa. "You are right I must hurry before something else comes to attack Dogo or even me." So Simu gathered up a reluctant Dogo, thanked Maziwa and set off for his cave. "Let me know what you find out," said Maziwa in parting. "I will, I will," answered Simu.

Kakere Kaito, the Mganga

8. The Mganga

Simu's trip back to Chepnall cave with Dogo and Changa was as uneventful as the journey out, much to his relief. They saw a serval cat, looking like a small leopard on the far side of a glade and several bushbuck that fled from Changa in good time, but nothing else. They met Bending Twig's troupe of colobus monkeys about half a mile up the mountain from Chepnall cave. Bending Twig announced herself with an enormous leap from a tree high up on one side of the path to a branch twenty feet lower on the other side. The branch bent and swayed, but did not break under the impact. Then she ran up the swaying branch as though it were a foot path, with a grace and agility that only the Colobus have. Simu and Dogo looked up in admiration, then waited for her to come down to the ground and jump on Dogo's back with a big smile. Dogo staggered a bit under her weight and laughed happily as she put a foot on each shoulder and held onto his head. He walked a little way with the monkey on his back, then bent forward and dumped her on the ground saying. "You're too heavy." "I'm happy to see you safe and sound," said Bending Twig, "no snakes, no sickness." "Race you to that tree," said Dogo sneaking a head start. He was fast for his age, but over a short distance no match for Bending Twig who jumped up the tree and chortled at him from above his head before rejoining her troupe. So the little group made its way happily down the mountain, across the open glade to the path down the side of the Bluff and then on to Chepnall cave, arriving in the mid afternoon.

Nothing seemed very serious on that warm afternoon with a few fluffy white cumulous clouds in a blue sky, the sighing of the wind in the cedar trees, green leaves, hibiscus flowers and butterflies by the stream. For a little while Simu allowed himself to relax and be at peace in the heart of nature as he looked across the plains to the blue of the Cherangani hills. It was a view that was part of his soul. It was the kind of place that fills the imagination of modern man living in the urban concrete jungle; a place of purity and peace in nature. But it was a place that the urban dweller can only visit. He has to love it and leave it, because he is not really willing to give up Western industrialized society which lives in cities, not forests and mountains. History judges societies by their great cities not their scenery. For Simu the natural beauty around him was as normal as water is to a fish, totally unremarkable. But there was a big downside to living in a state of nature. Being illiterate and having no knowledge of science, which explains so many causes and effects, Simu lived in fear of the unknown in a way that no well-to-do citizen of New York or London could appreciate.

The great fallacy of utopian dreamers is to think that one can live comfortably and happily in a state of nature without the benefits of industrialized society at hand. In addition to art and music, those benefits take forms essential to survival; a high powered rifle and modern medicine, for example. Those who do live in a state of nature, have no such benefits. They also live with fear. Fear of unmanageable disasters, plagues, droughts, floods, earthquakes, hostile attack, and the like, which are explained in supernatural terms for lack of any other explanation. In Kenya the supernatural was the world of spirits and magic. So spirits, good and bad, were as real to Simu as they were to the ancient Greeks. Twice Simu had faced life threatening disasters with Dogo and come to realize that he was helpless. Each time he had gone to the *mzungu* woman in the big white house with a red roof, hoping she could help in crises that tore at his heart, but were beyond his ability to solve. Twice the products of industrialized society, coming from far away, had saved Dogo. But now Simu believed that he faced a threat to Dogo that came from the world of the supernatural. Had he been asked he would have said that this was a realm the *wazungu* did not understand. Most of them did not take their superstitious beliefs seriously. He would have been correct at that time in history though the *wazungu* had believed in, and drowned witches in their day, saying that they were emissaries of the devil who was always at war with the spirit of the Christian cross. Like those *wazungu* of old, Simu did not think he could deal with witchcraft by calling on the spirit of the cross. His was an African problem to be dealt with in a way he could understand, a way that fit within his belief system. At that moment in Chepnall cave, Simu's belief in spirits and witchcraft made him feel most uncertain and very fearful. He knew little of them, but realized he could not fight the unknown. His anxiety made his stomach feel hollow. He did not know who was behind the threat to Dogo, nor in what form it would manifest itself. As he looked down the valley of Chepnall cave all he knew was that first he had to go to Endebess, then to the *mganga* called Kakere Kaito whim I shall call, Kakere. Deep down he was convinced that Kisharani had not taken the heiffer to Endebess. But he had to go and confirm this, and while he was there he would buy some arrow heads for Dogo. When his belief about Kisharani was confirmed, then he could justify in his mind going on to Kakere Kaito. Had he known how it would turn out he would have wept then. In the mean time the fear of the unknown lay heavy on his heart.

Simu did not tell Dogo of all his fears. That evening he simply said, "Tomorrow we will go to Endebess, and this time you will come with me." "Why can't I stay with Bossy and Changa?" asked Dogo who did not like Endebess. He was bored there. He had no friends there, no one to play with and nothing to do while Simu went about his business. "As I told you a few days ago I am worried that something wants to attack you. To be safe you must come with me." "Are you going to buy my arrow heads?" asked Dogo, "you said you would, you did." "I will try to get arrow heads and some cord for the bow too," said Simu. "Can Changa come?" said Dogo following up on his success with arrow heads. "No," said Simu firmly. "Definitely not. He would only get into a fight and some man might club or spear him." At this Dogo gave Changa a protective hug around the neck and received a wet face lick in return. This settled, Simu and Dogo went into the rock *boma* for the night pulling the thorn tree branch into the doorway behind them as usual. Changa stayed out as he always did. Like Bending Twig he liked to roam free. He had also left his mark on every tree and rock near Chepnall cave and instinctively protected his territory against all intruders. Simu slept easier knowing that Changa was on guard. Changa slept near the cave fire, but even though asleep part of his brain was awake, attuned to the night noises and smells. If anything strange were heard or smelt he would be instantly awake. In this he was like a human mother who wakes instantly to her child's cry in the night, but sleeps on through many other normal noises.

The next day Simu changed his plans, saying to Dogo, "I have changed my mind, today we will get honey and tomorrow we will go to Endebess." "Oh good," said Dogo who loved honey and eating bee grubs. They taste a bit like sour milk, but are quite nourishing. It does make sense to spit out the comb though. Simu's change of mind was quite sensible because honey fetched a much higher price per pound than salt rock. If he had it, carrying honey to Endebess was much easier. So Simu and Dogo spent the day collecting honey from several of Simu's honey barrels and did not set off for Endebess until the next morning. Changa started to follow them and was told immediately, "No, stay, you can't come." When this was repeated in a stern tone of voice, Changa felt rejected. His ears and tail drooped and he went unhappily back to the cave. When Simu and Dogo came back from Endebess he was not there. They did not see him again for weeks. He had gone to visit with his pack. If man did not want him he was comfortable with the wild; although his pack did not have much to do with him until the nasty smell of man left him.

Unaware of this, Simu and Dogo reached Endebess before the sun was overhead. The first order of business for Simu was to trade his salt rock and honey to the Indian *duka* owner every one called Patel. He was a small man with greasy palms, always on the lookout for ways to take advantage of the illiterate Africans with whom he dealt. He was amoral, rather than immoral. If you could persuade some one to pay more than the next person, or give you more of what he had to sell, that was a success, something to be proud off. In trade getting as much as you could was the only concept. Fairness was not an idea that was relevant in commercial matters. Taking advantage of a person's ignorance was good trading practice. But then he was a Dalit, an untouchable whose father had been brought to Kenya by the British at the turn of the century to build the railroad from Mombasa to Lake Victoria. What should one expect? Both the British and the African looked down on all Indians as dishonest traders. The exception were the Sikhs who were the only warrior class Indians they knew and respected. But in trade the Indians excelled. Patel was no exception. His was the only *duka* at Endebess. So he pointed out to Simu the usual deficiencies in what he had to sell. The salt rock was not salty enough and the honey had too many leaves in it and was of too dark a color. In the end Patel bought it for a third of what he would sell it for. He did not pay much in cash. For the most part he bartered sugar, *posho* and *chai* to the forest man. He was nonplussed by Simu's request for arrow heads. It was not something that he stocked. Without knowing how he would do it, he assured Simu that next month he would have arrow heads of the finest quality at incredibly cheap prices. Simu only half believed him and changed the subject asking, "In the last three moons have you bought a cow from a man off the mountain?" "Where would I put a cow in this shop?" answered Patel. "I do not deal in cows." It was a disappointing answer, but logical to Simu as he looked into the tiny dark shop about twelve feet square, packed with shelves with only one window, in one wall, where the counter was with bars above it. Customers stood outside and dealt through the bars.

So Simu went over to a group of several men sitting under a blue gum tree planted by the *wazungu* two decades earlier. He went through the usual formalities of "Hello, what is your news," and then asked, "In the last three moons did a man of my people from the mountain come here to sell a cow?" "What is it to you salt man? You do not sell cows," replied one recognizing him. "We have a man who is blaming his neighbor for stealing his money that he says came from selling a cow here. The neighbor agrees the cow is gone but says the owner ate it and did not sell it." The man you need to talk to is Kibet. If any cow is bought or sold here he knows." "Thank you. Where can I find Kibet?" "He lives in the hut by the river," said the man pointing north to a line of green trees that clearly showed there was a water course across the plain. So Simu walked up the road that led North to Kapenguria. As he approached the hut a couple of dogs leaped to their feet and rushed out barking. Simu ignored them. He was right. They stopped at a safe distance but kept barking. The noise brought a middle aged, tall man out of the hut. By his name Simu knew he was a Nandi, a cattle loving tribe like the Masai. So he felt more comfortable than would otherwise have been the case. Again he went through the formalities of greeting and then said, "They tell me you are the only man here who buys and sells cattle?" "That is true," was the answer, "do you want to buy a cow?" "No," said Simu, "I come from the mountain. We have problem with a man who says that he sold a cow here not more than three moons ago. Can you tell me if this is true?" "I cannot tell you if your man sold a cow, but I can tell you he certainly did not sell it here. You said just one cow?" "Yes." "Then I can assure you it was not sold here. Only once in the last three moons have I bought cattle and that was five head not one." Changing subject, Simu said, "Do you sell chickens?" "No, you have to go to that house there," Kibet said pointing to a nearby hut. "Thank you," said Simu, "may your cattle grow fat. Goodbye." "Goodbye," said Kibet. It was as Simu expected. Now he knew what he had to do. So first he went and used the rest of his honey money to buy two chickens at the nearby hut. He bought them alive because no one had any refrigeration and anything dead spoiled quickly. Their legs tied, he put them in his salt rock sack and set off for Chepnall cave with Dogo who complained that he thought he was going to get arrow heads that day and why were they coming back with chickens instead. "The chickens I need to give to another man. They have no arrow heads here. Your arrows will have to be wood, fire-hardened at the tip for now," Simu told him.

The evening was drawing in when Simu and Dogo arrived back at Chepnall cave. Bending Twig some how knew when they were coming and was there to greet them. Changa did not appear as expected. So Dogo immediately asked Bending Twig if she had seen Changa. His heart fell when with a sweep of her arm she indicated that he had gone North to where the triangular point of Mt Riwa sat like a blue diamond on the horizon. "Why?" asked Dogo. "We left him, so he left us," said Simu. "Perhaps it is just as well he is not here. Tomorrow we go to Miti Tatu and he could not come." "Will he come back?" asked Dogo. "I think so," said Simu. "When?" asked Dogo. "After one moon or two," said Simu, "he has left the mountain. If he were on the mountain he would sleep here. He has gone to walk far away on the plains." He then untied the chickens and put them in the back of the cave where they wandered about uncertainly, afraid to go out into the forest. Later in the evening he gave them the remnants of the *ugali* he made for the evening meal. Then, much to Bossy's disgust, he brought them into the rock *boma* when he went to bed for fear that some creature of the night would eat them.

In the morning Simu said to Dogo, "I cannot leave you alone so you will have to come with me to Miti Tatu." "Why are we going there Baba?" asked Dogo. "To see the Mganga, a man called Kakere Kaito." "Why?" "I want to ask him who it is that wants to attack you and why," said Simu. "How would he know?" asked the ever logical Dogo. "He is the Mganga who can see things that we cannot see, in the past, now, and in the future," replied Simu. "We must leave early, it is a long way and I am not sure where the man lives." Fearful of a possible attack on Dogo on the way, and because he was going into unfamiliar territory, Simu took his spear and his *panga*. The chickens he put in the salt rock bag hung over one shoulder. He knew Kakere would not work for free. Dogo carried nothing. So they set out around the base of the Bluff and then across the Rongai river towards the Kassowai, uncertainty and anxiety filling Simu's mind. When they came up out of the Rongai valley to the top of a ridge, Simu was much encouraged when he looked at the near horizon two or three miles away and saw three trees much taller than the rest, outlined against the blue sky. That is Miti Tatu, he said to himself. The Kassowai river will be at the bottom of the slope below the trees. The *Mganga* will live near enough to the river for his woman, or women, to be able to carry water up to his *boma*. Feeling much more confident that he would get where he wanted to go, Simu pushed on. Dogo was now tiring a bit and no longer running ahead. He fell in behind Simu who was constantly pondering the way ahead. Of course there was no road. Simu followed animal tracks through the forest going in the general direction where he had seen the three trees. They disappeared from view as soon as he went back into the forest. Mostly the tracks were old elephant paths which followed the contour of the hills and valleys because elephants hate going up or down steep inclines. Cutting through the thick forest was not a practical option. The elephant paths went back up into the mountain when going into a valley and then down the mountain coming out the other side. The zigzag nature of the trails made holding a direction uncertain. But two hours later Simu came out into a rocky glade where he could see the three trees on the near ridge. Seeing this he knew the Kassowai was at the bottom the valley.

Now he looked for trails going down the mountain to where the forest ended giving way to more open country with thorn trees and bush, with grassland in between where cattle and sheep could graze. Simu heard the cow bells about half an hour later. Dogo said he could smell them. Simu knew he could. When they saw the first of the cattle in the bush he said to Dogo, "Go and find whoever is watching them and then come and get me. I will wait under this tree. Do not go so far I cannot hear you call if you get lost." "I won't Baba," Dogo replied. He was thrilled to be given this responsibility. He ran off through the bush going through it as easily as any animal. He did a half circle around the herd and found the herdsman in ten minutes as Simu expected. The herds-man was one of Kakere's teenage sons. He did not see Dogo who was very cautious in strange situations. The cattle did not give him away. They had no fear of him and just kept munching and walk-ing and munching complacently. To Dogo the sound of their teeth was familiar and comforting. He found his way back to Simu as unerringly as he had come out. "I have found the watchman Baba. He is a young man." "Good," said Simu picking up his spear *panga* and chickens to follow Dogo. When they could see the young man watching the cattle Simu coughed to get his attention. In Kenya coughing is the accepted, polite, and non threatening, way of let-ting some know you are there when he does not realize it. The young man turned and saw them instantly, surprise registering on his face. He stood quite still, tense with caution, as Simu walked towards him with Dogo trailing behind. He too had a spear as one would expect in the bush where hyenas and leopards hunted. He was embarrassed to be caught unawares. The cough had told him that Simu's intentions were not threatening. Also Simu was alone except for the child. Had there been a group of men they might have been cattle raiders and he might well have been speared. This not being the case, he waited, but on guard, until Simu stopped a respectable distance away and went through the usual greetings.

This done he stated his business saying, "I wish to speak with Kakere Kaito. Do you know where his house is?" "That is my father," said the young man. Without another word he turned and called out, "Turana," "Oi," was the answer from about seventy yards away through the bush. "Come." In a few moments Turana appeared and stopped in surprise at seeing Simu and Dogo. "They have come to speak to our father, please take them there," said the first. Turana looked doubtful. The first said, "It's alright, it's just a man and a child." Turana nodded and beckoned to Simu. They were there in another half hour. The dogs rushed out barking when they were some distance away. Dogo dropped onto all fours and held his ground, stiff armed and quite still. Something about him brought them all to a stop looking at him suspiciously and uncertainly. Dogo then moved forward moving his head and making some wheezing, sniffing sounds as he had heard Changa do. The *manyatta* dogs seemed at a loss. When Dogo stood up and walked past them, they watched him silently, not barking. Simu watched too, surprised and pleased. When they reached the edge of the *Mganga's boma* Simu told Dogo, "While I talk to Mr Kaito, ask Turana if they have recently received a new heifer from a stranger. "Yes Baba," answered Dogo.

As they arrived, Simu had noticed four huts and immediately knew he was going to see an important man. Four huts meant three wives, that signified wealth. Kakere had his own hut, and each wife had her own hut too. This gave each woman her own territory. The arrangement had the advantage that it reduced jealousies because visits by the Kakere to any one wife were private. Turana announced the arrival of Simu and Dogo to one of the wives who was pounding maize in a hollowed out tree stump. She went into the largest hut and in turn announced the visitors to Kakere. He made no appearance for fifteen minutes as befitted a man of his importance. It also gave him time to dress up for his visitor. When he came out, Simu was not disappointed. Kakere was a big man. He was fat as well as tall. Of this he was proud and envied by others who saw in his fatness freedom from the specter of periodic hunger that haunted all of them. His weight was a visible symbol of his success. When his friends greeted him saying that he was very plump, he smiled and thanked them for the compliment. He was also envied for the three wives he could afford. This big man looked the part. In his left hand was a polished staff taller than himself made from the guriot tree. Around his head was a band full of eagle wing feathers. Beneath the head band, short, slightly graying hair showed, framing an angular face with high cheek bones and grey bearded chin. Around his neck was a reddish brown ruffle. Over the traditional blanket, worn toga style was a leopard skin cloak. In his right hand was a fly whisk made from the long black hair of a buffalo tail, bound on to a six inch shaft with silver wire. This too was a symbol of his authority. His eyes, muddy brown like a river in flood, never left Simu's face. They seemed to see in to him and through him as though he had no secrets.

This impression was reinforced when Kakere said, "Greetings man of the forest and father of one. What is your news?" "Greetings," replied Simu. I have come to ask for your help." "Put the chickens in that basket and come," replied Kakere as though it was the most natural thing in the world. He pointed to a basket and motioned Simu over to the shade of a thorn tree. "I have come to see you on a personal matter," said Simu. "My clan lives on the mountain above the trees." "And your problem is with one of your clan," interjected Kakere. Simu was impressed at the man's correct perception and continued, "Yes and I must first know if some one from my clan has been to see you in the last three moons?" "Many people consult me," said Kakere but none have come from above the tree line for a long time. You must have traveled fast to get here at this time." Simu explained that he had come from Chepnall cave. Then for the next half hour Simu told his story as Kakere asked a few questions. Simu was amazed that this man, he had never met before, seemed to anticipate his basic question, "Who sent the snake?" "Truly I have no secrets from him," thought Simu. "To answer your question I must go to the other side, to the land of darkness, in Makingene cave," said Kakere. "That is difficult and dangerous. I have to leave my body behind while I travel in the world of the spirits. If I cannot come back my body will not move again. Two chickens are not enough. Bring me two sheep and then I can do it." Had he thought he could get more from Simu, he would have asked for it. He added, "When you come bring also the boy." "Two sheep is more money than I have," said Simu, "I am poor." "Two sheep is very cheap for what you ask. It must be so, and leave the chickens too," answered Kakere without a trace of sympathy, and with a tone of dismissal. "I do not know if I can do it, but I will try," said Simu. So he left Kakere very disappointed that he was no wiser, and went to look for Dogo. He was in a hurry to get started to get back to Chepnall cave before dark. A minute or two later he found Dogo playing with some younger children behind a hut. Turana had disappeared. "Come," he said, "we must hurry."

Dogo heard the urgency in Simu's voice and came without complaint. When they were out of earshot of Kakere's *boma* Simu asked Dogo, "Did you ask the young man if any one had brought a heifer to Mr Kaito recently?" "Yes Baba," answered Dogo. "And what did he say?" "He said no one had brought a heifer to them in a long time." "That is good," said Simu. "Why?" asked Dogo. "Because it means I can trust this man as a *mganga*," said Simu without explanation. Then he pushed ahead as fast as he could walk, Dogo almost trotting to keep up. The path seemed shorter now that he was on the way home and knew where he was going. But still he worried. If he did not get to familiar territory near the Bluff before dark he would have to stop for the night for fear of getting lost. That meant they would be even hungrier than they already were not having eaten since morning. He would have to light a fire. That would be difficult without dry fire sticks made from the *dombier* plant. If he could not find a bone dry straight stick he might fail. Quite apart from the cold of the night there was the fear of wild animals that a fire would keep away. A fire would be the only light he had. A night in the forest without fire was not something he wanted to contemplate. Dogo sensed his concern and did not complain until much later about the hurried pace he kept up. As it was they had a scare when they bumped into a herd of buffalo that went crashing away with a great noise, quite different from elephant who would have drifted away as silently as ghosts. They jumped behind a tree while Simu scolded himself for not paying enough attention to what was going on around him. He knew they were lucky that they had not got too close to a buffalo cow with young calf. Had they done so it would have meant an almost certain charge by the cow in defense of her calf. Realistically that would have left one or both of them dead. Relieved he hurried on. As it was, darkness came as they approached the South side of the Bluff. Here Simu knew all the trails well. There was a quarter moon that night and no clouds. He could see enough not to trip over large rocks. Direction was not a problem as the sharp outline of the cliff that was the Bluff stood out against the sky on their left. They had one more scare from stampeding animals when they were quite close to Chepnall cave. Fortunately, this time it was a small group of waterbuck, elk sized animals with beautiful lyre shaped horns and white patches on the rump which identified them as they crashed away through the buffalo grass. In the dark the waterbuck were even scarier than the buffalo had been. For a few minutes this kept Dogo from thinking how tired and hungry he was. But as they went on he really struggled to keep up with Simu. "Don't go so fast," he complained, "my feet hurt." "I'm sure Bossy will be waiting for us," said Simu, hoping to divert Dogo's attention. It was not long before this prediction turned out to be true. The cave was dark, but familiar and reassuring when they arrived. Exhausted, Dogo gave a goat bleat that was immediately and enthusiastically answered by Bossy from inside the rock *boma*. Dogo's call to Changa was not answered to his considerable disappointment. So he focused his attention and hug on Bossy. Then it took some minutes for Simu to get the cave fire started up again from the embers hidden in the grey ashes of the morning's fire. He quickly made some *chai* and set the *ugali* cooking. Sitting by the warmth of the fire and with something hot to drink, Dogo felt much better.

Simu did not feel much better. Certainly he was glad to have reached the cave without incident, but this relief was overwhelmed by his worries about how to pay the *mganga*. How could he possibly earn enough money to buy two sheep? It would take him months selling salt rock from Chepnall cave. Meanwhile Dogo was at great risk. As he thought over the events of the day and the journey back, an inspiration came to him, he would kill a buffalo and sell the meat and hide. That should make enough money to buy five sheep. He would not normally attempt such a thing as he had no need for so much meat. Besides, even if he were part of a hunting party, spearing a buffalo was very dangerous and difficult. In thick undergrowth which hampered movement, a man would often be killed by an enraged buffalo. He could not leave Dogo an orphan. So he decided to use the falling spear technique as this would not put him in danger even if it might take longer. Also he could do it alone, and this he preferred.

The very next morning Simu said to Dogo, "Come, you are going to have fun today." "What are we going to do Baba?" said Dogo. "We are going to play in the mud," said Simu. A big smile lit Dogo's face. "You're going to make something aren't you?" replied Dogo. "Well yes," admitted Simu. "First I have to change my spear to make it heavy." As was traditional, Simu's spear had a long blade on one end, a wooden shaft in the middle and a long iron spike at the other end. "Why are you making the spear heavy?" asked Dogo. "Because I need to make a trap by hanging the spear from a tree," replied Simu. "You will see." He led the way down from the cave to the pool where Changa had first met his pack as a young dog. This was where many animals drank. Simu brought the spear. Now, with Dogo's enthusiastic assistance, he began packing the shaft of the spear with mud held in place by creepers wrapped in and around the mud. This he did until the shaft of the spear was a barrel as thick as his thigh, weighing about as much as he did. He could only just carry it. Eighteen inches of blade stuck out of the mud packed shaft. On the other end was a looped piece of cord from which he would hang the spear over a trail, bringing the rope down and around a tree on one side, and then across the trail to a tree on the other. The rope across the trail would be set high enough that only a taller animal such as a buffalo or elephant would run into it. When the buffalo's head pushed on the rope it would be released and the spear, twenty feet above, would plunge down. With luck the spear would cut the buffalo's spinal cord or a jugular vein in his neck. It took Simu some time to find a good spot, on a trail down to the water hole, with trees in the right position. With enormous effort he hauled the mud laden spear up over the branch and set the trap. Feeling pleased with his efforts he took Dogo the fairly short distance back to Chepnall cave. Dogo was impressed. "That could kill and elephant Baba." "Yes, may be it will, but a buffalo would be enough."

With high hopes Simu went back the next morning to find the spear stuck in the ground. The night had been stormy and the movement of the trees had loosened the rope. He sighed and spent the next hour resetting the trap. It was the morning of the third day when he felt a surge of relief and excitement as he came around a bend in the trail and saw a large animal dead on the ground. It was not an elephant or a buffalo, but a waterbuck whose big lyre shaped horns had caught the rope. The hit was perfect, the spinal cord severed just behind the horns. Simu had no regret at having killed such a handsome and harmless animal. His own survival and that of Dogo too, were of dominant importance in his mind. As he looked at the waterbuck's glazed eyes his only regret was that it was much smaller than a buffalo. Even so the hide and meat were enough to load down eight or ten men. Dogo was very excited. Never before had he seen Simu hunt and kill so large an animal. "We can eat for a month Baba," he said. "This meat is not for us," said Simu, "I have to sell it." "Why?" "Because I need the money to buy sheep." "Why?" repeated Dogo with childish persistence. "Because the *mganga* will not find out who is trying to attack you unless I give him sheep," replied Simu. "Oh" said Dogo, "can I eat some it?" "Of course, you can eat until you can eat no more." "I wish Changa were here, he would love it too," said Dogo. Simu smiled and gave Dogo a small wood handled knife so that he could help skin the waterbuck. Dogo felt terribly important and grown up. He was doing man's work.

Simu worked harder that day than he had in years, carving the animal up, and carrying it back to Chepnall cave in fifty pound loads. He made a forest man's back-pack out of inch thick creeper tied in a circle two feet across. More straps of dombier bark were tied across this frame like the stringing on a tennis racket. Then onto this base he tied heavy chunks of meat. Two more heavy bark straps around his shoulders acted as back pack straps. Each round trip took nearly an hour. By the third trip his knees were aching and his thigh muscles straining as he struggled up towards the cave. There the stream over the cliff was making a waterfall at this time of year, it being the wet season. Just below where the water hit the rocks Simu made a shallow pool with a dam wall made with stones and gravel. The water was very cold and about as deep as his knee. Simu put the hide and meat into it with stones on top to hold it down. Simu knew that the meat would keep there in the cold for several days. He hoped hyena would not find it. Underwater it will not give off any smell, he said to himself. He was right, but the site of the kill on the trail did attract jackals and other scavengers who quickly cleaned up all but the head, horns and some vertebrae. It was late evening before Simu finished, bone tired and bloody up to his elbows. As he worked he decided that he would boil and then dry out much of the meat, so that it would keep. Some he would cut into thin strips and dry in the sun to make *biltong* the equivalent of beef jerky, or waterbuck jerky in this case. That evening he carried thirty pounds of meat up the cave from his storage pool. Several pounds he put on green sticks to barbecue over the cave fire. He had been eating pieces raw all day, to keep himself going, but preferred it cooked. As soon as the barbecue was done he shared it with Dogo. Then he put the rest of the meat he had brought up into a *karai*. This was a heavy metal bowl looking like a giant saucer nearly two feet wide and about six inches deep. Normally it was used to carry earth on one's head. Simu used it to carry his salt rock. When washed out, the *karai* made a perfect vessel for boiling large chunks of meat. Simu boiled three loads that night. Dogo's job was to keep the fire stoked. This he did with great pleasure, feeling good with a full stomach, loving the warmth and basking in the feeling of security and contentment that the fire gave him.

In the morning Simu was up at dawn. He always woke as it began to get light, not so much because the light penetrated the *boma* but because his mind, even though asleep, was attuned to the morning bird song. Immediately he hurried down to his storage pool and was immensely pleased to find that no predator had raided it. Right away he brought up another load of meat to be boiled, and then another to cut into thin strips that he laid on the rocks to dry in the morning sun. Dogo happily helped cut the strips. "What are you going to do with all this meat Baba?" he asked. "Take it to Endebess and sell it," was the prompt answer. "I am going to take a load very soon." "Are you taking me again Baba?" said Dogo. "I want to very much but I am not going to," said Simu. "I will have to walk very fast to get there and back before dark and I want you to guard the meat against animals and birds that might eat it. Stay very close to the cave and be on the look out all the time. I do wish Changa were here, but he isn't. I will leave you my spear." He gave Dogo the deformed spear with the hook on one end. It was much bigger than Dogo, but not very heavy, so he could hold it parallel to the ground quite easily. "Nothing will steal the meat Baba," said Dogo fiercely making little stabbing motions with the spear. "When you have that spear nothing will dare to," said Simu. He did want Dogo to guard the meat, but said nothing of his deeper anxiety that Dogo himself might need guarding. He knew he had to take the risk of leaving him at the cave. Bossy was a small comfort, but Changa would have been much better. So Simu packed his salt rock bag with fresh meat wrapped in dock leaves and set off about noon for Endebess, walking as fast as he could. Two hours later he arrived and went not to Patel at the *duka* but to Kibet who was surprised to see him, but pleased that Simu came with meat, not quite as fresh now after two hours in a bag in the sun. Simu explained to Kibet that he wanted to trade the meat for sheep and though what he carried was not enough he had killed a waterbuck and would bring more the next day. Kibet believed him. The chunks of meat he carried obviously came from a large animal. The arrangement was that when the meat brought was as big as a sheep, he could take the sheep. It was simple logical barter. Simu correctly thought he had made a better arrangement with Kibet than he could have with Patel at the *duka*.

In five days Simu had bartered his meat for two sheep, a month's supply of *posho* for his *ugali*, some salt, sugar and tea. He was pleased, in fact very pleased. He put the two sheep on tethers and led them back to Chepnall cave. There they were poorly received by Bossy. In fact she totally dominated them. This was as it should be. As she said "This is my cave, and I am not letting you two sheep mess it up. I don't like your smell, so you sleep over there, and if you relieve yourselves in here you'll be sleeping outside and take your chances. Am I clear." "Baa" said the sheep submissively. As it was, the sheep were there only one night. The very next day Simu said to Dogo, "Come we are taking the sheep to the *mganga* today." "Are we going to have to hurry back like last time?" asked Dogo. "I don't think so," said Simu. "Oh good," answered Dogo. So they set out for Kakere Kaito, sheep in tow on two leads. One Simu held himself, the other he gave to Dogo which was hardly necessary as the sheep seemed obedient to Dogo. Now that he knew the way and what to expect, Simu found this second trip much less stressful. In fact he was almost cheerful thinking; at last I'm going to find out why Dogo is being attacked. The weather cooperated. The sky was half blue, half covered with thin layers and furrows of clouds that looked a ploughed field. It was not going to rain on them. Under the Bluff the buffalo grass had many green patches which attracted the sheep. Dogo had to pull hard on the tether to get his sheep to keep walking. The animal weighed as much as he did. Bossy they left at the cave, Bending Twig came with them as far as the podo trees under the Bluff and then left them saying, "I'm not spending the whole day traveling with you over the horizon." After they crossed the Rongai river they came to the broad elephant trail that leads up the mountain to Kitum cave where the elephants go in and use their tusks to dig their own salt rock. Simu saw fresh elephant spoor here. He was relieved that the elephants were headed towards the cave not across the mountain to the Kassowai where he and Dogo were headed. In one footprint he saw the sign of the cross. He stopped dead and trembled as if a ghost had walked over his grave. "What is it Baba?" asked Dogo, not seeing hearing or smelling anything threatening. "Look," said Simu, "that is the mark of the spirit of the *wazungu* which is in this elephant. That spirit saved you when you burned your buttock, and it led us to Changa when we found him. Remember? Changa was lying in his footprint." "Is the spirit bad?" said Dogo. "No, I don't think so," said Simu, "but one must be very careful of a spirit that one does not understand, especially when it travels in something as big as an elephant. I think this is a *wazungu* spirit. It lives in the little cross I have in the cave." "Is that those two sticks tied across each other that you keep in the back of the cave?" said Dogo. "Yes," answered Simu, continuing, "I don't understand how it can also be in an elephant at the same time. That elephant could easily kill us if it wanted to. If it is a spirit elephant it might not even be afraid of fire." "If the spirit is good, then why would the elephant want to kill us?" asked Dogo very logically. "If the spirit controls the elephant I do not think it would, but what if the elephant controls the spirit? Some *mganga* might then control the elephant and send it to attack us." The idea of being stalked in the forest by a phantom malign elephant sent a shiver down Simu's back. So he turned away from the path to Kitum cave and hurried on towards the Kassowai.

This time Kakere was alerted to Simu's approach by one of his several teenage sons. A big satisfied smile lit up his face when he saw the sheep as he came out of his hut. "*Jambo sana,*" "A very good day to you," he said to Simu. "Take the sheep," he said to one of his sons, "and let your Mother know she will have a guest tonight."

The boy's Mother was the Kakere's second wife. She enjoyed the variety that came into her life by taking care of clients who had to spend the night in her hut because they lived too far away. Kakere reflected that he was a good host conforming to custom. He was also happy to get detailed personal information revealed to his wife in pillow talk. This he used sincerely to give better advice, and, on some occasions, to protect himself from the machinations of others. He was particularly concerned to better understand Simu's case, as his situation, and his relationship to Dogo were quite unusual. He also shared Simu's belief that spirit forces were involved in the attacks on Dogo. It was natural to think that some evil doer was stirring the spirits to action.

And so it was, when Simu was settled and had eaten and Dogo was with the younger children in another hut, Kakere talked to Simu of the day that was to come. "As I have told you," he said, "I have to go to the darkness, to the other world where the spirits are. The nearest door to the darkness is in Makingene cave where the elephant tusk digs for salt in blackness, and the leopard in the dark eats the bush buck he has caught." "I thought the elephants ate salt rock in Kitum cave," interrupted Simu. "There too," said Kakere. "We will go to Makingene and I will travel there to the other world. You must guard my body when I leave to travel on the other side." "I do not understand your talk of traveling," said Simu. "My spirit travels, not my body," replied Kakere. "For now, keep in mind that I live in this world only by means of my body. Were my body to be destroyed when I were in the other world, then I would be locked for ever in the spirit world. So you must guard my body until my spirit returns to it. Keep the fire lit, and burning well. Creatures of the dark and evil spirits fear the fire. They must be kept back in the darkness away from my body and from you too, lest they swallow you and take my body. You cannot come with me to the world on the other side. In that world are eyes that see through blackness, feet that run like the wind, claws that catch you, and teeth that will tear from you the stone of fear you now feel in your stomach. I can hide from them or shield myself with my magic if I am prepared and watch carefully, but I cannot protect you, so you must stay in this world and guard my body. We will leave early in the morning; it will be a long day. Go now and prepare your mind to resist fear, so you do nothing foolish. It is too dangerous for the child. He must stay here." So Simu left and went to the hut of the second wife feeling small and ignorant, scared and helpless, in the face of the fearsome unknown. Wife number two had seen this before. She had sent Dogo to wife number three. Now she steadily set about giving Simu comfort and courage. By morning she knew all about the disease of the spots that had killed his family, about Bending Twig, hyena and the podo tree, Maziwa and Kisharani, the malaria attack, Bossy and the python, the killing of the waterbuck and his love for Dogo strong enough to make him go to the edge of his fear, the threshold of the spirit world. In the morning, before the dark had gone from under the trees, she left Simu sleeping and went to Kakere who listened carefully and thoughtfully. Wife number three also reported to Kakere her impressions of Dogo. "He makes noises like a sheep or a goat and like a colobus monkey too," she said. "We have no colobus monkeys here, but we have goats and he seems to be able to talk to them. One even let him take milk from her. When I gave him a piece of sugar cane to chew on he thanked me by licking my face as though he were an animal. In the evening he searched for bugs in my hair like a monkey might. He hears things I cannot hear, and smells things I cannot smell." "He is half animal," said Kakere, "I think that is the problem, but we shall see."

After Kakere and Simu had eaten, he said goodbye to Dogo telling him he would be back before dark. Dogo was not alarmed by this as Simu had always come home when he said he would. Besides Dogo was rather enjoying the attention of wife number three. He had met a woman only sporadically when Simu took him to visit with his Aunt Maziwa. Dogo liked these occasional visits. He had no memory whatsoever of his mother and no deeper understanding of the maternal function than the very simple if intense relationship with Bossy. However, something deep within him felt good when Maziwa picked him up and hugged him. But when Maziwa reprimanded him he felt hurt and uncertain. He realized that, unlike the situation with Bossy, he could not always anticipate if she would disapprove of what he did. But wife number three had not reprimanded him, so these thoughts were not in his mind as he happily said good-bye to Simu and watched him and Kakere set off that morning. Simu was as anxious as Dogo was relaxed.

It was the third hour of the day when Simu and Kakere saw the huge arch of the mouth of Makingene cave rising sixty or eighty feet out of the forest. In a few minutes they were standing under the soaring arch five houses wide. It made a giant semi circle coming down to a flat cave floor. This stretched back until it disappeared in gloom a hundred yards in. The floor was dry and dusty strewn with occasional chunks of rock as big as a room. There was a stale musty smell that grew stronger as one went in and the bat dung became deeper. Here and there were dried out little footballs of elephant dung. As none were fresh Simu concluded correctly that no elephants were in the back of the cave digging for salt. "We must gather much wood for the fire," said Kakere, his voice echoing as though in a cathedral. But he spoke in hushed tones as a sense of awe and uneasiness settled over them. It was a fitting setting for a gateway to another world. As Simu looked into the blackness, he shivered involuntarily. "We must start," said Kakere jarring Simu into action.

At Kakere's instruction they carried armfuls of sticks, and dragged heavier logs back to where the light faded and the cave floor began to rise up over large flat boulders which had fallen from the cave roof over the centuries. When they had enough to keep a fire burning for a whole day, Kakere tied sticks together in a bundle about six inches thick as one would to smoke out a wild bees nest. Then he took two fire sticks out of a quiver he carried and some very dry grass. In ten minutes he had smoke curling up from a little heap of sawdust about the size of the end of a pencil. Around this he very carefully arranged tiny bits of the dry grass on which he blew ever so lightly until it burst into a tiny flame. From this it was just a question of gently feeding the flame, and then lighting the bundle of sticks. With this as a torch Kakere led the way up and into the darkness. The mouth of the cave became a tiny dot of unblinking light at the end of a tunnel behind them and then disappeared behind the rock fallen from the roof. Further on Kakere stopped and said, "This is where I will go through the gate to the other side. Make the fire here." Simu did as he was told and spent the next half hour bringing the wood in. As the flames grew he saw they were next to one wall of the cave scarred with two foot long gashes from elephant tusks digging for salt rock. Behind him and on either side was blackness with the firelight moving over the outlines of rocks about fifteen feet away. Twenty feet above there was a huge fluttering of wings and squeaking as the smoke from the fire disturbed thousands of bats hanging like giant polyps from the ceiling. Their eyes glinted like red stars in a black sky. Simu wondered if they were real spirits or only messengers. He knew Kakere was right, only the light of the fire was keeping back creatures and things in the dark he could not fight, because they flickered and moved like shadows. Your *panga* could go right through them, like it would the smoke of the fire, and they would still be there. Despite the fire, Simu shivered and cold sweat dripped from his armpits down his ribs.

Now Kakere cleared all stones from the cave floor in a circle about ten feet wide around the fire. Then with green sticks, he had cut, he made an arch about five feet high at the edge of the circle of light. "That is the doorway," he said. Just beyond the doorway he divided and laid out the eagle feathers from his head dress, one row on the left one on the right, like the wings of a bird in flight. That done he looked with concern at Simu squatting by the fire, his face drawn and grey with fear and anxiety. Kakere walked over to him, took off his leopard skin and draped it over Simu's shoulders saying, "No tooth or claw will trouble you as long as you wear this, and the spirits will not come into the firelight. So keep the fire burning and watch over my body." He said this so calmly and confidently, Simu accepted it and felt far less apprehensive.

He watched in fascination as Kakere then took off everything except a loin cloth despite the cold of the cave. Out of a pouch that had been hanging from his waist he took what looked like dried peas and threw them on the fire. These popped and sputtered tingeing the flames blue green as Kakere began a chant, "Spirits of the mountain I am coming, I am coming. Spirits of the mountain let me see you". He kept up this chanting as he marched around the fire stamping first one foot on the cave floor then the other, sending up little clouds of dust. Seven times around the fire he went. Then he stopped before the gateway he had made and began to twirl around on himself. He began slowly at first then went faster and faster his arms flung wide on either side as though to help him spin. Then suddenly he clapped his arms to his sides and fell like a log through the arch. There his body lay motionless, face down between the eagle feathers.

As the minutes passed Simu began to worry whether Kakere lived, so still did he lie with his head almost in darkness beyond the fire light. Then he saw that Kakere was breathing very slowly, almost imperceptibly as though in a deep sleep. He realized Kakere must now be traveling in the world of the spirits as he said he would. For the next three hours Simu sat in that little circle of light entombed in the blackness of the cave. He listened to the bats fluttering and squeaking. He began to think of the mountain as alive, with himself buried deep inside it. He felt like a bug might feel deep in an elephant's lung, or a rat at the end of its burrow. An insignificant speck buried in enormous forces that could crush him in the blink of an eye should they realize he existed. This feeling of being entombed was only heightened when, after a long time, a deep thud reverberated through the cave as though something very large had fallen on the cave floor. Simu trembled and gripped his *panga* even more tightly, not being able to imagine any animal that could make such a sound. This passed and the silence became unbearable. Then he noticed that Kakere's body was sweating until his black skin shone in the firelight. As this happened his limbs began to twitch and small grunts and moaning sounds came from him. "He is like a dog that hunts in his sleep," thought Simu, "Except that he is traveling in places beyond my knowledge where dark forces live." He put new wood on the fire to push those forces back into the darkness.

As one hour rolled into the next Simu began to say to himself, "It is enough, enough, come back *mganga*, come back. Let us leave this place and go to the sun." After a long time this silent prayer was answered. Kakere's body stirred. He lifted his head, and then pushed himself up on one elbow. There he stayed for a minute as his eyes opened and he gathered his senses. Then he crawled back through the arch and squatted by the fire until its warmth brought blood back to his limbs. Simu did not speak out of respect for a master who has the courage to go into the land of the unknown. He waited until Kakere said, "Give me my leopard skin, I am cold and very tired." Simu handed it over saying, "What news do you bring?" Kakere did not answer this question. He replied, "We must leave this place. Take fire with you until we reach the light." And so they did. Kakere seemed exhausted and thoughtful as they set out on the return journey. He refused to say what he had seen or learnt, saying, "I must rest and eat before I tell you." So they walked in silence through the forest down elephant paths worn wide over the centuries, hearing only the sounds of the forest; the harsh cry of the hornbill, the occasional bark of an alarmed bushbuck and the twittering of smaller birds. In due course they came out of the forest into the more open country with bush and grass between the thorn trees and beyond that the beginning of paths made red by the uncovered earth where Kakere's cattle and sheep went out to graze. Dogo seemed to know that they were coming. Half a mile from Kakere's *boma* he appeared from under a creeper laden tree and ran smiling up to Simu, happy to see him back safely after he had set out so somber and serious. "Look Baba," he said, "I killed a lizard on the rocks with a stone. Can I eat it?" He held up the body of a lizard about ten inches long with a blue head and bright red wattles under its chin. "Why of course," said Simu, "but take off the skin first, the skin can make you sick, and then cook it on the fire." With these instructions, Dogo ran happily ahead to see wife number three while Simu and Kakere went to his hut to rest, eat, and then talk.

Buffalo

9. Prophesy & more troubles

When they arrived back from Makingene cave near dusk, Simu and Kakere rested in his personal hut. He did not satisfy Simu's curiosity until they had eaten and were comfortable. Then he said, "Even two sheep is not enough for the work I had to do, and the news I must bring you." Simu was silent, partly because he had no more sheep, and partly because he feared the news he was to hear. "I left my body with you," said the Kakere, "and rose on wings as an eagle above the mountain. When I was so high I was like a speck of dust in the sky, I could see three giant baskets on the earth below me, the past, the present and the future. The past and the future are miles wide, each as big as the bowl where the hot springs are at the top of this mountain. The present is much smaller than the other two. Each basket has in it many other baskets, each one smaller than the one before, and yet when you go into the basket it is wider than your eyes can see, even if you turn your head.

Each is like the moon, as small as a plate, but another world when you go there and see. I went to the past and the future. The present is just now. All the knots that tied up the baskets of the past have been undone before. Opening them again is not difficult, if you but know which basket to open, and where to find it. So first I went to the basket of the past. There I could see the podo tree where you found the boy you call Dogo. His real name is Sumatra, but another will tell you this. His Mother's spirit stayed in that tree where you found him. When the boy is troubled deeply, take him there to find that peace that only a mother can give; the goat cannot do this for him. The boy's Father was taken by the *sirkali* (the paramilitary police) to work far away beyond the peak called Riwa that looks like a blue tooth on the horizon. He will be in the land of the whistling thorn, where the dust devils play over the desert and the Somali *shifta* (bandits) have cloth around their heads and rifles in their hands. He will be there a long time.

The *Memsahib* in the white house with a red roof has helped you twice. She will not hurt you or Dogo. She has the power of the *wazungu* and part of this power is given to them by the spirit of the cross if they live by the book of the cross. This she must be doing because the spirit of the cross has done what she asked and healed your child twice. You would have to learn to read and study for many moons to learn how to use the spirit of the cross. I do not know how the spirit came to be in the elephant of which you have spoken, but I do know that the *Memsahib* did not put it there, nor did the Ndorobo *mganga* of whom I will speak in a moment. The spirit of the cross does not attack people; it is white magic not black. That elephant will not attack you or Dogo and may even help you. It is not controlled by any *mganga*. If he lives, the boy may one day call on this elephant for help. "What do you mean, if he lives?" said Simu sharply. "I mean what I say," said Kakere. "On this mountain there is a young man of your clan who wishes evil on you. He is helped, no, more than that, he is instructed by his mother. When they failed in their witchcraft accusations against you, then as you suspected they paid one heifer to an Ndorobo *mganga* to do their work for them. I do not know this *mganga*. But it was he who brought you and your boy the attention of the dark one in Suam gorge. Now I shall tell you of her and the future."

"The baskets of the future are different from those of the past or even the present. Bad spirits do not like you to see what they may do in the future. So the knots that tie the baskets of the future are very tight. With great work I was able to open only a few. There I was able to see only big things. The little things within them I could not reach. But I did discover that the python that attacked the boy was the spawn of the dark one who lives in the Suam gorge. As you know, that is the gorge cut two thousand feet deep by the Suam river to drain the crater of this mountain. When the night is cold the dark one comes from the gorge and rises above the mountain. She is as wide as two hands held up to the sky, like a giant snake with wings. She is black and icy cold. So I will call her Black Ice. No starlight shows through her long black body as she rises from the gorge and travels over the mountain. When the stars are hidden in a clear sky, you know she is there. She is the night watchman of the spirit world who keeps everything in its place and makes sure there are no intruders. Being very important, she does not act herself. She directs others to do what must be done. Her seed are not troubled by cold like normal snakes. She attacked me as an in-truder in the spirit world when I opened the basket of the future. I had to hide, and then I distracted her by starting the bush fire you saw on the plains as we came back down the mountain. When she went to investigate the fire I went to the gorge and found the spirit of the python you killed. That spirit told me that the Ndorobo *mganga* brought you and the boy to the attention of Black Ice who probably would not otherwise have noticed you. Your problem is that Black Ice sees the boy you call Dogo as you would see a wart on your skin, a blemish to be removed because he does not fit into the proper order of things."

"What do you mean?" asked Simu. "The boy is out of place in the nature of things, like a goat that wishes to graze with the cattle, rather than its own kind. He has never known a human mother, only a goat and a monkey. His spirit is half animal, half man. Black Ice sees him as having the body of a human but the mind and instincts of an animal, a creature of the forest. The boy was attacked not to be eaten, but to be removed. The attacks were not a matter of chance. They were matters of intention as you suspected. The boy is cursed, not by any man you know, but by the very heart of nature." "Cannot you not make magic to protect the boy?" said Simu. "No. Black Ice is far too big and powerful to be influenced or controlled by any *mganga*. If I knew which creature she might send to attack the boy I might make some magic to protect against that creature. But I do not know," said Kakere. "Perhaps Black Ice will forget about the boy, he cannot be very important and there are so many other things on the mountain," said Simu. "That is true," said Kakere, "but Black Ice has a memory better than an elephant. She may forget for a while, but she is part of the natural order of things and the laws of nature always work in the end. Black Ice does not give up. She will kill the boy sooner or later. My magic cannot change this, cannot fight it. What is, must be." "Then what can I do?" asked Simu in great distress. "Are you saying the boy must die?" "If nothing changes, the boy will surely die," replied Kakere. "Black Ice will send others to attack him, perhaps even man, who always kills what he does not understand. Whatever, or whoever, comes, sooner or later, the boy will not escape if he stays where he is. I have no magic powerful enough to protect the boy from Black Ice." Grasping at straws, Simu said, "What if I take him to live with my clan above the tree line?" "As you know that would only bring him closer to the Suam gorge, and to the young man and his mother who would do you harm," replied Kakere. "He must go far away from the mountain and hope he does not irritate some other spirit, or he must change so that he is no longer a thorn coming through the sandal on nature's foot. He must learn to think and dream like man not animal, he must be taught to be fully man." "I have taught him all I know," said Simu, "How can I change him to become fully man?" "You cannot," said Kakere, "You cannot teach what you do not see, what you do not understand. Any way no one can remove what the child has learned from the goat and the monkey. You could only build on top of it and perhaps cover it so that it is hidden. You must send the boy out of the forest to keep him alive and let another teacher build on the foundation that he has. There is no other way." "You have a tongue that cuts like a sharp knife," said Simu, letting his hurt turn to anger. "This child is why I have come to have purpose in my life, when I wake in the morning, when I dig the salt rock from Chepnall cave. I cannot send him away. A man cannot send away half his life." "You are a man not a woman, you cannot hold onto the boy and destroy him," said Kakere coldly. "If you would save the child you must do the necessary. He will not love you for it until he is old enough to have wisdom, by then you may be dead. Now hear what the future can be."

"You speak of your ties to the child. I speak of knots you must untie, of baskets that you can open if you will, so that the child may leave Chepnall cave and the forest. If he does not leave, then, as I have said, he will surely not live." "I will guard him day and night," said Simu. "I will never leave him alone." "You are a good man, but a simple man," said Kakere. "You will fail. Black Ice may take you first. Now be quiet, have courage, and listen to the only hope that you have. The spirit that lives on the wind that blows around the world will send a *mzungu* to your cave. The hair of his beard will be long and as white as his skin. If you surrender the boy to him, he will teach the child what you do not know. The magic of the *mzungu* will protect him. He will travel far beyond the reach of Black Ice and will learn all the *mzungu* knows. One day he will return to the place where he was born because the mountain will always call him. Living he will do great good for the mountain. When he dies, his soul will become part of her soul. This is what can be, if you let it be. You and I will not see it, for we shall be long gone." "You offer me only loneliness then death, what choice is that?" cried Simu in anguish, adding petulantly, "and for this I gave you two sheep." Ignoring him the Kakere replied, "The path is often slippery with mud, or sharp with thorns. It is in the nature of things. You must travel the path as best you can. But travel with courage as is befitting a man, even if you must be a warrior against your own desires. It is late, so spend the night here and go with the boy in the morning. More I cannot tell you." Dismissed, Simu left the hut so distressed, he forgot to ask Kakere when the *mzungu* might come. Politeness would also have required him to ask Kakere what fears and struggles he had encountered in the land of the spirits. But Simu was far too troubled, had too much of his own pain, to pay any attention to the troubles of another.

When he left Kakere's hut Simu went blindly into the darkness outside overwhelmed with his painful thoughts until he stumbled into a young thorn tree which he did not see in the dark. The pain of a thorn going into his leg brought him back to the practical present. Now he began to feel the cold of the night too. He backed away from the thorn tree. Cold and shivering he went to hut of wife number two. The outline of the hut roof was just visible against the night sky. When she heard his voice she untied the door and let him in. The children in the hut stirred but did not wake. Simu went to sit on a large stone by the small fire in the centre of the hut which gave out the only light. He could see a little trickle of blood on his leg and felt the tip of the thorn still there. He decided to wait to try and get it out until morning when there would be light. Wife number two asked him if he had eaten. He answered morosely in one word, "Yes." She picked up on his mood realizing that he was troubled by thoughts that shut her quite out of his mind. So she went off to the side of the hut where there was a sleeping shelf, pulled an old brown blanket over herself and watched Simu's dark outline against the dying fire light. She wondered what he had been told that troubled him so. She knew that it had to do with the child. As a mother she understood the anguish Simu must be feeling for his child in some trouble she did not understand. She watched him until she fell asleep. When she woke in the morning she saw Simu lying asleep curved around one side of the fire, now just warm grey ashes. She wondered what Kakere had told him to cause so much distress. The night before she had thought Simu a bit distant and a little strange, but comfortable enough to be with. Now she felt somewhat disappointed that he acknowledged her presence only as an after thought. But it was not her place as a woman to ask what troubled him if he did not volunteer it. So she held her tongue and did her duty by feeding Simu and Dogo when they were awake. Then they thanked her and went out into the cold morning when the sun was not yet far above the horizon.

When outside Simu sat on a log and worked on removing the thorn that had broken off in his leg the night before. It was just above the knee. He used another thorn as a needle to dig it out. It took him fifteen minutes of work. Dogo became bored and restless, saying, "Baba let's go, I am cold standing here." That was true. The sun was up but had not yet warmed the air. "As soon as I get this done," said Simu. He gave a grunt of satisfaction when he finally succeeded in removing about half an inch of thorn tip. No wonder it hurt he thought. With the thorn out, walking did not hurt, so Simu set a good pace on the now familiar path back to Chepnall cave. By the time they returned Simu had decided not to send Dogo away. Despite what Kakere had told him he rationalized his decision saying to himself, "I don't know any one to send him to." But he did take Kakere's warning seriously. He expected Black Ice to try again. He thought the attack would be another physical attack on Dogo, or possibly himself, by some creature of the forest. Here he was in his element. He said to himself, "I know this forest better than any man. For years I have lived here and have avoided all dangers. I will take my spear as well as my *panga* where ever I go, and I will take Dogo with me at all times."

The morning after they arrived back at Chepnall cave, Simu set up new rules for Dogo. He could no longer leave the cave with Bossy or Bending Twig whenever he wanted. He had to wait for Simu to accompany him. Very soon this led to considerable strain between Simu and Dogo. The cave had no toys or companions for Dogo to play with. The only exception were the hyraxes who lived in the rocks at the mouth of the cave, but Dogo soon became bored with Chok and any other hyrax brave enough to come close to him. He longed for the open air, the sunshine, playing in the stream and all the little lizards and other creatures he found outside. By the afternoon of the first day Dogo said, "I'm bored Baba, if I cannot go out without you then come with me now." "Let me finish chipping this salt rock, then I will come," said Simu. "You have been doing that all day," complained Dogo truthfully. "I will come in a moment," was the answer, and he did, saying to Bending Twig, "go ahead of us and let me know if you see anything dangerous." "Of course," said Bending Twig sitting on a rock and reaching out an affectionate hand to touch to Dogo's face, adding, "let the boy out of this gloomy cave." She then ran up into the trees and went ahead of them as they went down below the cave to find Bossy. For the next two hours or so Simu impatiently chaperoned Dogo as he played in the stream, added stones to the dam Simu had built to hold the waterbuck meat, chased butterflies and hunted lizards on the rocks. Bossy was grazing happily and everything seemed as normal as ever. Simu was very much on the alert for snakes, particularly pythons, but did not really expect to see one. I killed the one Black Ice sent, he thought. She won't send another if I am near. Bending Twig sat in the podo trees nearby happily munching on leaves as she looked over the sunlit open area where Bossy grazed and Dogo played. It was the usual warm comfortable scene. When the sun began to sink and the shadow of the cliff above the cave spread down the little valley, Bending Twig went off to find her troupe for the night and Simu said to Dogo, "Now we must find firewood for tonight's fire. Come." Dogo was used to this routine. He carried small dry sticks not too big for him to break off dead branches. He was happy doing this, partly because there were no other distractions and partly because he enjoyed feeding them one by one into the fire. Also he liked Simu's approval and wanted to please him. He also did things to please Bossy, but her range of activities was very limited and very much in the here and right now. She did not think about tomorrow. It was Simu who taught Dogo to think ahead saying, "It may rain tomorrow, so we must collect more firewood today and be ready." At his age Dogo could think about tomorrow, but anything more than a week away was so far in the future for him as to be beyond worrying about. Most of the animals of the forest were the same way. The meat eaters and the leaf eaters could not store food for tomorrow, or water for that matter, so they lived for today and did not worry about droughts or hunger tomorrow. Simu was not so blessed. He was desperately worried about what might happen to Dogo tomorrow or later. He did not appreciate it, but the ability of man to think about and prepare for tomorrow is what enabled him to survive more than any other creature. Even in modern societies with large safety nets those who do not prepare for the future do not do very well. At that moment, all Simu knew was that tomorrow he would have the same problem of Dogo being bored and wanting to go out.

He was right of course. The next morning Dogo was soon complaining about boredom and edging out to the mouth of the cave. "You can't go out without me," cautioned Simu. "Just onto the rocks Baba," said Dogo. Simu thought to himself, may be it's alright if he is so close, and if I check it out first; at least he will be able to sit in the sun. So he replied, "All right, but you cannot go off the rocks at all, and if the hyraxes give the alarm about anything you must run right back in." "Thank you Baba," said Dogo and began to walk towards the rocks." "Wait, let me check it out first," said Simu going out and up onto the rocks himself. Everything looked green and sunny and peaceful, so he turned to see Dogo was on his heels. "All right," Simu said, "but you cannot jump down on the ground." So Dogo sunned himself on the rocks and played with Bending Twig for a while when she came down to visit with him. He sat very still and watched the hyraxes, envying them that they could freely leave the rocks and climb trees to get green leaves to eat. He also wondered if they made mouse like nests in the cracks between the rocks where they lived out of view and in safety from larger predators. He watched them for a while then he was bored again. So he went back in the cave and said, "Baba, what can I do?" Simu thought for a minute then said, "I will teach you how to hunt flies." "How can I do that, Baba? They are too quick for me for me to catch," said Dogo. "Let me show you how to spear them with thorns," said Simu. He went and broke three large thorns off the acacia branch that he used at night to block the entrance to the rock *boma* where they slept. Going out to the rocks he stuck one thorn firmly into the base of another. "See," Simu, "the front thorn is the spear thorn. You use the third thorn to push hard on the base of the spear thorn. If you push hard enough the spear thorn will be like a tiny thrown spear." He then demonstrated, showing that with enough pressure the spear thorn would shoot off about two inches and, hopefully, impale the fly. He had Dogo spit on his knee to attract the flies and then try to impale them with the spear thorn when they came to drink his saliva. Dogo soon discovered that if the thorn hit the fly on the head it usually bounced off. Fly heads are relatively hard. The trick was to hit it in the softer abdomen. The fly would then take off buzzing furiously but moving sluggishly carrying the thorn in it. Dogo also found that the flies often took off in fright as he had to move his hands very close to them to get in range; less than two inches away. To solve this problem he scratched a scab on his other knee until a dot of blood appeared. The flies then became so engrossed feasting on this, he could move the thorns right up to them. Having got Dogo started Simu left him to it and went back in the cave. Thorn spearing flies amused Dogo for about an hour during which time he successfully speared about ten flies. Then this too paled and he went back again into the cave to bother Simu, reasoning, he is the one who will not let me go out, so he should find me something to do.

"Baba, I want to find the elephants and play with Tumbo. Why can't we go look for them?" "It is too late now," said Simu. "Well then tomorrow," replied Dogo. "There is nothing for me to do in this cave." Simu sighed inwardly, but capitulated. "Well alright," he said, "we will go tomorrow if it does not look like rain." "Where will we go?" asked Dogo. "To the elephant platform of course.

But I really do not like you playing the leg running game with Tumbo. If they kick him it may hurt him, but you it would break. You'd be squashed like a blade of grass under a man's foot." "Don't worry Baba, I'm very careful and his mother likes me." "They do seem to recognize you and know you are not a danger to them," said Simu. "I am not so sure about me however." "You just stay back Baba," said Dogo. "They know my smell and are not frightened by it. They speak in sounds you cannot hear. It comes from their stomachs. I know when they are happy and when they are annoyed. Then I stay away." This made sense to Simu. He had often heard elephant stomachs rumbling when they were not alarmed and eating. "I suppose so," said Simu. "Now let me finish my digging for today." So Dogo left him and went to look for amusement. He hit on the idea of dropping ants into the ant lion pits in the floor of the cave. These were small conical pits in the dusty floor about two inches deep and as much across. Hidden in the loose dust at the bottom was the ant lion, a bit bigger and chunkier than an ant with two huge pincers and a powerful tail that he used to flip dust up the side of the pit. The fine dust acted like a scree slope down which a wandering ant would slide to his doom. Dogo found ants on a branch at the front of the cave and carried them back one by one, dropping them into the ant lion pits and watching the ensuing struggle. It kept him busy unit dusk when Simu started on the evening meal.

The next morning was bright and clear. There were no clouds coming up from Lake Victoria to the South and East, so Dogo had a smile on his face. "Come on Baba! Let's go," he said. "Alright, alright," said Simu. He told Bossy they would be gone for some time and she should stay. Bossy was used to this from the times that Simu and Dogo went to deliver honey to Kisharani. She just said, "Baa," and went out to munch on grass. Bending Twig followed them down the mountain until the big trees were no longer close enough together for her to travel through the branches. There was no way she would come down into the bush and buffalo grass where she would be helpless. "Be careful," she said as Simu and

Dogo went on. Simu was being careful. He had his spear in one hand and *panga* in a home made raw hide sheath on his side. In his other hand he carried a piece of cloth, a *kitambaa*, in which he had placed cold ashes from the cave fire. He tied the ashes in the *kitambaa* made into a little pouch. When he shook the pouch whitish grey dust rose like smoke and floated in the air. The way it drifted told him exactly where the wind was blowing. If the smoke went ahead of him, he knew that all animals would know they were coming. If it went to the side or behind him, then it was possible that he might bump into the animal at very close range in the thick brush and elephant grass. A cow with calf would likely charge immediately. So great caution was advised. On the way out the wind carried their scent ahead of them and all animals moved away as they feared man and had no wish to quarrel with him. So Simu and Dogo arrived in due course at the open area above the elephant platform, an old lava flow making a cliff cutting off a valley. There were no elephants on top of the platform, so Simu and Dogo sat on the cliff edge and looked down the valley which alternated with patches of forest and open areas where there was too much rock near the surface for trees to grow.

It was a grand view running far beyond the valley at their feet which ended half a mile away when it joined the larger valley of the Kimothon stream coming down the mountain from their left. The far side of this valley rose dark green and forested to a near horizon over which could be seen a patchwork quilt of fields some tan colored with ripening wheat, others still green with maize not yet dried out for harvesting, all intertwined with thorn trees, patches of grazing and the green ribbons of water courses. The fields themselves merged into a hazy blue distance where the Cherangani hills rose high out of the plains. Simu and Dogo felt as though they were sitting on top of the world that clear crisp morning with the swifts whistling around their ears and the wind sighing gently in a stunted cedar tree. They were comfortable and at peace with nature. But Dogo was disappointed that they could see no elephants below them. "Where are they Baba?" he asked. "I don't know," replied Simu, "perhaps they went to Kitum cave to get salt in the night. Then they may have gone on South down the mountain. Perhaps they are just hidden in the forest. We must wait a little and see." He was right. After half an hour or so they heard a crack like a pistol shot come up from the forest in the valley below them. It was the sound a large branch breaking as an elephant pulled it down to eat it. Only an elephant could make a sound like that. "I hear them Baba," said Dogo, "let's go." They went along the top of the cliff to where it merged into the side of the valley, and then started down towards the place where they had heard the branch break. The wind was coming up the valley, so the buffalo did not smell them coming. They almost bumped into the small herd as they came out of the long grass into an open area on the edge of the forest. The first cow to see them gave a snort of alarm and rushed towards the forest with a great drumming of hooves. Instantly the whole herd was spooked and went crashing away. Then two bulls swung around fifty yards away and did their duty by facing whatever danger had alarmed the cow. First they lifted their heads and snuffed the wind trying to identify the danger. But the wind was from them towards Simu and Dogo, so they smelled nothing unusual. Then they saw Simu and recognized man, an ancient enemy who hunted them with spears and dogs from time to time. But they saw only one man and a child and no dogs, and knew they had the advantage. They were huge powerful beasts armored with a pair of horns shaped like giant military moustaches, a foot wide and two inches thick at the base on the animal's forehead, then spreading out and slightly downwards two feet on each side and curling up to thick blunt ends. Spears just bounced off this armored head which hit you like a tree trunk crushing your ribs. The neck carrying those horns was a thick as the bodies of three men and strong enough to toss a full grown lion six feet in the air. Simu knew that if they pressed their attack he had no hope of fighting them with just a spear and a *panga*. "Run, run," he shouted to Dogo, "climb a tree."

Simu headed for a tree about seventy yards away that looked solid and had a branch low enough to reach from the ground so that he could climb it. Naturally he outran Dogo even though Dogo was inspired by fear that ran from the pit of his stomach to the tips of his toes. He dashed through the buffalo grass and around small bushes ignoring scratches. After a short distance Simu's back disappeared in the grass in front of him. Dogo could now hear the drumming of hooves behind him. He realized that he was not going to make it to the tree Simu had seemingly chosen. Instinctively and naturally he set about saving himself if he could by darting sideways towards a small thorn tree not more than five inches in diameter at the base, its flat top about ten feet off the ground only a little higher than the buffalo grass. The tree split into two main branches at a fork about five feet up. It was a flimsy refuge, but better than nothing. This small tree was about twenty yards to the side of Dogo's line of flight. He was only half way there when the two bulls thundered over the spot where he had turned. He was lucky that he was small. The bulls had not seen him turn as he was hidden at that moment by a bush. They galloped past and went on twenty or thirty yards until one realized that the smell of man was now on the wind coming from behind him not on the trail through the grass and bush in front. He swung around, lifted his head and snuffed the air. In a moment he knew where the smell was coming from, just as a human can pinpoint the direction of a sound. He started trotting now upwind. The trotting turned into a canter when he saw Dogo swing himself up into the fork in the small thorn tree and then move up one of the two main branches which swayed and bent alarmingly. As the bull came under the tree he swung his head high trying to hook Dogo out of the tree with one of his huge curved horns. The horn hit one of Dogo's legs which was hanging down and hurt him dreadfully, but did not hook him. Dogo pulled his leg up in pain and looked down, terrified, at the buffalo now circling the small tree with a look that said, "I'm going to get you." Dogo remembered that look from the red rimmed eyes, the panting of the buffalo, the white stringy saliva coming down from it mouth, the enormous black nostrils flared in the excitement of the chase, and the huge horns swinging just under his body stretched out flat on the branch. What he did not remember were his high pitched cries of terror, "Aieeeee, Aieeee..." which echoed up and down the valley.

Simu reached his tree safely and was up it in a flash, just in time to see the buffalo take his first swing trying to hook Dogo off his flimsy branch. He felt relieved that Dogo had reached even a small tree and guilty that he had not stopped to try and save Dogo, even though he could have done nothing to help except sacrifice himself. He watched helplessly as the second buffalo came to join his companion in trying to dislodge Dogo. Dogo's cries pierced him like sharp thorns. He shouted and waved his arms hoping to distract the buffalo and divert their attention to him. The buffalo were having none of it. They had man only just out of reach of their hooves and horns. Had they been elephants they would immediately have pushed the small tree over, or simply reached up with a trunk and pulled Dogo out. They were heavy enough that they could probably have pushed the tree over enough to bring Dogo within reach. But buffalo do not think like elephants, so they continued to circle around Dogo swinging their horns as high as they could. But Dogo was just out of reach. Then one of them had an idea that would have worked but for a very surprising intervention. He reared up on his hind legs like a bucking horse and easily gained enough height to catch Dodo with his horns. On his first attempt he was too far back and missed the branch. He moved closer under the branch and was about to try again when an elephant trunk whacked him like a six inch lead pipe on his hind quarters. Tumbo's mother had heard Dogo's cries and recognized them as cries of distress. Moving surprisingly fast, but totally silently as elephants do, she had appeared out of the forest and come up behind the buffalo. Simu looked on in amazement as the mud-red colored elephant came to the rescue. Never had he seen such a thing before and he never expected to again. The second bull did not need a whack he just took off after his companion while the elephant circled around the tree as tall at the shoulder as the tree was high. Then she stopped and put out a long sensitive trunk to sniff Dogo on his branch. Dogo locked his hands around the end of the trunk in delight and held on as he was lifted out of the tree and put on the ground. Then out of the forest came a little rolly poly Tumbo, his trunk up in the air his ears flapping as he ran along his mother's trail and gave a delighted squeal when he found Dogo. Mother then led the way back to the forest with Dogo happily riding on Tumbo's back. Simu was too stunned to call out a warning to Dogo. He just came down his tree and walked over to where Dogo had been rescued. Then, not really knowing what else to do, he began to follow their footsteps towards the forest keeping an un-necessary but wary eye out for the buffalo. When the trail came to a patch of dusty bare earth he stopped suddenly and stared in amazement at the large elephant footprint in the dust. It showed, unmistakably, the outline of the cross that he had seen before. The elephant of the cross was Tumbo's mother.

Simu squatted on his heels staring, almost unbelieving, at the footprint. Then he remembered the words of *mganga* Kakere when he said, "You are a good but simple man, you will fail." This was in response to Simu's assertion that he would guard Dogo day and night. He saw now that some dangers he could not fight. Buffalo were one of them. Often they just crashed away with a great noise when they sensed man, but they were unpredictable creatures, sometimes turning off the path and waiting for man to follow and attacking from the side or behind. He knew what when disturbed they always turned down wind before stopping so that they could smell any one following their trail. It could have been just one of those things, but deep in his psyche Simu knew that Black Ice had put the two bulls in their path that day. He had no explanation for the intervention by Tumbo's mother other than Dogo's friendship with Tumbo, but supposed that her ability to thwart Black Ice was a reflection of the reality that the *mzungu* spirit of the cross was as powerful as Black Ice. Why that spirit should be in an elephant he had no idea. But he did see that Kakere was right. Attacks on

Dogo would continue and perhaps on himself too. Sooner or later one would succeed. Dogo's narrow escape that day left him with no choice but to heed the *mganga's* advice and sent the child out of the forest and so out of his life. The very thought left him feeling as though he had a ball of ice in the pit of his stomach. As he faced this heart rending truth he despaired of knowing how he would do it. Where could he send the boy, who would take him? As he waited for Dogo to come out of the forest, Simu considered going back to Kakere to ask when the spirit in the wind that blows around the world would bring the white haired *mzungu* to him. How long would he have to wait, how could he protect Dogo in the meantime? What he did not know was that titanic forces had begun to reshape Europe more than any one imagined at that time. The winds raised by the fires of Kristallnacht had already driven a *mzungu* from his home and sent him half way around the world. Now, I must tell you how this came to be and how he came to Chepnall cave.

Baba Max

10. Baba Max

Herr Doctor Rheinstein was a professor of philosophy who taught at the Universitat, Frankfurt am Main. However his first degree had been in anthropology. The study of the origins and evolution of humankind was an interest that would stay with him all his life. Africa had always interested him. He found that it dovetailed well with his philosophical interest in why man is the way he is and how that came to be. That he would live in Africa was, however, quite unexpected.

The professor had a commanding presence. He was a big man with a rugged face, white hair and trimmed grey beard. This was what you noticed at first sight. But, when you looked into those deep blue eyes it was like looking into the depths of an ocean. There was so much knowledge there, such a font of intellect and morality. When you sat with him and heard his deep voice, you automatically listened out respect. You marveled that a man could be so knowledgeable, but not in a bookish way. He was as much in tune with your own feelings, thoughts, and emotions, as he was wise. He was firm, but gentle, kind and generous. He put his heart into his teaching, and was very popular with his students. He had a very genuine interest in them. Every Sunday he and his wife Ruth would invite three or four to lunch. Ruth would carve the roast. She had started her career as a school teacher and liked young people. She often wore her dark hair in a bun particularly when working. When she let it hang to her shoulders she was a slim attractive woman of average size. Her nature was as generous as her husband's, but she was commonsense, loving and practical, rather than intellectual. She too, was well liked by the many students she entertained in their modest home where they lived with their two sons Aaron and Benjamin. The home was an apartment above a book shop they owned, on a side street in Darmstadt. There was a front door with a long pane of glass in it and a little bell than rang when you pushed it open. That put you behind the big plate glass window looking out on to the street. Rows of bookshelves ran into the back where a narrow stair case led up to the apartment which had two bedrooms and a living room. In the small back yard was a coal shed to fire the boiler and steam-heat radiators. A black coal scuttle stood by the cast iron stove in the kitchen where the family ate. Ruth ran the book shop while the Professor drove the thirty kilometers to the University in Frankfurt each day.

The Rheinsteins never made any public display of their religion, beyond attending the very modest synagogue in Darmstadt. This was a one room rectangular building about twenty feet wide and thirty long. On each side it had three big windows with arched tops, a tile roof, and whitewashed walls spattered at the bottom with mud from the street. Its furnishings were as simple and basic as the congregation that attended. There was no wealth here and no display of it. Apart from attending the synagogue, the Rheinsteins observed all other religious traditions and customs at home. They celebrated Shabbat every Friday evening and the major Jewish holidays, but always in private or with friends of the same faith.

They gave no offense to any one, and like every one else, struggled to make ends meet as the misery of the great depression, hyperinflation, and massive unemployment, left the populace searching for some one to blame for their woes.

Ruth asked why the Nazi party weekly newspaper, Die Sturmer (The Attacker) always proclaimed at the bottom of the front page "The Jews are our misfortune." The Professor's answer was, "Mein liebe, when people suffer unexplained or unexpected disasters, they ask why? Always they believe it is some body else's fault. They blame the sinners among them, or foreigners, or Jews, or infidels. Naturally, they pick on some one they think they can beat up on without too much risk to themselves. In this case it is us."

The life that the Rheinsteins had known came to an end on the night of the 9th November 1938. That night came to have a fairy tale name, Kristallnacht, or Crystal Night. In some ways it was a crystal night. It was cold and clear. The icicles glinted in the street lights and the stars shone bright. But it was no fairy God Mother who was out that night. Like the rivulets of water that precede a flash flood down a dry river bed, mobs of uneducated young thugs, orchestrated and encouraged by Goebbels, Hitler's chief of propaganda, presaged the enormous torrent of evil that was to come. When they left the opera in Frankfurt that night, the Rheinsteins did not know this, nor did they expect it in the civilized world.

When they started the drive back to Darmstadt, both Max and Ruth had a sense of unease as they passed several mobs of fifty or more young men marching down the streets chanting and shouting. They all wore brown shirts. Many carried pick handles. "They are growing like a cancer, these Nazis," said Max, "Soon they will destroy this country." "You mean they will destroy us; for the sake of the Fatherland of course," replied Ruth. "If we have to stop near them, wave and act friendly and unconcerned," said Max. "We do not have to carry Jewish identity cards until next January, and there is nothing in the car that will give us away." And that is exactly what they did. When stopped at a traffic light they waved to the mob surging by and smiled over hollow stomachs. Apart from this they left Frankfurt without incident and drove depressed, and silent down the tunnel their headlights made in the overwhelming blackness of the night on the road to Darmstadt. Their low spirits turned to great alarm when they turned down Frederikstrasse and saw their synagogue burning surrounded by a cheering mob. Three policemen stood on the side of the road behind the mob, doing nothing.

"Oh my God, today is the day Benjamin and Aaron were going to help the Rabbi," said Ruth. "You must do something Max, find out if they are there." With his heart sinking Max said nothing and stopped the car about fifty yards behind the mob. He saw immediately that the rafters of the synagogue were burning and half the roof had fallen in. "If there is any one in there they cannot be alive now," said Max. "If we push through these hooligans one may recognize us and we will be attacked. We can do nothing here. The boys are probably at home. We will go there first." "Dear God, hurry," said Ruth. So Max put the car in first gear and inched by until he cleared the crowd and could accelerate.

The streets on the way to the bookshop were silent and deserted at that hour. As soon as they turned off the alley into their back yard the Rheinsteins knew in their hearts that the worst had happened, but they could not acknowledge it. The back door was open, creaking as it swung in the wind and banging hollowly against the coal shed. Inside all was chaos. Overturned bookshelves leant drunkenly against each other. Piles of books lay all over the floor. A chill wind blew came through the shattered shop front window. Shards of glass littered the street and the floor. "Benjamin Aaron," Ruth shouted up the narrow stairs. Her voice echoed through the dark, cold, stairwell. She knew instinctively in that moment that the apartment was empty, that she would have no answer. "Call the Rabbi," said Max, and then did so himself. The phone rang and rang. No answer. The next call was to the Rabbi's brother Levi. Thank God, he thought as the phone was answered. "This is Max, are Benjamin and Aaron with you?" There was a long pause. Max could hear a woman sobbing in the background. Then Levi spoke slowly and carefully; "Max, the Rabbi and your two boys were at the synagogue, we do not have much hope." His voice trembling Max turned to Ruth and whispered, "Levi says they were at the synagogue." "Bring some clothes and come," said Levi. "Yes," replied Max, and hung up. He turned to Ruth and they clung to each other for a long time in that darkened shop as the tears ran down their faces and the cold wind blew through the wreckage. They did not hear the back door still banging. When they began to shiver Max said, "We must go to Levi's." Ruth nodded silently. They packed to two suitcases and drove to Levi's.

Levi pointed out that if the Rabbi and the boys had escaped the synagogue, they would almost certainly make their way to his house. If they had not escaped then nothing could be done until the mob went home and the fire burned itself out. Besides in the dark they could not search the wreckage well. So they waited until first light, and then drove in Max's car. Levi did not own one. It took them only ten minutes to find the charred bodies. For Max it was the darkest moment of his life, as though all were empty blackness in which grief and anger swirled through tears. Despite his anguish, he did what he had to do. They propped the bodies in the back seat of the car and drove back to Levi's house with a feeling that the morning was surreal as they passed newspaper delivery boys, the milkman and people going to work as usual, unaware of the horror of three blackened bodies in the back of the car. "How can they be unaware, indifferent, untouched," Max asked himself. "Is it ignorance or fear?"

When they arrived at Levi's Max went inside while Ruth sat in the car. One look at Max's face told the women the worst had happened. "They are in the car," said Max. Without a word, Levi went to the bedroom and came out with three white sheets. He put these on the dining room table, as he moved it and the chairs to one wall. Then he went out to the car where he and Max wrapped the bodies in the improvised shrouds and then brought them in to be laid out on the dining room floor. Within an hour Levi had organized a grave digging party. Fortunately the ground was not frozen. By mid afternoon the graves had been dug and a horse and cart borrowed from one of the congregation. The only motorized hearse was owned by a Nazi sympathizer. Willi and Hans who owned the shops on either side of the bookshop came to the funeral too, as did Frau Jacoby, one of Ruth's friends. This required some courage as mobs of brown shirted hooligans were still attacking Jewish shops.

German newspapers duly reported the events of the 9th and 10th November as a "Spontaneous uprising," by the German populace against the conspiracy of international Jewry to attack the Reich, as evidenced by the assassination of Ernst Von Rath, third secretary of the German Embassy in Paris. Von Rath had been shot a couple of weeks before by a young Jewish man, Herschel Grynspan, whose purpose was to avenge the deportation of his family from Hamburg to Poland. His Father Zyndel had come to Hamburg in 1911 where he established a small store. The pretext for his deportation and the confiscation of everything in his shop was the fact the he was a Polish citizen. It was no matter that he had lived peaceably in Germany for over a quarter of century. Seventeen thousand other Jews of Polish citizenship received similar treatment. Following the events of Kristallnacht many more Jews were arrested for alleged subversive activities and sent to concentration camps.

Max did not foresee the actual murder of millions of Jews by the German state. So far there had been political arrests and deportations to Poland, but no executions. But, he did make up his mind the day of the funeral. He said simply to Ruth, "We must leave Germany". Ruth was reluctant. "Our whole lives have been here. All our friends are here in Darmstadt, except for your university friends. Everything we own is here. Besides there is no country in Europe that will take us. That has been clear since the Evian conference last July. None of those thirty two countries want us." "If I were a doctor of medicine, not philosophy and anthropology, I could get a job at the big Jewish hospital in London," said Max, "and with a job offer I could get an immigrant visa." "But, you are not a doctor of medicine," replied Ruth. Max sighed, "I know," he said. "But I will speak to the British Embassy about the possibility of going to the Holy Land. My dear you must realize we have nothing left here. Our family and our shop have been destroyed. There are strong rumors that university teaching jobs will be denied to Jewish persons since the Nuremberg laws denied us Reich citizenship. Like many others, I will not have a job a year from now. I will ask the German Jewish Aid Organization if they can suggest anything." "I am not sure I want you to succeed," said Ruth. "If you do, I will have to build my life over again, make new friends, in a strange land." Like many others at that time, Max and Ruth thought of leaving Germany as an economic and life style issue, not a matter of life or death. Dachau had been built, but was used for political prisoners, those who opposed the Nazis. Only later was it to become an extermination camp.

The Rheinsteins never lived in the book shop again. For the first few days of mourning they stayed with Levi. This was just as well, because three days after the progrom, Max's neighbor and friend Willi called to say that the police had been asking where Max was. Apparently one of his students at the University had reported Max as saying things critical of the Fuhrer and therefore of the Fatherland. Willi had denied any knowledge of where Max might be and then immediately called Levi. Max and Ruth left Levi's that day and went to stay with other friends while they planned their escape from Germany. With a woman's intuition Ruth knew that if Max were arrested she would never see him again. Max had called the British Embassy about emigrating to Palestine. He was told this was not possible. Although he did not know it the British administration of Palestine regarded more Jews in Palestine as more trouble. The Zionists had not endeared themselves. The young man at the embassy was not unsympathetic however. He said that he could authorize emigration to British East Africa, in particular Kenya, which was looking for new settlers. If Mr. Rheinstein could produce a ticket for himself and his wife on the Union Castle steamship line from Southampton to Mombasa he could issue a two day transit visa allowing them to enter England to catch the boat.

With the help of the German Jewish Aid Organization, Max was able to get the tickets and the visa, but was now on the run from the German authorities who had come to Levi's home looking for him. The next sailing was nearly two weeks away. Max knew he could not stay that long a time in Darmstadt. The police had already found and confiscated his car. Traveling by train would be too dangerous as the railway police were now spot checking identity cards. So the decision was made to travel by bus to Koblenz, then Dusseldorf, and finally the small town of Emmerich on the Rhine just on the German side of the border with the Netherlands. Crossing the border normally was out of the question as the border guards would check papers and might well have Max's name on a list. So Max and Ruth decided to stay in a bed and breakfast in Emmerich while they explored a way to get over the border undetected. They had in mind buying a dingy and rowing down the Rhine at night. Traveling with no more than they could carry in their suitcases, they made their way to Emmerich and found a sailor's rest near the wharves on the Rhine. It was a place that asked no questions as it catered to transients, usually men who stayed less than a whole night. They were shown into a small dingy room with a floor of cracked linoleum, an iron bedstead and a bathroom down the hall. The sash window rattled in the wind which left black grime on the window sill. But the window did have a smokestack view over the Rhine. Looking at the commercial traffic on the river Ruth had an inspiration. "Max look at those coal barges chugging slowly along. See how they have a dingy in tow. Let's buy a dingy and hitch a ride." Max ran with the idea, "Yes," he said we could put a cover over it and hide underneath. I am sure we could find a dingy, but how can we get a tow from a barge?" "Put on your leather jacket and go down to the wharf, there must be a bar or a café where you can find a barge captain." So early that evening Max found a tavern near the wharf, called the Meerjungfrau or Mermaid inn.

The mermaid was not just a figure painted on a flat sign hanging under a light, but rather a three dimensional mermaid sculpture, rampant from the wall like the figurehead on the prow of a ship, a painted, bosomy torso with long hair falling naked to the waist. Inside, the bar was L shaped. The shorter part of the bar was separated from the main room by hanging strings of beads through which customers could see any ladies who might be drinking and or working that evening. Here the bar stools were upholstered and the stairs to the rooms above were carpeted. The main room was for men only. It had bare wood stools, oak benches and unvarnished tables. The rough men of the river drank here until the women behind the beads looked attractive enough to merit attention. "I don't fit in here", thought Max as he came in and walked up to the almost deserted bar. The middle-aged bar tender was one of those large buxom German women wearing a tight white blouse with a criss cross boot lace holding the front more or less together. Looking at Max's leather jacket she knew immediately he was no seaman. But as she chatted with him she found Max ruggedly handsome and much better spoken than her usual customers. She hoped he would become a regular. She was secretly disappointed when he said he wanted to meet a barge captain. "He does not look like a pederast. But, every man has his story," she thought. "He will tell me if he has enough to drink, but I wonder what his story may be, smuggling probably." Being generous and good natured she said simply, "I will introduce you to the right captain when he comes in, if he does." "A Dutch captain," said Max. "Yes he has a red license; he can go all the way from the Black Forest to the sea. If he comes in it will be about eight. Have some bread and pork rind with your beer while you wait." "Thank you," said Max as she turned away to deal with another customer.

It was about eight when the barge captain she was waiting for came in. "Max, this is Jan" she said. "Jan who if I may ask?" replied Max taking his hand. "Jan Van Rensburg," the short stocky man replied. "And who am I addressing?" "Max Rheinstein," was the answer. He should have given a false name, but did not. ""You must be Dutch," said Max. "Ya, how can I help you?" I have a dinghy I would like to have towed down the river to Amsterdam behind your barge," said Max. "What will be in the dinghy? I am not interested in smuggling." "Just my wife and I and our two suitcases." Jan's beer stopped half way to his mouth. He looked at Max steadily for a long moment. "There is some reason you do not just take the bus?" "I want to take my dinghy, and I cannot take it on the bus," replied Max. "Also I have no motor for it." "Towing a dinghy with two people in it would be most unusual. The coast guard on the border will certainly stop me and make me dock while they go through the formalities with you. It will take time, putting me off my schedule. I would not want to do that." "Could we ride in the barge with you?" asked Max. "Ya, that is possible, but the rules still require me to report all passengers to the authorities." "To the Dutch I do not mind," said Max. "And to the German border patrol?" asked Jan. "I would rather not," was the answer. "I do not know what your problem is," said Jan. "If you are not married to the woman you are with, that is one thing. If you are wanted for murder that is another." I am married to the woman I am traveling with, and I am not a murderer. It is my two sons who have just been murdered," Max blurted out with a break in his voice. "By whom and why?" "By a mob of hooligans," replied Max. The captain was no fool, he had read about mob attacks on Jews on Kristallnacht. His perception of Max changed immediately. This was no small time criminal, or hustler. Now he saw the pain, the unbearable sorrow, in Max's eyes. He said very kindly, "Let's move to that table over there, you can tell me about it."

Half an hour later the captain knew Max was telling him the truth. Had Jan been German Max would not have risked it. He knew it was a gamble, but he had to do something. The Dutch had a reputation for being neutral he reasoned; besides he had a good feeling about Jan. So it was agreed, he and Ruth would come to pier No 7 at five thirty the next morning and board the Sandvick before it left for the last leg of its run to Amsterdam with a load of coal. He and Ruth were to stay hidden in the small cabin. The border patrol made only spot checks and rarely stopped the Sandvick which was a regular.

Max was elated. He bought a salami sandwich and potato salad with a bottle of dark beer for Ruth, and hurried back with the good news. Now that the uncertainty was gone, their spirits rose enough to cure the empty, gnawing feeling in their stomachs. They very carefully set the wind up alarm clock for four thirty in the morning and paid their bill, saying they had to leave early. This was no surprise to the proprietor. Then they went to bed on the iron frame bedstead not noticing the stained mattress and chipped paint.

There was nothing dramatic about their flight in the cold darkness of the morning as they slipped silently along the streets like grey ghosts in the morning mist rising off the river. They found the Sandvick without difficulty. Jan made them sit down in the cabin so their heads stayed below window level. They were grateful for the hot coffee he gave them. Their suitcases he put in one of the rope boxes on the deck. Then he showed them the bilge trap door in the cabin floor. This gave access to a crawl space about two feet high next the engine. "If we are boarded this is where you must hide," said Jan. "If you cough or sneeze and are discovered I will deny all knowledge of you, saying you are stowaways." Ten minutes later they were on their way.

When they had been under way for about half an hour Jan said, "We are getting close to the border. If I am called on, I have to slow down while they come along side. They may or may or may not board, but I am not expecting to be called on." He was quite wrong. Ten minutes later a German police launch hailed them, "Barge Sandvick we are coming alongside to check papers. Have your cargo manifest ready." Jan grunted, "Can't they see I am carrying a load of coal? I don't recognize that voice. Get down there quickly," he said lifting the hatch in the cabin floor letting a waft of hot diesel and oil fumes fill the cabin. Max went down first and sat on his heels next the engine before shuffling sideways along it to make way for Ruth. Even squatting on their heels there was barely and inch of clearance above their heads. Then the hatch clicked shut above them and they were in total darkness feeling the thud, thud and heat of the engine, too hot to touch. Max wondered how long they could stand the heat and fumes and whether Jan could even hear them if they cried out. Then the note of the engine slowed measurably and they felt the bump of the police launch as it came alongside. Now that it was quieter, they heard a young mans voice saying, "I am Officer Hans Koch." "Goot morgen," replied Jan, "I do not recognize you." "I have just joined the river patrol," replied the young man proudly. "Saints preserve us from officious young men," thought Jan. But he said, "Here are my papers officer." "Take this rope and tie it to that bollard on your deck, I am coming aboard," said Hans Koch. "Welcome aboard," said Jan without enthusiasm. "Excuse me while I go to the wheel." Hans Koch studied the manifest without any idea what he was looking for. It said the barge was carrying a load of coal bound for the Gruithaven docks in Amsterdam. There was certainly plenty of coal on board heaped up in a black triangle rising several feet above the gunwale.

Not knowing what to do, Hans Koch walked over to the wheel house cabin, opened the door and handed the papers back to Jan. "May I see your barge captain's license?" he said. "Of course," replied Jan, thinking unprintable thoughts about young busy bodies without enough real work to do. "You drink a lot of coffee," said Hans Kock seeing the three mugs on the wheel house shelf. "Ya," replied Jan with a flash of fear, "I need it to keep me going when I start so early in the morning." Hans Koch looked around the wheel house which was about five feet by eight. He could see nothing amiss and did not ask himself why the captain did not use the same cup for his second cup of coffee. He was a city boy unfamiliar with boats. He was quite unaware of the bilge hatch he stood on. He looked out over the grey river, the heaped coal, and a sea gull sitting on the front rail. There was nothing for him to fix on. "These Dutch men are dull," he thought. "Very well Captain, you may proceed." "Thank you officer," replied the ever tactful Jan.

Once the police launch had cast off, Jan quickly opened the bilge hatch, much to the relief of Max and Ruth who were sweating heavily and half asphyxiated. Four hours later they were at the Gruithaven docks in Amsterdam. "We are forever indebted to you Captain," said Max. "May God protect you," replied Jan with feeling, wondering what it is like when you must go to strange lands with only a suitcase in your hand, uncertainty in front of you, and death behind you. He was a compassionate man.

The first thing Max did was hail a taxi and ask to be taken to the ferry offices. There he bought two tickets on the ferry to Dover leaving at 8.00am the next day. Then he and Ruth put their bags in 'left luggage' and set out to look for a cheap hotel in Amsterdam's red light district along the canals. He had heard of the plate glass windows letting you see into red velvet living rooms with only in-direct lighting and a woman ready to smile as you drew level with her window. She could watch you come up the street by means of a mirror angled out from the wall at the top of the window. He noted also the narrow houses with stable doors, the top open and the bottom closed, with a buxom woman leaning over it. Even if he had been alone he would not have been interested. It's just like I have heard it described, he thought.

The next morning they had a scare when they presented their passports for exit clearance from Holland as they prepared to board the ferry. The inspector flipped through them once, twice, then again. He looked up in frustration, "Where is the entry stamp?" he demanded. "I don't know," said Max adding, "All of us gave our passports to the bus driver when we reached the border yesterday. The driver presented them. Perhaps they had mislaid the stamp or missed ours by accident." "If you did not have English visas I would have to investigate," said the inspector. "But as you are leav-ing I suppose it does not much matter how you came in. You are not on my stop list." Here he was referring to the watch list of un-desirable and wanted people that all immigration control officers have at their finger tips. Ruth thought, "Thank God for Max. I feel so nervous and guilty I would stammer and stumble giving it all away." But all was well and in a few minutes their heart rates came back to normal.

In due course the ferry reached Harwich and Max mentally rehearsed his story for British immigration. When he presented their transit visas and reservations to Mombasa, Kenya on the Union Castle line he had no trouble. "Quite a few well to do chaps have gone out there you know," said the immigration officer pleasantly. "Good elephant hunting and wonderful climate in the highlands, much better than Tanganiyka where most of you Germans went." With these observations he sent them through cheerfully enough. From there it was a slow train ride to London's Kings Cross railway station where Max studied carefully the map of the underground rail lines across London. Ruth just followed where he led until they arrived at Waterloo station with its distinctive coal-smoke smell and blackened iron trusses. Fortunately, they were able to catch the four o'clock train from Waterloo to Southampton. There they knocked on the door of the first bed and breakfast they saw, and were happy to collapse in a room with twin beds, chintz curtains and a bathroom down the hall shared by all.

The Union Castle line, 'Empress of the Sea', sailed two days later for Malta, Alexandria, the Suez Canal, Mombasa and Capetown South Africa. Max and Ruth had a tiny cabin in steerage, well below the water line. Being so low down was an advantage when they hit stormy seas in the Bay of Biscay and the ship began to roll. The movement was less by half in the bottom of the ship. Even so they both felt very queasy and did not eat for a day. This they did not find to be a great hardship because the food, though edible, was as bland as only the English could make it. "How can they endure mashed potatoes, boiled peas and sausage day after day," thought Ruth. "At least our German sausages have taste and some meat in them, not just stale bread." The focal point of her good natured gripe, however, was the boiled strips of pork covered with bread crumbs and fried before being presented with a flourish as 'wiener schnitzel', accompanied by the inevitable boiled cabbage and mashed potatoes, varied occasionally with boiled turnip.

The passengers were, of course, predominantly English, or South Africans of English ancestry, and a few Boers. About a third were women and children, flesh and blood examples living to the marriage commitment, "Whither though goest I shall go;" in this case darkest Africa. Many were of the same mold as the men and women who settled the American West. Unlike today's young they did not expect to be given jobs, or welfare if they did not have a job. Those headed for Kenya intended to settle in the highlands, there to carve farms out of the bush and forest and bring the blessings of British civilization to those whom they perceived as illiterate savages. A surprising number were well educated country gentry bored with life in England. They were looking for adventure, and supported by the belief that they would be doing good bringing the skills and ideals of England to the natives. In the expansion of Empire, they followed the soldiers to build the railways, roads, farms, hospitals and towns of a modern state. They wanted to make a living, but believed that in so doing they would be bringing civilization to where it was needed.

One of such persons was the Englishman known to the Africans on his farm on Mt Elgon as Bwana Paws. As I have already told you, he was the son of the minister of the church in the tiny Suffolk village of Snailwell. He had grown up in The Old Rectory. Part of it was indeed six hundred years old. Fifteen years before Max and Ruth Rheinstein fled Germany; Bwana Paws had come to Kenya, ending a career as a gunnery officer in the British army. He had mistakenly believed that after World War I there would never be another major war. From this he concluded that there would be no excitement or promotion in the army. In the early nineteen twenties he discussed his career options with his childhood friend Tommy Howard de Walden. When there were difficulties in his family, Tommy had been sent to live with the minister in Snailwell for several years. Tommy and Bwana Paws became friends. Later Tommy inherited the title and became Lord Howard de Walden, a rather wealthy Englishman with extensive properties and a passion for big game hunting in East Africa. Lord Howard, as he was then known, suggested that his friend go to Kenya and manage his interests there. These included ten farms, some building land around Nairobi and a controlling interest in the colony's only daily newspaper the East African Standard. Part of the arrangement with Lord Howard de Walden was that Bwana Paws could own his own farm of 3,000 acres on the foothills of Mt Elgon. That was the farm where fate was to take Herr Doctor Rheinstein and his wife Ruth.

Max and Bwana Paws met by chance on the deck of the Empress of the Sea when it was tied up at Port Said, waiting for North bound traffic from Ismalia to clear the last stretch of the Suez Canal. It was still unbearably hot. The ship was not air conditioned. The cabins were stuffy little ovens. Most passengers, including Max and Ruth, suffered from prickly heat rashes. Taking a shower provided some relief, but fresh water showers were strictly rationed and too many salt water showers left you salt crusted and even more uncomfortable. So in the early morning, before the sun was too high, and late in the evening, all passengers were on deck, hanging over the rail hoping for a touch of cooling breeze.

The Arabs who preyed on tourists and travelers came alongside in little boats calling up to the passengers. "Hey Johnny, real silver, very cheap," as they held up tea pots and shiny bracelets made of tin. Another would be selling perfume allegedly made of ambrosia and beloved by Queen Victoria. Had the passengers been on the street one of the peddlers would have been extolling the delights of his sister described as, "White like Queen Victoria." They tended to be a little out of date in those pre transistor days when short wave radios worked on vacuum tubes. Then of course there were the usual carvings of Nefertiti's head and shoulders, green scarab beetles engraved with hieroglyphics that would cure all manner of diseases, model sphinxes, stone pyramids and all kinds of junk. Bwana Paws, hanging over the rail, said to his wife, "I'm glad they don't let them up on the boat." "Yes dear," she replied. "They are so persistent aren't they?" "All these Arabs from the bazaar are thieves," he replied. "They overcharge everything by three hundred percent. There's no decency in them. I think Arabs are born dishonest." To his great surprise the big man, with white hair and beard, standing beside them, said in a heavy German accent, "Nein, it is not in their genes. It is their culture." "I beg your pardon," responded Bwana Paws, "What did you say?" The big man with a deep voice continued, "They behave the way they do because they learn it as children, not because their blood is Arab." "You know about Arabs?" asked Bwana Paws skeptically. "I am a professor of anthropology in Frankfurt," was the reply. "We know about these things." "Well I wish you could change them. We've run the place for a long time and haven't been able to. Thieving scum." He added. The conversation soon drifted to where each was from and where he was going. Then introductions were made and the wives, carefully and uncomfortably, tried to establish if there was any common ground between them. From the English-woman's vantage point the first thing to establish was whether this German Frau, Ruth, knew how to behave correctly. She was quite convinced that only the properly raised English knew how to be-have correctly. If you did not answer your debutante party invita-tions in the third person you definitely did not belong in the club, whatever your merits as a human being might be. Nothing untow-ard occurred in the preliminary exchange of formalities so she reserved judgment. Had Ruth been English she would have been immediately stratified and classified by her accent. Only a speaker of Oxbridge English could be invited to dinner. Ruth's German accent hid her background, so it was hard to place her in or out of a socially acceptable category, which meant she stayed out. Not some one you could open up to.

As it took another eight days to get through the Suez Canal and down South to Mombasa, Bwana Paws and Max bumped into each other regularly on deck and gradually became acquainted. Bwana Paws needed a new farm manager for the farm he lived on, as well as another for one of Lord Howard's ranching properties. So it was not long before he said to Max, "What are your plans when you reach Kenya?" I don't really know," replied Max. "I am a refugee, so I must take what I can get, a teaching job perhaps." "I don't think so," replied Bwana Paws. "There are no universi-ties in Kenya and only one secondary school for Europeans. It is government run, and the government is pretty much appointed by the Colonial Office. They will not want a German with war on the horizon." "I am sure you are right," sighed Max. "Do you have any suggestions?" "Have you ever yoked an ox?" asked Bwana Paws. "I've seen it done on a farm in Silesia, but I have not worked on such a farm." "Pity" said Bwana Paws "But you can learn to do it in ten minutes. It's a job for the Africans anyway. How are you at handling men?" "Most of my life I have been teaching young men," replied Max, "I was trained in understanding why ancient man did what he did. Understanding the African will be no problem for me." "That's good, and I believe you," said Bwana Paws, "But there is one problem, you will have to learn Kiswahili. None of them speak any English, and for all of them too Kiswahili is secondary to their mother tribal tongue, Luo, Nandi, Kipsisgis and so on." "Are you telling me that there could be some way in which I could help you?" asked Max. Bwana Paws looked at this serious, solid man with a patriarchal appearance and made an instant decision saying simply, "Yes." On the plus side he saw an intelligent educated man who looked rugged and had held an important position as a university professor. From this he assumed Max was not given to drinking to excess and must be honest. What he did not know was whether this professor was too heavenly minded to be any earthly use. This was a risk he decided he had to take. This man was obviously well above a working class Englishman. Besides, when Bwana Paws had spent part of his military career in the British army of occupation on the Rhine, he had quite liked the Germans, especially a young woman, called Ingrid. He used to take her to the opera. So he launched into a description of what he did for Lord Howard de Walden in Kenya. The upshot of it all was that Max came to work for Bwana Paws, as farm manager on Mt Elgon, for a trial period of six months. Max and Ruth were as ecstatic as any refugees could be to find a house to live in, and work to do at a living wage. It was after the initial trial period of six months had passed, and he was comfortable with Kiswahili, that Max found himself talking to Simu at Chepnall cave. So now I must take you back to that cave.

Dogo

11. Mzungu

After Dogo was rescued from the two buffalo by Tumbo's mother, Simu realized that this first attack by buffalo in many years must have been inspired by Black Ice. He remembered then the *mganga's* words, "You are a simple man. Black Ice will send others to attack him." "Ah, it is true," he thought. When he brought Dogo back to Chepnall cave that evening and sat by his fire, Simu's soul was as black as the night outside the cave, but without any little points of starlight to give him hope. The wind came up and he listened to it sighing in the trees resonating with the choke in his throat. He realized that the *mganga* spoke truth; if the boy stayed in the forest he would surely die. If he loved him, he now began to accept that he would have to send the boy away from the forest, but it tore his heart in two. Caring for Dogo had become the focus of his life. He said to himself, "Why now that I love again is it to be taken from me. What have I done to be hurt so? I have lived within the rules of the forest never killing or damaging more than I needed to feed myself, always leaving enough bees alive in the nest to grow another hive. Why am I cursed?" As he sat on his rock by the fire, he curled his toes digging them in the dust of the cave floor, as he struggled with his thoughts. Painful as his sorrow was for the loss he must endure, there was an even worse thought; Dogo might be killed before he could send him to safety. "But where can I send him." He thought. "I do not know any people on the plains, only one two casual acquaintances by the *duka* and they are not of my tribe." The *duka* owner himself was a foreigner, an Indian. He was a man of low caste not to be trusted and unthinkable to raise an African child. All the other peopled he knew were his clan where Kisharani lived and it was Kisharani and his mother who had instigated Black Ice to set in motion the attacks on Dogo. Simu felt powerless in the face of malevolent forces he could not fight or run from. It was late in the night when he drifted into restless sleep filled with snatches of dreams of buffalo, pythons, mud and thorns, and serpents in the sky, all overshadowed by a looming darkness, like a thundercloud, depressing and ominous.

In the morning he decided that his only course was to hope that the second part of the *mganga's* prophesy would come true, the part when the *mganga* had said that the wind blowing around the world would bring a white haired *mzungu* to him who could save the child. At the time of the incident with the buffalo, Simu did not know that Max Rheinstein had already taken up a position as farm manager with Bwana Paws the husband of the *Memsahib* who had saved Dogo's life when she treated his burnt buttock with penicillin. The house Max lived in was about half a mile further down the mountain from the big white house with red roof where Bwana Paws lived. Had Simu known this he would have been much less worried. As it was he no idea when the *mzungu* would come, and there was always the nagging concern that he might not come soon enough, or possibly not at all, or even if he did come would he actually take the child. All he knew was that he had to keep Dogo alive, hope, wait for the *mzungu* and see what transpired.

That evening as they sat on stones by the fire one night, Simu tried to explain to Dogo his worries about Black Ice, but he had the feeling that Dogo understood and appreciated only immediate and visible threats, as when the buffalo had started towards them. An ongoing background danger that might not appear for a week or a month was not something he would worry about every day when he woke up. Despite his narrow escape Dogo was his usual cheerful self, saying, "Baba don't worry so much. Next time go a bit ahead of me so that I have more time to run away if you bump into something. The elephants won't hurt me, it's only the buffalo." "There are many other things bigger than you in the forest," said Simu. "Even some small ones can kill you quite easily. What if you get bitten by a cobra?" "You know that I leave snakes alone, Baba," replied Dogo truthfully. Conversation stopped abruptly when Bossy suddenly stood up and looked out into the darkness with an air of alarm, her nose twitching furiously. Simu reached instinctively for his *panga* as Dogo walked over to kneel by Bossy and stare into the darkness too. Simu's tension increased when Dogo stood up and ran into the dark with an excited cry. A moment later he half walked, half crawled, into the circle of firelight his arms tightly around Changa's neck. "Where have you been for so long? We missed you. Are you hungry?" Changa stopped by the fire to get warm, just like a regular dog, not a wild painted dog. With what looked to Simu like an enormous smile on his face he licked Dogo all over his head. He realized that it might have been a bit illogical, but Simu felt an intense sense of relief that Changa was back. If any one could smell or hear danger ahead it was he. Good though Dogos' sense of smell and hearing might be, he was still a child, and his sense of smell and hearing were far outclassed by Changa. Changa was a powerful hunter hardened by the wild. When at the cave he was very protective of Dogo. Few in the forest would bother Dogo if he were near. Simu smiled and felt good. He gave Changa the piece of meat he had been saving for tomorrow. Even Bossy gave a little Baa of acceptance. Hyena would not bother her with Changa around.

The next few days all was peaceful at the cave and Simu had much less trouble with Dogo being bored. In part this was because he had Changa for company and in part because Simu gave Dogo more freedom to leave the cave if he had Changa with him. This tranquility was not to last, however. The sun was half way up in the sky and Simu was making his second cup of *chai* that morning, somewhat gloomily wondering what to do about Dogo, when his thoughts were jarred into the present by the sound of a horse whinny and then another answering. It was a sound he had never heard before. It filled him with alarm. Were these some monstrous new creatures sent by Black Ice? The sound came from the path about two hundred yards below the cave. Fearful, worried and curious, Simu picked up his *panga* and spear and then, taking Dogo and Changa with him, slipped like a dark shadow through the trees down that very steep slope on the right side of the cave as you come out. He went around the lower chamber avoiding the normal path over the lower rocks for fear of being seen. When he was half way to the sound, he heard human voices. A wave of relief swept over him. Whether friendly or hostile, humans were within the realm of the known. That was much less fearsome than the unknown. Moving silently, he, Dogo and Changa crept through the underbrush until they could see two men and two large brown animals, each taller than a buffalo. Changa growled softly, but was silenced by Simu. He had heard of such animals, called '*farasi*', (horses) but had never seen one before. He had heard that the *wazungu* rode on them. The men were not riding them but holding the animals with ropes to their heads. When he saw the men Simu's stomach fell like the cold water off the cliff over his cave. He felt like a man condemned to die. A man with no hope, unaware of the dappled green and yellow leaves moving gently in the early morning sun and the butterflies flitting over the flowers. One of the men, the *syce* (groom), was black, but the second was a big *mzungu* with hair and beard as white as the snow that sometimes fell on the top of the mountain. Simu knew instantly that this was the man brought by the spirit of the wind that blows around the world, the man who could take Dogo. The time to break his own heart now seemed much nearer. He stood silent for several minutes, until Dogo whispered "Baba why are you crying?" Simu lifted a finger to his lips and did not answer.

The men tied the big animals to a tree with the ropes from the head. Then they started up the trail to the cave. The *syce* carried some sort of bag. The *mzungu* carried a rifle. It was common knowledge that these sticks that spat fire could kill you before you were in spear throwing range. So Simu decided to be very cautious until he knew what these men were about. He watched and stayed hidden as the men went up the trail and over the rocks to the cave. Arriving at the upper chamber, they looked at his fire and his tea in a blackened pot and knew that they had disturbed a man having his morning *chai*. Wondering if he was hiding in the forest or deeper in the cave the *mzungu* called out, "Jambo, come, we would talk with you". The *mzungu* leant his rifle against a rock, then they both sat down by his fire, rather brazenly it seemed to Simu. They waited for him to show himself. It was as one would wait for an animal to come again into the open after you have disturbed it. This was the first time any one had come to visit the cave. So Dogo was even more fearful than Simu. He had never seen a *mzungu* at an age when he was old enough to remember, though Simu had told him of them and their great power. He knew well the story of how a *mzungu* woman had healed him when he burnt his buttock. Like all his animal friends, Dogo was instinctively afraid of the new and strange. So he hung behind Simu with Changa, and hid when Simu decided to cough to draw attention and then show himself about fifty yards from the cave mouth. The men by the fire turned and saw him. The *mzungu* beckoned to him to come. Apart from this they just sat there quietly doing nothing, waiting for him to gain enough confidence to approach. They understood that he would be as hesitant and cautious as a wild animal you invite to feed from your hand. And so he was. Simu approached very gradually, ready for instant flight at any sudden or seemingly hostile movement. Finally when he came under the overhang of the cliff at the cave mouth, the *mzungu* smiled at him and motioned for him to sit, saying again "*Jambo, habari yako?*" or "Hello how are you?" Partly reassured, Simu sat very hesitantly and they began to talk, or rather, the *mzungu* talked. Dogo still hid with Changa, peeping from behind a rock fifty feet away, watching them.

The *mzungu* introduced himself as Bwana Max. In Frankfurt he had been known as "Herr Doctor." He thought of himself as an elevated person, and was not in the slightest bit embarrassed to attribute to himself the honorific title, "Bwana," or master. He introduced the man with him as Chegge, the man who cared for the horses, known in Kiswahili as a *syce*. This too meant nothing to Simu who knew nothing about horses. Apart from the formal courtesies of *Jambo, habari yako,* Simu volunteered nothing. In part this was because he was very nervous, but even more because he had no idea what to say to a *mzungu,* who might as well have come from Mars, for all that he had in common with him. So Max did the talking. First he explained that he came from Germany which Simu had never heard off. He assumed, correctly, that it was some place far away. Max said that he now worked on the farm of Bwana Paws. He did not know the Kiswahili words for farm manager, but it was common knowledge that Africans worked for the *wazungu* who did no work. So Simu knew that Max was in charge and gave the orders. It was Sunday, explained Max, so he did not have to work that day and had come to the forest. He said he was a teacher who studied things of long ago. He was interested in knowing how people lived, what stories they told and how magic affected their lives. He asked Simu how long he had lived in the cave. Simu answered, "Many years." Max asked, "Are you alone here?" "No," was the monosyllabic answer. "Who is with you?" asked Max. "A child," said Simu pointing to towards where Dogo was hiding. "Is the child's mother here?" asked Max, feeling a bit as though he were a police officer questioning a suspect. "No," was the answer again. This is hard work thought Max. "Will the child come to us if you ask him?" said Max. "He does not know *wazungu,* he is afraid," said Simu, speaking as much for himself as for Dogo. Max decided to change direction and for the moment give up questioning Simu about his family. He began asking about where Simu found food, and whether it had been raining much on the mountain. He had found that the British on the boat coming out to Kenya always made small talk about the weather, a good neutral subject that one could talk about without exposing anything about oneself. Simu responded better to this and Max learned that it had indeed been raining, but that in the dry weather the stream coming over the cliff above the cave would dry up and he would get water from the pool near the path below the cave. He then asked how Simu fed himself. "With *Ugali* and sometimes some meat from animals I trap in the forest," said Simu. "Do you grow maize?" asked Max. "No". "Then where do you get the *posho* (flour made of maize) to make your *ugali*?" "I buy it in Endebess," was the reply. "How do you get the money?" asked Max. "I sell salt rock I dig in this cave and take honey too," said Simu.

As Max was doing his best to get Simu to open up, Simu was more uncomfortable than Max. He was asking himself how he could talk to this white man about Dogo. He was not even sure that he wanted to. When face to face with a *mzungu* the vast gulf between them was very apparent to him. He felt very much as Max might have felt if he was meeting with a space alien and proposing to turn his child over to that alien. The world of the mzungu was a dark closed book to Simu. The unknown gave him great anxiety. How could he have any confidence that bad things would not happen. Would this man just sell the child into slavery? He had heard stories of slave caravans coming up the Karamoja trail past Endebess in years gone by. Would the child simply be made into servant, a scullery boy, known then as kitchen *mtoto*. Did the *mzungu* have a wife, how would she treat the child, and would she really want the child? How would the *mzungu* communicate with Dogo who spoke no Kiswahili? Would the child would be taught correct customs. Now that he began to actually think about the details of Dogo going to live with a *mzungu* outside the forest he began to understand how difficult and possibly dangerous it would be for

Dogo. It was only later that he began to worry about how difficult it might be for Max and whether he would want to do it. It had sounded so natural when the *mganga* spoke of it.

His thoughts were interrupted by Max asking him again if Dogo would come to them. "I do not think so," said Simu. Max knew from his anthropological studies that in societies where people are often hungry, sharing of food is a real demonstration of good will. So he reached over to the saddle bag the *syce* had carried up to the cave and took out a large tin which had on it a picture of a rugged looking naval man with a goatee beard, and an inscription reading "Capstan's cigarettes." Simu looked on curiously as Max opened the tin and took out what looked liked two sheets of white *ugali* shaped in a rectangle one on top of the other. It was in fact Max's lunch sandwich with butter and sliced chicken in it. Max cut it in half and handed one half to Simu. He saw at once that it was not *ugali* and was hesitant to eat it even though Max said, "Eat it is good." Max picked up the other half and munched on it to demonstrate that it was edible. Simu fingered his half, smelt it, then broke off a little piece and chewed on it like a squirrel might. It did taste good. So Simu nodded his head in appreciation and Max said, "Give a little to the child." Simu hesitated to expose Dogo to things from the world of the *wazungu,* but then thought he might as well see if Dogo liked *wazungu* food. So he walked over to where Dogo was hiding behind his rock, took a bite out of the half sandwich, to lead the way so to speak, and gave the rest to Dogo repeating, "Eat, it is good." Dogo came out of hiding. Changa, smelling food, came too and lifted his head to sniff at what was left of the sandwich as Dogo tasted it. Max watched with curiosity wondering why this boy had no mother. How he had come to have as a companion a wild dog, bigger and more dappled in color than the usual African village dog. The pricked up ears with rounded tops gave Changa a distinctive look. Max had not heard of wild dogs becoming domesticated. He did not realize that Changa was still mostly wild not relying on man for food. Then Max noticed Dogo sharing a piece of the sandwich with Changa. The affectionate lick

Changa gave in return told Max this was a close relationship. He watched as Simu spoke to Dogo and then beckoned him to follow Simu back towards the group by the fire. Dogo and Changa both came, but hesitantly and cautiously, as skittish as wild gazelles, on their toes, treading lightly, ready for instant flight. Max sat quite still, waiting until Simu sat down again by the fire with Dogo and Changa, both curious and nervous, a few feet behind him.

When they had settled down, Max reached again into the Capstan cigarette tin and brought out a piece of English toffee of the hard brown sticky kind. As with the sandwich, he broke it in half with some difficulty and held one piece out as an offering as he looked directly at Dogo saying, "Come it is tasty." Dogo did not answer in part because he did not understand, not speaking Kiswahili, and in part because he was nervous and overawed by these strangers. He made no move to take the toffee. So Simu did if for him, going through the same routine as with the sandwich, smelling and tasting it before giving it to Dogo. Changa pricked up his ears hopefully as Dogo took the toffee, but turned away as soon as smelt it, knowing there was no meat here. For his part Dogo had never tasted anything so good. He licked his lips very much as Changa would have done for piece of meat. It was the ice-breaker Max intended. Dogo now came and stood beside Simu looking with great curiosity at the long white hair, and sun browned hands and face, of this peculiar looking man, as strange to him as a white buffalo would have been. Even more peculiar were his eyes. They were the color of the smoke that rises from a bush fire. It was as though you could see through them and yet see nothing.

Trying to be friendly, Max asked Dogo his name and received a blank stare. "He does not speak Kiswahili," said Simu, "I call him Dogo." "Do others call him some thing else?" asked Max, wondering why Simu did not just say, "His name is Dogo." "I do not know," replied Simu. "Why is that?" asked Max. "Because I found the child in the forest when his mother died and I do not know who she was or who his father may be." "What is your name?" asked Max once again feeling a bit like an interrogator. "They call me *mtu wa shimu"*, (man of the cave), replied Simu somewhat evasively not revealing his given name. "Who do you mean by 'they," asked Max. "The people at Endebess," replied Simu. "Is that where your family live?" "No," said Simu, my family live up on the mountain and he gestured towards the Koitobos peak way above them on the crater rim. "I would like to meet them," said Max. Simu said nothing, so Max changed direction again. He told Simu that he would come again next week, and if Simu would tell him about his family and let him explore the cave, he would bring *chai* and sugar and give it to him. Simu said nothing, but wondered if this *mzungu* knew that fate had sent him to this cave to give him the opportunity to help Dogo if he chose to do so. He had no doubt that the *mzungu* could know this if he but asked one of his witchdoctors, but had he done so? If he did know, then what did he think about it? Did he have children of his own? If he did then would he really want to bring into his family an African child? Simu knew that most people do not want to raise other people's children. He had taken on Dogo only because his own family had died and Bending Twig urged him to. If his own family had been alive he would not have begun to consider it. As a *mzungu* this man could obviously afford a wife, perhaps more than one. It was very likely that he had children of his own and would not want to mess up his family with a strange child. As these thoughts went through Simu's mind, he looked in the face of this big bluff white haired, white man and tried to bring himself to ask the *mzungu* directly all that he wanted to know. But he could not bring himself to do it. One did not ask such questions of a stranger. The *mzungu* had, in fact, been far too forward in his questions, but then it was well known that *wazungu* did inexplicable things. So Simu just nodded his head as he listened to Max without paying too much attention to what he was saying. When the *mzungu* stood up and said goodbye Simu did likewise. Then Max and the *syce* disappeared down the steep slope towards the path.

After Max and the *syce* left, Simu tried to answer Dogo's excited questions. "Why did a *mzungu* come to their cave, where did *wazungu* come from, what was the white food the *mzungu* had given them, could Simu get any more of the small brown food that tasted a little bit like sugar cane?" and so on. To most of the questions Simu answered quite truthfully that he did not know. What he did not tell Dogo was that a *mganga* had foretold the coming of the *mzungu* and had also said that Dogo would have to leave the forest with the *mzungu* to be safe. Simu was pleased that the first part of the *mganga's* prophecy had come to pass. He had been waiting, hoping, but not sure, that it would happen. The arrival of the *mzungu* made the *mganga's* prophecies entirely credible. Up to that time one could have explained the attacks on Dogo as natural occurrences. Now that the *mzungu* had come as foretold, Simu found in that fact confirmation of the reality of Black Ice being behind the attacks. But this logic took him where he did not want to go; the attacks would continue and he had to send Dogo out of the forest to save him. He had half accepted this already, but now faced the reality of doing it. He hesitated, partly out of concern for his own loss and partly due to anxiety whether the dangers to Dogo would be as great with the *mzungu* as they would be in the forest. Would the child really be better off with this *mzungu*? Was it truly in the child's best interests? He thought he was doing a good job raising Dogo. Simu was far too close to Dogo to see or understand the limitations and distortions that the *mganga* had said made Dogo a misfit in the forest, an anomaly to be removed by Black Ice. What was wrong with the child? His survival skills in the forest and bush craft were superb for a child his age. He was quick and athletic. He could track animals almost as well as Simu. He was helpful and mindful around the cave. He seemed to be a quick learner. He was brave and not fearful. Could a *mzungu* really do any better than he? So, despite his underlying decision, Simu was ambivalent about surrendering Dogo to this *mzungu*. As it turned out events, soon to come, were to make the decision much easier for him.

As he had said he would, Max came back to Chepnall cave the next weekend. He wanted to because he was a professor whose first degree was in anthropology. He had a deep interest in what he saw as a primitive man. For him, Simu was a rare find, a man who actually lived in a cave, almost as a hunter gatherer. Max left the *syce* to watch the horses, thinking, correctly, that Simu might be more talkative if Max were alone. As he had promised, Max brought a pound of tea, the local brand being then known as '*Simba Chai*,' or lion tea. He also brought two pounds of sugar and half a dozen pieces of English toffee. The tea and sugar he presented to Simu as a gesture of friendship and goodwill. Simu was at first reluctant to accept them, not knowing what he would be morally obligated to give in return for such a generous gift. He was a man of pride and character, not yet cynical enough to take whatever he could get, and certainly not imbued with the culture of 'entitlement' that later came to be so ardently advocated by intellectual elites in developed countries. Simu was a self respecting man who did not think of himself as a beggar, so he naturally expected to give in return for what he received. But he was relieved, as he gradually came to understand that all this *mzungu* wanted, in return for his gifts, was Simu's life story. Tea and sugar for his story was a bargain he could accept with dignity. Without Simu being consciously aware of it at that moment, Max had opened the door to Simu telling Dogo's story. All Simu had to do was follow the lead Max gave him.

As Max came up the path to the cave, he was surprised to meet a goat coming down. It was a black and white goat with two surprisingly straight, horns. The goat stopped and looked at him curiously, then recognizing his smell from the week before just carried on browsing by the path. As he looked at Bossy, out of the corner of his eye, Max caught sight of a movement higher up the slope. Turing to look, he saw nothing until Changa moved his head. Max would have felt more comfortable if Changa had growled or barked in alarm, but he did not. Without showing any fear or concern he studied Max as a hunter would its prey. Max found that baleful stare quite unnerving. Another movement of leaves gave Max a glimpse of Dogo watching him too. Max felt a little bit alone, a white man with an urban background being watched in a strange forest. Unconsciously holding his rifle a bit more tightly, Max went on up to the cave. He did not see the Colobus monkey hidden in the branches of the cedar tree near the mouth of the cave. There was no one beside the gently smoking cave fire. As he looked around for Simu, Max heard the noise of a pick on rock coming from deep within the cave, so he called out *"Jambo,"* several times and then sat down to wait by the fire. Coming out of the darkness of the cave, Simu saw the outline of the big *mzungu* silhouetted against the window of light at the mouth. He came out slowly and carefully, gaining confidence as he came to see that the *mzungu* was alone. As before he coughed to alert the *mzungu* to his presence. Max turned, but did not see him in the dark. He just beckoned towards the blackness. When Simu reached him, Max went through the usual formalities of greeting and then suggested that he make a new brew out of the *chai* he had brought so they could share it. With some foresight for his own tastes, Max had brought his own white enamel mug, some sweetened condensed milk in a tin, and a spoon. From an anthropological point of view he was a little disappointed that Simu had a much blackened kettle and saucepan of obvious European design. The knee high reddish black earthen-ware pot full of water off to one side of the fire looked more like the real thing however. It's like a Roman amphora but without the handles he thought. The only other utensils lying on a rock were a well worn wooden handled knife, a flat wooden spoon like a spatula, a small clay bowl from the same place as the earthen-ware pot and two cups made from large bamboo stems. He eats with his hands thought Max, seeing no fork or real spoon. Had Max looked more closely among the many pebbles on the cave floor he would have found stone age knives and scrappers used by the people who lived in the cave forty thousand years before the beginning of recorded history. These were the ancestors of *homo sapiens* as we know him today. This would have excited Max had he found them, but that day his attention was focused on the living.

Max used his own spoon to put three measures of loose tea leaves in the kettle half filled with water. When it came to a boil the tea was quite dark and the leaves sank to the bottom when he let it stand a minute. Max poured the tea in one bamboo cup and his own enamel mug. Then he stirred in some condensed milk and two spoons of sugar. One tea leaf floated to the top of his mug. "I'm going to get a letter or meet some one new," thought Max remembering a saying learned at his mother's knee. The two men barely spoke as Max made the *chai*. To many the silence would have been uncomfortable, but not to Simu who had lived alone for so long. As one man would respect another, he gave Max the time to do his thing without comment. Max sensed that this man did not wish to chatter like a woman, so he held his questions and prepared his offering of friendship in silence. When he was done, he held out the bamboo cup and said to Simu, "Try it." Simu took a sip after blowing on the cup to cool it. Apart from his honey he had never tasted anything so sweet and good. "*Tamu sana,*" (sweet, very) he said nodding his head in approval. Max reached down and moved the brown paper bag with the sugar, the bag of loose tea and the condensed milk to Simu's side of the fire. "I said I would give you these if you would talk to me," said Max. "*Ni sawasawa,*" replied Simu, meaning, "that is acceptable." Max was pleased. His ever active mind was looking forward to something other than corn, cattle, machinery and managing a large labor force on the farm. In this cave he was experiencing in the now what he had only read about in his college anthropological studies.

On a hunch, he took a piece of toffee out of his Capstan cigarette tin and held it up. Without turning round he said to Simu, "Tell the child to come and get it." Simu beckoned to Dogo who was watching them from a rock about twenty feet behind Max. But as he did so he was impressed. How did the *mzungu* know the child was there? He said nothing as Dogo came very hesitantly to join them. Max smiled at Dogo and said "*Jambo.*" Dogo took the toffee from Simu, put it in his mouth and said nothing, keeping a cautious eye on Max. Max turned to Simu and started with the practical not the philosophical. "Where do you sleep?" he asked. Simu nodded his head toward the interior of the cave. "I would like to see it," said Max. Without saying a word, Simu stood up and started towards the darkness. Max reached in his saddle bag and took out a torch to light his way. Just where the light ended the roof of the cave came down to head height and the floor rose on the right to a platform coming up to just below Max's waist. The similarity to the second shelf in a giant chest of drawers was broken by two man sized pieces of rock jutting down from the volcanic tuff of the roof to touch the bottom of the shelf. Good support for the roof thought Max as he went on his hands and knees. Half crawling half crouching, he followed Simu into where he had built his rock *boma.*. The roof was up about four feet and black with the smoke of many fires. The front was walled off by a small fence of woven sticks, except for a narrow entrance. The fence came curving back a few feet into the *boma* making a shape like a capital C. From the droppings on the floor Max saw immediately that this was where the goat slept. Towards the back Max saw the sleeping places of Simu and Dogo with a couple of very brown blankets, two baskets woven from tree roots taken from where they trailed in a river and Simu's spear. In that quick look round Max had the impression these were all Simu's worldly possessions.

Coming out of the *boma* Max said, "Show me where you dig." Simu took him to the left side of the cave where the roof was high enough to allow one to stand up and walk a surprisingly long way into the back. There he saw Simu's pick looking like a giant six inch nail on the end of a stick. Max noted the pick marks on the wall and the roof. The volcanic tuff seemed quite soft for rock, except where there were football size chunks of black lava and light colored pieces of fossilized wood, the branches of trees shattered in some giant volcanic explosion millions of years before. He noticed many such pieces lay on the floor along with quite a few animal bones. "What are these?" he asked Simu. "Leopard ate them," was the answer. Max was not sure if the bones were old and predated Simu living in the cave, or whether leopard shared the cave with Simu. Probably these are old and were left here before Simu came, he thought. But now he understood the spear lying where Simu slept and the thick thorn branch that he pulled into the doorway at night. Max was in his shirt sleeves. The interior of the cave felt a bit too cool for comfort but not cold. Max imagined that the temperature did not vary very much and that it would be much warmer than being out in the open on a starry night when he knew there was often frost on the grass in the morning. It's amazing he thought how cold it can get on the equator when you are at 8,000 feet.

The inspection of the cave over, they came back to the fire at the front. The sun seemed brighter, the leaves greener and the sky bluer as they came from darkness into light and sat near the water fall over the forty foot high arch of the cave mouth. It is friendlier in the light thought Max, but still a very remote and wild place. How did this man come to live here like a hermit, he wondered? So he asked Simu. "You told me your people live high on the mountain above the forest, so why did you come to live in this cave?" "There was a sickness in our clan," said Simu. "My wife and three children died. I thought I would too. I did not want to live so I came to this cave expecting to die, but I did not. When my grief passed I wanted to live, but my heart told me that I lived only because I had come to this cave. So I stayed." "Do you visit now with your people?" asked Max. "Yes, I sometimes I go take honey to my niece." "Is the child with you now, part of your family from above the forest?" said Max. "No, but he is my family, he is all I have" said Simu. "I must tell you about him." As Simu said this, a tear ran down his cheek because he knew where this conversation would end. Max was quite disconcerted, feeling guilty that he might be treading where angels fear to tread. He wondered if the child had some fatal illness that was not apparent on first meeting. Why else would talk of the child cause such emotion? "If you must tell me," said Max, "then start at the beginning. How did you come to find him in the forest?" So Simu gathered his composure and started with Bending Twig coming to him. Then he told the story as I have told it to you, filling in details along the way as Max asked questions to get a better understanding. Max listened with fascination, and anthropological excitement, to the story of Bending Twig leading Simu to the child lying on its dead Mother under a podo tree, of the rescue from Hyena, the bringing of Bossy the nanny goat to Chepnall cave as a wet nurse, the attack on Dogo by the python, the visit to the *mganga*, his prophesy of Dodgo's death, and troubles with Kisharani.

An hour and a half later, Max sat on his rock by the dying fire, overwhelmed by the enormity of the implications of what he had heard, told so genuinely, so earnestly and at the end with so much sadness. He had come to the cave as an archaeologist to amuse himself on a Sunday afternoon as a digression from farming. Now he was presented with a story the truth and sincerity of which he did not doubt, but one that might make him a key player in a drama scripted by forces not only beyond his understanding, but in contradiction of the 'scientific method' with which he had been raised. He had wanted to study superstitions and myth. He was quite mentally unprepared to become part of them. He said to Simu, "So you think I am the *mzungu* brought on the wind that blows around the world." "There is no other *mzungu* here but you," said Simu matter of factly. Max had to admit to himself that there were very few *wazungu* in the Trans Nzoia district of Kenya at that time, and he not yet seen a *mzungu* matching his description either at the Kitale Club or at the rail head loading cattle. At that moment Bossy came into the cave and lay down not far away. Max found himself looking for blood on her horns. Then he looked at Dogo who had said nothing and did not seem in the slightest bit disturbed. Max wondered at this for a moment, until he remembered that Dogo spoke very little Kiswahili. He said to Simu, "How much of this does the child know?" "I have told him of the danger he is in from Black Ice, but I have not yet told him about you, my pain is too great." "I understand," said Max, "do not tell him until I know what I am going to do. That I cannot tell you until I have spoken to my wife." "You do not make the decisions?" asked Simu in surprise. "Caring for a child is a decision I cannot make without her consent, it is a decision for both of us." Simu was still surprised, but then it was well known that *wazungu* were strange. "You will speak to her?" asked Simu. "Of course," said Max. "Now I must go and talk to her." As Max started back down the hillside to the path where the horses were, he glanced back and saw a large black and white colobus monkey with Dogo at the cave mouth. He knew with complete certainty that it was Bending Twig, and marveled that such a thing could be. Christian theology had taught him that man stood apart from animals, on a higher plane, complete in the image of God himself, created not evolved. Now he began to see through the eyes of this cave man that, many centuries ago, man began his journey as one of the animals of the forest, in tune with a world of trees, other animals, and natural and forces beyond his comprehension. His story must true he thought. "How did that *mganga* know I was coming?" he asked himself. A shiver ran through his body as he passed under the trees and thought of Black Ice. It came from subliminal fear, not the cool of the forest. Max knew this and thought, "Like Simu, I am afraid of what I do not understand."

Two hours later as he came back the manager's house on the farm the dogs rushed out barking. Dusk was falling. Uncharacteristically, he ignored them being much too preoccupied with his thoughts. He gave the reins of his horse to the *syce* and sent him off to the stable. Then, as if in a dream, he crossed the verandah into the house forgetting to take off his shoes as he went in. Ruth was in the living room knitting in a large overstuffed arm chair. This was on one side of the stone fireplace where the house boy Kiprono had lit a fire. A pressure kerosene lamp hissed and glowed with a bright white light. It was at head height on a lamp stand. Electricity was unknown on the farm. She looked up as Max came in and said, "Did you have a good day mein liebe?" "I have had an extraordinary day," replied Max quietly and thoughtfully, as he sat heavily in the arm chair on the other side of the fire place. "That man in the cave, he opened up to me today and told me his life story.

The child I saw, when I first went there, is not his child. He found it in the forest by its dead Mother. He talks to monkeys. We have to take it, the witch doctor said so." "Slow down, let me get you a Tusker, and start at the beginning," interrupted Ruth. "What's all this about witch doctors, monkeys and a child?" "More than that," said Max. "Its also about a goat, a half wild painted dog, a python and a cold black spirit that lives in the Suam gorge just off the mountain crater until he comes out at night." "That's quite a menagerie," said Ruth. "My dear, this man Simu, and the child Dogo, may be a bridge to another world. The mythology is different, but I have met a man who experiences the spirit world in the same way that the Greeks did, or the old Germanic tribes, for that matter. For him, it is as real as a dream is to us, as we dream it." "Begin at the beginning and then tell me what this man told you, so that I can follow you better. This sounds like your place of anthropological dreams where time is never planned," said Ruth with a smile.

So Max spend the next half hour retelling the story to Ruth. Just as he finished his Tusker, Kiprono knocked on the door, and was bid come in by the one word, '*Karibu*'. He announced that the Bwana's bath was ready. "Go get cleaned up, we can talk over dinner," said Ruth. It was their custom to take a bath before dinner to wash off the dust or mud, as the case might be, of a day on the farm. A change of clothes, from shorts to trousers and a long sleeved shirt, drew a sartorial line between the master who ate the dinner and the servant who prepared it. Max was quite comfortable with this. In Germany he had been, 'Herr Doctor'. Pretending that all were socially equal would have been, for him, a deliberate distortion of the reality of things, just at it would have been for Kiprono. He spoke no English or German, so Max and Ruth felt free to talk at dinner even as Kiprono hovered at the end of the room waiting to clear their plates or fill a glass with more water. After a hot dry day, two or three refills might be necessary. Against this background of structure and routine, Max and Ruth talked of Simu and Dogo, without being fully aware of the profound changes that were about to occur, particularly in Ruth's life.

While grateful to be safe from Hitler and the Nazis, Ruth was also lonely and bored. The house work was done by Kiprono and the cooking by Ochieng. There was no book store to attend to, no customers to talk to. Bwana Paws' house was a mile away. His wife was correct rather than warm, and did not share her hopes and dreams with her. Conversation with the Africans was limited. None of them could read and write. Their conversation did not go beyond what they experienced, the weather, the land, cattle, snakes, rats, pains and illnesses, conflicts and witchcraft. Their only common language was Kiswahili, limited to a vocabulary of about eight hundred words as was to be expected when one cannot read or write. Did they even know that the world was round? Germany was just a place name. They thought it looked like Kitale, the only town, village really, that some of them had seen. She could not talk to them of the things that were important, or interesting to her. She knew the Swahili word for 'fight', but not one for war, country, nation, politics, concepts that were not part of language in an illiterate tribal society. What she could share with the Africans Ruth enjoyed, but she needed something more to interest her, to occupy her mind while she waited to see when it might be safe to return to Germany. During the flight from that country she did not have much time to miss Benjamin and Aaron. Now with time on her hands, having no teenagers to manage was an aching void. She did not envisage the cataclysm of World War II, but had she done so, it would not have changed what happened on Mt Elgon. Without being consciously aware of it, as she talked to Max about Simu and Dogo that evening, Ruth was ready to bring some thing more into her life, and she did.

"Simu believes the *mganga*. He believes that Black Ice will kill the child if we do not take him out of the forest. How do you see it?" asked Max. "Has he actually asked you to take the child?" asked Ruth, anticipating where Max was going. "Not in so many words," said Max. "He just recounted what the *mgana* said, that a *mzungu* with white hair would come and take the child and protect it. I wonder how the *mganga* knew that I would come? I doubt I had even arrived on Elgon when Simu went to see him." "Perhaps the *mganga* was thinking of Bwana Paws," replied Ruth. "Bwana Paws is a *muzungu* with dark hair, not white hair," said Max. Besides the *mganga* lives several hours walk along the mountain. Does he even know that Bwana Paws exists?" "You think the *mganga* really did see part of the future?" queried Ruth. "Yes," said Max. "I do not know how he did it, but I think he did. If he was right about me coming, then he is probably right about Black Ice and Dogo also. Bossy is Dogo's protector. She protected him from the python and an elephant protected him from the buffalo. I do not pretend to understand the mark of the cross in the elephant's footprint, just that it is, it's probably a co-incidence." "So you want to live to the prophesy?" asked Ruth. "I think so," replied Max. "Then the first thing you have to do is get Simu's unequivocal consent, and the second thing is you have to get mine, if I am going to take this boy into my home," said Ruth firmly. "Then please come with me to see Simu." And so it was set.

Later that evening when Ruth turned on her side to give Max a good night kiss, she was surprised and puzzled that his cheek was wet. For a moment she thought he must have washed his face, but remembered instantly that he had not. "What moves you so?" she whispered in the dark. "I don't know," he answered. "It is just a great sadness I feel, but I am alright," he added hastily. He lay silent and Ruth waited, not knowing what to say. Max went on, "Perhaps I see in Simu's story our own loss of Benjamin and Aaron and I cry for that. Perhaps I cry for Dogo who knew only a goat as a Mother." Ruth rolled over, put her cheek against his, and held him, her warmth running all the way down his body. Ruth felt her own tears as she said, "If we do it, then it will be to save the child. I cry for our loss, but also for this child whom the *mganga* says must lose all that he has ever known in order to live. I pray to God that we will do what is right." They lay in silence until Max said, "I am a product of universities, books and education, bricks and mortar, but today I had a glimpse of a man who experiences things on the cusp between nature and man; things supernatural that my educated mind does not want to accept. Man has always believed in, and been afraid of the spirit world. As a child I was afraid of the dark. That was an atavistic fear. Now, as I see in Simu, this man in a cave, the origins of myself, I am moved by a painful joy, as one who finds his roots might be moved. That too is why I cry." "I cry for my memories," said Ruth simply not really understanding him. So they slept.

Chepnall Cave

12. Leaving Chepnall Cave

After Max' second visit to Chepnall cave, Simu felt less anxious. He had told the *mzungu* the whole story. He knew of the need to save Dogo. There was nothing more he could do while the *mzungu* talked to his wife and they made up their minds. Simu worried that they might say no, but this was only a moderate anxiety because the *mganga* had inferred that they would take Dogo. A greater worry was that the *mzungu* might not decide for several weeks and in the mean time Dogo was at risk from Black Ice. So two weeks later when he went to the *duka* at Endebess to trade salt rock, he took Dogo with him. Bossy, as usual, remained at the cave with Bending Twig near by. Changa started to come with them, but Simu told him to stay as he always did, for fear that some one would recognize him as a wild dog and try to kill him. Changa accepted this but decided to go hunting. It was an exciting day for Dogo who for the first time carried a small pack of salt rock he could sell for himself. He was elated when he traded it for a box of matches. Dogo had been told of them by Simu, but had never before held these tiny sticks that could make fire. The concept of instant fire was amazing and fascinating; much faster and easier than using two sticks. So Dogo trotted along happily beside Simu clutching his box of matches as they made their way back to Chepnall cave. It was a dark overcast afternoon. Giant cumulus clouds were piled high across the sky threatening rain with their dark bases. So Simu and Dogo hurried towards home. They were nearly back having climbed up the to the podo trees by the elephant path just below the Bluff. It was very close to where Bending Twig had first seen Dogo as a baby. They were both very surprised to see Bending Twig racing up to them in great agitation. "Its awful, it's dreadful," she said. "What's awful?" asked Simu. "Its Bossy, she is in a tree." Simu tried to visualize this, knowing that when an elephant had pushed over a tree Bossy might walk along the trunk so she could browse on the leaves. "Did she fall and hurt herself? Simu asked. "No she's dead, she's dead and hung up in a tree." Simu's stomach felt as if a big stone had been dropped in it. Dogo let out a wail, "No baba! No!" "Where?" asked Simu. "Not far from the cave. The leopard did it. I hate him." This had the absolute ring of truth in it. Leopard always dragged his kill, or what remained of it, into a tree to keep it away from hyena and other scavengers. They broke into a jogging run and were sweating and panting when the reached the scene. The full impact of what had happened did not hit Dogo until he saw the half eaten body twenty feet above the ground. But, Simu knew instantly that Black Ice had struck again, removing the guardian that had saved Dogo from the python.

Simu climbed up the tree with some difficulty and dislodged the remains of the body. Only the head and shoulders remained. Just the shape of the head and horns told him it was indeed Bossy, let alone the black and white markings on her face. Dogo clung to the horns he had held so often before. Tears rained down his face as he looked with great distress at the wide staring eyes that blinked no more. He struggled with Simu as he tried to put what was left of the body in his salt rock bag until Simu gently said to him, "Let me take her home." When they arrived he covered the remains with big stones to protect them. He built a bigger fire than usual that night and asked Bending Twig to spend the night with him and Dogo in the little rock *boma*. Bending Twig did not want to. She loved the open tree tops and was claustrophobic in the cave. She had never slept there. But Dogo wept and clung to her so tightly she overcame her fear and did sit with him near the fire until it was nearly dark, doing her best to give him a little comfort, while Simu nursed his own sorrow. Being a solitary soul at heart, he did not feel the need to deal with his sorrow by un-burdening himself to another as so many do. Had he been able to do so it would probably have helped. But that was not to be. To Dogo's question of, "Why Baba, why?" he had only one unsatisfac-tory answer, "Black Ice." "What did Bossy do that she had to die?" demanded Dogo. Simu did not explain to Dogo that he was the ultimate target, that Bossy had been killed to make it easier to get at Dogo. He just answered, "It is in the nature of things." He did not want to burden Dogo with any sense of guilt for Bossy's death. But it was only now that Bossy was gone that Simu realized how a much a part of his life she had been.

His thoughts were interrupted by the return of Changa who appeared out of the twilight. Dogo enveloped him with his arms and cried until his neck was wet. He knew something was wrong, he could feel the tension. His response was to lick Dogo's face. Then Simu called him over to the pile of rocks against the wall of the cave. Changa smelt blood and knew what had happened even before Simu pulled the stones aside. He sniffed the body for only a moment and immediately caught the thick heavy smell of leopard. He looked up at Simu his teeth bared in a snarl. A low rumbling growl came from his throat. He and his kind had no love of leopard but Changa knew he could not fight him alone. Leopard was more than twice the size of a painted dog. A pack would chase leopard up a tree, but one dog alone stood no chance. Simu put the rocks back and went back to the fire. That night Dogo curled up next to Changa in Bossy's space in their rock *boma*. Simu did not expect leopard to come for the rest of his kill that night. His belly was full and would be for a couple of days. Never the less Simu made sure his spear was to hand beside him as he slept.

The next day was Sunday. Max did not have to work, so he had the *syce* saddle up three horses to go to Chepnall cave. They were English saddles of course in a British colony, one each for Max and Ruth, and one for the *syce* himself. The previous afternoon Ruth had gone into the kitchen and made more small squares of English toffee from brown sugar. The *Memsahib* cooking on the wood stove in the kitchen had made Ochieng distinctly uncomfortable; as though he were some how failing in his duties. Besides the kitchen was space for servants not the master or mistress. Ruth was aware of this but decided it was easier to do it herself than teach Ochieng how to. In the morning she almost filled the Capstan cigarette tin with toffee. She also packed extra lunch sandwiches in a brown paper bag, along with an extra mug, the spoon and the usual tea, condensed milk and sugar. She was excited and looking forward to meeting the cast of characters that Max had described to her, Simu, Dogo, Bossy, Bending Twig, and the painted dog Changa.

It was mid morning when they arrived on the path below Chepnall cave. There they left the *syce* with the horses and Max took the back pack and rifle as he led Ruth up over the rocks for her first visit to the cave. Its mouth looked dark and mysterious to Ruth, as she came out from under the trees and looked up the little green valley through the bright sunshine. She felt a mounting sense of anticipation and curiosity as she scrambled up the slightly muddy path and then over some head high rocks. She was glad she had chosen to wear trousers that day as there were tall nettles by the path. As they approached the cave mouth a small black child appeared and fled into the forest. Ruth was immediately taken aback by the fact that the child was completely naked. It was not that unusual in Africa at that time, but Max had not mentioned it, so it came as a surprise. The second surprise was that Simu looked smaller and older than she had expected. "Why did I expect a noble savage, a big strapping warrior?" she said to herself. She sat on a stone by the fire at the cave mouth and was silent as Max went through the formal ritual of, "Jambo, what is your news?" and the required response, "Jambo, my news is good, and what is your news?" Max then introduced Ruth as his, '*Memsahib*, who had come to talk to Dogo. If Max had said that he brought Ruth to carry firewood back to his house, Simu would have understood perfectly. As it was, he was surprised that Max had taken the trouble to bring a woman into the forest for any other purpose. Simu did not see this small brown haired woman as part of the *mganga's* prophesy, or as being important to Dogo or himself. But he remembered that Max had told him she too must agree if they were to take Dogo, so he was ready to humor her. Max started making small talk to Simu being unaware of the crisis that lay so heavily on Simu's mind. Max also wanted to give Ruth the opportunity to direct the conversation as she might wish.

As it was, Ruth paid no attention to Max's small talk conversation with Simu about the weather, honey hunting and when he might go up the mountain to see Simu's clan including Kisharani and Simu's niece Maziwa. Ruth's interest was in the child that she could now see peeping out of the undergrowth about fifty yards away. She rummaged in the back pack and came up with the Capstan cigarette tin and brought out a piece of the English toffee she had made. She then walked casually across the cave mouth to where the entrance on one side merged in to the forest. She ostentatiously put the toffee on a big stone then walked back and sat down by the fire to watch. She expected Dogo to remember the toffee Max had brought and come to get it. She drew her breath in with surprise as a big black and white colobus monkey came, seemingly out of no-where, picked up the toffee and ran over to where Dogo was hidden. First the monkey nibbled on the toffee then, not seeming to like it much, gave the rest to Dogo. He accepted it, making a noise half way between a click and a grunt, and then ate it. Ruth wondered about the meaning of the sound Dogo had made. She had the distinct impression that this was not a child with a monkey pet, but a monkey with a child friend. She knew immediately that it must be the one called Bending Twig.

Like Max, she said to herself "Mein Gott! The story is true." She began to understand why Max had been so thoughtful and excited. She was intrigued. Without then realizing it, she was hooked. Her next conscious thought, however, was that she would like to get Bending Twig's confidence too. So she began to leave the pieces of toffee closer and closer to the fire. The supply of toffee grew smaller as Dogo became less nervous until he and Bending Twig were quite close to the fire as they picked up the toffee. In the end Dogo began to take it from Ruth's hand though Bending Twig hung back. "What a handsome creature that colobus monkey is!" thought Ruth.

While Ruth was tempting Dogo with toffee, Max and Simu had stopped talking to watch Ruth. When Dogo ultimately joined them standing near the fire, Max decided to get serious in his conversation with Simu asking, "Has Black Ice been here?" "No, not Black Ice itself but one who was working for Black Ice" replied Simu. He continued, "Black Ice lives in the Suam gorge. It travels the mountain at night. You can see it as a long dark snake only when the lightning lights up the darkness or the stars are blocked out. But that is not important because this is a spirit that works through others." "Who was working for Black Ice?" asked Max. "Leopard," said Simu with a choke in his throat. "What happened?" asked Max, all of a sudden sensing Simu's anguish and nudging Ruth to be sure she paid attention to what Simu was about to say. "It happened yesterday when I took Dogo to Endebess to sell salt rock," said Simu. "I do not take the goat Bossy with me. I left her grazing down there as I do every day," he continued, pointing down the small valley so bright and peaceful in the sunshine. "When we came back Bending Twig told us that leopard had killed Bossy and left half of her in a tree. I brought what was left back here. It is under those stones," he said gesturing towards the pile of stones against the cave wall. "The goat was the child's mother when he was a baby. When he was bigger, it was the goat that defended him from the python. Black Ice used leopard to kill the goat so that he could attack the child. I am very afraid for him." Simu paused for a moment then continued, "Perhaps Black Ice will attack me first. If he does, so be it, I will fight." Max naturally thought like a man. He was action oriented so he asked, "Do you think Black Ice will use leopard to attack the child?" Without waiting for Simu to answer, Ruth acting on her woman's emotional intelligence changed the direction of the conversations saying, "It is very bad for the child, he must hurt much." She spoke this way because she did not know the Kiswahili words for 'terrible' and 'great sadness'. "He cried until he went to sleep with the dog," said Simu. In a fit of compassion, tears came to Ruth's eyes and she reached out as if to hug Dogo. He had not understood the conversation, and did not recognize the gesture, so he did not move and continued to stare curiously at this *mzungu* woman with hair so long, but brown not white like the man's. Ruth felt a bit disappointed that despite her best intentions she was unable to immediately reach across the gulf separating her from a child in emotional pain.

Max continued, "So you are afraid for Dogo?" "Yes," said Simu. "The *mganga* said that I would take the child. Do you want me to do that?" "I do not wish to lose the child," replied Simu with a catch in his voice, "but I must let him go with you, or he will die." "Will he come with me and the *Memsahib*?" asked Max. "He seems afraid of us." "He is afraid, because you are strange to him. Last night I told him you would come again. I also told him that you have a goat who is Bossy's sister. He misses Bossy very much." Hearing the word Bossy, Dogo let out a loud "Baaaaa" of a sheep or goat bleating. Max and Ruth both turned, startled, to look at Dogo who bleated again, a cry of mourning for his lost surrogate mother. "I would not have known it was not a goat," thought Ruth, its incredible, he sounds just like one. Max turned to Simu and said, "Yes we will have Bossy's sister; if the *Memsahib* agrees?" he added questioningly, looking now at Ruth. He tilted his head on one side, as if to say to Ruth, "The ball is now in your court." Ruth looked Max carefully in the eye and answered, "Yes, we will have Bossy's sister." And so a decision that would change the course of lives was made, without analysis or discussion, and perhaps a little too casually. Like so many very important decisions, it came from the heart, not from calculation, and for that reason it endured.

"Ask Dogo to sit with us," said Max. Simu did, and very cautiously, and hesitantly, Dogo sat on a rock beside the fire. Ruth held out her hand to him. He did not take it, but leant forward, sniffed at it as Changa might have, and then pulled back. "Jambo," said Max. Dogo was silent. "*Sema,*" or speak, said Simu. Dogo then responded in a small voice, "*Jambo,*" this being one of the few Kiswahili words he knew. Ruth took a chicken drumstick from her lunch box and offered it to Dogo. That was when a hopeful Changa came up beside Dogo and rubbed his head against Dogo's knee, never taking his eyes off the chicken. Remembering the toffee, Dogo took it and had a tentative bite. Ruth was elated by her first fleeting smile. He finished it quickly and gave the bone to Changa. He then made short work of the sandwich that Ruth had brought for him. "These *wazungu* have good things," he thought. He caught the eye of Bending Twig now sitting on a rock by the waterfall at the front of the cave watching the group by the fire. Bending Twig saw that he was pleased with the food and gave him an encouraging nod. As Dogo became visibly more comfortable and relaxed Simu asked the next question that was weighing so heavily on his mind, "When shall I shall I bring the child to see Bossy's sister?" he asked. Max answered, "The day after tomorrow Bossy's sister will return from a visit to her friends, come then." "Good," said Simu, "we will come the fourth hour of the day," meaning ten in the morning *mzungu* time. "Come for a visit for the day," said Ruth, "then bring the child back another day when he knows us." Simu nodded and said nothing, not really wanting to bring Dogo back once he had him out of the forest. In his head he was happy that the *mganga's* prophesy was coming true, but his heart felt hollow and empty as he accepted what he believed he had to do. Only modern man foolishly believes he can control nature and his own destiny. Simu was not a modern man. However reluctantly, he accepted the reality of forces greater than he such as drought and disease and *wazungu*; all brought by forces that could not be fought, only endured or used as best one could.

When Dogo's get acquainted visit to the farm had been settled, Max turned the subject back to leopard, asking Simu, "Would you like me to shoot leopard. I can kill him with this *banduki*," he said patting his rifle. "When would you come to do it?" asked Simu. "I could come seven days from now," said Max rather than saying next Sunday. He realized that Simu did not have a calendar and could not read it if he had one. Simu was afraid Max might delay Dogo's visit to the farm, so he said, "Let me bring the child to you first. Tomorrow I will bury Bossy's head on the cliff above the cave, the day after I will bring the child to you." "Why bury Bossy above the cave?" asked Max. "So that her spirit can look down the valley and watch over all who come and go from this place. That will make her happy, and I will be safer from Black Ice if she is watching," said Simu. "Are you worried that Black Ice will attack you?" asked Max. "Yes, until Black Ice hears that the child is no longer in the forest," said Simu. "Will leopard come in the night for what is left of Bossy?" said Max, concerned for Simu's safety. "He will not come tonight, he is not yet hungry," said Simu. "Tomorrow I will bury Bossy." This made good sense to Max, but left him feeling that it was a bit unfair that he could sleep with the comfort of a rifle to hand, whereas Simu had to rely on his spear and *panga*. "I would not want to live in this wild place with just a spear," he thought to himself. Then he turned to Ruth and said in German, "Let us have some more *chai*, finish our sandwiches and then go back to the farm." Ruth nodded in agreement.

As they rode back to the farm, Ruth asked Max, "Are you going to ask Bwana Paws for the goat?" "Yes, I will offer to buy it from him. He has quite a herd of sheep and goats." "I feel so strange offering a boy a goat not as a pet, but as a companion or a comforter," said Ruth. "I take it that the goat was Simu's idea?" "Yes" said Max. "With a goat as a wet nurse, do you think the boy believes he is a goat?" asked Ruth. "He sounds like one." "No" said Max. "At his age he looks only outward. For him bleating like a goat is normal, like talking. He does not think about what he is. He just learns from what is around him, be it a goat, a monkey or a man." "But if he learns from a goat and a monkey, as well as man, will his brain develop partly as a goat and monkey brain? Will his thought patterns be different from those of ordinary people?" asked Ruth. "Yes, we are going to be dealing with a half feral child," answered Max. "Very few feral children have been found or studied. As anthropologists, what we know is that if a child is not taught language and normal human patterns of thought by the time he is about ten years old, he loses the ability to ever develop fully into the main stream of normal human behavior, even if he is taught to talk. If the capacity to think like a human is not developed in early child hood, it can never be fully developed. Dogo can think like a goat or a monkey already. This would serve him well enough if he were to live as one in the savannah or the forest. But it will not help him with mathematics, politics, law, or a hundred other concepts that humans have and animals do not." "Are you saying it is too late?" asked Ruth. "No, the child is still young," answered Max. "But the *mganga* saw the problem; the child is a misfit in the forest, neither fully human nor fully animal." "I hope there is still time," said Ruth, "at least most children do not learn law or politics until they are older than ten. Do you think leopard will attack the child?" "Not in the next day or two. Simu says he will not be hungry for a couple of days. Any way leopards do not usually attack humans."

The next day Max bought a goat from Bwana Paws who said, "Take whatever one you want. I think 30 shillings is the going price." Max did not try to explain why he wanted a goat. Bwana Paws assumed he was going to eat it. He picked it out personally; a black and white nanny goat with fairly straight horns, to look as much like Bossy as possible. The goat was brought and put in a small fenced field by the farm manager's house. Meanwhile Ruth hurried to get the guest bedroom in the house cleared of stored boxes, the cobwebs taken down and the floor swept. The bed was a simple wood frame with rawhide straps across to hold one mattress about three inches thick made of the fiber from coconut husks.

Not quite up to the standard of a bed and breakfast in the Black Forest, but functional. Kiprono made it up with white sheets, a pillow and a grey blanket. He thought the Memsahib must be having trouble with her Kiswahili when she said it was for a child who was coming from the forest. "There aren't any *wazungu* children living in the forest," he said to the cook, Ochieng. It never occurred to him that the child would be black.

The next morning at about ten o'clock as he had said, Simu came to the kitchen at the back of the house, holding a small black boy by the hand. Max was out at work on the farm. Ochieng assumed he was a man looking for work and told him to go away. Hearing the exchange Ruth came out, and to the complete astonishment and disapproval of both Kiprono and Ochieng, explained that the child hiding behind the legs of this forest man would be coming to live with her and the *Bwana*. Kiprono and Ochieng, considered themselves several cuts above farm labor and in particular, 'forest', people. After all, they wore cotton shorts and shirts with no tears or holes in them, not a blanket or animal skins. Also they were familiar with the white man's ways and had daily access to *Bwana* Max, the boss of all the farm labor. They were, so to speak staff in the Kings court, well above the peasantry. For the *Bwana* to take in this bush child was a total affront to their status. Dogo could expect no warmth from them. This was hard, but in a way good for Dogo, as it kept him firmly in the world of the European not the African. He learned the ways of the white man faster.

After the initial formal greetings outside the kitchen, Ruth told Ochieng to make '*chai*', with three cups, toast and marmalade, and bring it to the front verandah. Inviting this unwashed forest man dressed in only a blanket into the house would have been incongruous, more uncomfortable for him than for her. It would have been like visiting the King in Buckingham Palace dressed in a sweat suit, with hair uncombed. Even the verandah was a stretch. Simu had seen a chair when visiting Endebess to sell his salt rock. A man had been sitting in one under a tree having his hair cut. But, Simu had no chairs in his cave, nor did Maziwa's manyatta higher up the mountain. He simply copied Ruth as she sat in one of four chairs around a simple wood table. Dogo was now wearing his only pair of very dirty shorts. He climbed up on his chair like a monkey and then squatted with both feet on the seat, hoping for treats like this woman had given him at the cave. With his small inquisitive black face, all one had to do was put white fur on his sides and you would have a colobus monkey, thought Ruth. When Kiprono brought the tea she watched Dogo stir in the milk with his knife holding it in his fist like one would a stick. Not wanting fingers in the marmalade jar, Ruth herself put some on a piece of toast and offered it to Dogo. He took and ate it appreciatively as he held it with both hands. Then to Ruth's great consternation he walked over to her side of the table and affectionately licked her hand. "Oh my God," thought Ruth, "that;s the way animals show affection and say thank you. I have a long way to go with this one."

As soon as Dogo finished his toast, Ruth suggested that they go and visit Bossy's sister. Dogo's face lit up at that. So the three of them left the verandah and went to a shed a hundred yards down the line of gum trees leading to the house. The shed had bales of straw at one end and two stalls at the other. Bossy's sister was in the last one. "*Busi*," said Dogo, meaning goat in Swahili. From then on this goat was known as Busi. Dogo was as quick as squirrel, going up and over the sawn half logs making the side of the stall. He landed as lightly as a cat on all fours in the stall and gave a small affectionate bleat. The goat lifted its head, cocked its ears and walked over to Dogo, who waited for it to come. They rubbed noses, then the goat nudged Dogo gently with its head and Dogo pushed back, making little sounds. They played for a few minutes and then walked up to the door obviously wanting out. "It will eat grass," said Simu. Ruth opened the door. Dogo and the goat walked out together in perfect harmony. The goat began grazing and Dogo sat on his haunches and watched it until Simu called him. Dogo came reluctantly. Ruth led the way back to the house and put Simu under a tree outside the kitchen.

With a piece of toast in her hand she led Dogo into and around the house. To him it was jus a funny rectangular cave with lots of chambers and stuff in it. He had always slept on a pile of grass on the dusty floor of the rock chamber that Simu had built in Chepnall cave. Warmth came from an animal skin over him, or the small fire Simu made in the chamber, blackening the rock roof with soot. The bed in his room did not mean anything to him, nor did the idea of sheets. After the tour, Ruth rewarded him with another piece of toast. She had the distinct impression that Dogo's attention had been on the toast all the time. She was right. The tour done, Ruth was a loss for what to do next, so she went out the tree where Simu waited. There she asked Simu to explain to Dogo that he was going to live with this *mzungu* in the house. He did, speaking seriously, slowly and gently. "You must stay here with Mama Ruth," said Simu. "Busi," said Dogo. "That is his truth," said Simu, matter of factly. Ruth nodded, and then led the way back beyond the shed to where Busi was grazing. They watched as Dogo ran over and nuzzled her with his head. "Now is the time for me to go," said Simu biting his lip fiercely. "You do not take the child?" asked Ruth in surprise, thinking that this was just a get acquainted visit. "It is safer for the child if he stays," said Simu with conviction. Ruth had not discussed this with Max, but made a quick decision that this day would be no worse than another and Dogo seemed happy enough with the goat. So she said, "*Kwa heri*, we will come to see you when the moon next shines." "It is good," said Simu with a choke in his throat as he turned to go down the brown road between the gum trees and then into the open, a small, lonely figure, dwindling into the distance, walking in bright sun but with an unbearable ache in his heart. Ruth's emotions were almost as troubled as Simu's, but whereas his was sorrow for his loss, hers was anxiety.

Ruth worried about Simu leaving thinking, "What will the child do when he realizes Simu has gone, how will I get him back to the house, how defiant will he be, will his reaction be flight not fight? Didn't the books say these were the two basic responses of the jungle. Is Dogo's mind so full of goat and monkey that there is not enough room left for human things? Or is the human mind, as some said, like a book with as many pages as you want, and all you have to do is write on them?" Half aloud and half to herself, she said, "I don't really believe that, I think the mind is more like a piece of metal that has to be hammered into shape, fashioned to fit in with other people and behave correctly." For his part, Dogo seemed quite unconcerned. He ignored Ruth who felt quite foolish standing by the edge of the road watching a child climb easily in a small thorn tree while a goat grazed nearby. She said the herself, "I'm not going to spend the rest of the day like this, some-one else can watch the goat graze." So she went back to the house and found Hoya, the gardener, and told him to go watch Busi and Dogo. Hoya had no idea what was going on. He just said, "Yes *Memsahib*," and left to find the goat and the boy, thinking there was no knowing what strange instructions a *mzungu* might come up with. They did things for incomprehensible reasons, but you were wise not argue because they paid you and their magic was stronger than yours.

After supervising the ox teams ploughing in one field and harrowing in another, Max came home for lunch as usual. "Did Simu come, and how did it go?" he asked Ruth. "Yes he came and he left Dogo." "I thought this was to be just a, get acquainted visit," said Max. "That's true, but when Simu saw how happy Dogo was with the goat, he just said he was leaving. I didn't argue, thinking what's going to be different another day?" "Where is the child now?" asked Max. "Out with the goat. Hoya is watching him." "Have you got any lunch for the child?" "I've told Ochieng to make some ugali, and I had hoped you would carve some chicken, he seemed to like that. I am not sure, though, that lunch is part of his routine." Ruth was right. It was mid afternoon when Hoya came back to the house leading Busi on a raw-hide tether. It was the end of his work day and he wanted to go back to his hut. Dogo walked happily alongside Busi and Hoya. He felt comfortable with this quiet bare foot man who just let him be. They both liked the earth. In the months to come Dogo was to spend many happy hours digging, making mud bowls and planting with Hoya in the garden.

When Hoya reached the house with Busi and Dogo, he tied Busi to a Jacaranda tree on the lawn and waited by the verandah outside; knowing that he was not allowed in the main house and that Kiprono and Ochieng would not let him into the kitchen. Kiprono went into the living room and told Ruth that Hoya and the child were outside. Ruth told Hoya he could go to his hut. She then asked Kiprono to bring the ugali and chicken from the larder and put it on the table on the verandah. She thought to herself, "I will get this child's confidence by feeding it. That is what I would do with an animal. I hope it works." Max had gone back to work on the farm, so now Ruth was alone with Dogo, full of uncertainty and anxiety. Dogo squatted on his chair again, ate with his hands until it was all gone, then simply left to go to Busi who was lying under the Jacaranda tree. Without hesitation he peed on the lawn then curled up beside Busi and dozed off in the warm afternoon sun. At that moment Ruth realized Dogo would defecate on the lawn to if he felt like it never having used a toilet. As she though about this, Ruth was surprised that Dogo did not seem nearly as anxious as she was. "I suppose he is used to being alone with a goat while Simu is away in the forest," she said to herself.

In the mean time a very heavy hearted Simu came back to Chepnall cave. As he clambered up over the rocks at the mouth of the cave, a flash of black and white signaled the arrival of Bending Twig. Seeing Simu alone she ran back down the path to find Dogo thinking that he was trailing behind amusing himself chasing butterflies or climbing on a fallen tree. But no, he was nowhere to be seen. She went down to the road that ran around the mountain there and looked both ways. Nothing! Alarmed and frustrated, she ran back up the path to the cave. Anxiously, and angrily, she gesticulated and jibbered at Simu as he sat on a rock trying to start up his fire again. "Where is the little one?" she demanded. "With the white man, the mzungu," replied Simu sadly, pointing down the mountain. "When will he come?" asked Bending Twig. "When the moon is next big," said Simu. Hurt and bewildered, and not understanding why Dogo was with the white man, Bending Twig retreated to a branch in a cedar tree outside the cave. In the end she grew hungry and went off to eat, but each morning she came to see if Dogo had returned.

When Max came back in from the farm again at the end of that first day, he immediately said to Ruth, "Where is the child?" "Out with the goat," replied Ruth. "Is everything all right?" asked Max. "Well he's been with the goat all the time except when he was on the verandah eating. He doesn't seem to be afraid of me any more. I think it's because I feed him. But if he's not eating he ignores me. The goat is his security blanket. You're the anthropologist; tell me how I replace a goat in this child's mind. I'm not going to walk around on all fours." Max was silent for a moment as he thought. Then he responded, "Think of the brain as being like a honey comb. The child's brain is already a much larger honey comb than the goat's, both in actual size and the number of cells per cubic inch. If each cell is like a slot, it may be empty or full, depending on what the child has been exposed to and therefore what he has learned. This child has been exposed only to a goat and an illiterate man who lives in a cave. So many slots are still empty. You and I have to fill the empty slots. We have to teach him so much more than a goat or a cave man can." "I would not argue with that," said Ruth, "but I am not so concerned with information in slots as you put it, as with the emotional connection, with his wanting to be with me and you rather than a goat. How do I do that?" "I agree," said Max, "the emotional connection is most important and feeding him is probably a pretty good start. That's what you would do with a dog to gain its confidence. This goat is not in milk, so we are lucky there. But right now we have to get him back to the house before it gets dark, feed him and put him to bed." "Good luck," replied Ruth. "You know as well as I do that until now he has slept on pile of leaves in a cave next a goat and a man." Ruth hesitated and then said, "I'll send Kiprono to find and bring the goat back,

Dogo will follow the goat." Somewhat reluctantly, Kiprono did as he was told and brought both back to the verandah.

Ruth then told Kiprono to take the goat back to the shed. He resented being told to deal with the goat, believing that it was a job for the "*mpagazi*' or farm laborers, not a man important enough to work in the *Bwana's* house. But he went. Ruth motioned Dogo into the house saying, "*kuja,*" rather than, "come." Max made a mental note to talk to Ruth about speaking always in English not Kiswahili, or even German. Kenya being an English colony that must be right he thought. Probably because he associated her with tasty things to eat, Dogo followed Ruth into the house cheerfully enough. Ruth looked at his dusty bare feet and bits of grass stuck on his bare back from sleeping on the ground, and made an instant decision to try a bath, or at least a wash. Before she could start on this, Dogo saw a glass paper weight on the desk. It was one from Venice with red, green, blue and yellow flowers deep inside an egg shaped piece of glass. He was fascinated by it. He had never seen stone in the river as colorful as this, or one so shiny and clear. Ruth held her breath, fearing he would drop it, as he picked it up and then sat on the floor to examine it. In a minute or so he became bored, left it lying on the floor and went on an exploration of the room. She was impressed by his curiosity, as he climbed on the chairs, the sofa, and a coffee table and then was momentarily startled when a book he pulled off the shelf fell open with its pages fluttering. The fireplace he understood and made a little grunt of satisfaction as he put his hand over the ashes to see if they were warm. When he finished his tour, Ruth held up a piece of chocolate and walked down the corridor to the bathroom. Dogo followed quickly and watched as Ruth turned on the taps. Dogo was comfortable with water, having played often in the stream that came over Chepnall cave except in the dry weather. He had no problem getting into this big pool to play in it. He loved the fact that it was so much warmer than the stream. Ruth repeated the word bath several times, touching the bath tub. She was surprised, and very pleased, when Dogo tried to imitate her and came out with "Baas." He was immediately rewarded with a small chocolate square. She sat him down, splashed the water over him, rubbed soap on his back and knew he liked it when he licked her wet arm like a dog might lick your face. The goat taught him that she thought. The rest of the bath was a success. There was a short fright, however, when she pulled the towel off the back of the bathroom door revealing a full length mirror. Dogo jumped back when he saw two more people in the room. Ruth touched the mirror, saying soothingly, "It's all right." Understanding the tone of voice, if not the words, and with some hesitation, Dogo came forward and touched the mirror too. He watched in fascination as the finger from the other side came to meet his finger. He spent the next ten minutes experimenting there.

Ruth left Dogo playing with the bathroom mirror and went back to Max in the living room. She did not take any special notice when she heard the bathroom door close, but it was not long before she heard the door rattling and Dogo crying out in anguish. In a moment she was there and opened the door to see Dogo by then hiding at the other end of the room as far behind the tub as he could get. He was looking with alarm at the door. Ruth walked over, picked him up and carried him out as he clung to her obviously afraid as she approached the door. When she arrived in the living room, Max asked. "What was the matter?" "I'm not sure. He seems to be scared of the door. Perhaps it was the mirror, but he seemed to be getting used to it." "I heard the door click shut," said Max. "My guess is he found himself locked in unable to get out. He's never opened a door, never used one, and does not know how to turn a handle. Then there's this person behind the glass that won't let him out. It was pretty scary for him. When he stops crying show him how a door works." So Ruth did, showing him how to press down on the handle of the French doors onto the verandah and then push. She was surprised how soon Dogo could do it. "He's very quick on the up-take," said Max. "Now try him on a door with a knob not a handle." Ruth had him try on the bedroom door which had a round brass handle. It took Dogo a

bit longer to learn to grip it hard enough, but, in the end he succeeded and smiled happily when Ruth praised him. He still kept
well clear of the bathroom door which had that person inside of it.
Later in the evening Ruth was not so sure that it had been a good
idea to teach him how to open doors. But for now, she had a great
sense of accomplishment.

Kiprono brought in some firewood and lit the usual evening
fire in the fireplace. Dogo was delighted and immediately squatted
down on the hearth warming his hands until the heat made him
move back. Max looked at the half naked child squatting by the
fire and saw this image repeated in the African bush down the generations that came before. For a moment he felt an atavistic urge
to sit himself by a fire in a cave, secure in that circle of light beating back the darkness. The thought passed and he said to Ruth, "I
will go into Kitale tomorrow. Where can I get him some clothes?"
Ruth answered, "Let's take him to Endebess. It's just a few houses,
but it's only six miles away and there is an African there who makes
clothes on a sewing machine with a foot treadle. I don't want to
expose him to all those people in Kitale. Besides I would feel awk-
ward and uncomfortable with this child I do not know." "Right,"
said Max, "now let's get him fed and to bed." "I imagine he is used
to going to sleep fairly soon after it gets dark," said Ruth. Let's
feed him first, put him to bed, then eat ourselves." "Good idea,"
said Max, "we don't normally eat until eight anyway." At that moment Kiprono brought in the hissing pressure lamp they used in
the evening. Dogo backed away from it until he went out of the
verandah door and stood outside looking in cautiously. "He may
associate the hissing with some sort of giant python," said Max, "he
was attacked by one." Kiprono thought to himself, "I am right, this
forest child has no business in a *mzungu* house." His instinct was
to chase the child away into the darkness, but he did nothing, and
said nothing as he put the lamp on its usual head high stand. Ruth
went to Dogo and encouraged him to come in behind her, saying
in quiet soothing tones, "It's alright, it's alright." When Dogo saw
that the lamp made no threatening movements, in fact it did not

move at all, he gained confidence and very carefully followed Ruth in. Kiprono left disappointed that the child came in. Ruth said, "Max please go to the kitchen and put some *ugali* and chicken on a plate and bring it. We will feed him by the fire here in the living room. He always ate by the fire in the cave." "Right," said Max and did as he was asked. Dogo was of course quite comfortable with a man bringing him food.

Dogo much enjoyed his meal. The *ugali* he was used to, but large pieces of chicken were a complete novelty. When he was done Max said, "So far so good, now what?" "He should go to the toilet before he goes to bed, said Ruth and you are going to have to teach him how. He pees on the lawn without any embarrassment, and I bet he will defecate on it too. He has no idea what a toilet is for. I can't demonstrate, but you can." "They say a picture is worth a thousand words," said Max, "and that is especially true when one cannot understand the words. So I'll do it." Max took Dogo down to the bathroom, washed his hands without a problem and then did his demonstration. Much to Max's surprise Dogo copied him instantly seeing Max's action as being the same as Changa peeing on something to leave his mark. Dogo had, of course, long since learned to copy Changa. The toilet was one of the old style with a tank up near the ceiling and a pull chain. It made quite a roaring noise when Max flushed it. Dogo fled to the other end of the bathroom and fumbled with door handle until he opened it. As before with the lamp, he did not flee into the dark, but stopped to evaluate the new threat. When Max did not act in any way alarmed, he was reassured. Speaking English, Max said, "Bedtime," as he beckoned Dogo down the corridor to his new room and was followed by Ruth. "Sleep" said Max, once again demonstrating by lying down on the bed pretending to sleep. "Tonight, let's not bother with pyjamas," said Ruth, "I don't have any his size any way." She pulled back the covers and motioned Dogo into bed. He went hesitantly and she covered him up. "Don't kiss him good night," said Max, "if you do anything lick his face." Ruth gave him a shocked look, but said nothing and went to open the window to give Dogo fresh air, as she said. Pleased with their apparent success they went back to the living room and talked as they waited for Kiprono to announce that dinner was ready in the dining room.

"Do you think Simu is right and the child really is at risk from Black Ice? Does Black Ice exist?" asked Ruth. "I don't know," said Max. "But Simu clearly believes it, and from our point of view that is all that matters at this moment. If we were to send the child back to the forest, Simu would see it as our imposing a death sentence on him." "Isn't that a bit extreme," said Ruth. "Everything that has happened to Dogo could happen to any one living for years in the wild of an African forest." "The thing that sent Simu to the *mganga* in the first place was the python being so high up in the cold of the mountain," said Max. "He knew that was not right. Then the *mganga* made a prophesy and attributed the abnormal behavior of the python to an evil spirit. Man has done that since time imme-morial, often saying that a particular person or group put evil into motion. Look how often the Jews have been blamed for natural disasters. These people are very superstitious. They believe in evil spirits. Don't many of us Europeans believe in horoscopes? Then you get a soothsayer or witchdoctor whose predictions come true, and even I am tempted to believe that some can see what I cannot see. How did that *mganga* know that I would come, that I would be a big man with white hair, when it would be more likely to be brown or black?" They chewed silently for a minute until Ruth asked, "Do you think the *mganga* was right in saying that the child is a misfit, an anomaly, in the forest and that is why Black Ice wants to eliminate him?" "As I have said before," replied Max, "the child is half feral. It is as useful a working hypothesis as any other. The *mganga* said if Simu wanted the child to live he had to get him out of the forest. I do not think you would disagree that the child is much safer with us than with Simu." "I suppose you're right," said Ruth thoughtfully. "What about the elephant with the mark of the cross on its foot?" "I expect that is co-incidence. I know that most priests would say so because they firmly believe, mistakenly in my view, that man and animals are totally distinct, that man was

255

created and did not evolve from an animal such as an ape. But would I bet my life on it? No! Would I have told Simu to ignore his dream of the *mzungu* woman being able to help Dogo with his burnt buttock? Again no." "Well," asked Ruth, "what about that part of the *mganga's* prophesy that the child will learn all the *wazungu* can teach him and return one day to do good on the mountain where he was born?" "That part of the prophesy is up to us," said Max. "Thank God the child does not seem to have emotional problems. Even without them we have an enormous task. You will have to carry most of the load to start with. Because he is a boy I will carry more later. Let's look in, make sure he is all right before we to bed." So when they finished dinner they went down the corridor and opened Dogo's door very quietly. There was enough moonlight; they could see the room and the bed were empty.

They looked at each other in stunned, shocked silence. Then Max said, "I think I know what has happened, we are going to have to have a goat in the house for a while."

And so it was.

4729810R0

Made in the USA
Charleston, SC
08 March 2010